THE LAST VERSE

Also by Caroline Frost

Shadows of Pecan Hollow

THE
LAST
VERSE

A Novel

CAROLINE FROST

WILLIAM MORROW

An Imprint of HarperCollinsPublishers

THE LAST VERSE. Copyright © 2024 by Caroline Frost. All rights reserved. Printed in the United States of America. No part of this book may be used or reproduced in any manner whatsoever without written permission except in the case of brief quotations embodied in critical articles and reviews. For information, address HarperCollins Publishers, 195 Broadway, New York, NY 10007.

HarperCollins books may be purchased for educational, business, or sales promotional use. For information, please email the Special Markets Department at SPsales@harpercollins.com.

FIRST EDITION

Designed by Michele Cameron

Library of Congress Cataloging-in-Publication Data has been applied for.

ISBN 978-0-06-326548-6

23 24 25 26 27 LBC 5 4 3 2 1

For country music songwriters, my favorite poets

THE
LAST
VERSE

PROLOGUE

She sits alone on a cold, hard chair, still as the dead. Round eyes closed, lips a sliver, face a crushed rag of linen, she looks all of her sixty years plus fifteen more. Feels it, too. She is worn down, by time, by hard living, and by the memory of the night that brought her here. She has spent every day replaying a moment that would come to define her, one most would be desperate to forget.

The sounds of others talking, fighting, bartering, paper the walls, a backdrop of noise. When her mind is quiet and solid as the concrete underfoot, she begins to hum. She hums to warm up her voice, murmuring those dank bands to life. The sound is sleepy and hungry, the intimate call of a lover reaching across the sheets. *Are you awake?* Thirsty, she runs the spitting sink, catches a handful of water and sucks it from her palm. It tastes of pipe. She clears her throat and hums again. She'll need all day, she thinks with a pang of fear, to get this engine running. But she hasn't got all day; for the first time since she can remember, she's got somewhere to be.

She rolls the sound from a gentle rise down to a valley and up again, soft strokes until her voice gathers strength. Then she hums a melody that will shuttle her from one end of her range to the other, pausing just shy of the note she can't reach, waiting for her vocal cords to stretch and relent.

Finally, she sings.

And the voices around her stop.

Who is this crone, so beloved and yet unknown? To see her on the street you might tuck a small bill into her palm or flash a kindly smile and walk on. But you do know her. Have spoken her name, sung along with her at your high school dance, your hometown football game. To the sound of her voice, you walked down the aisle or buried your loved ones or rocked your baby to sleep. You can't explain why her music hits you square on a nerve, why certain notes send chills across your skin and make you want to stop what you are doing, stop time, and call someone you love before all of it goes away. Her music takes you from the gates of heaven to the darkest hell and back again because she knows. She's been there. And all she's ever done, all she knows to do, is render it in song.

I

CHAPTER 1

It was any old Sunday at First Tabernacle, a relatively new congregation of charismatic Christians worshipping in a rented annex, where folding chairs stood in for pews, ceiling fans and flytraps adorned the low ceiling, posing a threat to anyone over six-foot, and light filtered not through colored glass but bottom-dollar windows from Sears.

Nineteen-year-old Twyla Higgins mouthed the words to "Walking in the Light of God" while she wrote an original song in her head, a skill she had honed over these eight years of singing in the choir, how to tune out the sounds around her and be somewhere else entirely in her mind. This was her refuge—not choir, and definitely not First Tab—but writing songs. It was like sitting in the hull of a wooden boat in the pitch black, being moved by a rhythm so much larger than her it must be God. Her body and mouth followed remembered rhythms, while her mind worked out something beautiful, sad and strange. The melody flirted, teased her from behind some opacity, presenting itself then flitting quickly away before Twyla could seize it. She was nearly there. Then someone jostled her from behind and she almost stepped off the riser, breaking the concentration she needed to capture the song. She became aware of the din around her. Entire bodies pressed up against her own from the front, the back, and both sides, their musk and scented soaps penetrating her hair and clothes, odors that would linger until she scrubbed them off. She willed away the distractions, desperate to be immersed again, but like a fleet-footed deer, the song vanished. So often, in the beginning at least, it was like this. More hunting than craftwork.

Eager congregants sang along, hands to cheeks, hands to heart, hands to the sky, arms flung over themselves, contorting, wiggling, jerking to the Spirit. The scrum of singers amassed around her, driving her deeper into its center. Smothered in the cheap yellow satin of her choir robe, she stuck out her elbows to make room for herself. She regained her composure and swayed to the beat, an up-tempo arrangement in a falsetto register she never would have chosen for herself, for anyone. She'd told the choirmaster just this morning he ought to deepen it by an octave and slow it down. To thank her for her feedback, he'd given her solo away.

She glimpsed her mother in the front row all decked out in her floral chiffon church dress and matching hat, ankles crossed and feet tucked beneath her chair, clapping in time. Her eyes were closed in reverence and adoration, a signal to others that she was swept up in the spirit of the Lord, though from time to time she opened them slightly to peep at Twyla, no doubt monitoring her for a hair out of place, a smile lackluster, and, upon discovering one or the other, she would pat her hair or screw her fingers into her cheeks as if to say *Smile, baby, smile.*

After the closing hymn was sung, the congregants greeted each other and filed toward the fellowship hall. Twyla helped Hazel, who called herself the "organist" though she merely played the organ setting on the keyboard, fold up the chairs and collapse the choral risers. She had designs on the afternoon but first needed her mother and Lloyd to get sucked into conversation, as they often did, to give her enough of a window to bike to the record store before her mother and stepfather returned from church. Elvis Presley's latest album was out and she had been counting the days until she could hear it.

She had always liked Elvis's music, but when she saw his Christmas special the year after Daddy died, she fell in love. Her mother had gone to bed early and Twyla had sneaked out of her room, lonely and bored. She turned on the television and saw Elvis, all decked out in leather with a big guitar on his lap. She sat there for an hour, watching Elvis at his best.

Relaxed, inspired, spontaneous. How he had teased the crowd, one false start after another, winking, vamping, and loving the feel of the audience hanging on every flick of his pinkie. He layered the effervescence of his early career performances with weathered maturity, the zeal of a second chance. Though he was every bit the showman the world had fallen in love with, what struck her most was how he made love not so much to the audience but to the music itself.

She and Hazel rolled the risers to the adjacent multipurpose room, muscled them on end, and leaned them with a clatter against the wall. She looked around and saw her mother pursue a pressing conversation out the doorway and into the fellowship hall. Seizing her moment, she said goodbye to Hazel, let herself out a back door, and followed the side of the building through clumps of uncut grass to the tree where she'd left her bike.

It was mid-August and Texas hot. She concealed herself behind the thick trunk of an oak tree to remove her choir robe, though she was fully clothed underneath. It was the sort of thing that could be taken, here at First Tab, as an act of seduction. She bunched up the robe and stowed it in the basket, then hiked up her plain, butter-colored dress to her knees and secured it with a rubber band so it wouldn't get eaten by the chain. Just as she pushed off for the sidewalk, her mother sauntered out.

"Twah-la, baby," said Faith, hand outstretched.

Twyla stopped and released the knot in her skirt, lest her mother accuse her of inciting the desires of passersby.

"Come on inside now and talk to whatsis-name—oh, you know—the Nichols boy. His momma says he's organizing a mission to El Salvador or San Salvador or somewhere." She opened her hand and shut it like a baby grabbing for a bottle, her charm bracelet making music on her wrist. When Twyla failed to step forward, her mother clapped twice. "Come *on*."

Twyla ran through her Rolodex of excuses and did some quick math on the last time she'd used her period to get out of fellowship. Three weeks. A little dicey but plausible enough.

"Mother," said Twyla, and lowered her voice to lady-talk levels. "I just started my monthly."

She gave her daughter an impatient look, then rummaged through her handbag. "Well, didn't you bring anything for it?" she said in a strained whisper.

Twyla bit her lip.

"No, Mother, and if I wait too long it'll make a big old *mess*."

Faith shook her head, skeptical and sour. She licked her palm and ran it down from Twyla's hairline to the back of her head, reglueing a flyaway. Every morning Faith French braided Twyla's thick, honey-colored hair in two surgically precise plaits and lacquered the curly sprigs with hairspray. Twyla was aware she had grown too old to be groomed by her mother, but this time between the two women was calm, close even. It was one of the last vestiges of the time Before. Twyla worried if she stopped letting her mother do her up in the morning this last comfort might disappear. Still, she longed to wear her hair free and wavy, the way it looked when she brushed it at night. Mother said loose hair is for loose women. Tuck it, tie it, glue it down if you have to.

Faith kept her frosted-blond hair blown out and sprayed into a dome so steadfast it could sustain gale-force winds without the slightest shudder. She was very pretty, Twyla's mother. She kept her hourglass figure, plumped slightly by motherhood—in her lower abdomen, on the backs of her arms and in a fleshiness at her armpits, the outer curve of her thighs—in a way that seemed to please most men who encountered her. The way their gaze would roll down the middle of her body, how she'd look away to let them. Twyla wasn't supposed to focus on such things, but she was proud of her mother's beauty. Even if she envied it.

Her stepfather, Lloyd Finch, barrel-built and handsome, chewed on a powdered donut and approached them with bovine curiosity, two coffee cups nearly disappearing into his porterhouse hands. When he sensed trouble between the two women, he stopped all movement and assessed the nature of their dispute.

"Next time," her mother insisted, pointlessly, "bring a pad with you."

Confirming danger, Lloyd set one foot behind him and spun on it, making haste to the samovar.

"I'll be sure and set the table so it's done for supper," Twyla said as a peace offering.

Recognizing defeat, Faith patted her daughter's pudge. "Well, can you at least *suck in*, Twyla? I'll give you some water pills when we get back."

Twyla's face reddened. She wanted to grab her mother's hand and twist it. "Yes, Mother," she muttered, and before Faith could get another word in, she pedaled away.

The farther she got from church the better she felt. She pumped her legs as fast as she could in her church shoes, homely flats chosen because they were the only dress shoe she could find in extra wide. She swiveled down winding neighborhood streets to the main road, which at this hour was mostly empty. Much as she hated biking, especially in the hellish heat of summer, she couldn't afford to drive. She was saving up for an apartment, at least as far as the other side of town, and didn't want to spend a cent that wasn't necessary. Sometimes she dreamed of getting farther than out of her house—out of town, or state, or even farther than that. But ambition in these suburbs revolved around a tight nucleus of family and church. Most girls her age had married, a few worked. One had left town to join the anti-war protests in California, prompting a feverish wave of nightly prayer circles. No one had heard from her in over a year, and some thought she had gotten into drugs. That was the general attitude about leaving. That you'd run into trouble and never be heard from again.

CHAPTER 2

Free for a moment, the wind at her back, she cruised the mile and a half to the New Groove record store. With luck, her mother and Lloyd wouldn't return for an hour or more. Time enough to catch up with Eli and listen to the new Elvis album, *Moody Blue*. His version of "Unchained Melody" had been playing on the radio nonstop, and the first time she heard it, it had utterly devastated her, caused her to lie on her bed and submit to the force of its melancholy. Every time he belted out an "Oh, my love," all the armor she wore to make it through the day turned to water. Elvis had her by the soul.

Before her father died, Mother had played his early albums on the weekends, the up-tempo songs, like "Hound Dog," "I Got a Woman," and "Love Me." The purr, wobble, and pop of his voice, the playfulness with which he sang, made him easy to love from an early age. As Twyla grew older, the ballads appealed to her more and more. She didn't think she'd had a particularly complicated or difficult life, but the soul and the sadness in his music shaped her. She sometimes felt she was receiving not just his heartache but the pain of others passing through him, like he was channeling all the woes of humanity. When she started writing her own songs around ten years old, she felt something similar. Emotions she never knew she had, yearnings, sailed through her and into her music. How they came, who they belonged to, she didn't know. Absorbed from the world around her? Or were they built into living, like original sin, but for suffering?

Twyla leaned her bike against a streetlight in front of New Groove. When she saw the state of the storefront, she lost her breath. A flattened cardboard box taped over a busted window, blue powdered glass dusting the sidewalk below, and sprayed on the painted brick, a hateful word. Twyla had been coming to this record shop since it opened five years ago, amid the settling of the dust of the civil rights marches. Eli, equipped with a business degree off the GI Bill, had raised enough money through his church, family members, and a lucky win at roulette on Lake Pontchartrain to make his dream come true. Though he had a steady stream of business from all over town, not everyone was pleased to see a success story in a Black veteran-turned-pacifist.

She swung open the door and rushed up to the counter.

He was on his knees buffing the display window, a spray bottle of Windex in one hand and a chamois in the other.

"Twilight! My girl. What's new, baby?"

"Eli, what the heck?" Her face was hot with concern, and her voice came out louder than she'd intended.

"Oh," he said, bored. "The li'l love note?" He brought out a pouch of tobacco, papers, and a box of matches, readying to roll himself a neat cigarette. "I'm waiting for Marylou to come back with the solvent and some steel wool."

"So y'all're okay?"

He seemed remarkably calm. Last time this had happened he'd chased the pair of men, tackled one to the ground. Instead of arresting the vandals, the cops had thrown Eli in jail.

"I'mma make like George Harrison and Hare Krishna myself outta trouble." He drew off his cigarette and blew out a billowing, milky cloud. "Peace and love, baby, peace and love."

Her alarm now calmed, she let her eyes scan the new-releases display. A few other godless music lovers browsed the stacks. The Elvis section was empty. She turned to Eli, hopeful.

"Sold out, honey. I tried to hold one back for you like you asked, but Marylou sold it when I wasn't in the shop."

Her lids fluttered closed in defeat.

"Eli, no . . ."

"Well, cheer up now, we'll get another case next week."

"I can't wait another week, I just can't."

Eli looked down his nose with forbearance, then promptly changed the subject.

"You should listen to some real music," he said. "That boy is counterfeit."

Twyla knew where Eli was headed. He'd made sure she knew Elvis was cashing in on Black music. He'd made a good case for it, too, enough to make her feel guilty but not enough to keep her from loving him.

"You can't lecture the heart," she said. Eli shrugged. "Okay, you win," she said. "Play me some Sister Rosetta."

Eli clapped his hands together and stepped over to the rock 'n' roll section with a little swagger in his step. "That's what I'm talking about." He selected an album and led her to a row of narrow booths with glass windows. Inside each booth sat a turntable on a little platform, and a pair of headphones hung from a hook. Before he opened the door he held out his hand and pushed his John Lennon glasses up his nose.

"Sorry, baby, you gotta pay to play," he said, buckling his arms in front, as if bracing for pushback. "New policy."

Her stomach knotted. "Oh, come on, Eli. You know I'm saving—"

"Just fifty cents a listen, one song or the whole album, doesn't matter. Fifty cents to get in and twenty-five for each album after that."

"Fifty cents a listen!" she said, a little sting at her eyes. She usually spent an hour in the booth, eyes closed, drinking in the sounds of her favorites. Johnny Cash, Willie Nelson, Patsy Cline, Janis Joplin, Charley Pride, Loretta Lynn. She was hungry for these sounds. They soothed the rash of living with her mother, the ache of her confinement. She handed two quarters to Eli.

"That's how it goes," he said, unconcerned, and wove around the maze of displays to the counter where he recorded something in his ledger, tapped a sale into the register, and dropped the fifty cents into the drawer. She settled into the booth and set the needle down.

Something about the Elvis disappointment and Sister Rosetta's husky spirituals made her homesick for her father. She could remember his playing "Clementine" as quietly as he could to lull her to sleep, his particular way of just barely brushing the guitar strings to coax out a whisper of a tune. She had tried and failed to replicate the sound.

Music hadn't always been contraband in her house. Twyla's daddy had been in a traveling bluegrass band. He played guitar mostly and backup fiddle and taught Twyla everything he knew. He wasn't a technical player, but he showed her how to use a few well-ordered chords and the saddest notes to tell a story with sound. *A music teacher might call it bad form*, he'd say. *But when you're famous, they'll call it your signature style.*

Everything changed the year she turned nine. It was sunny, one of those shocking clear days in May, when the heat never fully sets in. Daddy hadn't lived with them since she was eight, but for a year he came back every few weeks for a whirlwind of presents and special time together. But by the spring of 1967 he'd stayed away longer than ever before and after a month with no word from him, Twyla had a sick feeling in her stomach that wouldn't go away. To cheer her up, her mother had let her stay home from school on a Monday to watch Elvis and Priscilla's wedding coverage on TV. They'd curled up on the sofa, commenting on every detail. Mother even teased Twyla's hair up in a beehive to match Priscilla's.

The next morning she was feeling well enough to go back to school. Mother sat reading a ladies' magazine, her bare feet tucked beneath her, ashing a cigarette into a teacup while Twyla ate her cornflakes. The phone rang. Mother hopped up so fast she stubbed her toe on the doorframe where the wall-mounted phone hung, and she yelped and held her toe, then reached up and answered, laughing at her own clumsiness.

"Higgins residence!"

From Twyla's seat at the table, the voice on the other end could be heard but not understood. Mother said *yes* and her smile disappeared as the voice kept talking. Then she went very still and faced the wall, one hand strangled by the telephone cord. When the call ended and she turned around, her face was a hard mask. Twyla had never seen it like that before, colorless, empty. She pleaded with her mother to say something but she drifted out of the kitchen and into the bedroom, closing the door behind her.

Police arrived and spoke to Mother, and the men from Daddy's band, the Sundowners, came, too, hats pressed to their chests, looking somber and watchful of Mother. Aunt Ginny showed up and took Twyla to get ice cream. Twyla remembered licking that chocolate ice cream cone, how she could feel the cold on her tongue but couldn't taste a thing.

There was no memorial for her daddy, not even a burial. No gathering to honor him, to play his music and say goodbye. Twyla begged her mother to see his body, to touch him one last time, play a song on the guitar he'd left behind. She wrote a three-page eulogy and showed it to her mother, but Faith wouldn't even read it nor trouble herself to explain why. Faith just carried on like nothing had happened. But Twyla could see she was different, her manner clipped and cool. As far as her mother was concerned, Daddy never existed.

"Hey, Eli?"

Eli was busy unboxing some new arrivals and loading them onto a rolling cart.

"Mm-hmm?" he said, absentmindedly.

"I'm in the mood for some Mickey Higgins."

He stopped what he was doing and glanced at her with sympathy in his eyes. Then he returned to his work.

"You know where it is."

She found her daddy's album in the bluegrass section, under *S* for Sundowners, and studied its cover, three men posed midsong on a wooden stage under a moony spotlight. Daddy on guitar. She dumped the contents of her coin purse into her hand and counted her change. Not even five bucks.

"I think I'll finally buy it today," she said. "How much?"

Eli made a face, like *If you say so.* "Well, sticker says $6.98." He thumbed the patch of hair below his lip in thought. "So for you . . ." It sounded like he might cut her a deal. Older record, probably no one would want it but her. She had listened to it here more times than she could count, but today she felt the need to own it. Even if she had to hide it from Mother. "For *you* it's $6.98, just like everybody else." Her heart shrank back down to size. "Now get outta here with that poor-me white girl face! *Shiiit.* My shoes have seen harder times than you." He continued to mumble in dialogue with himself as he took up his unboxing again.

Her cheeks blazed with the heat of his reprimand. She hadn't asked for a deal, but he had seen her hoping for one.

"Sorry, Eli, I'll see you next Sunday. I'll bring more money next time." She looked at the clock above the door. Her parents would probably be home soon. She made a *C* shape with her hand to funnel the coins into her purse and pinched the clasp shut.

Eli looked over at her, annoyed at something that was known only to him. He pointed to the sound booth.

"Well, throw it on the turntable and have a listen, I don't care. As long as you buy it next time, it's fine with me." He seemed both bothered by his decision and relieved of some burden. Twyla smiled, not just at the chance to hear the Sundowners, but at the fact that whatever wrinkle she had pushed up between her and Eli had been smoothed. She glanced at the clock again, wondering if she should risk her parents finding the house empty and wondering where she was. Much as she wished to avoid a confrontation with her mother, she did not want to turn down Eli's offer. She put twenty-five cents on the counter and took the album to the booth she'd been in, then pulled the record from its sleeve and laid it on the player.

"Would you like me to play it out loud?" she called out to Eli.

"Won't bother me if you do," he said and kept busy at his cart.

She set the needle carefully on the first groove and the wheel began to spin. The crackle before a song played always excited her. She leaned back against the wall and closed her eyes. The old murder ballad began with a howl. Some primal call, a signal meant to travel a great distance. Then the skitter of banjo hook, pure Appalachian wizardry, guitar layering in, and the sweet fiddle last. Daddy belted out the first verse.

> *Went out one night to make a little round*
> *I met Little Sadie and I shot her down*
> *Went back home, jumped into bed*
> *.44 pistol underneath my head*

How his voice tugged at her. Plain, loud, and weathered by time and circumstance, he was not gifted, only moved to sing. And that was what drew her to music of any kind, the raw will behind it. The shattered feeling that pressed against the artist's heart, begging, *Please, don't let me stay broken. Make me beautiful.*

She imagined the trio in a run-down recording studio, lamplit and smoky, rugs layered on the floor to dampen the sound. All of them pulled up close to each other, microphones at their instruments. Daddy with his clear flask of whisky, what she had innocently called his mouthwash for its amber color and the way he would take a sip and swish it around his mouth before swallowing. His fingers picking those strings, the economy of movement, his laid-back style. The intricacy of sound flying up from his guitar, now hers.

What she wouldn't give to sit in the studio with him. She remembered the time he was playing a show near the Stockyards and at the end of their set the crowd had lost their heads, clapping and hooting and bawling for more. He had hopped off the stage and plied his way back to where she was sitting on her mother's lap, and he had taken her into his arms and brought her back to sing with him. The cheering surged when he set her down and handed her the mic. She hadn't a moment to get nervous, because right then the band started up with "Train 45" and the song she knew so well just came right out. If she'd had a second to think she might have frozen, but the spirit of the song got to her first. The fiddle chimed in sounding like the whistle of a steam engine, the banjo plucking a railroad beat. She sang with brio, slapping her thigh in time, ruffled skirts swishing, and glanced up at her daddy when it came time to harmonize. This was how she remembered Mickey.

There were other, darker memories, too, but she hadn't understood what was happening, nor been given words to describe them, to make them real. Only an unkind feeling between her parents, a bottomless longing for them both, and a sense that all of it was slipping away.

Twyla said goodbye to Eli and left the store. She pedaled home singing "Little Sadie" on a loop, hoping she could trap the sound of it. But the more she sang it, the sound in her head merged with her own voice, and her daddy's, like an echo, faded with every turn.

CHAPTER 3

When Twyla rounded the bend on their cul-de-sac she saw her mother's prized station wagon, a blue Ford Country Squire with wood siding, hogging the driveway, with Lloyd's humble pickup parked obediently on the street by the mailbox. They had beaten her home.

The family's postwar ranch-style house resembled all the others in the neighborhood—grass front yard, driveway and attached garage, brick-and-siding combo. But theirs had the distinction of a raised, built-out attic space, lifting their roofline about two feet higher than its neighbors. This amendment had been an expensive one, but her mother had pressed her stepfather so mercilessly that he finally gave her what she wanted. She would never admit it to a soul, not even herself, but her mother had to have, in every situation, the upper hand. She suffered from any perceived inferiority, and the foil to her complex was most often her daughter, Twyla. Twyla who had not smiled enough as a baby, who spoke late, toilet-trained late, who had always, to her mother, looked odd. Not *odd* odd, but who never seemed to look and behave like she ought to.

The greasy smell of pork on the grill traveled from the backyard. Chops and applesauce. Lloyd hunted for sport, so there was always a fresh cut of meat. Her mother didn't cook, just opened cans and microwaved their suppers and made a show of plating them on their nicest Corelle.

As Twyla stood at the curb in front of her house, her mind raced for an explanation for her whereabouts that was both truthful and also protected her from having to explain why she wasn't in bed nursing cramps. How she was received today depended on the contents of Mother's conversation at the fellowship hall. Any moment Twyla wasn't at work, at church, or helping Mother, she was considered to be open to the devil's influence. And indeed, any chance she got she did the very thing her mother feared. She turned the knob on the radio or biked up to New Groove and listened to music. Songs of lust and love, sung by addicts, cheaters, hussies, and drunks. Songs of fornication, adultery, and sin of every sort. But these songs were beautiful, and they touched places deep within her. Twyla didn't see how anything that made her feel so alive, so human, could be sinful. She snatched a handful of primrose growing wild on the strip of grass between the street and the sidewalk, steeled herself against whatever storm awaited her, and resolved to tell the truth. She wiped her clunky shoes on the mat and let herself in.

Grill smoke seeped in from the backyard and mingled with her mother's rosewater eau de toilette. Faith met her at the door with an earring in her hand. The way she pressed her lips together like she was holding back a smile, it seemed she had something to say.

"There you are. I've just gotten off the phone with Pastor Horton," said Faith, clipping the gumball-size fake pearl back on her lobe. She didn't even ask where Twyla had been. "It's a real shame you couldn't stay for fellowship, Twyla."

"Yes, Mother," Twyla said, hoping not to delve into the details of where she had been. "Here, these are for you." She handed her mother the fistful of primrose.

"Wanna know why?" Her mother took the bouquet absently, wheeled around, and led Twyla into the living room. She dropped the flowers on the coffee table. "Well, I'll tell ya. I was talking to that Coby Nichols, as you know, and I was just so impressed with him. He's very ambitious. And like I said, he's planning a *mission* and has the *full support* of First Tab."

"That's real nice, Mother," Twyla said, anxious to get off the subject of Coby, a guy her mother had been pushing her toward since he joined the church two years ago.

"He was saying he's looking for able bodies, you know, for mission stuff."

"Oh, I don't know, Mother—" Twyla said, once she saw where this was going.

"So I volunteered you." She grinned and paused for Twyla's reaction. "Can you stand it? I would chaperone, of course, and Lloyd said he didn't mind sparing us for a couple weeks. I'm sure Hazel can cover your shifts at the daycare, she's always looking for extra work, isn't she? And all we have to do is pay for our airfare down to San—to El—oh, shhhugar, I forgot which one it is again. But I'll find out before I book our tickets. Oh, *Twah-la*! Can you think of anything more exciting than this? A chance to see the world, spreading the Word of God?"

Twyla blinked hard to set her brain to what her mother was saying. "You want me to go down to Central America with you and Coby Nichols?"

"Well, there will be a group, Twyla." Her mother scowled. "You make it sound so sordid."

Twyla didn't think she'd suggested anything sordid, but she did sense an agenda. "How are you going to pay for those tickets, Mother? All the way to Central America, that's got to be hundreds of dollars."

Her mother waved her off, as if brushing away a housefly. "I'll buy my ticket, and you've got plenty of savings for yours, and if there's anything we can't pay for, I'm sure Pastor will pass a basket for us." Faith looked perplexed, an expression she often wore when her enthusiasm was not immediately shared by others. "Twyla, it's a mission! Saving *souls*. What about this is not just sending you over the moon?"

Twyla took a breath and steadied herself. She couldn't argue when her mother was hot with a fresh idea.

"Mother, can we talk about this after supper? I need time to think, and I'm hungry."

Faith huffed out so forcefully Twyla felt it on her face.

"Honestly. This is just like you to mope around your whole life acting like you're chained up in a dungeon, and when an opportunity for adventure falls in your lap, you look it up and down like it's trying to bite you."

Her mother made a fair point. Setting aside the fact that she would have to represent a cause she didn't support in a language she spoke poorly, she could see the upside in getting the heck out of Fort Worth. Apart from summer trips to Port Aransas to see Aunt Ginny and her cousins and the odd drive they used to take to one of Daddy's gigs, Twyla had scarcely been farther than Dallas. She was curious to see new ways of living and working, but she was scared, too. What if they thought her small and stupid? What if she got a taste for the outside and wanted more? As far as she could tell, the only thing that was going to get her out of her parents' house was getting married or paying her own way. Twyla was relieved to have dodged trouble today, but now she'd have to get out of this mission trip. All her savings, and with them her hopes of moving out this decade, would be dashed.

"All right, Twyla, we'll talk about this later, but you're as good as signed up far as I'm concerned."

Twyla sighed and deployed her tactic of appease and delay. She went back to her room while Lloyd finished cooking the last of the chops. Long gone were the Johnny Cash and Loretta Lynn posters, the Elvis shrine on her side table with a framed picture of him on *The Ed Sullivan Show*, hips midswivel. Those wood-paneled walls were stripped of the things she loved, replaced with a single image of a fair-eyed Christ washing the feet of Judas.

A feeling came over her, now familiar but with fresh potency: there was no place for her here. No place for her music, her body, her questions. She needed out. From the back of her closet she removed a shoebox filled with her savings, a mess of bills and coins. She counted her money, discouraged, as she remembered the seventy-five cents she'd spent at Eli's. There was $339 and change, not enough to stay gone for long. She pulled out her guitar, a pretty Martin from the thirties, her father's only splurge after the band cut their first album. It was used when he bought it and had only grown more beautiful with age. She admired the flame in its rosewood body and fingered a silent song without plucking the strings. Then, as if beckoned by the curl of her fingers, the song she had been trying to write in church surfaced. A lyric appeared. "Let this hunger be not sated," and she jotted down a simple melody in her song bible. She was desperate to play what she'd written to hear how the lyrics sounded against the melody, but the strum of the guitar would draw her mother's attention.

She spent some time playing with the song and teasing out its verses. Once she had a little something to work with, what she called a song baby, she closed her songbook and put away the shoebox that contained all her hopes for getting out, moving on, growing up. Then she sat on the little tufted stool at her vanity and looked herself in the mirror, praying for the courage to tell her mother the truth.

In her reflection she saw a woman dressed up like a child. She wore a drab wool jumper over a white blouse and loafers on her feet. Dull and desexed. Her face, with its small, downturned mouth and round, gray eyes, was mostly plain. But her hair, in its natural state, was striking. Honey-gold in color, long and unruly, with fine curls around her forehead and at her temples, ones her mother wrestled down every morning.

"Mother, I've been praying on it," she said softly, humbly, to her own reflection. "I'm not going on that mission with Coby. I just think . . . I *believe* that I have a different calling." Her big eyes and breathless delivery were unconvincing. She hardened her face and tried again, this time with her diaphragm. "My calling is music." And though the declaration brought embarrassed tears, every word she said was true.

CHAPTER 4

Twyla sat down at the back of the church daycare and scribbled the beginnings of another song. The kids were all laid out in their sleeping bags in various poses of slumber. Ratty animals in their clutches, thumbs in mouth, butts in air. Three hours into a six-hour shift, Twyla was already hankering for the weekend. Since Sunday, a whole fleet of songs had been coming to her, steady and strong, so many she couldn't keep up. She was scared if she didn't write them down, she would lose them forever. Daddy had often said every song is like a soul that wants to be born. If one came to her and she didn't bear it forth, it would just go visit someone else. So she kept a sheet of plain paper folded up in the pocket of her sturdy blue dress and jotted down whatever she could until she could transfer it to her song book. Some she took down like dictation. Others she coaxed and coddled. Every once in a while a song came stillborn. Sometimes those were the ones she was most certain of, and when they didn't work she wondered if it was a failing of her own.

The inspiration could come from anyplace. It could be the rhythm of the dishwasher—*shhh tt-tt shhh tt-tt shhh*—or a little saying she would turn sideways that became the conceit of a song. Earlier today, one of the three-year-olds came up to her humming "Row, Row, Row Your Boat," but he had the notes mixed up in the most surprising way. She sat with him repeating the notes he'd sung, making a beat with patty-cake hands, and as he sang his part she harmonized the last measure. It was silly, but when she imagined the ditty supported by drums, sweetened by a cool fiddle, and sung at half-time, she thought it worthy of the radio.

"Oh, Twyla, you look like you're about a million miles away," Cecile said, hoisting a wakeful toddler to her hip. Cecile was a good Christian, the kind who didn't have to trumpet it from every rooftop but who genuinely enjoyed Christ and church and did the right thing when no one was looking. She was twenty and recently engaged to her long-distance boyfriend, a dental student at Baylor. It was the success story of the year among the church group, and Twyla was privately jealous of the fact that Cecile would get to leave Fort Worth for wherever her future husband's residency took them.

Twyla's real-life experience with boys was poor to nothing special. There was her first fixation, an older boy named Corey Baldwin. He had a shaggy Beatles cut, thick brown hair swept to the side with sideburns, wore his bell-bottoms low, and listened to Jimi Hendrix. He was a rare combination of popular and kind.

Then she was set up with Warren Oster, the anxious son of her mother's Bible study friend, who stuttered and stroked the yellow hair on his arms. They drank Cokes at the kitchen table, making shapes with the condensed water on the yellow Formica tabletop while Lloyd watched *Gunsmoke* and Mother sat next to him, eavesdropping. This was the extent of what her mother would allow. Twyla longed for someone to look into her eyes and feel who she was, to know the shape of her hands and hold them with care, for the love in her heart to be shared with another. She wondered if the other girls were curious about these things, too, but feared her asking would provoke horror, suspicion, or pity.

There was a time when she could have brought her questions to her mother. But just when she was beginning to notice subtle changes in her body and in the contents of her thoughts, her daddy died and Mother found Jesus. It was as if her mother had disappeared overnight and been replaced by a zealous counterfeit. A few months into her new passion for Christ, Mother announced she was changing her name from Betty to Faith. She went straight to the court clerk and filed the paperwork. Twyla was horrified. She tried to talk her out of it, but her mother ignored her, resolute.

It was around this time that Twyla came home from school to a bonfire in her front yard. The smell of burning plastic and thick black smoke had drawn the neighbors outside to watch Faith as she tossed her ladies' magazines, lingerie, bottles of booze, and Harlequin books into the fire. Twyla tugged at her arm. "Mother, don't burn those things—"

"Twyla, don't try to stop me. I'm doing a deep clean." Faith shook her off. "The devil has burrowed himself all around our home, and I'm digging him out!"

There was a wheelbarrow full of items set to be torched, many of them belonging to Twyla. But far worse than the loss of her belongings was her mother's plucky optimism as she lorded over the blaze.

Then Faith opened a cardboard box full of records.

Twyla froze. "Mother, no." She went to the box and pulled out Bob Dylan, Woody Guthrie, and Creedence Clearwater Revival, then Dolly Parton and Elvis, and held them to her breast. "You can't."

Her mother rubbed a circle on Twyla's back. "I know, baby," she said. "Devil comes wrapped up in pretty paper sometimes." To Twyla's horror, she lifted the box and set the whole thing on the bonfire, shaking up orange sparks and embers. Twyla wanted to drag it out and save her music, but her mother was so steadfast she could see it wasn't any use. She slipped the remaining records from Twyla's arms and set them to burn.

By some miracle, Mother spared Daddy's guitar. She said to Twyla, "You can keep it, baby, but all I ask is that you play it in praise of the Lord." At the time, Twyla would have done anything to save that guitar, so she agreed to restrict her use of the guitar to gospels and hymns. She took comfort that her mother wasn't so far gone she'd take the thing most precious to her, that it was a line, maybe the only one, she'd never cross.

Before Christ, Mother had always pecked at Twyla, corrected her posture, her handwriting, her mismatched clothes, the sullen music she listened to. But in her own way, she had been right there with her daughter. After Christ, the thing that felt like such a betrayal was the handing over of all these responsibilities, the morality, the social instruction, much as she'd loathed them coming from her mother—giving it all to the church. So now these personal matters between them became the jurisdiction of strangers with suffocating and absolute laws. Mostly Twyla just missed her company, ganging up on Daddy and making him take them shopping or setting up a home salon in the cramped bathroom, with Mother lying in the tub and Twyla working on her hands, then her feet, then daubing Pond's cream on her face like icing. And because her mother left her for Jesus so soon after Daddy died, it was like Twyla lost them both at once.

The children began to stir and raise their mussed heads from their pillows. Cecile instructed them to put away their bedrolls and join her on the circle rug for snack and Bible stories. These barbed memories had their tines in Twyla. She, too, rose, as if from heavy sleep, and shook them away.

CHAPTER 5

When Twyla came home from work, she stripped off her white smock apron and found her stepfather on his recliner, cracking pecans into a bowl on his belly, watching the five o'clock news.

"What's for dinner?" she asked out of earshot of her mother. Lloyd shrugged and looked at the bowl of nuts, then back at Twyla.

"I don't know, baby, but I'm snacking just in case." Twyla went toward the kitchen in search of food but paused when she heard someone on the television say Elvis's name. She turned around and stood behind her stepfather to see what it was about. She hoped it meant he was coming to Fort Worth. He'd been singing in Vegas for ages, it seemed. If he was coming to town, maybe she could figure out a way to go without her mother knowing. Her father changed the channel to a baseball game.

"Lloyd, put it back, would you?" she said.

"Come on now, the Rangers are playing, lemme just get the score here." There was some complication in the tone of his voice that made her walk up to the television and turn the dial to channel 2. The young newscaster cleared his throat. "Again, reporting here the tragic death of the King of Rock 'n' Roll, Elvis Presley. Dead at forty-two."

Dead? The word landed on Twyla like a foreign object.

She sank to the ground and fixed her eyes on the TV, reached her hand out to the screen. Cheeks hot, eyes wide, a sickly feeling in her gut.

No.

How could Elvis be dead? He was younger than her mother. He was the King. All those nasty rumors came to mind, of appetites insatiable, drugs, women, fits of rage. She had shucked them off, disbelieving, just like she now tried to deny the truth of his death. Not Elvis. Lloyd looked up from his recliner and, seeing her face, set the remote on the table and went to her. He squatted and hovered a hand over her back, then, when she tipped toward him, he patted her, saying nothing, and it was this gesture that uncorked a spring of tears.

Mother came in barefoot, wiping her wet hands on her apron. She looked at the television, then at Twyla and her stepfather, and clucked with dismay.

"Your love for so-called great men comes so easy, Twyla. Doesn't matter what they do, does it? Delivered the devil to every home in America. Roused the desires of adolescent girls. Treated that innocent Priscilla like a show pony, grooming her from a filly and parading her around. Not to mention the pills and the gorging—it's like that man is trying to tick every last deadly sin off his list. Meanwhile, you barely give *me* the time of day." She drew down the corners of her mouth like she was trying not to cry.

How could her mother talk about him so cruelly, when all he had done was bring people joy? He wasn't perfect, but he was tenderhearted, took care of his parents and his friends. She was tired of feeling like what she loved was wrong. Like she couldn't decide anything for herself. She went cool and had a powerful urge to put some distance between her and her mother. Then, she had an idea.

"I have to go see him," Twyla said, willing her eyes to look at her mother square and steady. "To pay my respects."

Her mother laughed and looked at Lloyd to back her up. "Is she joking?"

For whatever reason, her stepfather did not retreat, but shrugged between the two women and took a side. "Well, if that's what she wants . . . She's long grown, sweetheart."

Faith's mouth dropped open a little. "She's unmarried and naive as

a country mouse, Lloyd. She's not going anywhere, certainly not to wor-
ship a fornicator with a bunch of groupies and burnouts."

Suddenly Twyla wished she were as reckless as her mother imagined
her to be.

"Gosh, Mother," she said, getting up and taking a step toward Faith.
"You make it sound fun."

"You're not going." She was trembling. "And I swear if you try to
challenge me on this I'll take away your—"

"My what, Mother?" Twyla said softly, defiant but sad. "You gonna
take Pearl?" She shrugged, went to her room, and brought out the old
rosewood guitar, in the headstock a simple mother-of-pearl inlay of the
North Star. She held it out to her mother. "Go ahead. You won't let me
play anything good anyhow." She could feel her own powerlessness in
those words. She was a grown woman, behaving like a child. But this
was how it went between her and her mother. Faith bossed her around
because she wouldn't stand up for herself. Twyla was terrified if she went
her own way, her mother would cut her off just like she had her daddy
and every other person in her life who didn't line up with her way of
thinking.

"I'm not trying to take anything away from you," Faith said, more
gently, "but if you're living under my roof, you've got to stay in line." She
dropped her arms to the side and pushed the guitar back to her daughter.
"Ask any mother if they would give their teenage daughter permission to
take a bus *out of state* to go mourn with a bunch of strangers over a dead
druggie *sex* symbol."

It hurt to hear her mother reduce the situation in this way. The cal-
lous use of "dead" in particular seemed designed to prick.

"Mother, I've got my own money, you know. I can pay my way."

"Not your Salvador money, no ma'am," Faith said.

"I never agreed to the mission trip," Twyla said, her voice a cool growl.

Her mother looked perplexed, then glanced into the kitchen at the
sink full of dishes and the supper that wasn't done and began to untie her
apron.

"That's *it*. You've killed my appetite." She threw the apron down. "You're on your own for supper."

Lloyd exhaled, then picked her apron off the floor and coaxed Faith toward the hallway that led to their bedroom.

"Why don't you go lie down, sugar," he murmured to his wife. "I'll take care of it." Faith whispered something to her husband and patted him on the hand, then disappeared into the dark of the hall.

Twyla stood there watching with familiar hatred and amazement at how her mother manipulated a situation in her favor, recruiting Lloyd to make her the victim and Twyla, somehow, the difficult one. A scream welled up in her throat, one she imagined could fill up the room and shatter the windows. But she didn't make a sound.

It occurred to Twyla that an opportunity to leave might have presented itself. She considered the viability of a quick getaway. She had plenty of cash to buy a roundtrip bus ticket to Memphis and pay for the three or so days she'd be gone. It would take months to replenish her savings, but Elvis was worth it. Without hesitation, Twyla went to her room, wrestled a paisley zippered bag out from under a stack of boxes in her closet and laid it open on the bed. She stuffed inside it a tangle of underwear, ankle socks, and two days' worth of outfits. She removed the false bottom she'd added to a shoebox, took out a hundred dollars and some change, and stuffed it in her coin purse.

Twyla's head jerked up at the sound of a knock on her door. She shoved her bag and guitar into the closet and scanned the room for anything else that would expose her plan. Mother let herself in and sat down on the pink patchwork quilt. She was in her nightgown, an elaborate, Edwardian-looking frock with a high collar and yards of diaphanous cotton.

"Twyla." Her mother sighed and flopped her hands in her lap. "I know I don't say this very often, but I hope you know that Lloyd and I only want the best for you. And if we keep you close and if we're hard on you . . ." Twyla wasn't making eye contact, and seeing this, her mother rose and stood behind her daughter, taking the two braids in her hands. She removed the elastics and pried apart the woven thirds of her hair so it fell away in shiny waves. Twyla closed her eyes.

"If we're hard on you it's because of how precious you are. Every night I pray for you, Twyla, for happiness to come your way." As her mother's fingers worked through her long, thick hair, breaking up the hairsprayed mass at her scalp, gathering the strands and then fanning them across her back, Twyla craved more. Faith was a master of energetic movement. She could start a party, or suck all the vigor from it. Here she was using her biggest gun, maternal seduction, to pacify her daughter. But knowing her mother's ways didn't make her immune. As a result of the simple ritual, the thrust of Twyla's Memphis plan dwindled.

Her mother rebraided her hair, loosely now, then kissed the center of her head, and looked at her in the mirror.

"I guess I'll go eat after all, since Lloyd went to the trouble of cooking," Faith said, and left with her white gown billowing behind her.

Twyla was tempted to stay home, watch the funeral on TV, keep saving. Patch things up with Mother and maybe even figure out how to do the mission without paying for it. She'd keep working toward her dream of moving out.

She held up her hand and rubbed her thumb against the pads of her fingers. Used to be she had thick buttons of skin built up from all the guitar picking. It made her feel like a real musician, like the road-worn men in the Sundowners. Daddy would be sorry to see that she had let the instrument, and her fingers, go fallow. He would have wanted her to go to Memphis—heck, he would have taken her there. She put her guitar safely in its case and closed the lid. Then she pushed her things, and herself, out the window into the azaleas below.

IT TOOK HER THIRTY MINUTES to bike to the Greyhound station, guitar case lashed to her back, the travel bag stuffed in the basket in front, and when she arrived she had worked up a mean smell. An older man with a gray mustache and a cowboy hat stood in a lit ticket window, staring straight out like a very detailed mannequin. She parked her bike against the wall and went to the window.

"Is there a bus going to Memphis tonight, sir?" She was conscious of herself, this being the first time she had tried to go anywhere by herself, let alone leave home. If a person could beam light made of excitement and fear, she thought she could blind him with it.

The man reanimated. Without speaking he looked at a list in front of him, squinting, then put on the pair of glasses that hung from his collar.

"Yes, ma'am," he said, and looked up, finger still pinned to the bus information should he need to consult it again. "She's leaving at 8:47. Drives through the night and arrives around 7:00 a.m. tomorrow. Thirty-four dollars, cash or check."

Twyla nodded, trembling. She removed her coin purse with its bloom of tens, fives, and ones and paid for her ticket. Leaning forward through the window, he pointed her in the direction of her bus, then handed her a slip of paper. She stuffed a few bills into the depths of her pocket and put the rest in her duffel, gathered her things, and headed toward her terminal.

The bus was already half full, mostly white men, cowboy hats removed and stowed on their bags overhead. Elvis sang "Kentucky Rain" on the radio, and her throat lumped at the sound of his voice. A pale woman with a beehive, slightly off-kilter, crocheted an intricate length of lace. A pair of Black twin brothers, identical down to their potbellies and the close trim of their hair, sat in the middle of the bus. Not resigned to the back, but not yet daring to claim a seat up front. Twyla secured her bag and guitar above a seat in the back and sat down to wait the twenty minutes until departure, the whole time fearing her mother would come running onto the bus and pull her off.

The bus finally grumbled to life and the vibrations and smell of gasoline filled the cabin. She jittered with adrenaline. She was weightless, giddy, yet frightened. It occurred to her that the weight of permission, of her mother's approval, had been as much an anchor as a shackle. Now she was free to choose. And free to fail.

As soon as she rested her head against the window fatigue rolled in like bad weather. She prayed for sleep. Sleep to soothe her troubles, sleep to wash it all away. With any luck, she wouldn't wake up until Memphis.

CHAPTER 6

Twyla woke up to a chalky mouth and a headache and lusty thoughts
of food. She had been so wired from her escape, so worried about the
fallout, that she had been up most of the night. Now just a few miles
outside of Memphis, the warm air churned in through the open windows and others around her began to stir, prompted perhaps by some
inner sense of closeness to their destination. Her legs stuck to the vinyl
on the seats and her feet steamed in their socks, which had loosened and
gathered under her heels. She felt so unfresh, she swore if there were a
cold body of water nearby she would jump into it, clothes and all.

A vendor awaited the arriving bus with shaved ice, cold Cokes, and
ham sandwiches wrapped in wax paper. It was such a welcome sight to all
that by the time the bus was empty, so was the food cart. Twyla devoured
a sandwich and sipped her Coke, making it last. The weather was already
hot but the air sparkled and the birds chattered and it seemed everywhere
she looked were saturated greens. Trees bushy and taller than any she had
seen in Fort Worth, no animal smell of the stockyards, but a summer
perfume of warm leaves and gasoline.

She could hardly believe, standing here among strangers, that she
had carried out her last-minute plan. A plan that she now remembered
did not include the particulars of her mission, namely the how and the
by-what-means. She flagged down the guarded-looking woman from her
bus and asked if she was going to the funeral, but the woman bustled

forward, shaking her head no. The sandwich lady didn't know where to point her either. Finally, she went over to a line of three taxis parked under the shade of a tree.

"Excuse me, sir?" she asked one of the cabdrivers, and the man looked up from his reading. "How do I get to Graceland?"

"Oh, sure," he said thoughtfully. "It's a shame what happened to him. Anyways, I could take you for cheap, it isn't far."

"If I can walk, I'd rather do that."

"It's about three miles. Go down Brooks Road just here, then left on Winbrook Drive, take a right on Winchester Road, then left on Highway 51—they call it Elvis Presley Boulevard now, but old habits, you know? You'll see the signs." He went back to his paper and Twyla hoisted her bag straps over her shoulder to lighten the load.

As she walked, she passed car dealerships, a Motor Inn, flags half-mast and marquees reading "Rest In Peace Elvis." Even with the heat and her luggage, the physical exertion of the walk kept her mind focused and the hour went by quickly. Soon she merged with thousands of people making the pilgrimage to Graceland. The sight of so many fans filled her with camaraderie. She was moved to see the range of those who loved Elvis: an elderly man in creased slacks helping his wife brave the high grass in her good shoes; a chain of schoolchildren holding hands, flanked by their teachers; a loud procession of bikers in leather, moving slow as hearses. Rockers, hippies, wanderers, squares, people of many colors and ages all here to pay respect to the King.

They rounded a corner and the walking stopped. She heard someone say they'd reached the gate but she couldn't see it and pressed forward, slipping between people, ducking here, wiggling there, until she reached a lawn of flowers, not planted, but laid down in their florist cellophane. Behind the offerings, the famous musical gates.

A rush of antiseptic cologne announced itself from her right. She turned and saw a lanky, good-looking man about her age wearing a tight T-shirt, sleeves rolled over his biceps, dyed black hair greased into a ducktail. He raised his eyebrows and waved a little hello. She looked away, embarrassed to be caught staring. Someone jostled her from behind and the man reached out to steady her.

"You okay, miss?" he said.

"I'm all right." The person behind closed in on her again, trying to see past her, but she pushed back this time, holding her ground.

"Your bags look heavy," he said. "Lighten your load?"

She shook her head and pulled them closer to her.

"I get it, it's cool." He took a comb from his back pocket like they did in the movies and secured a loose strand at the crown of his head. "I'm Benny," he said, palm outstretched.

She felt wary of his interest, but shook his hand firmly like she'd been raised to do. "Twyla," she said. Her mouth was sticky and her voice hoarse.

"Where you coming from?" he asked, raising his voice to cut through the din. "I just drove thirty hours straight from San Diego." The comb he'd been holding in his left hand he slipped back in the pocket of his Levi's, which were cuffed at the ankles. "I think I cried all the way to Phoenix." His eyes watered a bit as he looked out at the gates of Graceland. "Man, I loved that guy."

The thought of him driving alone in tears put her at ease, and she smiled. The crowd shifted again and nearly split the two apart. Benny maneuvered around a man with a child on his shoulders and made his way back to Twyla.

A woman at Twyla's side was weeping violently, and for a moment it all struck her as funny, how tightly we cling to what we love. She giggled out of discomfort and he gave her a curious look.

"Are you dressed up for the funeral?" she asked, flicking her gaze up at his vintage Elvis hair. "Or do you always look like this?"

He scrunched his face up in acknowledgment that he had a Look.

"I sing in a rockabilly band. Benny Rose and the Boutonnieres." Twyla perked up to hear he was a musician. "My bandmates—Julio and

Cam—lazy bums didn't want to drive. They're flying out to Nashville to play a gig at this place, the Exit/In?" He paused as if expecting a reaction. "Supposed to be out of sight."

"I'm a singer, too," she said, but he didn't hear. She felt funny saying it out loud, like she was trying on a new pair of shoes. Did it even count if she'd never really been on stage?

"You what?" he said.

Before she could answer, someone behind them cried out, and the crowd began to shift forward. The gates creaked open and people spilled over the flowers and toward the gate. There were men in uniform shouting at everyone to fall in line.

"I can't believe it," Benny said, eyes fixed on a point she could not see.

She asked him what he meant, and he had to swallow something down before he could speak.

"They're going to let us view his body," he said. "I heard people saying they would open the casket, but I didn't want to get my hopes up." They walked forward, funneled into line by the men with guns. There was a tension in the air, of feeling brimming over, and it was unclear if that feeling would spill in the direction of order or of mayhem. Twyla held her breath. There were hundreds of people in front of her. There was no telling how long this would take, or how many people would be allowed to enter.

For the next two hours, she waited, sweating in the pummeling heat. Dog-day cicadas crackled in the trees, chiggers and ants made snacks of her ankles. Around her, people wept, sang, fanned themselves, prayed, some even fainted. Her tongue was dry and fat in her mouth, and she had to pee so badly, in her sunbaked delirium she entertained the idea of wetting herself and might have done it, too, if Benny with his friendly black eyes and California smile hadn't been there. All that idle time led her to second guesses. What would Faith do when she found her missing? Had she called the police? Would she even go after her? Part of her wanted to be chased, and the other wanted to run so far away she could never be found.

Finally, the people between them and the front door of Graceland dwindled to two and it was nearly Twyla's turn. The air-conditioning in the house blew through the open front door and cooled her skin. She could see the grand staircase ahead and smelled cinnamon and vinegar. She felt at once an intimate closeness with the singer to be here in his beloved home, and a sense that she should leave as quickly as she could. The line processed to the right through panels of peacock-stained glass into a white-carpeted room. On one side of the small room was the piano, and her eyes filled with tears for the songs that wouldn't be written.

Then there he was. Tucked into his satin-wrapped bed. A sliver of his face, hair inky black, his plump features almost infantile. Twyla's arms lifted, reaching out, without her intending, and a guard gently pressed down to contain them within the velvet ropes. As she took in the sight of the body, more effigy than man, she was struck by the emptiness of the room, the lack of life. He really was gone. The line continued to move, pushing her along and out of sight. Even though it had been only seconds, she did not wish for more time. It was all so much more than she could have hoped.

Upon exiting the house, her immediate physical demands—rasping thirst and bursting bladder—overpowered her wish to contemplate her moment with Elvis. She was stuck in a thick, somber line toward the front gate and there was no easy way to leave the property. She darted away from the line to a landscaped cluster of bushes, gathered her skirt, and, without shame, relieved herself. When she was done, she inserted herself back into the line. An older woman whispered over her shoulder, "I just might follow your lead."

Then a bank of people suddenly heaved into her and she stumbled knees-first onto a pile of trodden bouquets. Others fell around her, people shouted and cried out in pain. A big woman climbed over the man in front of her, skirt hiked over her girdle, collapsing him to the ground. Twyla scrambled between legs and over the bed of flowers, seeking out pockets of open space, until she finally made it to the wrought-iron fence, and pulled herself up to stand. It was then she realized she had left her bag and her guitar behind. She looked back at the chaos, searching for Benny and her things, but they seemed to have been swallowed by the crowd. She'd be trampled if she went back, so she followed the fence line and clawed her way out of the rush of people for what seemed like an eternity, until she finally reached an outcropping of pine trees. She sat down on a bed of dry pine needles and caught her breath. She marveled at her own foolishness. Not four hours in this town and already she'd lost her clothes, her cash, and her guitar. She made fists and pressed them into her eyes, furious, crushed.

She wondered then if it was worth it, the strife with her mother, losing Mickey's guitar, for a ten-second glimpse at her girlhood crush. Pathetic was one way she could feel. So why did dead-broke-thirsty-on-the-side-of-the-road feel so much better than home?

"Hey!" someone said.

Benny appeared, his ducktail splayed out and wagging. "Twyla, you're okay!" he said, beaming with relief. "I thought we were doormats there for a second."

She laughed, and tears wet her eyes, her feelings all sputtering close to the surface. She was so relieved to see Benny that it wasn't until he laid them at her feet that she noticed he had saved her paisley bag and Pearl. She picked up her guitar case and held it to her chest. He sat cross-legged beside her and whacked her on the back like he was congratulating her.

"Man, that was wild!" he said. He pulled out the comb and handily reworked his hair into its cool swoop. Twyla dabbed her tears and, seeing him put himself back together, laid a hand over her own braided hair, patting the wisps away from her face.

"Hey, listen," he said, motioning with a jut of his jaw. "You wanna get out of here? I'm parked in the shade down the road a bit. I have a cooler of beer and sodas. We can climb on top of the van and watch the procession above the crowd."

Twyla could just imagine what her mother would say. Wandering about *unchaperoned* with a musician? Mother did not condone hanging out, which was idle and would lead to bad ideas, drug use, and, of course, sex. It sounded fun as hell. She looked at her plain smock dress and her supportive shoes and wished she didn't look so straitlaced.

She smiled, then followed Benny a few minutes' walk to his van. He opened the rear doors and clawed around in an icy cooler, and when he turned around he was holding two cans of Coors.

"I guess I'm out of Cokes," he said. She let out a nervous laugh and Benny sprayed open a beer for her. She hesitated, having never tasted alcohol before, then blew the foam off the bottle mouth and took a sip that turned into a long, quenching, bubbly draft. It was starchy and pleasantly bitter. Alcohol was forbidden at home, but she remembered the smell from the time Before. It smelled like Daddy.

She sat with Benny on the roof of the van, sipping, chatting a little, observing crowds of people approaching Graceland, some bereft, others thrilled, or numb, or curious. After two beers, she felt goofy, her arms long and rubbery. She found a place in the grass to lie down and absorbed the new feeling, sank into the damp earth, rubbed mulch and grit between her fingers, embraced by an all-over wonderment. It frightened her to think she could feel so changed. She couldn't believe this was the devil's brew she'd been warned about. A belly full of beer was like a hug from the inside. She wondered if it was Satan she was feeling, or God. Or a simple gust of freedom.

Then a thousand heads turned, and a strand of cars crawled by, men in shades at the wheel. People pooled in the culvert and along the street to watch the hearse go by, many holding hands to their heart. Someone sang out the first verse to "In the Ghetto" and other people joined, a few at a time, until a raw chorus of voices had formed and the vibrations rolled across the crowd. She could feel them in her cheeks and chest, the music and the way that Elvis made people feel. Known, loved, a little less lonely. Flanked on all sides by others, she remembered the crush of singing with the choir, anxious and out of place. Here she enjoyed the feeling of blending in, merging into the whole.

Her thoughts turned to Mickey. All the questions her mother wouldn't answer returned. Why did he die? Was it painful? Was there anything they could have done to help him? Had he died alone? And the question no one but Mickey could answer, when he was close to the end—had he thought of Twyla? She had battered her mother with these questions in the days following his death, but Faith had ignored her until finally whipping around with blood in her eyes and blurted the only morsel of an explanation she would give. *Dammit, Twyla! Daddy is dead for reasons I can't even understand. How can I possibly explain them to you?*

Word of mouth took them to a bonfire in an open field where hundreds had parked their trucks and vans with tailgates open. Benny and Twyla joined the mass of people sitting on the roofs of their cars and blankets in high grasses. Twyla grew heavy with regret that she would never see her idol alive, never touch him or hear him sing. She saw a flash in her mind of Elvis in his coffin, one closed eye, a cheekbone, the arch of his upper lip, his hands strangely folded. Seeing life absent, his waxy repose, she thought she had found what she needed. Proof to set her fretting mind at ease, that he was indeed forever gone. All her life wishing for a moment with him. And here she was, realizing it was Daddy she had wanted to see.

Tipsy and tired, Benny and Twyla crashed head to tail, like canned fish, in the safety of the van. Once in the night she parted the cheap tapestries and slipped out to drink some melted ice water from the beer trough and when she returned she laid her head next to Benny.

When she woke the next morning she could feel him warm and damp beside her. She rolled slightly toward him and he lifted his arm and laid it over her and pulled her to him without waking. She smiled, burrowed closer. All the little gallantries and kindnesses gathered in her mind and she began to wonder if he might be interested in her, and in thinking this way wondered if she were interested in him. He was creative and friendly and hadn't gotten fresh with her. And he was a musician. She imagined traveling with him and the band, writing songs in their downtime, maybe hopping onstage for a duet. No one she knew except maybe Coby Nichols had any interest in travel. Her mother's

scheme to take her on that mission trip to El Salvador seemed like ages
ago. She wondered if it was the beer she drank or if there was a change
underway already. Had she, so quickly, grown out of her home?

Benny stirred again and held her, this time with more intention. Her
forehead touched his cheek. She could smell the malt of last night's beer
and glanced at his lips, now so close they were blurred. *All they want is sex,
Twyla. Anyhow, anywhere.* Her mother's admonition, a chant. Men were
sex-crazed wolves and she their prey. But she had never addressed the fact
that Twyla herself had appetites. In her experience, men hadn't pursued
her at all. What was so wrong about loving on someone, holding them
close and being held? She tilted her chin up and kissed him, tasted his
sour and salty lips, and without fully waking he kissed her back, lapped at
her tongue with his and brought her so close their teeth clicked together.
Then his eyes opened and, seeing her, he pressed her suddenly, but not
unkindly, away from him. He looked at her through a layer of sleep, confused. He said her name with a downward tone, and her sensitive ears
heard the pitch of his refusal.

"Twyla, I'm sorry," he said, propped up now on one elbow. "You seem
like a great girl." She looked down, shook her head to signal that he didn't
have to finish his sentence. She wanted to vanish. She pushed herself up
to sitting and looked through the nicotine haze on the van window. All
men wanted was sex, but not from her. What was she missing? Catching
her faint reflection in the window, she studied her plump cheeks, round
stone-colored eyes. A sad, small mouth. She couldn't recall anyone saying
she was pretty, but she knew she wasn't ugly. Maybe he thought she was
too young, or innocent. Or was it this stupid grade-school frock? These
braids. She yanked at the elastics holding her plaits together and fingered
them apart, shook her hair out into a wild wavy mane. She could scarcely
stand the feel of this dress on her skin.

"Look, I'm sorry," he said again. "Nothing personal. I just don't like
you like that." Then he touched his heart and smiled. "Do you know what
I mean?"

She didn't understand, she just wished he would drop it. She had a sudden urge to tear off and set fire to everything she'd brought from home.

"Hey," she said. "Any chance you got an extra T-shirt in there?"

He tipped his head to the side, questioning, and gestured to her bag. "What's wrong with the clothes you brought?" he said.

She sighed and shrugged. "They don't fit anymore."

He reached into the canvas duffel behind him and drew out a plain red T-shirt, thin and faded with wear. She looked around for a place to dress in private, but, deciding she wasn't in any danger of being ravaged, turned around and pulled her dress over her head, then unbuttoned her blouse and removed it, too. She could feel his eyes on her back, keenly aware of the rolls at her waist, and wondered if he liked them or didn't. Then she heard him crawl into the front seat and start fiddling with the radio. The red shirt felt snug around her breasts and smelled stout with cologne. She fished around in her own bag and tugged on a pair of blue pedal pushers. Old-fashioned but better than her homely dress.

Part of her was ready to go home. She'd take the first bus to Fort Worth and tell her mother in the morning that she was moving out. Minus bus fare, she might still have first and last month's rent. If she signed a lease, she'd be locked into figuring something out. She would have to do better, make more money. Maybe even move to Austin, join a band. She smiled to think such a leap was within reach. The idea of facing her mother after disappearing for two days filled her with itchy angst. It was one thing to fantasize about telling her mother off and moving out, and another to follow through. She feared if she went home Faith would drill into her with those insistent blue eyes and break her will. Then again, she had already left, hadn't she?

"Listen," Benny said, climbing out of the driver's seat. "I gotta be in Nashville by noon. I wish I could stick around for the funeral, but, you know, a gig's a gig."

"Oh, you're leaving now?" There was hurt in her voice. She wondered if he would make an offer, a ride to the bus station, or something to eat.

"I meant what I said. I think you're great. If you ever make it out to San Diego, give me a call."

"Yeah," she said like she knew how it was. He wasn't making any offers. She was on her own.

"Welp," Benny said. "I gotta split. You good?"

"Super," she said and slid out of the van and into a tangle of grass and sticker burrs.

Twyla's insides turned over at the thought of being here without a friend. Suddenly she wished someone would tell her what to do. She thought back to that moment in her room, Mother's hands in her hair. *Every night I pray for you, Twyla, for happiness to come your way.* But happiness wasn't coming for her. She had to go out and find it.

The engine turned over. She ran up to the driver's side where Benny was putting the car into gear.

"Benny, wait," she said. He rolled down his window with a look that said, *Make it quick.* "I need a ride."

She ignored the whiff of irritation on Benny's face, the one that wondered how long he'd be stuck with her. She had made up her mind. She would hitch a ride to Nashville, if not with Benny, then with someone else. All these years writing songs, and here was her chance to make something of it.

"Come on, Benny."

"I don't know, Twyla, we're just there for the gig and then we head back home. I don't—"

"I can handle myself," she said. "It's just the ride I need." He made ditches of his brows as he thought it over. She stared a hole right through him, willing him to say yes, even as she realized she was asking him to throw her off a cliff.

CHAPTER 7

Twyla dozed on and off for the three-and-a-half-hour drive to Nashville, but when they entered the city limits she rolled her window all the way down and stuck out her head. She didn't want to miss a thing. Gorgeous trees, limber and swishing in big gusts of wind. A great classical building with many columns, one that looked straight from ancient Greece, presiding over a vast lawn. A group of boys played in the magnolias, spiking their seedy cones at each other. They cruised down past the bungalows and modest office buildings on Sixteenth Avenue, the heart of Nashville's music industry, and she marveled at how her favorite songs had been forged in such ordinary surroundings. The whole town was much smaller than she expected, no bigger than Fort Worth. But the atmosphere was charged, radiant. Music trailed out of bars and restaurants, musicians passed on foot with instruments in tow, marquees on every storefront barked out the next big thing.

They filled up the van and split the gas money, then cruised downtown. At the end of Broadway she glimpsed the Cumberland, a wide, churning waterway that divided the town. Benny pulled up to a record shop on lower Broadway.

"This is where I leave you." His eyes skittered from the bag at her feet to the car door. She lingered a moment, not quite ready to launch. Outside the car a disheveled woman picked through an overfull garbage can. Her shirt was in tatters but on her feet were brand-new cowgirl boots in dazzling peacock blue.

"Any ideas where I should go?" she asked. It was a pathetic question. Even she could hear it.

"It's Nashville, baby. The city is yours—go out there and grab it." His voice was falsely upbeat. When she looked back at him, the lost feeling in her heart was reflected on his face. Sympathetic eyes, his lips set hard against each other. He glanced at the time.

"Well, why don't you come on out to grab a bite with us before the show. I'll introduce you to Julio and Cam."

She lunged across the seats and gave him an awkward hug.

He shrugged her off and she got out of the van. "I'll pick you up here at seven."

THE BUILDINGS ON BROADWAY WERE a mix of elegant, turn-of-the-century redbrick storefronts with tall, arched windows and junky-looking businesses hawking their wares in sputtering neon light. She let herself stare at the images of nude or nearly nude women advertising peep shows at the adult arcades. She could hear her mother crying *Sodom and Gomorrah* at the sight, but it wasn't so bad in the light of day.

Then she walked by the Ryman Auditorium and kissed the door of the original home of the Grand Ole Opry. She passed pawn shops, furniture stores, bars, souvenirs, a guitar shop, and a boutique selling custom western wear. She slowed down to look in the window at a woman's suit being fitted to a mannequin by a man with a pincushion strapped to his wrist. The cream-colored suit was embroidered with cacti and prickly pears and beautiful desert birds. She imagined slipping it on, stepping onstage to a blast of lights and cheers. Anything, even this, seemed within reach in Nashville.

She found a hot dog stand with a striped awning and bought a tall lemonade and a foot-long with chili and minced onions, which she ate, gratefully, standing in the shade of the awning. With sore feet and a full heart, she made her way back to the famous Ernest Tubb Record Shop to wait for Benny.

Tubb's was the home of the radio program the *Midnite Jamboree*. The names and the sounds that came out of this room were gigantic, but the space was surprisingly intimate. Framed photos of all the country music greats lined the walls above shelves and shelves of records. A banner announcing Tubb's thirty-year anniversary was strung across the room. There was an Elvis display set up at the front of the long, narrow shop with albums and pictures and little offerings that people had placed around it—packs of gum, handkerchiefs, silk flowers, and tchotchkes purchased in the store. She thought of Eli back home and wondered what he'd say about the strange journey that had landed her in this particular record shop, at this moment in time. Maybe he wouldn't think anything of it, but she hoped he'd be proud. Then she remembered her promise to return with the money for the Sundowners album and realized, with striking clarity, she would not be home anytime soon.

"Excuse me, miss," someone said from the other end of the store. She turned and saw a man in his twenties with wolfish good looks. She took in a world of details in a glance: dark, curly hair that appeared clean but not brushed; an outfit that was young-outlaw country, a pearl-snap shirt and brown leather vest, silver-and-turquoise cuff; an orthodontic smile, white and straight; broad chested and built strong.

"Are you Twyla?" he said. How in the *world* did he know her name? She crossed her arms across her chest.

"That's me," she said. "How did you know?"

He held up a slip of paper and came toward her. He walked squarely, legs a little wide-set. If Benny was a six, this guy was a ten straight out of bed. She could barely see his eyes behind his tinted aviators but she'd bet they were tens, too.

"Here," he said and handed her the paper, which was folded and labeled with her name. "A guy came looking for you and left this."

Benny, she thought with a start. Had she gotten the time wrong and missed him? The stranger left her alone without comment.

She flipped open the letter and read:

Twyla, tonight's gig fell through—Linda Ronstadt came to town so we got bumped—but we booked a headliner in Atlanta. Driving there now, couldn't wait. God Rest the King! -Benny

She crumpled the letter. Dumped.

The handsome guy returned with her bag, her guitar, and a can of beer. A pang of homesickness hit her when she saw Pearl. He set her things on the ground in front of her and held out the beer.

"Shit," he said. "Was that your ride?" He seemed half caring, polite but removed. She was grateful for the gesture, though, and took the beer and sipped it, considering what her next move would be, whether to spend her remaining money on a bus ticket or a room.

"Kind of," she said and lifted the beer. "Thanks for this . . ." She raised her eyebrows to prompt him for a name.

"Chet Wilton," he said with a nod. He was keeping his distance, but there was a tension there. Of intrigue or attraction, she didn't know. He sure wasn't hitting on her. She looked down at her short pants and legs that needed shaving. And those horrifying loafers that stirred up a hatred for her mother. *Oh, it's a blessing to be homely, Twyla*, her mother had said one day at the shops when she'd denied Twyla a pair of low-heeled pumps. *When you find love you'll know he's in it for the right reasons.* It had never been a comfort to know her plain looks would weed out all the men who enjoyed a beautiful woman. In moments like these, she got the feeling her mother was trying to keep her a rung down.

"How far are we from the nearest Greyhound station?"

"Not too far," he said. "Going so soon?"

She laughed a little bitterly. "I came to Memphis for the funeral," she said.

He nodded.

"I hadn't planned on coming here at all."

"There's only one reason anyone brings their guitar to Nashville," he said.

She didn't want to admit to her ambition yet, but why not? It didn't quite feel like shame, more that it was all so new to her, this business of going after what she wanted.

He looked at the clock on the wall. "Hang tight," he said. "Closing time."

"Oh, I can go," she said gathering up her things. "Sorry to trouble."

"No, no, stay for a bit if you like, use the phone. No need to rush." He locked the register and flipped the CLOSED sign.

He produced another beer from behind the counter, cracked it open, and took a foamy sip. He leaned against the wall and lifted his chin at her guitar. "You a picker?"

"No, I just mess around. I write songs mostly." Her daddy was a picker, but she didn't think of herself that way.

"That counts, doesn't it?"

She shrugged and gulped her beer, cool going down, but warm where it hit her stomach. She was beginning to enjoy the taste, its malty and bitter notes, and the feeling of fullness, but what she loved the most was the way it reminded her of her freedom. She would not be here, sharing a drink with a stranger, had she stayed at home.

"Here," she said, feeling encouragement from the beer. "I'll play you one I'm working on now." She flipped the clasps on her case and lifted the top.

"Look at this beauty," he said, then he took the guitar from her.

"Hey, now," she said. He might as well have plucked a baby from her arms. She kept her eyes on him, watching, but he handled the guitar gently. He picked a simple melody, then felt his way around the guitar. He had a nice smell, warm and spiced, like he'd just walked out of a bakery.

"That was my daddy's guitar," she said after a while. "He called it Pearl."

"Country music?" he said.

"Bluegrass. Old band called the Sundowners. They were about to get big in the early sixties and then kind of . . . dropped off."

"No shit," he said, brightening. Then he handed Pearl to Twyla, went to the wall, and flipped through some records. He held up the album she'd listened to just a few days before at Eli's. "This him?"

Her gray eyes went wide. "You're yanking my chain," she said. She went over to him, took the old record in her hands. The sight of Mickey in this new place cheered her right up. "You've heard of them?"

"Hell, yeah," he said. "I dig that old-time shit. Rough around the edges, you know? Not that slick Nashville sound."

She pointed to her father. "That's him, that's my father."

He ran his hand through his hair and grinned. "Who woulda thought I'd be hanging out with Mickey Higgins's daughter tonight."

She smiled back, shy and pink in the cheeks. "And playing his guitar," she added.

He looked closer at the album cover, at the pretty little Martin with the North Star inlay, and took off his tinted aviators. When he looked back at her, she saw his eyes for the first time. He had thick lashes, irises dappled green and brown and gold. She had never understood the term "bedroom eyes" until this moment. Not sleepy, but relaxed and seductive.

"Listen, I have to go," he said, glancing at the clock.

"Oh," she said. She didn't want him to go. He pulled the shades over the storefront windows and shut off the air-conditioning. She gathered her things and stood by the door. She had the embarrassing impulse to follow him around tonight. Perhaps she could ask him for a place to stay, or at least to point her in the right direction.

"You work here every day, or . . . ?"

He looked confused. "Oh, no, I'm just covering for a buddy of mine. I'm a musician." He pointed to a flyer on the wall, a woodcut of his face with "Chet Wilton Band" in a curly western script. Thinking back to the way he'd played her guitar, she was a little surprised to hear him say he was in a working band. His picking was proficient, but lacking in artistry. If *he* could make it, maybe there was a chance for her, too.

Twyla was about to ask if she could see him play when he pushed open the door and stepped outside. He held it open for her and she followed him out to the sidewalk.

"Well, I better run," he said. "Good luck to you and the same to Pearl."

She smiled over her disappointment. Another acquaintance gone so soon. And there was the question of where to sleep tonight. She willed herself to say something. But her jaw was locked shut.

He held out his hand and she shook it, then he said goodbye and was gone.

CHAPTER 8

Twyla glanced up and down Broadway. Country music floated out the open doors of bars and honky-tonks. A clock tower read ten after seven. Twyla counted her money. After paying for food and pitching in for gas, she had forty-seven dollars left, enough for a few nights in a motel or a ticket back home. She started walking, hoping the movement would ward off the nerves. She told herself to keep it simple. First, she'd have to find a place to stay. Then she'd try to get a job.

She walked up and down the gridded streets, looking for a motel. The first she found was too expensive, twenty dollars a night; the next had no vacancies. Finally, she saw a group of girls her age hanging around under a sign that read EXCELSIOR BY THE HOUR. The girls wore fancy clothes without brassieres and teetered on dangerous-looking heels. Their eyes followed her as she passed them and stepped inside the lobby.

The lobby was merely a thick-paned booth inside a narrow hallway, which led to a sagging staircase. Inside the booth, a jowly man with black hair and gray roots played solitaire. She cleared her throat to announce herself. Without looking up, he pointed at a sign: $1.25/HOUR CASH ONLY. She smiled, relieved. The price was right. At an hourly rate she could catch five or six hours' sleep and spend the rest of her time looking for work. Never mind the water-stained plaster, this funky smell. She could afford it. It was perfect.

The motel clerk led her up the stairs to the fourth floor and down a narrow dim hallway lined with a lumpy red carpet. He opened a room at the end near the shared bathroom and left her with the key. Slightly wider than a twin bed, it was more of a slot than a bedroom. The white sheet pinned to the window let in dusky light. But the linens seemed clean. She stowed her things under the bed and lay down, then fell swiftly to sleep.

SEVERAL HOURS LATER SHE WOKE up to someone screaming. She sat upright, uncertain of where she was. She clocked the open window, her shoes beside the bed, the chain lock on the door. Motel, Nashville. Another scream, a woman's, followed by a man grunting words she'd never heard but the meaning of which was obvious. Her whole face scorched and she remembered sounds she'd heard coming from her mother's room on Saturday nights. She was repulsed. But she was interested, too. She listened as the voices rose to a violent crescendo and then tapered to silence. Too alert to go back to sleep, she got up, used the toilet, brushed her teeth, and rinsed her armpits. Then she gathered her things and paid for the four hours she'd slept. It was already midnight, but there was still time to go out and look for work.

CHAPTER 9

Twyla made her way down Seventh to the brightest strip of Broadway. She'd find an all-night diner or a bar and ask for a job. She'd keep asking until someone said yes.

After just a few blocks she stepped into the doorway of a bar with an empty stage and an ax throw. A bartender with a droopy mustache and tattoos on his forearms waved her in.

He slapped down a coaster and asked what she was having.

"Actually, I was hoping you might have some work for me."

She couldn't believe she'd just come out and asked for it. She held her breath to wait.

He clicked his tongue and revealed a flash of gold on a tooth.

"Working woman, huh?" He raised a beer to his lips, soaking his mustache in foam, then set it down, now half empty, on the bar.

"What are we talking about? Barback? Bussing? Waitstaff?"

"Whatever you need, sir. I just need a job is all."

He smiled down at something, a private thought. "Whatever I need," he said. A chuckle and then a hard look that sent a ripple of fear across her skin. She mumbled an apology, then quickly left the bar.

She hurried down the sidewalk, stunned. She felt naive and stupid. What had she said to put that mean glint in his eye? She suddenly wished for the safety of her job at the daycare, for Cecile's cheery prattle and the sounds of children at play.

But it was too soon—or too late—to retreat. She followed brightly painted signs advertising "Irma's Famous" and turned into an alley where a plump, aproned elderly lady in cat-eye glasses leaned against the door, smoking. She looked like she belonged in a school cafeteria more than a bar.

The woman gave Twyla, bag in one hand, guitar case in the other, a once-over. "You just get in today, little mama?" she said.

Twyla had to think about it for a moment—was it only today she arrived? It felt like days ago.

"Yes, ma'am," she said.

"I'm Irma," the woman said.

"Twyla."

"You got a place to stay yet, Twyla?"

"Sort of," she said, not wanting to advertise her lodging, suddenly ashamed.

"Bless your heart." Irma shook her head. "There's a boardinghouse for young ladies. Cheap and clean. I'll get you the number."

Twyla gave her a small smile and thanked her.

"Lord, if I had a nickel for every lost soul that walked through that door. Lemme just finish this ciggie and I'll fix you a drink." She pinched the cigarette and sucked three times in a row, then killed the butt under the toe of her flats. Then she led Twyla inside. The bar was smaller than it looked from the street, its walls and ceiling papered with tobacco-stained photographs and ballpoint pen graffiti. A three-foot cloud of cigarette smoke loomed over everything. Hank Williams yodeled on the jukebox and the forty-odd seats were half full. There was a bulletin board with many layers of advertisements for used instruments, amps, voice lessons, and celebrity tours of Nashville.

"If you're looking for a job, you can start right there," she said, pointing to the bulletin. "Everyone passes through here at some point."

She brightened. Some flyers had a fringe cut into the bottom where you could take a phone number. She pulled five numbers and tucked them into her coin purse for tomorrow.

An old salt at the bar tipped his hat at her. "This one's on me, Irma," he said.

Twyla didn't get the feeling he was hitting on her but didn't care to tempt a situation. "No, thank you, I'm all right."

"Newcomer's special, comin' right up!" Irma said. She pulled a beer off the tap and filled a shot glass with whisky, then gave them to Twyla.

A reedy woman with heavy kohl and a Jane Fonda shag offered her a cigarette. Twyla shook her head.

"Relax, sister," she said, lighting the cigarette Twyla had refused. "No strings attached. Isn't that right, Wallace?" He didn't look over, just kind of waved his hand in confirmation and went back to his drinking.

The woman stretched out her arm to Twyla. "Mimi." She wore a tank top without a bra and had let the hair in her armpits grow long. She had the allure of an aging French actress, disheveled, cigarette thin, and nonchalant.

Twyla shook her hand and gave her name. She sipped a scant teaspoon of her beer and let the whisky be.

"You should come back and put your name in a hat on Monday for Writer's Night—you are a writer, right?"

"How'd you guess?" she said.

"You don't seem like you enjoy being looked at," she mumbled over her smoke.

Twyla thought about that and answered quietly, "Sometimes I don't, sometimes I do."

"No offense," the woman said. "I'm in the business myself. Or once was. Writers are the good ones." She sipped her beer and looked thoughtful. "It's the singers you have to watch out for."

Twyla wanted to ask if she'd worked with anyone famous, but played it cool, hoping she might offer more details as they spoke.

"Is everyone in Nashville in the music business?" Twyla asked.

"No!" Irma shouted across the bar. She swizzled a Tom Collins and licked the spoon. "*Some* of us work for a living."

"Oh, please," Mimi shot back. "Irma, country music bought you a coupe de ville and a four-bedroom house in Brentwood." Irma shook her head like she wasn't going to comment. Mimi returned her attention to Twyla.

"So, what's your story anyway?"

Twyla took a breath and considered how to answer. "I took a bus to Memphis a couple days ago," she said. "To pay my respects."

Mimi's eyes watered up. She wiped at them, smudging her kohl. "This only happens when I drink."

Twyla teared up, too.

"Goddammit," Mimi said and raised her glass. Twyla toasted and they both drank. "Did you see him? In the flesh?"

Twyla nodded. They sipped in silence for a moment.

Irma took Mimi's drink before she was finished. Mimi reached after it but Irma had already dumped it in the sink.

"You can fix me a fresh one, then," Mimi said and Irma raised her eyebrows like she should reconsider another drink. "Not that it's any of your business, but in case you were just about to judge me, I'll have you know my son doesn't come till next Tuesday."

"I love kids," Twyla said. "How old?"

"He's four. He's so goddamned cute I could kill him. I only get him three days a week, though, and I'm always hustling trying to find work."

"That must be hard. Three days a week, I mean."

Mimi teared up again and the left corner of her mouth went down. She cleared her throat hard and picked up the last of her cigarette from the ashtray and finished it in one long drag.

"My row to hoe," she said on the exhale.

Irma leaned over her side of the counter, her bosom perilously close to the maraschino cherries, and passed Mimi another drink.

"Mimi, ain't you always talking about needing some help around the house and look after Ollie?"

Mimi shrugged off the question.

Twyla sensed an opening. It was a little early to make a play, but the woman seemed nice enough. And the sooner she could get out of the motel, the better.

"I could watch him for you."

Mimi looked at her strange. "You're sweet, but I don't know boo about you."

Twyla shushed her nerves and pressed forward. "That's true, miss, you don't know me and I don't know you. But maybe you could give me a trial run."

Mimi turned slightly to Twyla, as if she might be open to persuasion.

"I worked in a daycare back home. I'm good with kids. If you can give me a place to stay, we can get to know each other better. I'll clean up or cook, whatever you like."

"She can hustle, cain't she?" Irma said, amused.

"Look, I'm not just gonna leave you with my kid." Mimi tapped the bar next to her drink. Irma filled her a glass of soda water. "But"—Mimi drew a gusty breath and let it out—"if you need a place to crash, for a night or two, until my son comes, be my guest."

Twyla tried not to look too eager or grateful, but found herself smiling at Mimi.

"Now, if you're looking for some kind of leg up in this town, you can forget it. Even if I wanted to open doors for you, which I don't, you should just know I have no pull around here anymore."

"Three hots and a cot—that's all I need." She'd heard her Daddy say that to her mother once. She couldn't remember why but it had stuck with her. Mimi gave a little reluctant laugh.

"Sure, fine," she said and slid a five across the bar to pay her tab. "Newcomer's special. Come on."

MIMI'S HOUSE DIDN'T MATCH THE colonial two-story brick houses in the woodsy neighborhood near Radnor Lake. It was modern, low and angular, like sheets of slate jutting out of the earth. Though it must have been a statement house when they'd built it, the whole place bore the shabby, crumbling patina of deferred maintenance. The peeling orange front door was flanked by a floor-to-ceiling glass pane through which you could see clear across the house to the backyard swimming pool. Beside the door sat a flowerpot full to the brim of barren soil, the shriveled stems of dead plants, and cigarette butts, and the dim front porch light fixture lit in silhouette the scattered bodies of june bugs and flies. Lloyd, a compulsive fixer, would have been both maddened by the disrepair and ecstatic at the task of improving its condition. Her mother would simply have delighted in judging it.

Mimi opened the door into the sparely appointed court of the foyer and the living and kitchen areas, which had the air of something missing. Bare picture hooks on the walls, a black leather sofa on a rug with no other seating to fill out the large living room, dirt-strewn plant saucers absent their potted plants.

"You lucked out," Mimi said, stepping out of her ankle-high leather boots one by one as she flipped on lights and made her way to the kitchen. She filled up two dark green tumblers with water and dropped into one of them a pair of antacids. "Want one?" she said, holding out the box of Alka-Seltzer. Twyla shook her head no. She removed her ugly shoes and set them neatly by the door, then wished she could have kept them on. Her socks were cruddy and so damp she had to take care not to slip on the terrazzo floor.

"Not one hangover since I started doing this," Mimi said and shook her head as she stared into the fizzing glass. "The one good thing my ex left me. Besides Ollie."

When the antacid bubbles subsided, Mimi shimmied two aspirin out of the bottle and downed them with the tonic in three loud gulps.

"You were saying I lucked out?" Twyla reminded her host.

"Oh, yeah," Mimi said. "Here, follow me."

She led Twyla away from the living area into a long, dark, carpeted hallway. On their left were three doors spaced apart. On the right a glass wall that looked out into the overgrown yard. The two backyard sconces showed the rough sketch of a long rectangular pool but yielded little de-tail, only the feeling of encroachment by the overgrown plantings and trees.

"You lucked out, my dear, because I was just about to toss the mat-tress," Mimi said. "Just drag that sucker to the curb, bedding and all. Too many bad memories wrapped up in those sheets. Lucky for you," she said and belched into her fist, "I was too lazy to act on my drunken whims." They passed a small bedroom with a twin bed and a little Howdy Doody lamp and baskets of toys against the wall. She pressed her hand to the doorframe as one would the back of a loved one.

"That's Ollie's room," she said, then gestured to the room next to it. "This'll be where you sleep." When the lights went on, she could see this had been Mimi's room. A king-size bed, low to the ground with built-in side tables and bedside sconces, dominated the longest wall and faced sliding glass doors that led to the backyard. "You've got your own entrance here to come and go as you like."

Mimi yawned and ruffled her hair, turning as she spoke. "I'm gonna hit the hay, Newcomer. Help yourself to whatever shit-all I have in the fridge and just *please*, don't wake me in the morning. I get up when I get up."

"Wait," Twyla said, Mimi already at the end of the hall. "Where are *you* gonna sleep?"

Mimi gave a weary look at her old room. "I haven't slept in there since I kicked him out. Can't stand even to look at it. I'll be in the guest room past the kitchen. But like I said—"

"Don't wake you in the morning," Twyla said. "I won't make a peep. Thank you, ma'am, thank you so much."

Mimi dismissed the show of gratitude with a wave of her hand and Twyla closed the door. She took in the elegant lines and subtle furnish-ings of this room, its casual expanse, and then thought of the motel room she'd slept in hours before. It was then she decided she would make her-self indispensable to Mimi.

CHAPTER 10

After Mimi went to bed, Twyla took the shower of her dreams. She soaped and scrubbed and let the nearly too-hot water fall over her until it turned lukewarm. She dried off with a washrag she found in the bathroom drawer and dressed herself in a clean blouse and pedal pushers, for she had forgotten to pack a nightgown. She tumbled into Mimi's plush, enormous bed and slept deeply, unselfconsciously, and dreamt of nothing. When she woke up around seven a.m., she felt dumb and disoriented. Then, remembering Mimi and her kindness, she got to work tidying up.

She gathered into a laundry basket all the clothes that had been strewn about the house, loaded crusty dishes into the dishwasher, and swept the hardwood floors. She pumped a whole bottle of Windex on the windows and wiped them down, then opened the sliding doors to refresh the smoky, stagnant air. When she finished cleaning, she ate a slice of toast with margarine and then showered a second time just to feel the water on her skin.

At eleven thirty, Twyla was brewing a pot of coffee when Mimi scuffed in from the living room with a breakfast cigarette between her lips. She wore black jeans and a threadbare tank top and her hair was matted in back.

"Lord have mercy, Twyla," Mimi said, still squinting at the late-morning light. "You do not kid around, do you?" Twyla couldn't tell if she was pleased or just taken aback by her efforts.

"I can do a deep clean anytime you like, but I didn't want to make too much noise. I hope you don't mind my taking the liberty."

Mimi put on a friendlier face. "Oh, no, please, this is . . ." She picked at the snarl behind her head absently as she looked around. "Well, I knew it was a dump but I didn't realize how much until just now."

Twyla took two slices of bread out of the breadbox. "May I fix you some toast?"

Mimi was still waking up and looked confused. "Honey, I don't need a cook."

Twyla knew she was overdoing it. She decided to make a more direct appeal.

"I've been thinking. I know you said I could crash for a night or two—and I'm so grateful for it—but do you think I could stay on a few more days until I find my footing here? I promise I'll earn my keep."

Mimi took a drag and laid her smoke in an ashtray that looked like it had been stolen from a diner. "Let's just take it one day at a time," she said. "You seem cool, but I've been wrong before."

Twyla felt a wave of disappointment but nodded her understanding as she pulled the plastic seal off a tube of frozen orange juice concentrate. Mimi watched her opening and closing cabinets for a moment before telling Twyla to stop and pointed to a lower cabinet. "Should be a pitcher in there somewhere."

Twyla mixed the juice and poured the coffee she'd made earlier, smeared some margarine on the toast, and put the plate on the counter in front of Mimi. Mimi waved her hand to invite Twyla to share with her and they ate for a bit in silence. Twyla felt the woman's questions gathering in her mind. *What's your story, kid?* And she wasn't quite ready with an answer. Soon she would have to decide what she was doing here. Would she try to get up and sing somewhere, would she have the guts to put herself out there? She didn't know much about what it took to be a working musician, but she knew it was hard to break in. The very thought of it embarrassed her, how little she knew and how dearly she wanted it, and she wished her daddy were here to guide her. Mimi had already declared herself unwilling to help. Twyla hoped she would change her mind, but it was too soon to press the issue. She had the sense it would be wiser to prove useful to Mimi before asking for favors.

"So," she said, gathering the dishes. "Can you tell me about your son?"

Mimi looked more alert than she had all morning. She scrunched up her nose and her eyes, the mere thought of him filling her with unbearable love.

"Oliver. My boy." She laughed the tiniest laugh. "I miss that joker every single day. You know he's been gone for a month? Went to see his grandmother in Virginia. Even when he's here I'm missing him because I know he's about to leave."

"Is his daddy nice?"

Mimi dealt a loaded expression. "Nice, no. But he's a good father mostly. I'm the screwup in this family. Kind of let things slide lately." She gestured around the house. "Well, you saw the way I live."

Twyla cleared the breakfast plates and slotted them into the dishwasher. "Everybody needs help sometimes."

Mimi refilled her coffee cup. She sipped—too hot—then blew on it, thinking.

"Fine, fine. You can stay at least until Tuesday. If Ollie likes you, and if Dean doesn't hate you, we can talk about something a little more . . . steady."

Twyla resisted the urge to throw her arms around Mimi. Instead she wiped down the counter and grinned at the distinct feeling that things were beginning to fall into place.

ALL WEEKEND TWYLA HELPED MIMI prep the house, stocking the fridge and pantry, changing out all the fizzled lightbulbs, putting new batteries in Ollie's toys. By Monday, the house was transformed. Cozy even. The two women were loading bags of garbage bound for the dump into the trunk of Mimi's ice-blue Dodge Charger Daytona, when Twyla remembered what Mimi had said about Writer's Night. She had been hoping for encouragement from Mimi, some bend in her rule about not giving Twyla a leg up.

"So, I was thinking about going to Writer's Night at Irma's," Twyla said cautiously, sliding one foot onto thin ice.

Mimi continued muscling the last bag in the trunk. "Uh-huh," she said, also cautiously.

"Do I just show up? Or what's the . . . procedure?"

Mimi brought down the trunk door and tried to close it, but it was too full. "You know," she said, frustrated at something, maybe the trunk, maybe Twyla. "You throw your name in the hat. You get picked, you go up. Pretty simple."

Twyla nodded and joined Mimi in pushing on the trunk door. "Yeah, okay. I can do that. And is it acoustic . . . or do I need to bring anything special?"

Mimi jumped up and brought her weight down on the door, forcing it to click shut. Her dark hair, damp from the effort and the summer humidity, licked curls all around her face.

"Goddamn, girl, I told you I didn't want any part of this. So you can keep your hedging questions to yourself. Here's what you need to know: if you want to make it in Nashville, you have to figure it out yourself. Anything good that comes out of your career is gonna happen because you cracked your knuckles and got your hands dirty. You start off expecting handouts, you can *forget it*. And even if you get what you're looking for, and everything goes your way—even if you're Patsy fuckin' Cline—they can take it away from you *like that*." She kicked the tire of her car and stormed inside. Twyla could see that this outburst had roots. Where they came from, she could not know for sure but guessed it had something to do with Mimi's ex-husband and this fancy, run-down house. Still, it hurt to be dressed down after she'd spent her weekend helping out.

Twyla gave her a moment, then followed her inside where she found Mimi sitting on the edge of the neglected pool, her feet skimming the leaf-strewn cover. Twyla stood awkwardly at the sliding door, wishing she had someone else to ask. Then she remembered how she had gotten here, from Fort Worth to Memphis to Nashville, Tennessee, with a few bucks and more courage than she'd had in all the nineteen years before. *Feet-first, Twyla.* She took a map from the Charger glove compartment and found the intersection she'd remembered from the other night, Fifth Avenue and Broadway. Using the guide she estimated they were about six miles away, an hour and a half by foot if she booked it, faster if she hitched a ride. She stepped out of her dirty clothes and showered quickly. Then she dressed in the only clean clothes she had, her smock dress and blouse, and avoided the mirror. After stashing a five-dollar bill in her pocket, she grabbed her guitar and headed out.

Mosquitoes flitted around her body, landing, sucking as she walked down the front path. She could feel the tingle of an itch about to happen in a dozen spots.

"I'm not trying to be an asshole," Mimi said from the front door. Twyla turned around. "But it looks like you dressed yourself on your way out of a burning house."

Twyla soured her face. Mimi laughed and motioned for her to come back in. "I'm sorry for bitching you out. I should keep my mouth sewn shut." Then she squared Twyla by the shoulders and gave her a good once-over. "But lord, woman, give me some background on this getup. You a Jehovah? What is the deal?"

Twyla told her she came from a churchy family and left it at that.

"All right, we're going shopping," Mimi said and led her to her bedroom closet. It was a whole room unto itself, packed with clothes of vivid colors, slacks in shades of citrus, blouses in florals, paisleys, geometric patterns, stripes in every direction. At first, Twyla selected some gray slacks and a white button-down blouse. She held the outfit in front of her body and studied her reflection. It was a comfortable look, sensible. She would not be concerned with hemlines or attention. She would be able, as always, to move around without being noticed. Mimi scowled and told her to put it back.

"What are you, eighty years old? I've got half of Harveys department store in here and none of it fits me anyway. Go wild. Honestly, anytime you want." Then Mimi left her alone.

Running her fingertips along the hanging dresses, Twyla felt textures from corduroy to denim, to polyester to silk. She strained to imagine the need for such variety, felt physically stressed at the thought of trying to select one outfit out of such abundance. She finally settled on a pair of high-waisted bell-bottom jeans, a psychedelic-print blouse in sherbets. She found some black Keds in the closet that were a size too big but fit fine with some thick socks.

After dressing, she turned around to look at the shape of her butt in the mirror, a "3" lying on its side. It wanted to burst out of the jeans, bulged at the pockets. She faced forward again; her abdomen pressed at the zipper, and the flesh at her waist spilled over the sides. The top she'd selected revealed her shape in a way she had never seen before. There was a harmony to the balance of her breasts and her hips, the softness of her belly, the leonine waves of her hair. It made her angry to see herself this way, as desirable, lovely, because for so long, she had been made to think she was plain. Her mother had surrounded her in dull, untouchable fabrics, had insisted on clothing that deflected interest, had strangled her hair into braids so tight they lifted the outer corners of her eyes and pulled the skin of her forehead till it shone. Standing here now, she wondered if perhaps her mother had been afraid of a girl who knew her strength. But why would Mother hold her back? Why steer her away from playing the music she loved, from looking like a woman who wanted to be seen?

She found Mimi standing by the door, holding her keys.

"I have to go to town anyhow," she said. "So don't think I changed my mind. I'll take you to Fifth and Broad. You can find your own damn way home."

CHAPTER 11

"Why do you think they let Gram sing over Emmylou like that?" Twyla asked. A popular duet by Gram Parsons and Emmylou Harris was playing on the car stereo as they drove to town.

Mimi shook her head. "Beats me. I always thought his vocals were pretty feeble. He sounds even worse next to Emmylou."

"So why's he so much louder?"

"It *is* his album," Mimi said thoughtfully. "But, I don't know, maybe that's how it was between them, too. Some women choose to let their man step forward. Even if they're holding back the goods. But keep listening. She knows what she's doing."

Twyla felt a little slap of anger thinking about how she'd let her mother speak over her so long, how everybody let her mother take charge. She brooded quietly, blocking out the song completely. Then Mimi patted her knee.

"Listen here," she said and turned up the volume. "She's picking it up. Hear it? She was just biding her time. She wasn't gonna hang back forever." They listened as Emmylou's voice swelled, then soared. "She takes over in the end."

Mimi dropped her off at Irma's, the bar where they'd met. The swamp cooler in the window dribbled chilly air and a crowd of fifty or so filled the floor, some seated in folding chairs around tables the size of a steering wheel, others standing by the bar or gathered along the walls.

But for Irma and a few old-timers posted up at the back of the bar, the crowd tonight skewed younger. At one table a group of big-haired women in leather fringe and custom boots pressed their heads together in conversation, while a nearby group of cowboys looked ready to make a move. A man with a fiddle rosined his bow while his teenage son played a pair of spoons.

Twyla wished there were someone to hold her hand and wish her luck, but tonight she was on her own. She wrote her full name on a matchbook flap and dropped it in a cowboy hat. She was proud to see her daddy's last name and hoped he'd be proud, too. She found a place to stand in the back and watched as Irma called the first act. Her whole body tightened at the possibility of hearing her name. Her only experience performing had been in the safety of the church choir, and though she had dreamed of a moment like this, she now wondered if she would know what to do when the moment arrived.

"Lydia Giles," Irma said into the microphone, and Twyla relaxed for a moment. A lean, long-haired brunette in a slip of a dress took the stage. She strummed out her opening chord and took a breath. Others carried on chatting and drinking, but Twyla couldn't look away. The woman closed her eyes, calming her nerves. She took another breath and let it out slowly, seeming to reset herself. Then she played a raucous lick, stamped her boot in time, and got to singing. She had a strong, silky voice, a charming delivery. The song was funny, about a woman who spends all morning getting her hair done at the beauty salon only to have it messed up by her lover. The crowd stopped chatting. Each time she came to the end of the chorus "So I'm sending you the bill!" she'd hoot, and they'd hoot back to her. She was sensational, a natural. And Twyla was jealous.

The song she had prepared was slow and understated. She had chosen it because it was easy to remember and made Eli misty when she had played it for him last spring. But here in this bar she could see it would be suicide to play the song in a room like this, people drinking and carrying on. Lydia Giles had set the tone. Twyla scrambled to recall a lighter number she knew well enough to play without thinking. She came up short. They were all, in this light, maudlin. Dirges. Moony, saccharine, unfit in every way. Her chest tightened, hands clamped around the neck of her guitar as if strangling it. What would she sing? Even the lighter songs she had written with Daddy were old-fashioned, simple, heavily bluegrass. Front-porch ditties. She remembered the chord progressions but the lyrics escaped her.

Nine people followed Lydia Giles. No one quite as strong as she, but they enjoyed the good humor of the crowd and kept their numbers brisk and cheerful. Around eleven p.m., Twyla started working her way around the crowd to remove her name from the hat. She had decided to work on a new song, practice it to death, and come back next Monday. Or the Monday after that. She was trying to wriggle past a cluster of young men at the bar when Irma called her name.

She closed her eyes. She could leave. Just duck out the door. They'd move on to the next name. But then she'd be the girl who didn't show when her name was called. Worse, *she'd* know she had chickened out on her first little shot in Nashville.

She lifted her guitar to signal she was coming and the crowd parted slightly for her to approach the stage, people at the tables tucking their feet under so as not to trip her. The audience seemed friendly, if a little drunk. She stepped up to the small stage, a shipping pallet filled out with two-bys and painted black. She sat on the wooden stool, adjusted the mic to her height. There was no time now to choose another song. She would sing the one she'd prepared, but play it faster, lean into the guitar. She'd have to start strong. Push through the nerves. She thumbed the strings lightly and could hear that her guitar remained, thankfully, in tune.

She laid her hand on Pearl, the song gathering up like a swell.

Then she drew up her pick and ripped into the strings.

She strummed like a mariachi, muscular and loud, giving herself an extra measure to make sure she remembered the lyrics. The audience tuned in. She skated her fingers down the fretboard, plucked the A string and bent it hard. People straightened up at the bluesy flourish, and Twyla relished the way she had made them react with a tug of her finger. She bent it again and was about to launch into the opening verse when the A string snapped away from the bridge and whipped her across the right side of her face.

It smarted like a bee sting. Tears of pain and mortification sprung from her eyes and the room blurred. A long, white-hot welt appeared on her cheek. She tried to keep playing while she decided what to do. It was stupid of her to play so hard, showing off, trying to sound big just to stand out. She hadn't thought to buy an extra set of strings.

From the side of the stage Lydia Giles held up her instrument.

"Here, honey," she said. "Use mine."

She wished she could dissolve straight into the floorboards. The offer, so kind, made Twyla feel even more pathetic. She couldn't refuse, but as she rose to accept Lydia's guitar, the whole song she was about to play vanished. The tune, the lyrics, the chords. All of it. Her mouth hung open, hand dropped to her side. Then she turned her downcast eyes toward the exit, and stumbled for the door.

Once in the dark of the alley, she sat down against the painted brick and let 'er rip. Tears, sobs, snot. Cold words against herself, for going too hard, for grandstanding when she should have waded in. She tried to summon Mickey's wisdom, but all she could hear was her mother's voice. *Serves you right for thinking you could just step up on stage like you knew what you were doing. Serves you right for leaving at all.* Pearl lay at her hip like a sympathetic hound, quietly supportive, waiting to play again.

Red-faced and puffy from crying, alley water soaking the cuffs of Mimi's bell-bottoms, Twyla wandered out in search of food. She pulled the city map Mimi gave her out of her pocket and, seeing Printers Alley was nearby, walked to Fifth Avenue and headed uphill toward Church Street. She followed Church to the east until she heard the jangly sounds of music and laughter and tucked into the alley. Bright signs in neon and blinking lights were crammed into the narrow passage among unsightly wiring and pipes running down the stone and brick buildings on either side. Women in spaghetti straps and tight jeans, men in polyester shirts stood in groups smoking, talking loud over the music blasting from the dozen businesses lining the narrow passage. George Jones's Possum Holler, Johnny Paycheck's the Country Showcase, Skull's Rainbow Room, the Black Poodle Lounge. She knew she should walk right into one of these joints and slap her name down on a list, but she was stung from her performance at Irma's. For the first time since she left, she felt homesick. The outfit that had felt so becoming earlier that night was now unbearably tight. She wanted a big, billowy nightgown and her old quilt, soft from many washings. She wanted her mother to braid her hair, to put it back in place.

She stepped inside a phone booth and pushed a dime into the slot, then dialed her home phone number. It was eleven thirty there, too, and her mother would be long asleep. She'd wake with a start and think the call could only mean bad news. Maybe it did. She worked herself up to say she was sorry as the tone trilled and silenced, trilled and silenced. Then her mother picked up.

There was a lightness in her voice. She did not sound bereaved or angry in the least. Plucky church music played in the background. What was she doing up so late? Twyla couldn't speak.

"Hellooo?" Faith said and waited. "Speak now or I'm hanging up."

She mouthed the word *Mother*. Nothing else came.

At that moment someone outside the booth slammed his hand against the window. A muted shout. Twyla jumped, gasped, and hung up on her mother. The man had pressed his forehead to the glass and looked directly at Twyla, grinning, his black eyebrows a sinister V. Without taking her eyes off him, she fumbled for the receiver. If he came for her she could try to fight him off. Then the man stepped back from the glass, waved his hand, and shouted again, this time clearly. He was saying her name. He looked familiar from this new vantage, but he'd stepped out of the light that was cast from within the booth. He pointed at his chest and shouted again.

"It's me!" he shouted. "From the record shop. Chet Wilton!"

She settled a little with relief, and when she stepped outside the phone booth and he hugged her like an old friend, the fright from moments before subsided. He smelled sweet with alcohol.

"You been roaming the streets since I last saw you or what?" he said.

She gave a polite laugh. "No, but I was headed that way."

His expression was stretchy, exaggerated. He was plastered.

"Did you have a show tonight?" she asked. She hoped at least he'd been anywhere but Irma's. There was nothing to indicate he had seen her at Writer's Night but the thought of it made her shudder.

His jaw tightened and he looked away.

"Naw, I was supposed to play a little set at the *Rainbow Room*, but they bumped me. Fuckin' Waylon Jennings."

"I love Waylon," she said, and his face crumpled like he was going to spit.

"He thinks he's hot shit," he said. "Outlaw, my ass."

Chet looked her up and down. She stood up a little straighter and tucked in her stomach.

"You're lookin' good, missy."

She went red from hair to heel. Before, on the floor of the record shop, he'd sent off a brotherly vibe. Now something flared up between them. He stepped closer and she noticed he was holding a plastic cup full of ice and cola and, she guessed, something with a kick. He held it up for her to take a sip. She touched her lips to the cup and swallowed a mouthful of cold, watery booze. Mickey had used to drink bourbon and it had smelled like this tasted. Like sweet gasoline.

"Oh no," he said, his eyebrows reaching toward each other. "Have you been crying?"

She flushed again, this time wishing she could hide. She didn't want to revisit the Writer's Night fiasco. He took her by the hand and led her away from the din.

"I'm starved," he said. "Can I buy you some chicken?"

"I could eat," she said, grateful for the change of subject. "But who's open at this hour?"

Chet nodded toward a staggered line of people waiting outside a window over which hung a yellow sign that read GERTIE'S HOT CHICKEN.

They joined the line and once Chet had paid, they carried their wax paper bundles to a bench where Broadway dead-ended at the river.

"All right," he said, unwrapping his chicken, "I have to ask. How come you were crying earlier?"

She hadn't wanted to talk about it but it felt good to have someone care. She took a big breath and let it out.

"I went up at Irma's," she said. He raised his eyebrows, like *How'd it go?* "Started off strong but then my A string gave up and . . ." She drifted into the horror of that moment. "I ran offstage like a coward."

"You choked! Oh no . . . oh man, I'm sorry." She touched the weal on her cheek. "I've been there, you know," he said.

"Really?"

"Hell yes, it's a rite of passage. You know what? I'm proud of you."

Words Mother had never spoken. She shrugged, blushing.

"I am! It takes guts to get up there."

"But I ran out like a child. It was awful. I keep replaying that moment, wishing I could have calmed down and played that lady's guitar. I could have played a cover, or 'Amazing Grace,' anything but dive for that back door like a bomb was about to go off." Chet was laughing now, trying to keep the chicken in his mouth. She must have let her discomfort show because he reached out and squeezed her arm.

"Don't get bent outta shape, Twyla, I'm laughing *with* you."

She looked down and took another bite of her drumstick.

"So, what were you going to play tonight?" he asked.

"Just something I wrote a while ago. Most of my stuff is kind of . . . moody. I was trying to sing it happier. Seemed like that was what everyone wanted to hear."

"Are you crazy?" he said. His face in the dim light of the streetlamp was pared down to its shapes. Square jaw, a faint cleft at the chin, high forehead, and smooth, strong eyebrows over drowsy, darkened eyes. "Don't play down to the audience. You gotta bring them with you. You're the artist. They don't know what's good for them or they'd be up there singing."

Artist was a new word for her. Even her daddy had never called himself an artist. Seemed a little high and mighty, but she wasn't going to correct him. She liked his idea that the artist was in charge. The audience at her mercy and not the other way around.

Then, on cue, her mother's refrain: *A man will say anything to weasel his way into your pants*. And her whole mood soured. She hated her mother for putting it in her head that any time a man complimented her, it didn't count. And what if he did want her? Why couldn't she feel good about being wanted? It never ceased to amaze her how relentlessly her mother could assassinate her joy. She wasn't even here and she was ruining the moment.

"After tonight I can't even imagine going up on stage again," she said.

"Was that your first time?"

"Pretty much," she said. "Not since I was little and played with my father. Mother says it's vain to sit up on stage by yourself, everybody's eyes on you. She'd rather stick me in a church choir."

"Your momma doesn't know how good it feels," he said. Then he nudged her leg with his. "Will you play one for me?" he asked.

His touch rippled up her thigh. Was she really here, she wondered, eating good hot chicken with one of the most beautiful people, let alone men, she had ever seen? And was he hitting on her?

"That depends," she said. "You got an extra A string?"

"I just might," he said. "I keep an extra set or two in my car. How 'bout I go check?"

She nodded, and he took off jogging. She could hear shouts and music from Printers Alley a few blocks away, many songs and voices clashing, bank buildings and other businesses all dark and aloof above the late-night carryings-on. Before long, Chet reappeared with a packet and a pair of pliers in his hand. Without asking he removed the dangling string from the bridge and fed the new one through, replacing the pin, then threaded the tune-key post and tightened the slack. It was a gesture more intimate, even, than playing her instrument. If not for the way it felt to watch his hands at work, it might have been an outright violation. After he finished, she laid Pearl in her lap and brushed her fingertips across the strings, one by one. The high E string a little flat, the new A string quite sharp. She adjusted the pegs until the notes rang clear and true. The Cumberland rolled behind her. Unnerved by his gaze, she focused on her strings and found a rhythm with the toe of her shoe.

She sang "I Miss You When You're Here," a song about her mother. Halfway through the song she stole a glance at him. His expression had changed. Not flirty, but pained. Overcome, even. She knew she should have played something lighter. He reached out and gripped the neck of the guitar, muting the strings.

"That bad, huh?" she said, trying to make light so the hurt didn't show. Then his hand slid over Pearl and gently took the guitar away from Twyla, setting it down on a patch of grass. He turned back toward her and cupped her cheeks with both hands and drew her face close to his. He paused there to let his desire be known to her, in his breath, in his searching eyes. His hands were warm where they touched her cheeks and she could feel his fingers in her hair. Then he kissed her. He didn't turn his head sideways as they often did in the movies. His face was pressed to hers, noses aligned, foreheads merged. There was thrust behind the kiss, like he was pushing into her headfirst. She felt as though dipped into thick and gorgeous warmth. She finally thought to do something with her arms, which had been stunned, slack at her sides, and wrapped them around his neck. Without effort he scooped her into his lap. Now she ran her fingers through his loose curls, down his neck, his back, marveling at his strength, how much more of him there was. In his arms she felt supple, palpable. Under his hungry kiss she felt wanted.

She was so immersed she lost track of herself, her surroundings. There was no concern that someone would see them, how it might look for a young woman to be seen straddling a man in a public park. If the Cumberland River had emptied itself onto their heads she might not have noticed it. But after a few minutes he stopped kissing her and smiled, apologetic.

"Damn, Twyla, you got me good."

She tasted his neck, the spot behind his ear. He laughed and pulled her in tight.

"There's nothing I want more right now than you."

"That's a pretty good start to a song," she said, frustrated, breathless, so full of wanting she could barely look at him. "Can I use it?" She made a note to fiddle with some lyrics later.

"But, it's just, I gotta be somewhere. And you're the kind of woman that'll make me late to things."

Her cheeks burned, even as she enjoyed it very much. She reached for Pearl, perhaps for comfort or to put a chastity barrier between her and Chet.

"Come on," he said. "I'll give you a ride. Where are you living?"

"Nice lady named Mimi Dewitt took me in. It's just for a couple of days, till I find a place of my own."

"Sounds like you might be sticking around for a while," he said, helping her up. He held her hand all the way to his mallard-green Bronco and even on the ride to Mimi's house. They kissed good night, and when he finally drove away, she fell through the doorway with numbed lips and cheeks rubbed raw.

CHAPTER 12

The next morning, the day Ollie would arrive, Twyla lay in bed for an hour thinking about Chet. She rolled the evening over in her mind like a candy on her tongue. His eyes up close, the glint of hazel when he'd look at her, the scruff on his jaw, and how soft his hair felt when he buried his face in her neck, smelling her, tasting her skin. Things he had said came back to her like verses.

How did you do that? he'd said, his lips against her collarbone. *How'd you make me love you with a song?*

She knew it was foolish to think he meant it. But how else could she describe what happened between them last night? He had touched her with care, not groping lust, had shown restraint without concealing how powerfully he'd wanted her. She had always put her heart into the songs she'd written. Was it possible this love had reached him? Had touched some part of him that might one day belong to her? A song began to nag at her. Up-tempo. Pop music. Not her style at all.

> *Get me to you*
> *I undo you*
> *What am I to you*
> *I see through you.*

The images and words came together like an abstraction, and anytime she tried to nail down a feeling it came out sounding trite. It was awful.

She hoped to God she didn't have to choose between writing songs and being in love.

AT NOON ON THE DOT, the doorbell chimed and Mimi ran to it. A decent-looking man in a western suit stood waiting, one hand behind his back.

"Mimi," he greeted her.

A little boy, small for his age by Twyla's calculations, emerged from behind the man. He had long, straight, bowl-cut hair and was sucking his thumb. Mimi had tears in her eyes and took a knee, arms outstretched. Ollie hesitated, then walked into her arms and let himself be hugged. Mimi looked like she wanted to squeeze him harder but held back enough that the boy eventually laid his head on her shoulder.

"How's your mother?" Mimi asked. The man grunted something in the affirmative. "And what's-her—"

"*Marjorie* is fine." He cleared his throat and peered around the foyer and into the living area. "You finally hire a maid or something?" he said.

Mimi's expression soured a bit, though she did not let go of Ollie, and said into his hair, "No, I did not hire a maid." She stood up and brought Ollie onto her hip. "This is Twyla Higgins; she's from Texas. She'll be staying with me, helping out around the house, till she finds a place of her own. Twyla, this is Dean."

Twyla held up a hand and said hello.

"Tell me, Twyla," he said. "Do you use drugs?"

Twyla started to answer when Mimi cut her off. "Deano, leave her alone. She's clean as a mountain stream."

"I'm only asking because I know you didn't, Meems." Turning back to Twyla: "You done any hard time?"

Twyla no-sirred him and almost mentioned that she was a song-writer, then decided, based on Mimi's loud opposition to giving her a leg up, and her poor opinion of her ex-husband, that she had better not.

Dean edged deeper into the house and looked around. He picked up the potted fern and set it back down, making sounds of approbation.

"Ollie," Mimi said, turning away from her ex. "This is Twyla. Can you say hi?"

Ollie waved his fingers. Then he ran over to the play area.

"Twyla," Dean said, having finished his inspection. "Could you give us a minute?"

She looked at Mimi, who shrugged and nodded toward her room.

"Nice to know you, sir," she said and then waved at Ollie.

As she went down the hallway she heard Dean announce he had some rules for when Ollie stayed at Mommy's house. He sounded more controlling even than Faith.

In the quiet of her room Twyla noodled around on a song and kept one ear on the conversation from the living room. Tense murmurs became sharp vocal jabs. *None of my business.* She turned the portable radio on the dresser to the static between stations to block out the noise. When bickering turned to full-on yelling, she put down her guitar and stood next to the door. From what she could gather Dean was running offense, with Mimi trying to block insults. Mimi trying to prove herself; Dean picking her apart like a carcass. It was unsettling to hear this tough, no-BS woman letting this guy needle her, and in front of their son, too. She considered intervening to spare the boy the worst of this fight or stop it altogether. What this would do to her chances of staying on at Mimi's house was unknown, but she couldn't stand the thought of that little boy witnessing such ugliness.

She turned the doorknob as quietly as she could and was about to step into the hallway when she noticed movement outside. She went to the window for a better look but there was nothing. A breeze ruffled the treetops. Perhaps it had blown something across the yard. She was about to return to her eavesdropping when the pool cover shuddered and something poked up at its edge. Her whole body tightened. She opened the sliding door and approached the pool. Watching, listening. Then the cover rose again, more pronounced this time. She looked toward the living room and saw the sliding door slightly ajar, wide enough for a very small body to slip through. She ran for the pool and reached down to lift up the cover, but it was tied to a ring in the cement. She looked over the pool to see where the boy might have fallen in. She tore at the rope, but it held fast, so she wriggled into the gap between the cover and the side and plunged into the deep end. Fallen leaves had steeped and made tea of the water, and she couldn't see where he was. She went still, hoping she could sense him, and sank slowly toward the bottom. It occurred to her that she hadn't called for help. She used the last of her breath to scream in the water, sending a signal to Ollie. Then she felt the water moving to her right and saw, vaguely, his shape in the water. She kicked in that direction, reaching out with her hands. She felt his arm and snatched an elbow, yanked him to her body and held him close with one hand while she pushed off the bottom toward the edge of the pool. The gap was too small for the both of them, so she fed his languid body up toward the crack of sunlight. She felt the panic of low oxygen and struggled to lift him. There was nowhere to put her feet. She kicked with all her strength, inching him up, hoping at least he had reached the surface and could breathe. Feeling faint, she struggled to stay buoyant. She hoped he could hang onto the side while she went up for air. Suddenly, Ollie slipped up and out of her arms and disappeared from view, one sneaker bobbing behind. Summoning one last burst of strength, she clawed her way into the opening and inhaled and dragged herself onto the warm stone coping.

Her eyes burned and she couldn't see clearly, but she heard Mimi hyperventilating. Inside the house Dean shouted at someone. Sputtering, she rubbed the water out of her eyes and blinked hard to get a read on the situation. There was Mimi, leaning over a lifeless Ollie, her hands on his cheeks. She pushed Mimi to the side and immediately began CPR as she had been trained at the daycare. She pinched his nose, tilted his head back, and sealed her mouth over his, breathing twice. Then she gave swift compressions to his little rib cage. Mimi never let go of Ollie's hand. She was crowding Twyla, but she just kept up her compressions until it was time to breathe again. Dean ran from the house and said the ambulance was on its way. Twyla felt the calm of trust steady her hand and settle her mind, focusing only on her movements, not Ollie's lavender features, how limp he felt between her hands. She refused to do the math of how long he might have stopped breathing, but after ten rounds of compressions, doubt crept in. *What if I was too late?* She carried on even as her chest tightened and eyes filled with tears. This beautiful boy.

Then Ollie convulsed. Twyla pulled away, and Ollie spewed pool water and began to cry. He spewed again, this time his breakfast Cheerios, and she tipped him on his side. Now they were all crying. Dean and Mimi went to Ollie and touched him like he would shatter, caressed his cheeks, chest, kissed his hands, cried into them, into each other. Twyla went inside shaking and brought back a stack of towels, wrapped them in layers around Ollie, then collapsed into a chair and fell quietly to pieces.

IT WAS WELL AFTER SIX the next morning, after Ollie had been released from the hospital and they'd begun draining the pool, when Dean finally left. For the tenth time, Mimi checked in on Ollie, who now slept in his bed surrounded by stuffed animal guardians. Then she knocked lightly on Twyla's door. She let herself in and sat on the bed, eyes gleaming with gratitude.

"How's Ollie?" Twyla asked. Though she had known him only minutes, she felt a savior's fealty to the boy.

Mimi gathered up a big sigh, like she'd been holding her breath awhile, and smiled. "He was in fits a few hours ago, but now he's sleeping like a newborn."

"That's real good," Twyla replied.

"Listen, honey," Mimi said. She opened her mouth, then seemed to reconsider her words. "I worked really hard to stay out of debt." She took Twyla's hand and squeezed it till her fingers buckled. "But I want you to know . . . for what you did for him? I will never forget this." Mimi's eyes brimmed with tears. She blinked them back and swallowed a sob. "You need something, *anything*, just come to me."

"You don't need to say that," Twyla said, embarrassed by the intensity of Mimi's words.

"Goddammit, get in here," Mimi said and tugged Twyla upright so she could hug her. "He'd be dead if you hadn't—" Twyla shook her head as if to stop Mimi from going down that road. They sat in weighted silence.

"Twyla," Mimi said after a moment. "Did you see him go in?"

She shook her head. "Not exactly." She told Mimi what she had seen, how she wasn't sure if she could get him out in time. She didn't say how close she had come to drowning, too.

Mimi talked over her tears. "Dean and I were fighting over the goddamn electric bill. That's why I haven't been using the pool, because it's too expensive to heat and I can't afford a service, and I'm too stupid to keep up with the chemicals—and Christ, the cover was supposed to keep him *out* of the pool, not—" She rummaged in the pocket of her robe and pulled out a snubbed-looking cigarette and a lighter. She lit up and took a moment with her smoke. The pump whirred outside the big glass windows. They had decided, after inspecting and securing its ties, to leave the cover on after draining.

"Well, needless to say," Mimi said, standing, "you're hired. And come Friday you'll have a little spending money, too. It's all worked out with Dean. First time in my life he didn't give me shit for asking for money." Twyla smiled in thanks. "I hope you stay as long as you like. Or at least until he's eighteen."

Twyla laughed wanly. She was anxious to move, to discharge the fright. She left the bed and went to the door.

"How about I fix us some coffee?"

Mimi put up a hand and nudged Twyla out of the way.

"I'm making *you* coffee. Or breakfast, or goddamn lobster thermidor if you want." Twyla smiled, lightened by the gesture, and let Mimi take the lead, relaxing for the first time since Ollie's fall.

CHAPTER 13

On the afternoon following Ollie's fall in the pool, while Mimi fixed ice cream sundaes, the phone rang. Twyla was showing Ollie how to play the alphabet song on her guitar, and he inspected the movements of her fingers with intense fascination, like they were curious insects traveling across the frets. Mimi held the receiver across the counter. "It's for you." The women exchanged unknowing expressions.

Twyla went cautiously to the phone.

"I hope it's okay I looked you up," a man said. It took Twyla a moment to recognize the voice. Chet Wilton. He even sounded handsome.

"I'm not listed," she said.

"But your boss is." She remembered telling him about Mimi Dewitt. "Did I overstep?"

"No, you didn't," she said and looked, grinning, at Mimi. Mimi mouthed, *A boy?* Twyla nodded.

When he spoke again she could hear the smile in his voice. "I was just wondering where you wanna go on our date tonight," he said. "Or should I pick?"

She turned toward the wall to hide the color in her cheeks. She was torn. Her body was saying yes but she felt it was too soon to be leaving Ollie.

"I can't go out tonight," she said. "I need to stay here. It's a long story."

She looked to Mimi to show her she wouldn't be leaving her, not after all they'd been through. "Maybe another time."

Then Mimi hopped up and took the receiver from her. "You can pick her up at seven," she barked and hung up the phone.

WHILE MIMI PUT OLLIE TO bed, Twyla got herself fixed up for Chet. She tried curling her hair so it waved away from her face like Farrah but it ended up looking more like Shirley Temple caught in a hurricane. She yanked a brush through her hair to smooth out the curls, and it fluffed out full and high. She gave up and braided her hair, not *tight*-tight, but in loose plaits on either side of her head. From Mimi's closet she selected high-waisted jeans and a snug western shirt with embroidered roses climbing up the front and across the shoulders. The thorns appeared sharp enough to prick.

Chet arrived at seven in his shiny Bronco, smelling of spearmint and shampoo. He opened the door and helped her climb into the cab, then they tore off toward town. He wore a white shirt and leather vest and a rodeo buckle the size of a hubcap.

"Bulls or broncs?" she asked.

"Huh?" he asked, then noticed her looking at his buckle. "Oh, ha, neither. My dad bought this at auction for one of his charities."

"That sounds like rich-boy talk to me," she teased. "How many charities does your daddy have?"

A flare of umbrage crossed his face. "Oh, my parents aren't rich," he said matter-of-factly. "They're wealthy. The money's in assets, and they don't like to spend it."

"Rich, wealthy, same thing."

He looked at her, briefly, like an irritant. "Rich people show off their money. Wealthy people don't need to. Rich people spend money to get things done; wealthy people use their relationships. It's not my world, you know. I'm a musician. But it's where I come from."

Twyla considered this distinction with amusement. "How do you get the assets if you don't spend money to buy them?" she asked.

Chet adjusted the mirror, caught his reflection. "Usually, somebody has to die."

HE TOOK HER TO THE Parthenon and they sat on the northwest-facing steps to watch the sun set. They shared a six-pack of beer and a bag of hot dogs from Phranks N' Steins, though Twyla was so full of happy nerves she barely ate, stealing glances at the handiwork of Chet's jawline, neck, and chest. A toothless old cowboy stood by his open case playing guitar, trying to sing Hank Williams but all the words went soft in his mouth. Watching him brought up forgotten memories of Daddy. How no one mentioned his rotting teeth. The funny smell on him toward the end, the way his skin would purple and blotch.

"Do you have any money for him?" she asked Chet, feeling a surge of concern for the man. She had forgotten her coin purse on the dresser.

He forced a hand into the tight pocket of his jeans and pulled out a five-dollar bill. He left one weighted down by a full can of beer in the man's case. The old man tipped his hat and mumbled his thanks, then packed up and left.

"You always leave five-dollar bills like that?" Twyla had been thinking he'd leave a dollar at most.

"Only when I'm trying to impress my lady," he said.

The words smacked her in the gut. *My lady.* Chet didn't acknowledge the largeness of the moment, and Twyla told herself to be cool, take it casually. He pulled out his guitar, a flashy-looking twelve-string with a bloated back.

"How come your guitar is so funny looking?" she asked, then wished she'd taken a moment to shape her question more tactfully.

"This here's a Glen Campbell Ovation." He said it like she ought to be familiar with the make, but it was new to her. "It's made of this special carbon fiber here that makes it ten times more durable than your old-fashioned wooden guitar." He handed it over to her. "Here, feel that. It's light as a feather."

"Sure is," she said. Light, yes, but she found the material lacking in character.

"You could play all night on that motherfucker. Hardly even need a strap to hold it up."

She turned her attention from the guitar to the man holding it. The play of his muscles as he strummed was mesmerizing. She allowed herself a moment to stare, then turned her gaze on his playing. The baritone he was shooting for was a bit of a stretch for his natural range. Though his speaking voice had only a light Tennessee twang, he sang with a southern working-class inflection.

She threw out a line to match the rhythm of the tune he was playing.

Hey, pretty boy, how'd you get so cute,
With those Maybelline lashes and a pout to boot.

He grinned and pinched up his brows, surprised but charmed. She went on.

Spent an hour in the bathroom fixing up my face,
But I could never live up to the likes of you.

He laughed and riffed a little, returning her volley, then she threw out another verse and he played it right into the song. They laughed and fumbled through a few lesser verses before sketching out a fun little tune. As they wrote together, she had the sensation of meeting and merging with a part she didn't know was missing. Was it Chet? Or the music they were making? Here was the creative joy she had been missing lately. It was the first time she had written a song with someone since Mickey.

Their repartee seemed to open Chet up. He talked about his family—the glory of high school football, followed by two seasons of warming the bench at Vanderbilt; his parents, Gail and Chester, and what it was like growing up in the Wilton household. Dad was exacting and intimidating, but when called to action, a good enough father. His mother he described as nervous and prone to exaggerated fears of the opinions of others. Sometimes she became so paralyzed she couldn't leave the house and would hole up in her den with a gin rickey and a deck of cards and play solitaire until it was time for bed. He said his parents never forgave him after he quit college two credits shy of his finance degree to indulge his music dream.

After they'd finished the beers, Chet led her back to the Bronco and drove a few minutes until they reached a vacant alley. He turned off the car, killed the headlights, then turned the key halfway so he could play the radio. The windows down, she could hear and smell the city just beyond the two buildings. A honky-tonk nearby jangled with a loud house band; beer, smoke, garbage, and the murky scent of the river perfumed the cab. Chet pulled a bottle out of the glove compartment and climbed into the back seat.

He didn't ask her to come sit in back with him. Didn't have to. And though she wanted him, she demurred. How many times had her mother painted the landscape of the back seat of a boy's car to her? The den of sin, a sure path to fornication. The site of a young woman's undoing. She thought of the other night, how easily she had slipped onto his lap, how right he had felt between her legs, under her lips. She couldn't tell if she was being consumed, or was the one consuming, or if they were both being slurped into the mouth of desire—or the devil—itself. Was that the evil her mother had been warning her about? Why would a loving God punish them for the nature He had given them?

"You know, I've never been with a woman like you," he said. He leaned against the seat, knees fanned out, waiting.

"What do you mean by that?" she asked. In her head, she supplied hoped-for answers. *As beautiful as you, as sweet as you, as talented as you.*

"A woman I could sink my fingers into," he said. His sure, heavy-lidded gaze lit her up.

She shifted in her seat as his meaning sank in.

"You calling me fat?" she teased. She would have taken offense if offense was intended, but he looked ready to eat her.

He shook his head. "I'm not calling you anything. I'm telling you I can't stop thinking about touching you," he said, with the slightest pitch of helplessness in his voice. He looked her over, took his time, lingered on her collarbone, breasts, the soft rise of her abdomen, then back to her eyes. This body, long hidden, shielded from sexual interest, shamed by her mother's sly comments about calories, flattering cuts, and healthy portions, was the object, and vessel, of desire.

"I've been hungry all my life and didn't know till I touched you."

You give them what they want, they'll lose interest. Her mother's voice again, another one of her confusing mottos. Did desire really work like that—once satisfied, erased entirely? Was Chet here, wanting her, because she hadn't gone all the way? And if they did tonight, would he move on to someone else? And what about what *she* wanted?

Right now, she wanted only him. He was a wilderness she wanted to explore. Thighs thick as timbers, the cliff of his chest, his features carved from soft stone. She could feel him beneath her, taste the beer on his tongue and the salt at his temples. *This hunger.* She lifted herself from the seat.

Then someone rapped at the window. Twyla jumped, Chet cussed. A security guard shone a flashlight in on Chet and held it there until he climbed back into the driver's seat. "No parking here, kids," he said with a backwoods drawl, and slapped the rump of the Bronco as he returned to his patrol.

The run-in with security seemed to break their lusty trance for a time. They found a place to park and started walking. Twyla suggested going to Printers Alley and seeing a band. Chet said the clubs were too loud, they wouldn't be able to talk. As they meandered, she told him about Fort Worth and her Christ-crazy mother, her meek stepdad, and the father she never buried. She started with the good stories, the ones brightest in her memory. The daily guitar lessons after supper, how his knobby hands would dance across the strings. When she would come home upset about a fight with friends or a run-in with a mean teacher, he would tell her to put it in a song. *All that heartache is your material*, he'd say. *How we gonna have songs without sorrow?* And since then she never felt completely hopeless, because whatever struggles she faced could be made into music. How, toward the end, he'd doze off in the middle of a song, and she'd take his guitar and pick up where he left off, put her own spin on what he'd started and hope somewhere in his sleeping mind he could hear her. But the good seemed wrapped up in the painful, and she drifted into stories about her last days with him. He'd stopped going to the job at the meat-packing plant and filed for disability after the accident with his hand. How he'd come home with his fist all papered in gauze. He'd taken medicine to help the pain, and slept so much he wasn't changing his dressings, and how after a week or so, it began to stink. He lost the hand, the job, too. He spent more time sleeping on the couch than playing music, and even the Sundowners stopped coming around to visit. Then one day he wasn't on the couch when she came out for breakfast. He hadn't told her he was leaving or left a note. She'd told herself he'd gotten a gig that couldn't wait. And the next they heard of him, months later, was the call that he was dead.

"Almost like he went off to die like an old hound," Chet said.

Twyla wiped her tears and saw her mascara was running. "You really think so?" She hadn't thought of it that way. It was difficult not to take it personally, that she hadn't been enough to live for.

"I just wish I knew more about what really happened. No one even told me how he died or who was with him. Not knowing makes me think it was awful."

Chet glanced at his watch, then turned to her, looking apologetic.

"Oh boy, we're gonna have to race back to the car," he said, having left the previous conversation behind. "I got band rehearsal in thirty minutes."

Twyla was thrown by the abrupt pivot. "Rehearsal? It's so late."

He shrugged. "My bandmates have jobs; we meet when we can meet," he said. "You'll see how it is one day."

Chet rushed Twyla back to Mimi's. At the front door, Chet kissed Twyla hungrily and loaded his hands with her ass.

"Don't make plans for Saturday night," he said and headed back to his car.

Her hurt feelings lifted at the promise of a date. "What are we doing Saturday?"

With a rakish smile he climbed into his seat. "We're going to church."

CHAPTER 14

Thursday and Friday dragged by. Mimi had taken a temporary job mixing jingles for an advertising agency, working regular hours and networking at night. With Mimi busy and Ollie at his dad's, Twyla was both bored and agitated. When she tried to write, nothing came. She couldn't focus on anything but the memories of kissing him, his voice in her ear, the sure grip of his hands. She had always imagined the force behind her music as a beam of light; she feared it had shifted away from songwriting and onto Chet.

By Saturday, she was so anxious to see Chet again, she'd been in and out of the bathroom with an aching stomach. Mimi made her drink an Alka-Seltzer and helped her find something to wear. She selected an orchid Halston jumpsuit with billowy legs and thin straps that crisscrossed her back.

"Never wait around for a date," Mimi said, zipping her up. "You're busy. You're squeezing him in. It's basic supply and demand."

"I don't know how to show anything other than what I'm really feeling," Twyla said, assessing her profile in the mirror.

Mimi looked troubled in an understanding way.

"Just trust me, kiddo. You feel what you feel, that's okay, you don't have to lie. But don't tell a goddamn word of any of that to him. It'll scare him off. I'm not telling you how it ought to be, I'm telling you how it is." She fanned Twyla's hair over her shoulders and gave them a squeeze.

"Now let's play some cards and make like you're not sitting by the door waiting for him to call."

Mimi mixed herself a concoction of Ovaltine, cream, and peppermint schnapps, then led Twyla over to the wooly carpet and dealt out a hand of rummy.

"Mimi, don't you ever think about meeting someone new?" Now that Twyla had a taste of love, she couldn't imagine not wanting to feel that way all the time.

Mimi made a meld of a 6, 7, and 8 of diamonds, then laid down her 9 of clubs.

"Love looks sweet on you, Twyla, but I'm forty years old. I'm too tired for all that."

"Forty isn't so old," Twyla said. She picked up Mimi's discard and put down a four-card run. "You've got half your life ahead of you, or more. Don't you want someone to spend time with?"

"I got no time for anyone but Ollie."

Twyla had a crappy hand, but she didn't mind. "That's how I always felt about music," she said. "But now I'm starting to think I was missing out on all the good stuff."

"Always starts off good," Mimi said, but Twyla didn't take heed of her tone.

"All that time I was writing about troubles," she said, "now all I can think of is love."

"Love comes in all flavors. Some of 'em cherry sweet, some of 'em bitter."

Twyla got over herself for a moment and thought of Mimi. "What happened with you and Dean, anyway?"

Mimi considered her cards, looking rueful. "All those clothes in the closet, I don't even know who that person was. Dean bought me those, did you know that? Picked out every last piece. He has taste, I'll give him that."

"That was nice of him." Mother and Daddy would always fight after one of Faith's trips to JCPenney.

"Oh, he wasn't being nice," Mimi said. She slapped down another meld. "He was sexing me up for his clients. All the studios did it, had to have a pretty face at reception to draw people in. The thing was, I was a sound engineer, not a secretary. I mixed every album he produced from 1960 till we split last year." She looked troubled. "I was one of the best, and now I can't pay someone to give me a job."

"People won't hire you because of him?"

"He put a stink on me. Put out a call to every studio on Music Row and told them I'd been stealing from the company. But I wasn't stealing, I was paying our bills. He wined and dined our artists, sent ridiculous gifts for every possible occasion, upgraded our equipment every couple years because he couldn't stand not having the best. And the newest. And the prettiest. He was bleeding us dry. The notices were pouring in so I dipped into our personal savings to pay down our debts. Maybe I should have told him what I was gonna do, but he had no shame about owing money and he would have tried to talk me out of it."

"Dang," said Twyla. "You should write a song about that."

Mimi laughed and took a long swig of her drink and gargled it. She was getting tipsy. "I don't have the gene," she said. "All that time working with songwriters, seeing how they put them together, hearing them change right there in the room. Couldn't write a song to save my life." She got up to mix another drink. "My skill is knowing what a song is supposed to sound like, and pulling the best of it forward, balancing the levels until it's just the way it was meant to be."

"I never thought about that side of things," she said. They played a few turns in silence.

"I've been hearing you picking behind that bedroom door," Mimi said after a while. "Weird stuff. A little glum to be commercial." Mimi paused, choosing her words. "But, it's good. I mean—you should keep at it. People with far less talent and character than you have gotten record deals. Remember that."

"Actually, I've been a little blocked since I met him," Twyla said. "You think that'll pass?"

Mimi went serious. "Twyla, listen to me, do not let yourself fall apart for this man." There was heat behind her words. Twyla held her gaze. She knew Mimi was right, but her feelings seemed unstoppable.

Mimi looked like she was about to say something when the doorbell rang. She tipped the last of the fudgy sediment into her mouth and left her glass in the sink.

"Shit, Twyla. Don't mind this cranky old bitch. I'm happy for you. I hope he's real good to you."

CHAPTER 15

When they arrived at the new Opry House Twyla understood what Chet had meant when he'd said he was taking her to church. The previous location of the Opry had been a tabernacle before it was home to the Grand Ole Opry, and though the new building, opened just a few years before, was not nearly as beautiful as the Ryman, it was holy for what went on inside. To Twyla, this whole town was blessed. People making music everywhere, writing, singing, playing their instruments. Some to get famous, maybe, but she'd wager most, like her, were driven by devotion.

"This show is gonna be out of sight," he said, pulling into a loading zone. "A bunch of big names are there—Dolly, Carl Perkins, Bill Monroe—and they're doing a tribute to Elvis."

"Elvis?" she gasped. She shouldn't have been surprised—they'd been playing his songs in every bar, on every radio station, in every store since he died. But to witness his tribute at the Opry sounded like something from her dreams. Twyla got so excited she felt sick again.

Chet unscrewed the top from a mason jar of greasy liquor.

"Here," he said and passed it to her. She took an obliging sip and it scraped its way down her throat. She passed it back. "Nasty," she said, laughing, gagging, giddy to think she was minutes from seeing her heroes.

He slipped a bag of powder from the cupholder and scooped a mound with the long nail of his index finger. "Just a little sunshine for my moonshine," he said and snorted the powder. He tipped his head back and pinched his nostrils.

Her eyes must have gone wide.

"Don't worry now. This is pure Colombian. Safe enough for a baby." He sniffled and wiped his watery eyes. She recalled with amusement the slogan of the anti-marijuana campaign poster at First Tab: *Misery! Shame! Despair! The weed with roots in Hell!* She wasn't sure what she believed about them, but was skeptical of both extremes.

"Look, I think I can get us in through the back door. I gotta go in there and get the lay of the land, though, talk to my guy."

"Sorry," she said, confused. "You *think* you can get us in? Don't you have tickets?"

He tucked his chin back, defensive. "I don't have tickets *yet*, but one of the stage managers owes me a favor. He said he might be able to get us backstage with the talent." He made a move to get out of the car and when she started to open her door, he signaled for her to wait.

"Hang tight, okay? It's better if I show up alone. I'll come get you in a few."

He kissed her and disappeared into the alley behind the concrete-and-brick building. She tried to put aside her disappointment that he would get her hopes up without securing tickets. Only minutes ago, going to the Opry was a dream. She wouldn't even let herself consider the possibility of meeting these artists backstage. It would be enough to see them from the audience, to drink in the sounds of live music, knowing they would be broadcast all across the country but that she was hearing it fresh and up close. She felt high sitting there, thinking that in moments she could be bathed in music. She tuned the radio to 650 just in case the show started before Chet got back.

Ten minutes had passed when she got the urge to snoop in his things. There was a country club sticker on the windshield she hadn't noticed before; a set of golf clubs and a shoeshine kit in back. She had a giggle when she saw his car was registered to a Chester Wilton III. She knew he came from money, but that name made him sound like royalty.

In the cupholder she found the little baggie he had dipped into before he left. For all her mother's lectures on drugs, it turned out they weren't so scary. Chet had seemed so natural and unashamed about doing cocaine, and as far as she could tell, using it hadn't caused him to sprout horns or a barbed tail. She wondered if it wasn't more like coffee. A brightener. She licked her pinkie and coated it in the powder, then touched it to her tongue. It tasted of diesel and aspirin. Bitter, and wrong. But also, like the smell of a permanent marker, chemically appealing. Her mother had warned her of so many of these monsters—boys, drugs, booze—and yet she was learning they hadn't any teeth.

After thirty minutes the show started. She didn't want to miss anything but she began to wonder if something had happened to him. She shut off the engine and walked in the direction she'd seen him go a half hour before. There was a set of dumpsters near a loading dock and a staircase that led to a door that looked very locked. She tried it anyway, then knocked as loudly as she could. Nothing. She went around front and asked to buy a ticket.

"Sorry, hon, sold out." She could hear the sounds of the show murmuring through the doors. It was too blunt to hear what was happening or who was playing, but it was the best she was going to get tonight.

"Can I stand in back?" she asked.

The woman in the ticket booth gave her a look of practiced sympathy. "I'm afraid not. You'll have to go listen on the radio like everybody else."

Back in the car she started running scenarios, from the plausible to the outlandish. And the only sensible explanation was one that made her very angry. He clearly had only been able to get the one ticket and instead of coming back, trying another time, he had stayed to watch the show without her. She shut the radio off with a bitter twist. She couldn't stop her head from racing. If he was ditching her, she wasn't gonna sit around and settle for scraps. She saw the oily-looking moonshine on the seat and unscrewed it, jerked back from the fumes. She might as well be sipping from a gas can. But she was too hopped up to just sit around and wait for him. Maybe a few sips from the jar would pacify her. Not too much. She didn't like the morning after too many drinks, the spikes in her head, the day-long slump. It was a new world for her and one she was trying to figure out how to handle. She held her nose and took a long mouthful, pushed it down her throat like an egg. It burned hard, deep in her middle, burned away the doubt and the anger. It burned bright like inspiration and left her wanting more. She downed another egg and it cracked open, hot in her gut.

She found a fruit pie on the back seat and tore open its wax paper jacket, thinking about what she was going to say to Chet when he came back. In her mind she was clever and he contrite. She chewed on her fantasies and gooey apple pie until the moonshine knocked her out like a babe full of milk.

WHEN THE DOOR OPENED AND slammed shut, she jerked awake and saw Chet looking cheerful as a wren.

"Twy," he said. "You shoulda *been there.*"

She squinted at him and then at the clock. It was well past three a.m.

"*Everyone* was there. Barbara Mandrell, Bill Monroe. Tammy sang a tearjerker with Dolly —I watched the whole show from backstage. Then we got drunk in the greenroom and shot the shit, and when the stage manager kicked us out, Bill invited us back to his house, and *man* was it a kick, just carrying on, drinking, playing cards. Man . . . you really shoulda seen it."

"I shoulda seen it?" she said, not believing he could be this earnest without any apology. "I *coulda* seen it if you'd brought me with you."

Chet cocked his head to the side, perplexed. "Twyla, I would have brought you along if I could. They were at capacity. I had to call in a favor just to get in myself."

"Do *me* a favor and take me home."

He looked at her hard like he was willing some sense into her.

"Twyla. I tried like hell to get you in. And I've got a promise from the stage manager that we can get you a ticket next month. They oversold, see? And the fire marshal . . ."

She tuned him out. She'd had enough platitudes and not a single apology for leaving her alone in his car all night.

Chet took her chin in his hand, more gentle in his expression. "Baby, I'm surprised you're not happy for me. Your beau just played poker with Guy Clark."

She pulled away, but she wasn't so mad that the word "beau" passed her by. Was he her beau? This was only their second date, but it did feel like they were moving quickly into something more. The softening that began, smudging the rough edges around her heart, was involuntary. She wanted to stay angry, but she felt a loosening between the shoulders, an unclenching of her jaw. Though the softening was out of her control, she did not reveal it to Chet. She would play angry as long as it took for him to admit he'd done her wrong.

Seeing his kindness unreturned, Chet took off his hat and spun it into the back seat, revved up the engine. He surged forward, then back as he maneuvered out of the parking spot. They didn't speak during the dark, breezy drive out of the city toward Mimi's. By the time they pulled up the wooded road they had both cooled off enough to say good night.

"Twyla, I'm sorry, all right? I guess I should have let you know what I was doing. I couldn't have gotten you in but I didn't have to leave you in the dark."

She was relieved to have an apology before saying goodbye.

"So," she said, "how'd you get backstage anyway?"

Chet gave a guilty look. "I slipped the doorman a tenner."

"Ten dollars? Shoot, I thought you said wealthy people didn't have to pay to get stuff done."

He looked at her as if she'd called him a bastard. "I'm not wealthy," he said firmly. "My father is."

She took this in without anger, but wondered at his need to make this distinction. His was a world she did not understand. "So," she said, appeasing him, "did your poker partner sing 'Desperados Waiting for a Train'?"

He smiled. "You know he did. And you know what I told him after I beat him? I said I'm seeing a girl that's gonna blow the lid off of Nashville."

"You didn't," she said and told herself he was teasing. But she beamed at the thought. Had her name touched Guy Clark's ear? She was sure it hadn't, but she remembered making music with Chet on the steps of the Parthenon, how easily they had thrown that song together, and saw for a bright moment the two of them onstage under a blue light singing a love song of their making. She wished she could kiss him before he left, but it was too soon to give herself over after what he'd done. She let herself out before he could get to her door, thanked him for supper, and went inside.

AN HOUR LATER, UNABLE TO sleep, she was sitting on her bed working out harmonies to their "Pretty Boy" song when she heard sticks snapping underfoot. She put down her guitar and went to the window, cupping her hands around her eyes to better see into the dark. She felt her eyes and ears straining. Could be deer. Out here in the woods there were plenty of night-prowling creatures. Then she heard several more steps with the sound of a human gait followed by the suction of the sliding door. She drew her breath, sharp and quick, and saw a figure press against the curtains. She dashed for the door to the hallway but her hands fumbled with the slippery knob. She had just gotten it open and swung it wide when someone grabbed her from behind, one hand around her waist, the other across her mouth, muffling a scream.

The intruder muscled her to the bed and laid his body weight on her. She thrashed, attempted to scream for Mimi, but he had her completely contained. Then something, his smell maybe, calmed her enough to turn and see his face.

"Goddamn, woman," Chet said, half whisper, half yell. "I was trying to Romeo you and you took off running like I came in with a hatchet!" He flipped her over but kept her pinned at the wrists.

"How did I know you didn't have one?" she said. "Let me go!"

"No sudden moves, okay?" He let go of one wrist, and she smacked him on the side of his head, hard enough to numb her hand. The pumping of her heart made her want to run.

"How did you even know which room I was in? If you'd jumped in on Mimi—"

"Well, I don't know, maybe because you're surrounded by windows. Damn."

"Let me go." He removed his other hand from her wrist and held her gaze. They remained there looking at each other with enough adrenaline between them to lift a tractor. Chet seemed to notice Twyla, nude under the tissue of her borrowed nightgown. She took him in, too, ragged but sultry, from a long night of drink and smoke.

"Did I just blow it twice in one night?" he said, his voice softer now.

She wanted to say *Yes, you maniac* but shook her head *no*. He inched his face toward her, not knowing whether she would strike again. The closer he got the more she wanted to be touched by him. Her knees parted and Chet filled the space between them. He kissed her, slid his hands beneath her nightgown and lifted her up. The scruff on his face was soft, the skin on his neck, his lips, his earlobes, all of it maddeningly made for her. She'd once stood over a side of brisket fresh out of the smoker and carved it away, one slice at a time, unable to stop. It was luscious, fatty, smoky. Her appetites unleashed, she had let herself go after what she craved, as much as she could hold. Chet surged into kissing her more deeply. *Send me to hell*, she thought. *I don't want to live without this.* She sloughed off her nightgown and was not ashamed. He undressed to the waist, then lowered himself over her. She arched toward him and, wanting to see him better, shifted her weight so she was on top. He ran his hands over her like a blind man, over her breasts, her belly, and finally on her ass and clutching like he'd never let go.

And then, like a bucket of icy water overturned, they were all in the room. Faith, arms pinned across her bosom, tsking at naked Twyla; Pastor pacing across the carpet, screaming "Fornication!"; Mimi cross-legged on the dresser looking jaded and cynical. She stopped kissing Chet and held him at arm's length.

"You have to get out of here."

Chet looked genuinely shocked, like he'd never been denied a thing in his entire life. He flopped his head on the mattress, deflated. "You gotta be kidding me," he said to the ceiling with a touch of drama that made it easier for Twyla to stay strong.

"Soon," she said, "but not tonight."

He looked pained, almost heartbroken.

"You'll live," she said, liking the edge of power she had over him, however temporary. His hands, still tucked into the folds at her hips, rocked her over his groin. She closed her eyes and let him, warming right up again. He shut his eyes. She admired his neck, the thick straps of muscle on either side of the knuckle of his Adam's apple. She wanted to lap up the salt on his skin and bite, to mark him. Instead she swung her leg over like she was dismounting a horse. His chest rose and fell with a deliberate breath. Then they went to their piles of clothes and dressed.

"You know, sweetheart," he mumbled as he buttoned his vest. "It's 1977. Women have sex whenever they want. It's not such a big deal any-more."

She approached him from behind and tucked her fingers in the front of his waistband.

"It's a big deal to me," she said.

CHAPTER 16

The urge to call home again finally came about two weeks after she'd left Forth Worth, on a day unseasonably cool and clear, when Twyla was not homesick at all, but perfectly content. Ollie would be starting preschool the following week, and she had a day of indulgence planned for him starting with lunch at the old Elliston Place Soda Shop. She hoisted him up on the swivel chair, spun him around fast till he was a blur and let him peter to a stop. He begged for more and she spun him again. His laughter drew warm looks from other customers.

"Last spin, then no more once we've eaten or you'll lose your lunch."

She looped an arm over his shoulders to keep him from slumping off the chair from dizziness. Then she ordered a chocolate Coke float for him, vanilla Dr Pepper for her. As the soda jerk delivered their baskets of oozing grilled cheese, she noticed a phone booth at the back near the restrooms. It was then that she felt an urge to make contact with who she was, and where she came from, before Nashville. She'd come here without a plan, and things had begun to fall into place. A nice job, a beau. And though her music wasn't flowing the way she had hoped, she knew every musician had to take their licks. Much as she begrudged them, her mother, Fort Worth, and even First Tabernacle were a part of her. She couldn't bear to go back, but she wanted now to reach in and touch the pieces of her she left behind.

She warned Ollie not to leave his seat, then, keeping her eye on him, let herself into the phone booth and called home. It rang once, twice, and Lloyd picked up on the third. She was relieved. *Hello* came more easily with him than with Mother.

"Twyla *Higgins*," he whispered intensely, "where the devil have you been?"

"I'm not sure I want to say," she said. "But I'm safe."

He breathed out a little sigh. "That's good. You still in Memphis?"

"No." She waited a moment, not sure yet what she wanted, or how much she wanted to share. "How's Mother?"

He laughed a little bitterly. "Well, heck, Twyla, she's all but written you off." The phrasing stung. "I mean, you know, she's got them praying for you at church. They all think you're off doing drugs or selling yourself. I know that's not like you, but your mother's convinced." She wasn't as far off as all that, Twyla thought.

"Look, I'm not supposed to say this—in case you're out there getting high, but . . . do you need any money?"

"No, Lloyd, I have a job—"

He didn't seem to hear her. "I admit it's a little tight around here, but I can scrape something together if you're in a bind."

"I don't need your money, all right? I'm doing real good."

"All right, Twyla." He seemed to want to say more. "You getting enough to eat, though?" he asked.

She smiled. "Well, no one's feeding me venison," she said. He laughed. "But I'm eating plenty."

She heard her mother from the living room, distant but unmistakable. "Nice of her to grace us with a phone call," she shouted. "She isn't getting fat, is she?"

Her comment felt like a kick to the shins. She tried to convince herself it was only her mother's pride and not a lack of caring that kept her from picking up and hearing her missing daughter's voice.

"You can tell her I'm not any fatter than I already was." A stab at herself to deflect Mother's.

Lloyd repeated her message. Though there was cruelty in her mother's laugh, Twyla took pleasure in having turned the blade of her mother's insult away from herself. Then her mother came in for the last word.

"Well, that's as fat as anyone needs to be." Twyla took the hit and grew angry. She wanted to ask just how her mother felt when she found out Twyla had defied her and left, and whether she had the nerve to be proud of her daughter for taking a risk, for going after what she wanted. But the words inside her head stayed trapped, and Twyla played her part in their dance: she looking for praise, her mother determined to withhold it from her. She hung up still wishing for connection but feeling more certain she might never find it at home again.

She looked over at Ollie and, finding him content and sipping his float, she dialed the operator and asked for New Groove record store in Fort Worth.

"I thought you were coming back to buy that album," Eli chided when Twyla said her name. His tone was light but truthful.

"I'll get it to you, Eli."

"Sure, sure," he said. "How come you ain't been coming around? You that hard up?"

Twyla filled him in on the last two weeks. She told him about Mimi and the drowning, about choking at Irma's and running into Chet and how he knew about the Sundowners and Daddy. Eli laughed in disbelief. "You *would* find yourself some obscure-bluegrass-loving fool." Twyla smiled at his low-key endorsement. It felt good to talk to a friend.

"How's business?" she asked.

Eli cooed like he often did when he had a good story to tell.

"Oh, boy. Those yahoos came back to mark up my storefront again. Same ones as always. I called the cops with them standing right there, and they just kept on doing what they was doing, thinking those cops would never come to help out a Black man. What they didn't know now was I got me a new friend. Deputy sheriff type of friend, see? Fought alongside him in 'Nam and just found out he got transferred to Cow Town. And when he showed up and made them motherfuckers clean up my windows, I poured myself a cocktail and watched them till that glass was so clear you'd like to walk right through it. Once they finished, they thought they was off the hook, but my man cuffed their asses and hauled them downtown. I took a picture right then, the big stupid one getting tucked into the police car looking like he was reaching out for his mama. Got it framed behind the register right here. Look at it every day."

Twyla laughed like her heart would break. She missed Eli, and the shop, and she was glad somebody was standing up for him.

"So you really made it to Nashville?" he said when the line went quiet.

"I made it *to* Nashville. But I haven't made it yet."

She was quiet for a moment. Ollie had finished his ice cream float and was blowing straw paper rockets at passersby. It was time to say goodbye. She knocked on the glass and waved at Ollie, signaling that she was almost done.

"Be good, Twilight."

She smiled. "Aren't I always?" Though in fact she had decided she didn't want to be good anymore.

CHAPTER 17

Twyla had been avoiding Chet's calls for several days since he'd broken into Mimi's house. Her desire to sleep with him had left her wanting more space and time to reflect on what she was about to do. She didn't want to make this decision while under his spell. Even though she wasn't bound to the teachings of her church, it was ingrained in her that her body was a special gift not meant for just anyone. Twyla now understood that she had wanted this from the first time she met him, on the floor at Tubb's records, when he held Pearl in his arms and told her how much he loved Mickey.

Tonight, the first of September, she strummed her guitar in Mimi's living room, coaxing a love song from its strings. Mimi had stayed out late the night before and had fallen asleep on the sofa next to her, drawing breaths in a perfect four-four meter. Accompanied by this gentle metronome, Twyla homed in on her first decent song in weeks.

She was so absorbed it took her a moment to notice a sound that seemed to be coming from down the hall, a slight, but regular, tapping. A dripping gutter, maybe. She put down her guitar and tucked Mimi's feet to the side so she could rise without waking her. The tapping resumed, five in a row, this time a little louder. She followed the sound, wary, all her senses bright and ready. When she entered her room and saw Chet at the window, she felt a spike of adrenaline followed closely by pangs of joy.

She flipped the latch and slid the door open as quietly as she could.

Chet gathered her up in a long hug. It felt like eons since she had seen him last. She smelled him keenly, the leather vest and his starched collar, the oily polish on his boots, something rich and herbal on his cheeks. She recalled with a catch in her throat how vividly her father would smell after a long separation. She could detect every bar he'd played in, every meal he'd eaten, every cigarette he'd smoked.

"I missed you," he murmured into the flesh of her neck.

"Goodness sakes, it's only been a few days," she whispered and closed her bedroom door to the hall. She wanted to believe his heavyheartedness was caused by his yearning for her, but it appeared he had something else on his mind.

"Something wrong?" she asked, though she did not sincerely want to hear his answer.

"It's nothing, I just had it out with one of the guys." He laughed to himself like there was more than what he was letting on. "Can't seem to shake it."

"Oh," she said. "Sorry. You wanna talk—?"

"Old news!" He clapped his hands together signaling a new conversation, a direction Twyla was more than willing to follow. "Listen," he said, "let's get out of here. I could use a drive."

Twyla thought of the song-in-progress she'd left in the living room, and the good night's sleep she'd been craving. She thought of the stacks of laundry and household chores and errands she'd slated to complete the next day. But prudence was no match for desire.

She went for her house key, locked all the doors, and followed Chet to his car.

Chet took her on a circuitous, aimless drive. He punched through the radio stations, finding nothing to his liking, then finally turned it off. He took sharp turns and seemed unconcerned for the comfort of his passenger. She wished to ease what bothered him, to smooth the creases on his forehead, to be the reason for his relief.

On the western edge of town they passed a sign advertising pleasure boats for rent.

"There!" she said, pointing. "Let's go there."

Chet slowed down and parked on the side of the road.

"You want to go on a boat?"

"Sure," she said, now clear about her intention, now sending him the message with a graze of her hand to his thigh, a shimmer about the eyes. "It'll be fun."

On receiving her signal, his mood instantly improved. He turned the car around and headed back to the marina.

They arrived at dusk just as a middle-aged man smelling faintly of fish was locking the gate.

"I'm closed up for the night," the man said, and wiped something from his hands into a cruddy rag. Chet stood fast like he belonged there. It was seven thirty, well after the stated closing time on his sign.

"Sir, I'm in a pickle," Chet said. "I've promised this lady a boat ride. Can't you keep the lights on for another hour? Sign says you're still open."

"Sorry, son, I've got to be somewhere. Come back tomorrow." He slung the rag over his shoulder and started for his office door when Chet passed him a wadded-up bill.

"How about this? You let us sneak out for a bit and I'll pay you double."

The man gave him a weary look.

"We'll tuck it back in right where we found it," Chet said. "You won't even know we've been here."

He sighed, having simultaneously made and regretted his decision. "All right, take your pick. You've got one hour."

Twyla picked out a sunny yellow rowboat with matching oars and a small outboard motor, and, perched across from each other, they shoved off into the graying night. Chet rowed out and let the current carry them downstream. Light faded into darkness. Twyla admired the shush of the river, the rustling of millions of leaves overhead. Any lingering doubts about her decision swirled into the eddies behind them.

Chet stuck an oar in the water and veered them to shore, where the boat surfed to a stop on a muddy bank. A canopy of kudzu and trumpet vine draped over low branches gave her the impression of being in a cave.

"I got something for you," he said. "For writing songs."

She smiled. In the dusk his face looked like a charcoal sketch. He withdrew from his vest pocket a slender box wrapped in Florentine paper. She held the gift, its existence alone a treasure. She pried apart its wrapping with ginger fingertips and opened the box inside. In its velvet bedding was a silver fountain pen, aglow in creamy moonlight.

"This is too much," she said, not yet daring to take the pen in her fingers.

"Read it," he said. He seemed to be probing her for a reaction. "It's engraved. I was thinking you could use it for writing your songs."

She squinted and rolled the pen until she saw an etching on its barrel, two words with the weight of gold.

For Twyla.

"This is . . ." She scraped around for words that wouldn't come. She thanked him, her gaze stitched to a tear in her jeans, afraid of how she'd feel if she met his eyes. When she finally looked up he kissed her.

As he lowered her down to the blankets he'd draped on the floor of the boat, she almost wished he hadn't given her anything. She had already made up her mind to give herself over to him tonight; now it seemed transactional. A thing for The Thing. But her sentimental heart was touched by the gesture. Not the price, but the thought. He'd planned ahead, he'd personalized. He believed in her. And if the price and the beauty of this gift reflected his feelings, surely he loved her.

With all these thoughts on her mind she had barely noticed Chet untying her top, kissing her ear, her neck, her collarbone. She dropped back into the moment. Her skin reacted to the cold and to his touch. She kissed him back. Chet propped himself above her while she searched for a comfortable position between the two bench seats. He shrugged off his vest but left his shirt.

"Take it off," she said.

He smiled, with a playful guilty expression. "I'm cold."

Twyla, naked and covered in gooseflesh, laughed at his nerve. She propped herself up on her elbows, now leaning against one seat with her feet pressed against the other. Chet, unbuckled and unzipped, kneeled between her legs and lowered himself down upon her. As he did, the boat wobbled, listing heavily to her left, so that water sloshed in and wet her bottom, and Twyla's arms shot out in some stabilizing reflex. Chet seemed calm and in control. He shifted his weight slightly to restore balance to their vessel. She inched his pants down and felt him warm on her abdomen. He paused, caressed her cheek. She wasn't sure how she'd imagine her first time, but there was something furtive and delicious about sharing this moment with him, afloat in their private skiff.

"Next time we'll get a bigger boat."

She laughed and slid her hands on the warm dough of his rear end. He leaned down to her, intense in his gaze, and his hair brushed her cheek, got tangled up in their kisses. She gathered up his dark hair and tied it back with an elastic she wore on her wrist. He laughed a little into her kiss. "How do I look?"

She smiled, then, sensing him waiting for a sign to go forward, widened the span of her legs and settled underneath him.

He pressed down on her. There was a profound tightness followed by a dull stab of pain. She opened her mouth to cry out but the sound did not come. Perhaps sensing her tension, he moved slowly. Soon there were hints of pleasure, a lessening of pressure, an ease of movement. She kissed him, laid her hands on his neck and brought him close, ready now for more.

Then a searing flash of light.

"What was that?" she said, startled.

Afterimages bloomed in purple and green. Was it lightning? A late-season firework? Chet was too consumed to acknowledge her question, but she was certain she hadn't imagined the light. She wondered, amused, if pleasure could be so intense you could see it. That was it, then. She'd seen the light.

Soon, the heat between them and the rocking of the boat carried her away, and in minutes he brought her to a feeling so perfect, she was, for a moment, furious it had to end. She continued to rub herself against him, bringing tides of sensation, like aftershocks to the first wallop of pleasure, and they collapsed, he on top of her, in the cradle of the boat. Panting, giggling weakly.

Then he shifted over and onto his side and, quicker than she thought possible, he fell asleep.

Twyla lay there in a bed of her own frustrated desire, wishing he would wake, but also savoring the feeling of him heavy next to her. There in the drifting vessel, she took in the stars and sounds of night creatures. Little branches snapping, leaves rustling. The natural world carrying on as always.

ONCE UNLEASHED, TWYLA'S HUNGER FOR sex was insatiable. Any minute she wasn't working for Mimi, she was with Chet. In every seat of his car, under bridges, in bathrooms, closets, on park benches, and once, after closing, inside a listening booth at Tubb's. At night they said sweeter things, dreamed about the future, wrote sappy little verses together before one of them dozed off. But her own songwriting halted. Every morning before chores she would warm up her vocal cords, pick up her beautiful pen, and try to write, then return to the guitar and brush out familiar songs on its strings, hoping to jiggle something loose. But the lyrics, sentimental at best, only eked out, and there was no magic in them. Hearts were set aflame, love was forever, and promises unbroken. She cringed at the sight of them on paper, didn't dare sing them aloud. She finally decided to take a break from songwriting. She had never had to exert force on her music. Maybe all she needed was to surrender to what was happening. When she had some distance or perspective she might be able to render it in song. A part of her hoped she never got far enough from being in love to write about it.

CHAPTER 18

About two weeks after their night on the river, Chet stopped calling. On the third day with no word from him, she couldn't wait any longer. Mimi was working late, so after Twyla put Ollie to bed, she dragged the phone into her room. It was only then she realized he had never given her his number. He had pursued her with such enthusiasm that she had no reason to call him.

Now it dawned on her how little she knew of him. She hadn't met his bandmates or any of his friends or even seen where he lived. Where had her mind gone? Where was her curiosity? He had seemed like an open book, rambling on about music, shows he'd played, people he'd met. She'd never been around a man who was so willing to share about himself, so extroverted, not stoic like Daddy, or retiring like Lloyd. Even Eli shielded her from his private struggles, the war scars she knew were there. On occasion her father had shared stories from the road, how he and the Sundowners were robbed at gunpoint of all their equipment, how he'd bargained for Pearl in exchange for the truck and he'd wept from relief. She could still hear the sound of ice rustling in his watered-down whisky. But he always told these stories in the second person. *He* never got scared, "you" did. She'd tasted intimacy with Daddy but never gorged on it. With Chet she had confused confessional with monologue.

The dial tone clanged from the receiver in her hand, signaling her to hang up. She didn't know how long she'd been sitting there stewing in a sense of feeling wronged. She tried to talk herself out of the worry that started up, that maybe he'd booked a gig, or the Bronco had broken down, or his phone stopped working, but even she could hear the desperation in those excuses.

"It's only been a few days," she said aloud now to calm herself. "Everything's just fine."

But it wasn't just worry. It was need. And it pounded at her.

She went to the kitchen and flung open the fridge. Sandwich meat and cut-up vegetables for Ollie's lunch. A loaf of bread. A Tupperware of onion soup dip and a pot roast in its Dutch oven. She pulled everything out and spread it haphazardly across the counter. Then she made a strange sandwich of everything and tore into it, working her jaws.

THAT NIGHT TWYLA BARELY SLEPT. And when she woke the next morning, still without word from Chet, she feared he might be dead. As she went through the motions of fixing coffee, juice, and Grape-Nuts for breakfast, Mimi flagged her down.

"What in God's good name has gotten into you?" Mimi asked, then poured herself some juice.

Twyla filled her in, hoping Mimi would reassure her, but when she finished, Mimi just looked back at her pityingly.

"Shit, I don't know why he's not calling. It could be a lot of things. Don't waste your breath crying over him. Boys like that, they just don't last. And honey, in my book, that's a good thing."

WHEN CHET FINALLY CALLED IT had been eight days since their last visit, and Twyla, dry and bitter, could muster no joy at the sound of his voice.

"Twyla, hey," he said with too much gentleness. "Listen, I'm sorry I've been a little tied up lately. I've been busy with rehearsals and . . ."

She let him speak, numb and out-of-body as he rattled off a merry list of his activities since last they spoke. She couldn't tell if he really thought she had no reason to be cross, or if he was avoiding discussing it. What irked her the most was the sense that if she let loose her hurt she would only push him away. The resulting state was a sort of paralysis. She couldn't move beyond the anger that huffed just behind her teeth, but she couldn't share it with him either.

She felt ants in her hand and when she looked down saw that she had wrapped the phone cord around her wrist so tightly that her fingers were blue. She uncoiled the tourniquet and shook out her fingers while she gathered her thoughts.

"Well?" he said.

"Sorry," she said and tried to access the last thing he had said. "What was that again?"

"I'm headed out for a few weeks. We leave right after my show tonight. I'll call you when I get back from tour, okay?"

"Tour?"

"Twyla, were you even listening? Look, I have to go. When I get back to town I'll give you a call."

She was too stunned to speak.

He hung up before she could ask where he was going, or why he couldn't call from the road, leaving her shocked that she could feel worse than she had before.

Hearing his voice, though, had dosed her with energy. The kind that made her want to move, or fight, or tear something apart. Tour? Those things took weeks of planning—why hadn't he mentioned it before? Why hadn't she been to any of his shows? She considered her next move. One option was to fake nonchalance and white-knuckle their time apart, playing Mimi's game of supply and demand. But this didn't feel right. She feared he would forget about her, forget the promises he'd made, to cut a record with her, to introduce her to his manager. She wanted to go to his show tonight. If she didn't come, it was like she was saying it was okay to treat her like she was nothing.

She wandered into the kitchen and opened the fridge, not hungry but needing something on her tongue. She found a beer at the back that had the consistency of slush and drank without lowering the can from her lips. Her teeth pounded, the roof of her mouth ached. Then she went to the bathroom, stripped and stood under a cold shower until she could think straight. There was something rigorous and bracing about bringing her body temperature down, making it hurt, that calmed the chatter in her head. By the time she had dressed, the question of what to do about Chet became suddenly clear. She would not wait around for him to call in a few weeks. She would go to his show tonight and talk to him. If he was done with her, he would need to tell it to her face. This way, she could fall apart, then carry on.

She opened up Mimi's closet and scanned for the right outfit. If she was getting dumped, she wanted him to know what he was missing. She strapped on a crocheted halter top and the jeans that shaped her big ass just right. She brushed out her hair and let it hang wild around her shoulders. Mimi appeared in the doorway smoking a ciggie.

"You're going out to get that man, aren't you?" Mimi said.

Twyla nodded.

"Even though he's on his way out."

Twyla bit her lip, ashamed but not deterred. Mimi took a long drag and exhaled.

"Welp, it's gonna make a hell of a country song, I'll tell you that."

Twyla smiled.

"I guess you'll be needing my car." Mimi rooted around in her pocket and tossed Twyla the keys. "Don't forget to let her warm up and don't rush the clutch. Handle her nice and easy and she'll be an absolute kitten. Or a wildcat if that's what you're going for."

CHAPTER 19

Twyla wove between glittering and cowboy-hatted hopefuls, dodging their elbows and denim-wrapped butts, to the bar and said hello to Irma. Irma tossed her a generic nod, not recognizing her face, and shouted "Beer only tonight" followed by an icy Budweiser spun expertly down the bar. Twyla fumbled the catch and knocked the beer to the floor. She wiped off the grime and let it settle a moment, then pulled the tab and took a long, fortifying sip.

After a retro set from the 1940s, three old cusses doing their arthritic best, the emcee bounded up to the mic and announced the Chet Wilton Band. Twyla abandoned her slot at the bar and pushed her way up toward the middle of the crowd. Chet let his band take the stage before stepping up. He flicked a signal to the sleepy tech manning the spotlight. A little to the left. Then he smiled and slung the guitar strap over his shoulder. Women in the crowd took note. Lips wrapped themselves around cocktail straws, eyelashes lowered just so, painted fingernails shushed the talk of lesser men.

She drew a breath. There was a sense of transgression, like she should not observe without being known. Having never seen him perform, it occurred to her only now she hadn't thought him capable. He had swagger enough, sure, but technically he was a blunt, intermediate musician. The first song was a country take on "Paint It, Black" by the Rolling Stones. A little cheer rose at the famous intro, now on a slide guitar—a stylish choice—instead of the sitar used on the original recording. Chet played up the crowd, teasing here, stoking there, but she saw through his charisma. She could practically hear him counting the beats, calling out the chord changes in his mind. His bandmates were career players, far stronger than Chet, and they made him look good. They covered for him when he dropped a note, let him take the glory while they held down the rhythm.

The audience was hooked. Twyla envied his energy. Musical ability wasn't everything, apparently. The band kept playing a zippy background tune, killing time while keeping the audience alive. As the song ended, he locked eyes with someone whose face she couldn't see. Chet stretched out his hand into the front row and pulled a woman onstage. She tugged her hot pants up to a waist the circumference of an infant's and waved to the audience. She wore an indigo bandanna top tied between her breasts and a coordinating cropped suede jacket, studded with rhinestones. When she turned around in a whirl of hair she outshined every living being in the room. Leggy and tall with Barbie-doll dimensions, luscious black waves, and determined eyes, she had Lynda Carter looks with a Julie Newmar cunning.

Chet leaned intimately into the microphone and glanced, then winked at his onstage companion. The woman kissed the air with jammy lips.

"Everybody put your hands together for a talented singer, the prettiest girl in Tennessee, and the future *Mrs.* Chet Wilton, Lorelei Ray!"

Twyla stood there staring, as if trying to verify with her eyes the appalling thing she had just heard. Suddenly dizzy, she reached out and clamped down on someone's shoulder to keep from losing her legs. The band struck up the opening to a love song, a syrupy-slow one, heavy on the steel guitar. This woman, unknown to her moments before, now locked eyes with the man she loved. In the cozy space around the microphone they sang, and ruined, one of her favorite songs. And as she backed away from the stage, she swore Lorelei met her eyes as she sang, "Are you lonesome tonight?"

Someone bumped into Twyla and knocked her beer back, spilling cold foam onto her breasts and all down her front. Her eyes were shot full of tears, and the room felt suddenly too crowded, too loud. She started burrowing her way to an exit. On her way to the door someone blocked her passage and slid a hand around the curve of her waist.

"Slow down, sister," a man said and began to sway with her. "Got time to dance with an old cowboy?" He smiled to reveal a chalk-white row of dentures. "They're playing our song."

She shoved him aside. He snatched after her but she was too fast and made it to the door. She fell into the cooling night air and sat down on the curb. People were drinking and smoking in the alley and thankfully paid her no mind. She wished she could cry but was too furious.

The future Mrs. Chet Wilton.

He had said those words with such ease and inevitability. To a crowd. She was humiliated. She looked at her outfit, which now seemed ill-fitting and dated. In no world, this one or the next, could Twyla compete with that woman. Lorelei Ray was a walking mannequin with a Hollywood shimmer. She seemed feisty and confident, larger-than-life. Perfect for him.

Her guts turned as she wondered how long he had been with that woman. Had they been together while he was courting Twyla? Or, was it recent, a whirlwind affair? The thought of both possibilities broke her heart. And as she ran the course of their relationship over in her mind, she now understood why he had always avoided crowds, claiming he had wanted to meet in private. It wasn't privacy he had wanted. It was secrecy. Perhaps he had been hiding Twyla from the world because he was engaged to another woman; or perhaps he just didn't want to be seen with someone so terribly ordinary.

She could feel her mother's pointed disdain. *Well, what else did you expect, Twyla Jean?* she'd say. For going out on her own, for straying from God, for getting mixed up with sex and booze. Mother might as well be here, hand at the nape of Twyla's neck, rubbing her face in a stinking pile of her mistakes.

In fact, no one was here. Only Twyla.

If she had been given a chance to do it again, would she have said no to Chet? Taken it slow, approached with ladylike caution? Told him she wasn't that kind of girl? To what end? She would have ended up as lonely and frustrated as she was now but she wouldn't have had the chance at bliss. She never would have tasted him, felt herself lifted and held. She wouldn't have been the object of his craving. Then she thought of the silver pen. Why would he go to the trouble of giving her such a personal and costly gift if she was just a fling? Even if it hadn't lasted, and even if she hadn't been the only one, he *had* cared for her. She had to believe it was true.

CHAPTER 20

A few weeks later, she'd cried enough tears to fill a bathtub and written so many horrible songs she wondered if she ought to give in and go home. She might have considered leaving more seriously if Mimi hadn't been so understanding, so quick to pull her to the kitchen for a cup of coffee and a cry. She wished that her mother, not Mimi, were the one offering comfort. But how could she confide in a woman who was so terrified of Twyla's feelings, and her own? A woman who would not admit to noticing her daughter was gone? She hadn't heard from Chet or even seen him around on the rare occasion she went into the city, though, of course, she had looked. It had been easier to hole up at Mimi's, distract herself with her household duties and caring for Ollie, and wallow in her self-pity.

As she sat at the edge of the empty pool, strumming some nonsense on her guitar, getting nowhere, she warmed herself with recurring thoughts of Chet coming back to apologize. Finding her despondent, he'd beg her forgiveness, probe her for understanding, and kiss the life back into her. She'd push him away and make him prove he would stay. She would toy with him, lord her power over him until he crumbled, and send him away. Then she remembered Lorelei, that prize filly, and realized he wasn't ever coming back.

She said it to herself then, out loud: "He's never coming back."

What surprised her in that moment, once she had spoken the words, was the little bubble of hope rising in her chest. Hope that a greater wisdom had orchestrated all of this—Nashville, Chet, even Lorelei—that all of it was happening for reasons beyond her, and that her salvation was to return to what she knew. She didn't know how to go home, or how to talk to her mother; she didn't know how to make it in Nashville; she didn't even know how to fall in love anymore. But she knew one thing.

Even if Chet didn't love her back, music always would.

A little lyric twinkled. *Do you love me after all I've done?* She sang it out a couple different ways, one mournful, the next bittersweet. Then she wrote down two verses of a song that had a shot at being decent.

"What took you so long?" she said. To herself, perhaps. Or to inspiration. And a smile crept over her face as she remembered, finally, what she was made of.

That one little line turned into seven songs. Twyla wrote with her whole heart, pouring into her lyrics all she'd experienced since climbing on that bus to Memphis. Elvis in his casket, rockabilly Benny, conversations with Mimi, nearly losing Ollie, and, of course, Chet. She worked out her songs on the guitar and then, when they were ready, jotted down the lyrics and a few messy notes with the fancy fountain pen. Days ago, in a fit of anger, she had made it as far as a pawn shop on Broad, ready to sell the pen and be rid of him for good, when she remembered something lovely *had* passed between them, and even if it had to end the gift was a reminder that he had cared.

Twyla rolled up to Writer's Night in Mimi's Daytona and found parking right in front of Irma's like it was waiting for her. She bought a Coke, dropped her name in the hat, and tuned her strings one last time. Next to her a boy in a Sunday suit picked his afro and patted it down. He must have been thirteen or fourteen.

"What are you playing tonight?" she asked him.

His voice cracked adolescently when he tried to speak. He swallowed and cleared his throat and tried again. "Something I wrote for Bo Diddley," he said and pointed to a junior electric guitar.

There was something unbearably beautiful about the guts, or the innocence, of taking the stage so young, so liminal, and to show a room full of people his love of music. It was enough to split her heart at the seams.

"You scared?" she asked.

He put away his pick and she could see his hands were shaking. "Mama said you ain't scared, you ain't living."

She smiled and wished him luck. From his show of courage, she summoned some of her own. She brushed aside memories of the Writer's Night humiliation, of her weeks-long slump, of the heartache, the pride of living through it. Tonight, she arrived focused, prepared, and alert to the work ahead of her.

After a couple of middling acts, Irma drew her name. The crowd was antsy. They seemed ready for a winner. She sat down onstage, cleared the nerves from her throat, and gave her guitar a warm-up strum.

"This one's called 'After All I've Done,'" she said.

The mic popped. She gave it a little room and got ready to sing.

Her eyes closed, she imagined the lyrics on her eyelids. Then when she felt sure they would not elude her, she drew a breath and played. The first chord came out dull. Her fingers were stiff. She shook out her hand and started again, this time playing from her shoulders, her hips, and her voice rang out like the crack of a leather whip. She lost herself then, in the music, in its loping rhythm, in the appreciation coming now from the audience. Drinks set down, chins rested on fists, heels catching the beat. All of it, the audience, the music, her guitar, every soul in Nashville it seemed, had joined together. For three and a half minutes they were all on the journey together; there was no separation, no worry, nothing to take her away. And as she steered the song from nostalgia into rage into weary hope, she saw those emotions reflected in their faces. Where she went the audience followed. She had never felt power like this.

When she played the final chords, she knew it was good and it came to her not like a thought, but a deeper wisdom, that this here was her purpose. Every moment, every turn, had led to this stage, this song. And the applause that followed confirmed it. Someone handed her a fresh full beer. She took a sip and set it down on a table, not wanting to mellow her pride. She thanked the crowd and stood up to a fresh wave of cheers. The entire room belonged to her—every pair of eyes and ears, every beating heart, was Twyla's. She reeled, she bowed. She wanted more.

Against a tide of smiles and "hot damns" and "atta girls," she worked her way to the bar and ordered a Coke.

"A song like that deserves a real drink," someone next to her said.

She looked up and saw Chet. Though it had only been a few weeks, she barely recognized him. His shoulder-length waves had been cut short and slicked down like a businessman, face shaved smooth but for the razor burn on his throat. He wore a plain blue Oxford shirt over his old jeans, and that stallion energy was now gelded. All the questions she wanted to ask, all the insults she could fling, all the ways he had hurt her, mobbed at the base of her throat. If she thought there was a chance of a relationship with him, she might have let them loose. But she had already crossed this particular bog, and from the other side, he didn't look quite worth the trouble.

"I know about your girlfriend," she said. She wanted him to be ashamed. To apologize.

But he just cast a mean look around the room, then knocked back his first of two whisky shots.

"Lorelei and I split up," he said. She drew in a tight breath. She held to her conviction that they were over, tightly, as if it might slip from her grasp. "But you probably don't want to hear about that." Second shot went down. "Or maybe you do." He wiped dribble from his chin. "Maybe I just made your fuckin' day."

"Maybe, I don't care what you've been up to," she said, too quickly, hoping what she said was true.

He seemed not to have heard her over the noise of the bar or his own rumination. "The tour was a big fat flop. Six cities, twelve dates. Pretty good crowd in Memphis, half that in Atlanta, then I don't know . . . Word got out and all of a sudden Denver cancels, Dallas . . ." Even his voice seemed different, slurry and lacking in bass. "After that I said fuck it. I broke up the band and started working for my father."

He looked smaller with his short hair, everything stooped and turned inward. She couldn't believe this was the person she nearly lost herself to.

"You quit the band? What for? Everyone takes their licks—you said so yourself."

He shook his head, embarrassed, and gazed down the barrel of his shot glass.

"I didn't sign up for empty rooms. But that's not the worst of it. After I quit, and I'm finally making money, Lorelei convinces me to write her a check for her album, pay for a goddamn backup band, new outfits . . . Shit, she hasn't even written any music yet. As soon as the check cleared she dumped my ass."

Twyla allowed herself some pleasure in his misfortune. In the weeks since they'd stopped talking she had begun to see him more clearly. Reaching the conclusion that he didn't understand music, wasn't in it for the right reasons, had helped her move past the hurt and let him go. Now it seemed she had been right. When music got tough, instead of trying to get better, he folded.

"You did good up there," he said.

She let out a soft little laugh. No one, especially not him, needed to convince her she had nailed the song.

"Is that some kind of way of saying sorry?" she asked.

Then he reached out for her, brushed the hair away from her cheek and drew her gaze to him, the murky green and gold of his eyes enthralling. The audacity, and the familiarity, of his hand on her skin cast a flush over her whole body. Her throat pulsed in time with her heart so forcefully she feared he could read her arousal. She lost command of her thoughts and was swept into helpless, compulsive wanting.

He jutted his chin toward the door. "Let's get out of here."

The answer was no. She had come too far since the night her heart fell out of her chest to give him one more second of her time. He didn't even deserve to share this moment with her, her first solid win since she came to Nashville. Common sense told her to get herself home, to hole up in her room and tough it out. Or, like Mickey had said, to put it in a song. But her common sense was crushed, splattered, pulverized by the mass of her desire. Right or wrong, she couldn't say no to the best feeling she had ever known, even if it might also mean the worst.

She looked at the clock above the exit. Only eight thirty. An innocent hour. He paid for their drinks, motioned with his eyes to the exit, and left. She hated that he expected her to follow. And worse, after all he'd done, she hated that he was right. As she pushed through the crowd, she tried to justify her choice, that she was in control, and that she knew as well as he did that this time would be their last.

CHAPTER 21

Twenty minutes later they pulled up to the marina.

Chet, who had not spoken during the ride over, turned to Twyla. His eyes were bleary from drink, and sad.

"I'm not asking you to take me back," he started.

She crossed her arms and turned slightly away. "Why in the world would I—"

"Please, can we just pretend nothing happened? Just for tonight?" She didn't know what to say. The seduction was taking a strange turn. More out of curiosity than attraction now, she followed him out of the car. She considered whether it would be possible to wade into him without full immersion. Without the cold and the wet and the awful sinking. So long as the drive she felt was physical, she decided it wouldn't hurt, just this once.

The marina was closed but the boats were all there for the taking, just a locked wooden gate that gave way to a flick of Chet's crowbar. He helped Twyla into the same yellow-painted boat where they had first made love. He shoved off the dock and rowed several minutes in silence before laying down the oars. The moon cast its dim silver hue over the darkness. Chet pulled Twyla toward him. His hands found her, moved surely under her clothes, rediscovering the swells of her shoulders, belly, breasts, then settling at the helm of her hips. His short hair bristled under her fingers, so strange, manicured like a tidy lawn, chaste as a church boy, but his smell was the same. His kiss was, too.

He repeated how good she felt, how much he had missed her, missed this, like a chant, a return to himself. He handled her fleshiness with appetite, taking care with his movements so as not to tip the boat, for this time they were not moored, but floating, adrift. He peeled off her jeans and underwear, untied her halter. Her body glowed silver in the moonlight.

Then he had his pants around his knees and she straddled him. He clutched her behind and sighed as he sank into her.

"That's what I love about you," he said. "You're all woman."

She did not want to talk or think. She shushed him. But he kept going.

"Not like Lorelei," he said. "There is such a thing as too perfect, you know? Always dieting, always weighing herself. She's like a goddamn sprig of parsley."

This time she put a finger over his mouth. "Can you please stop talking?"

"Not you, though." He slapped her thigh. "You're the meat and potatoes." He grunted and tried to pull himself deeper into her but she pushed him back. She had had enough talk of Lorelei. But Chet kept going.

"She is one crazy bitch, and she's got this one-track mind. I mean, *obsessed*. Nothing and no one better get in her way. She'll light a stick of dynamite and drop it right in the middle of your life. *Blam*."

"Stop, Chet."

"She'll fuckin' track you like an animal. She'll make you wish you were dead rather than deal with her bullshit." He shivered in remembering something. "I just don't get why I love her so much."

She shoved him back and pulled a tangle of jeans to her breast.

"What is so wrong with you," she said, "that you think you can say something like that to me?"

Chet looked mean, his eyes in shadow. He was very still.

"I think we better get back to the car," she said, hoping to rupture this threatening pause. But he held fast. She noticed he had begun to tremble, and not from the cold.

"Chet, take me back, now," she said, louder.

She wanted out, away from him. She imagined rolling over the side and swimming away.

"Look, I don't know what's going on with you, but can we just get back, please?"

Finally he spoke.

"It's your fault she broke up with me, you know." He moved in and took her by the arms, the rage smoking off of him. "Even after the tour she stayed with me. I thought we were good. But then she found out about you."

His grip was so tight she thought her arms might snap. She strained away from him.

"Two years with that bitch, for nothing. Now I'm stuck working a fuckin' *banking job*, kissing my father's ass."

He shoved her down and loomed over her.

She couldn't get out from under him. And it pissed her off.

"It's probably for the best," she said through her teeth. He stared her down, debating something, then, his fury seemed to pass just as quickly as it came. He took the oars in his hands, swung them round and dug them into the water. After a minute, he cocked his head, puzzled, some suspicion ignited.

"The fuck did you mean by that? *What's* probably for the best?"

She should keep quiet. He was ready to go back, things were cooling down. It was safer to stroke his hurt feelings, and swallow her own. But she couldn't, and wouldn't, do that anymore.

"I meant it was probably for the best that you went to work for your dad," she said. What she wanted right now was to cause him pain. "I mean," she said, holding his gaze, "you didn't think you were gonna make it playing *covers*, did you?"

She didn't know the oar was coming her way until it knocked the breath from her lungs. Then he shoved her up against the front bench, hands around her throat. She reached up and clawed at him, locked her guitar-strong hands around his neck, but he didn't seem to feel a thing. She kicked and swatted her arms around, searching for something to stun him, at least enough to get him off of her, but he outweighed her by a hundred pounds. She couldn't breathe, her throat clamped shut by hands that, moments ago, had touched her tenderly. The shadowy grimace on his face bleached as her vision winked out and she felt herself fading. She groped around the bottom of the boat for something, anything, a key, an oar, a splinter of wood she could lodge in his eye, but all she found were her pants. She tried to cry out, a thin, rasping sound, though of course, even if she could call for help, there was no one around to hear it.

Then she felt the edge of something thin and hard. A bolt of hope.

As he screamed in her face, she wriggled her fingers in the pocket of the jeans and found the silver pen. She fumbled with the cap, trying to unscrew with her thumb and forefinger. He cried out again, this time in anguish. A glimmer of humanity. Then his grip loosened. She saw his lips move. He was saying something, but she did not hear his words. Just the sound of blood pulsing in her ears.

She only meant to fight him off.

The cap finally spun off the pen and her arm swung up like it was spring loaded. She sank the pen into his throat, once, twice, and on the third strike she left it in the flesh under his jaw. He let her go. She gasped, sucked in great breaths, and as her vision returned she watched him raise a hand to the pen. His expression curled down in horror, and he pulled at the pen weakly, pried it out and let it fall, releasing a thin pulsing ribbon of blood. Twyla gaped, numbly watching the scene unfold as if she weren't square in the middle of it.

Then Chet slumped sideways and tumbled headfirst into the river.

Whatever shock had riveted her to the boat released her into action. She dove after him. The muscle memory of Ollie's rescue from weeks before was fresh. She waved her arms around, hoping to bump into him in the black of the water. If he sank to the bottom she could miss him. Then her foot snagged what may have been his shirt. She dove down, groping around until she felt his hair and grabbed a handful, yanked him up, then took hold of his shirt and kicked upward, an inch at a time, until she finally breached the surface, gasping like it was her first breath on earth.

When she brought him up, he coughed and sputtered.

"Chet!" she said. "Are you okay?" Moments before she had nearly killed him and now she was praying he would live. He moaned, eyes rolling around, unfocused. She kicked harder to keep his mouth above water. By this time the boat had drifted to an eddy by the bank. They were only twenty feet from shore, but he was heavy, even in water. She couldn't fight the direction of the river or they both might drown, so she lugged him sideways, kicking them over bit by bit, until a strong rush of water pulled them downstream. She had him around the neck. Even in the moonlight it was clear he was bleeding badly.

They were ten feet from shore when Chet began to thrash. She lost hold of him, and he went under. She stared at the spot, already smoothed over by the current. She was barely strong enough to tread water and feared she would not have the strength to go after him again. Then, with a spray, he resurfaced. She screamed and lost half her breath. Then he swung his big arm across her face, knocking her under. She fought to find the surface and finally came up for air but he quickly forced her down, using her body to keep himself afloat. She tried to get out from under him, kicking, clawing, but the water slowed every punch she threw and his hold on her was too strong. Then her foot grazed the silty floor. They were close to the bank. She thought if she could push off the river bottom she might be able to dart out from under him. It would take what little strength she had left. She let out some air to sink farther down, then pushed with her legs. It wasn't enough. She was out of strength, out of air, out of hope. The urge to inhale was strong, and her muscles had turned to jelly. As Twyla inched out of consciousness, she was less afraid. She saw a baby suspended in fluid, breathing without air. At peace. It struck her as a natural, beautiful thing. Her limbs flooded with warmth and calm. She stopped fighting. Then she opened her mouth and inhaled.

CHAPTER 22

If anyone had been watching, they would have seen a man slip beneath the river's glossy, black surface, and in his place a woman burst from the depths in a spume of water and sound, choking, retching, whimpering as she paddled her way to the water's edge, clawed through mud, and collapsed on the bank. Quivering and panting and bringing up river water, she did not celebrate having evaded the drug of drowning, how breezily she had sunk into giving up, but now, racked with chills so violent her teeth kept piercing the meat of her tongue, she feared she may have survived drowning only to die of the cold.

One more second and she would have joined him in the river. But she would not die tonight. The current had plied her from under him and she floated to the surface, to air, to life. Slowly her shaking subsided, blood returned to her extremities bringing with it sensation and a burst of energy. She scanned the area for Chet, straining to see, listening, finding nothing human. Then her thoughts appeared in blunt, rudimentary blocks. *Find the boat. Wipe it down.* She rose like a swamp creature, mud matted into her hair, clumped and smeared on the tops of her arms, her belly, her thighs, her cheeks, and all down her back where she had lain writhing. This primordial maiden pitched down the bank, staggered through razored grasses and bramble.

A half mile downriver she saw the yellow boat eddying in a stand of cypress. She went to it, secured it to a tree trunk. The river was safe and still in this protected cove, yet terrifying. The river that had nearly killed her must also rinse her clean. She waded in up to her knees and crouched down, feet planted in soft mud, water up to her shoulders. Quickly as she could, she scrubbed her skin, tipped back her head to loosen the mud from her hair, then squeezed and rinsed over and over until only the finest grit clung to her scalp. She could not submerge her face. Even the feel of cold water splashed on her cheeks shortened her breath.

Then she found her blouse in the bottom of the boat and held it to the moon, revealing black splotches of blood. She dunked the garment in the water and scrubbed it over a river rock, dunking and scrubbing and holding it up to the moon. When she had rinsed out the blood, she made a pail of it and ferried water to the boat, dumping it on every surface, swirling her garment over the lacquered wood. She carried out this task with the same quotidian dutifulness she would in cleaning the bathtub.

She observed her actions at a remove, as if through the wrong end of binoculars. She braced herself under one side of the boat and lifted, dug her toes into the mud until the bloody water rushed onto the banks and drained back into the river. When she tried to get dressed, her hands shook so violently she could barely fasten her top. She worked her legs into her sopping jeans, and secured the straps of her shoes. Then she started up the outboard motor and worked her way slowly upstream. When the marina was in view, she killed the motor and drifted silently into the slip. It was still dark, early morning, and no one was around when she tied up to the dock. She found a bucket of rags near a bare spigot and wiped the remaining fingerprints, shoe marks, drips from her clothing, from the boat, until she was certain she had buffed away every trace of what she'd done. She slid the pen in her pocket, arranged the paddles crisscross like the others, and walked away.

Just as she made it to the Bronco, a faint sundusted light over the horizon. He'd left the keys in the ignition, so she turned it on and drove it over rough ground to a wooded area where it couldn't be seen from the road, then she whacked away the tire marks with a stick. With her last clean rag, she rubbed down the seats, handles and hard surfaces, shook out the floor mats, and retrieved her guitar. By the time she was finished, the sun was out. With Pearl on her back, she started the long walk to Mimi's. She trudged ahead, numb to the blisters forming on her heels, while the new sun dried her clothes.

It wasn't until she started up the wooded drive to Mimi's house that her surroundings began to materialize. And once she could smell the hot pine needles underfoot and feel the salt of her sweat running into the scratches on her shins, and hear the squirrels jeering at the crows across the treetops, memories of the night before clambered back. How his hands pinched off her breath. The swift thrust of her arm and the way the pen sank into his neck like a meat probe into a roast. The taste of mud, the burn of water in her lungs. The bliss of waiting to die.

She raised her hands to her throat, to the spine-deep bruise and a crushed feeling at her trachea, and she imagined her own body as the scene of the crime. There would be tells. She arranged her tangled, bushy hair around her face and neck, grateful, for once, for its wildness. Her clothes were dingy but dry. Her face was another matter. If she could only slip in before Mimi woke up, there would be time to conceal the marks of what she'd done, and what he'd done to her.

Just then the front door opened and Mimi stepped out, still wrapped in a robe and caressing a mug of coffee. Her expression begged questions Twyla could not answer. They stood there a moment, Twyla's eyes cast at her feet. If she even tried to explain she might give something away, so she hoisted her guitar over her back and limped past Mimi into the house.

"Twyla?" Mimi asked.

Twyla paused in the entry, afraid to look or speak.

"Where the devil is my car?"

CHAPTER 23

After paying for Mimi's cab to pick up the Daytona downtown—Mimi had recognized without comment that Twyla was in no state to fetch it herself—Twyla locked herself in the bathroom and ran the shower. She inched backward under the boiling spray, still shy of the water, of its power over her. Then, facing away she braced herself on her knees and heaved. The thin contents of her stomach coiled down the drain and the aftertaste was so vile she braved the water to rinse it clean. She cupped her hands and gargled, spat, gargled, and spat, but the taste was a stain on her tongue. Her lungs and sinuses burned from breathing silty river water, and her nails were thick with grit. Her whole body ached like she'd been fed through a wringer, but the ache was welcome. Pain relieved her from the agony of her memories.

Now clean, at least on the outside, Twyla looked herself over with medical remove. Juicy blisters on her heels and under her ankles and feathery hash marks on her shins. There were two jam-colored blotches at her throat where he'd leaned on his thumbs, a spray of red pinpricks around her eyes. She could cover some of the bruising with makeup, but the hot red splashes on her eyeballs would be impossible to hide. After applying some off-color foundation she found in the bathroom drawer, she dressed in loose pants and a turtleneck. Then she lay on her bed and slept. She slept as if under a stack of blankets, nearly smothered, and

dreamt of swamps. Mimi woke her up two hours later. She lurched out of
bed, hair damp and hot.

"Rough night?" Mimi said, giving her a pointed once-over.

It was impossible to meet Mimi's eyes, as she realized this was the
moment to confess.

Twyla sat back down on the bed, panicked. She hadn't given any
thought to what would happen next. She had been dragging herself from
one moment into the next, staving off obsession, trying to forget. It was
only vaguely real to her that she, with her own hand, had killed someone,
and in this vagueness she felt she was able to survive. Telling Mimi, or
anyone, would bring that reality crashing brilliantly to life.

Mimi rapped her trio of rings on the doorframe. "Earth to Twyla.
Come in, Twyla."

Twyla flicked her eyes up at Mimi, reminded of her presence. "Yeah,"
Twyla croaked. Her voice was mangled and it hurt to talk. "Rough night. I
might have overdone it."

"I can hear that. I hope you didn't sound like that last night?" Mimi
said.

Twyla looked at her, unable to guess what she was prompting her to
say. "Last night?"

Mimi looked incredulous. "Writer's Night, for crying out loud? Did
you go up?"

Was it only last night?

Tell the truth.

All she had to do was open her mouth and say three words. The rest
would follow as it should. She could just open her mouth and let it go.
But the consequences for murder, the questions, the shame on herself, on
her family, were too many and too harsh to imagine. How could she bear
it? She was certain the ordeal would kill her. And no action of hers could
breathe life back into Chet.

"Yeah, I went up," she said.

"And?"

Another voice, distinct from the one she heard by the river, spoke again. This one seemed to beg.

Tell the truth.

"Better this time," she said. She needed more time to think. "I opened my mouth and sound came out."

Mimi laughed. "That's super, kid. I knew you could do it. It'll get easier every time."

Twyla was struggling even with simple sentences, and not only because of her bruised trachea. Every word she uttered seemed to have implications.

"So, listen," Mimi said. "Ollie's coming over today at noon. It's not my day but Dean and what's-her-tits needed a favor. I'm doing a pickup gig filling in for an old friend, so I need you here with him. Can you do that? I'll bring supper when I get back. Whatever he wants."

She was barely listening but had grasped a blurry idea of Mimi's instructions.

"Watch Ollie?" Twyla said. "Yeah, of course." She was anxious to stop talking and start moving. "I'll get started cleaning up." Chores would keep her hands busy and give her a moment to think things over. She started to edge past Mimi in the doorway, but her boss took her by the arm and squared up with her.

"You sure you're okay?" she asked. "You seem kind of . . . squirrelly."

Twyla's insides fizzed up like beer. Mimi would find out on her own if she didn't fess up. She took a breath. "Yeah, I'm okay," she said. *Don't lie.* "Just boy trouble."

Mimi's interest only seemed to grow at this. Her eyes widened and she took both of Twyla's hands in hers.

"Ugh, sorry, sweetie. You'll have to fill me in after we get Ollie to bed," she said. Twyla's heart pounded. "I want to hear all the gory details."

TWYLA WAS SITTING UNDER A shedding walnut tree, numb and blank-minded when Dean pulled up in his sporty Mercedes. As Ollie climbed down out of the car with a little red backpack and his stuffed elephant dangling from one hand Twyla was seized by opposing urges, to hold him and to hide. Given what she'd done, how could she be trusted with Ollie?

"Hiya," he said. His shy blue eyes peered up at her from behind the edge of his fresh bowl cut. She didn't belong here. She was bad, the worst kind. The river stench rose from her pores. Dean rattled off a list of instructions from the passenger window and Twyla must have answered him because he gave a thumbs-up and did a three-point turn out of the driveway. Ollie scuffled over and sat in the chair next to hers. For a long moment they sat in silence.

"Twyla, what is this fizz?" he said, running his hand over the arm of the green plastic lawn chair. "And how did it get there?"

"Hm?" she said, half listening. "Fizz?"

"This fizz here," he said. "This fizz that tickles my hand."

The sweetness of his question drew Twyla out of her rumination. "Oh, I see. That's static electricity."

"*Electristity?*" he said, wide-eyed. "Like lightning?"

She smiled. "Like teeny-tiny lightning."

"Can I *eat* it?"

She smiled. "No, you can't eat it."

"How come? *Why* not?"

"'Cause there's nothing to it."

This seemed to satisfy his curiosity. Then he crawled off his chair and into her lap and tugged on her turtleneck.

"How come your winter shirt is on when it's summer outside?"

The warmth and weight of his little body thawed something in hers. She rested her cheek lightly on the top of his head, her eyes pricked with tears, and she marveled at how one could hold so much goodness and horror in one moment.

"It's not summer anymore, Ollie, it's autumn."

"But it's making-you-sweat weather." He pointed at the damp patches under her arms.

She looked and chicken-winged her arms to air them out. "Okay, you got me, buster. Here," she said, changing the subject. "Wanna race to the trees and back?"

Ollie instantly slid off her lap and assumed a sprinter's position.

"Ready, set, go!" They ran to the end of the long lawn. She wanted to let him win but her legs were not her own. They pumped, drove her forward and upward and far away. When she reached the point where the grass ended in a stretch of forest, she wanted to keep going deeper, but, remembering Ollie, turned around and ran toward the house, sprinting at full speed, turning again at the house and back to the trees until her lungs burned and she doubled over, coughing. She coughed so hard it brought forth a splash of liquid that tasted of algae and rot and all at once she was back underwater, fighting toward the surface.

Ollie caught up to her. "No fair," he said, outraged. "You went grown-up speed." His voice was a drill to her ears. She thought she might be ill again.

"TV," she said, panting, and pointed toward the front door.

Ollie didn't need to be told twice. He ran toward the house and disappeared inside. Within seconds she heard a dish soap jingle. She dropped to her knees and rested her forehead in the prickly grass, high on the fresh blood that surged through her veins. Somewhere right now Chet's body was submerged in the Cumberland. Or had washed up, lungs soaked with the same dank water she tasted now. Would the police be coming for her? She tried to imagine all the moving parts of the evening, to track her movements and his. He had found her at Irma's and they'd left, one by one instead of together, split by the crowd. From that point on they hadn't seen a soul. All the businesses near that part of the river had been closed for the night and there was no pedestrian access that she knew of. Once she left the marina she may have been seen on the road, but likely would have resembled any other hitchhiking dreamer with a guitar across her back. She'd seen a dozen girls with the same silhouette since she'd gotten here.

In fact, there was nothing she could think of that tied her to Chet at all. Though it had pained her at the time, there was now relief in the knowledge that she had been kept separate from the rest of his life. She was ashamed of the cool calculation with which she was processing the night's events. Impassive, rational thought wasn't like her. She usually dove in, feelings forward, sorting things out by intuition more than cunning. Some analgesic pall kept her emotions vague and distant. But she was also glad for it. She repeated her bottom line like a psalm.

Nothing I do can bring him back.

And she didn't think it was wise to throw herself to the authorities without getting her story straight. If she went at all. The fact was, Chet had attacked her, with malice, and she was certain she had done what anyone would do: defend her life. With a matter-of-factness (that, for one humbling moment, reminded her of her mother), she repeated these statements as truth.

It was settled, then. She should carry on as normal for now. Do her job, keep her nose clean, and stay far from town.

Momentarily calmed by this plan, Twyla poked her head in the living room to check on Ollie. The TV was on, but he wasn't there. She called out to him—no answer. Her heartbeat doubled, and she passed through each room, scanning, calling. Flung aside curtains, checked beneath beds. She went to the empty swimming pool, peeked under the cover, eyes slow to adjust to the change in light. Only leaves and a stagnant puddle of rainwater.

"Dang it, Ollie!"

Back in the house she went for the front door, thinking maybe he had followed her to the yard and been playing in the trees. But when she stepped into the foyer someone jumped out from behind the front door.

"Boo!"

Twyla screamed louder than she thought possible and her hands went for his neck. Ollie clapped his hands to his ears. When she realized what was happening, she pulled him close, squeezed him tight. Then she held him at arm's length to scold him.

"Ollie, you shouldn't—"

His face melted into tears. He stood there crying, arms slack at his sides. She wanted to cry, too, but she took him back in her arms and stroked his hair, and she lied and lied to him that everything was all right.

CHAPTER 24

For seven hours, Private Investigator T. Lynn Struthers sat in her beige Volkswagen bug waiting for Mr. Broken Back to waltz out and do cartwheels across the grass right where she could snap an incriminating photo and submit it to her client—his employer—for the rest of her pay. Not that the seventy-five bucks would even tickle the debt she'd been hoarding, but it would buy her groceries through the end of the month.

Struthers was fifty-two years old with sensible short gray hair and the paunchy-strong look of a retired volleyball pro. Long, weight-bearing legs, arms that remembered being muscular. Her once-crosshatched abdomen now felt like pudding when she pressed it, as she did now, with her fingertips. It had been three days since her last bowel movement and her already not-so-svelte midsection was bloated and tender.

As if she had pressed a release valve, her viscera suddenly churned and gushed.

"Lord have mercy," she muttered. "I'm gonna take a shit."

She swept the littered floor with one hand while wrestling down her sweatpants with the other. She found an empty Big Gulp, tore off the top, leaned over the steering wheel and made a tiny toilet of it.

As her meager luck would have it, Mr. Broken Back chose that moment to cruise up on his bicycle, handlebar mustache fluttering in the breeze.

"Oh, you *would* come out now," she said. "Just hold tight, sucker. Don't move." She found a wad of paper napkins and took care of things sort of slapdash, then glanced down to look for a safe place to set the cup. When she looked back at the man, he was hoisting his bike into the bed of his truck. The money shot.

"Shit, shit!" she said, and, fearing she would miss her chance, let the cup fall. She snatched up her camera, advanced the film and scanned for her subject. She scanned left, right, then she looked above the viewfinder to see Mr. Broken Back bounding athletically up the steps and into his house. She released the shutter just as he closed the front door behind him.

Seven hours down the drain. She brought her fist down on the dash and roared.

Goddamn workman's comp cases were sucking the life out of her. It wasn't the long stakeouts—she had loved them during her time on the police force—it was the lack of purpose. There was no honor in being a professional tattletale. But these were the only jobs that she, a middle-aged, disgraced *lady* detective, could tolerate that didn't involve typing pools or skirt suits. At her peak, she'd been a detective in homicide, worked twice as hard as any of those clowns in the MNPD, closed so many cases they should have cast her in bronze and put her on a plinth. Not that she was a genius, but she did have two assets in spades. A feeling person's knack for human behavior and an insatiable, compulsive itch to know what really happened.

She'd been hustling to make rent ever since her very ceremonious termination last year from the Metropolitan Nashville Police Department for provoking one of her perps into violence. A wife beater through and through, this guy had shrugged off a slew of domestic assault charges like a cardigan sweater. He was a real whiz at making them hurt without leaving a mark. She worked off the clock so she could nail him, staking him out nights just so she could catch him with something they couldn't look away from. And this guy, they seemed determined to let him slide. Wife beating without injuries? Half the police force had probably let the back of their hand fall onto their wife's cheek once or twice. Why go after a man like this when there were real bad guys to catch, bad guys who didn't look so much like them?

Well, she took things into her own hands.

She knew what time he left for work and made sure she was in the neighborhood one morning when he drove by. She pulled Wife Beater over for speeding (he wasn't), dragged him out of the car to conduct a search, and planted a gay porn magazine under his seat because that was the greatest fear of a guy like this. It seemed like every drop of blood in his body flooded his face when she pulled it out and riffled its pages. When he forcibly calmed himself, she did something she knew would push him over the edge.

She straightened his collar to get close, and at nearly six feet she stood eye to eye with him. She spoke intimately, quietly, out of her partner's range.

"Grady, if you want to shut your wife up, you don't have to hit her. I know a better way."

He was all chin and he lifted it higher to look down his nose at her. "Is that right?"

"Yeah, that's right. If you really wanna shut her up"—she looked left and right—"you should eat her pussy."

Grady broke into a laugh, whether from amusement or scorn she couldn't tell.

"I don't do that shit," he said.

"You might think about changing your policy," she said, then leaned in and spoke right next to his ear. "Last time I was down there it worked like a charm."

At that he took a swing that was meant to be a bluff, but she turned her nose right into his knuckles. Currents of blood ran down her mouth and neck and saturated the white undershirt she wore beneath her police-issued navy blues. She refused to clean herself up, so when she carted him into the station everyone could see in red and white what had happened. She was counting on that trigger in every cop that gets pulled when somebody attacks one of their own.

She counted wrong.

SHE PULLED INTO A GAS station to wash her hands and dump the Big Gulp in the trash. While she was there she called her answering service from a payphone. As she tugged the folding glass door shut behind her, a curvaceous woman in a tube dress pounded on the window and tapped on her imaginary watch.

"I just got here, sister," Struthers said over her shoulder. "Damn, hold your horses."

The woman soured her face and leaned her fleshy back against the glass, revealing a tattoo of Kermit taking Miss Piggy from behind.

"Charming neighborhood," Struthers muttered and dialed her service.

"Hello, Ellen," she said to the woman who answered the phone. "You working the night shift?"

"Yes, ma'am," she said. "Three messages for you. You got a pen?"

Although it had been six years since she heard from her son, every time she checked her messages, she held her breath for his name. "But nothing from Francis, I'm afraid." The daily disappointment scooped a hole in her middle every time she heard these words. The disappointment never got easier over time, the hole just got bigger. She retrieved from her pocket a notepad with a pen stuck through the spiral and held it to the window.

"All right, Ellen. Shoot."

"One from your landlord—"

"Stop right there, I know what that miser is gonna say and I don't need to hear it from you. What's the next one?"

"It's from First Tennessee Bank about the loan—"

"Boy, you're full of good news tonight, Ellen. Next."

"Last one might be a goodie," Ellen said. "He asked me to take dictation. Older fella, genteel-like. Here's what he said: 'Chester Wilton *the second* calling to request your services in finding our son. Please call at once.' And then he leaves a number. You ready?"

Something in her flickered to life. She was a sucker for a new case, and she needed the money bad. She took the number, thanked Ellen, and blew a kiss to the woman waiting for the phone.

A new case. A fresh start. Nothing better.

Struthers dialed the number she'd scribbled in her notepad and was asked to hold by the polite but chilly woman who answered.

The line clicked back on and another woman spoke.

"Yes, Mr. Struthers, this is Gail Wilton, thank you for calling—"

"*Detective* Struthers is fine," she said and waited for the inevitable confusion, embarrassment, or outrage when the woman realized Struthers was not a man. Mrs. Wilton only paused briefly and continued without drawing attention to the mistake.

"Detective, we are just in pieces. I—I don't know where to begin, but let's meet in person." Her voice had the timbre of nasal swelling. "Can you come tonight?"

"I don't mean to be crass at a time like this, Mrs. Wilton, but it's a hundred dollars once I set foot outside my door."

"Detective," Mrs. Wilton said with measured indignation. "I am certain you have nothing to be worried about. Can you come quickly?"

Struthers had been stiffed by rich people before. In fact, they were the worst, because they couldn't relate to, or even imagine, a state of being broke. But she held her tongue. From what she could tell, this family was big money, and she couldn't afford to give them any less than the service they expected.

"We live at 1000 Chickering Road," Mrs. Wilton said, then continued with a sour twist, "When you arrive, Mrs. Malcolm will direct you to our accountant for any further *billing* concerns."

They have staff to handle their money, she thought. *Woopdy-doo.* Then she made a note to charge them through the nose.

"I can be there in thirty minutes."

IT WASN'T THE FIRST TIME Struthers had been to Belle Meade, but it never ceased to amaze her how money hung in the air here like a scent. In the flamboyant azaleas, the geometric boxwoods, the football field lawns and rambling driveways, and absence of eyesores—dumpsters, billboards, litter—reserved for the rest of humanity. Was the *air* cleaner here? She'd wager it was.

The house could not be seen from the street, but after a long drive past the security hut down a corridor of ancient, towering hedges, it appeared before her in its gleaming, sprawling decadence. A three-story, white-painted brick house built in the Federal style with stately columns and wings upon wings extending from the main building. Discreet lighting accented centenarian chestnut oaks, walnuts and sycamores, giant magnolias with their cone-heavy branches skirting all the way to the grass. Money made on the backs of the slaves who built this place just sitting here, self-fertilizing.

She wanted to snoop so bad she could taste it, but she parked her shitbox car (all the uglier against such elegance), brushed the flakes of gas station strudel off her sweatpants, wishing she'd stopped at home to change, and raised the lion's head knocker to announce her arrival. But before she could bring it down, the great black lacquer door swung open and a maid in full servant garb greeted her.

Struthers waited in an equestrian-themed parlor of cozy dark greens and gilded edges and saddle leather. She inhaled, again, the smell of money. Sweet pipe tobacco, cut gardenias, and prime rib with Yorkshire pudding, she guessed, priding herself on her olfactory acumen. But she wouldn't live in a house like this if someone paid her. Not just because she couldn't, in good conscience, sleep at night knowing she could probably solve hunger in a midsize town with the yearly operating budget of this household, or that she didn't enjoy the company of the disgustingly wealthy, who had never been required to develop anything so common as a personality. No, when she looked at a house like this, it made her sad. If she had all the money in the world, what the hell would get her out of bed in the morning? A maid drawing the curtains? No, sir, she would rather shower in a sink and shit in a cup.

Still, she thought, if rich people were good for one thing, it was hiring people to do things they couldn't or didn't want to do. She was more than eager to relieve them of their burden, in exchange for enough money to pay off her creditors and finally get back in the black. She might even be able to pick and choose her clients instead of hunting workman's comp fraudsters for these corporate blowhards.

The pocket doors behind which she had been sitting slid open to reveal a Nordic, long-faced man with hair somewhere between white and blond. If he had any worries at all, he hadn't decided to let on. Faded blue eyes dripped downward at the outer edges and met the corners of his mouth in a smile, even when his face was resting. A few steps behind him was a thin woman with a tidy bob, the ends tucked under, and secured by a wide headband à la Jackie O. She wore cropped gray pants and a sapphire cardigan, buttoned top to bottom. On her feet, she wore a dainty boat shoe. Both the Wiltons were sun-weathered in a sporty way, like they'd spent their days between the tennis courts and the open sea.

They all shook hands cordially. Mr. Wilton offered Struthers an overstuffed club chair and the Wiltons sat in synchrony on a tartan love seat. Mrs. Wilton raised a stripped and ragged thumbnail to her lips as if she would bite it, then lowered it primly to her lap and clasped it tightly with the other hand. She'd allowed herself one nail to gnaw. The remaining nine fingernails were filed to thin white crescents and buffed to a gleam.

After exchanging an excruciating, but socially necessary round of pleasantries covering the unseasonable heat, the Kentucky Derby, and a brief survey of local politics, Struthers whipped out her notepad and asked how long their son had been missing.

"We last saw him at family supper," said Mrs. Wilton.

"And that was?"

"Here at the house last Monday, just this past."

"And did he seem different to you? Worried? Not himself?"

"Not in the least. He was our Chet. In fact, he's never seemed more like himself."

"How's that?"

Looking pained, Gail glanced at her husband before answering. "He'd gone astray for a few years after college. Consorting with a bad crowd. He thought he would try his hand at music, which we permitted but did not support. Chet isn't particularly talented, but he's a handsome boy."

"Meaning?"

"Well, he lasted longer than we thought he would," said Mrs. Wilton. "Playing other people's songs and such. It was a childish dream. I think he was rebelling. We were very strict with him in some ways."

"Too permissive in others," Mr. Wilton added and opened a burled wood box inside which lay an antique pipe with an ivory mouthpiece. He sprinkled some tobacco in it and tamped it down with his finger, then repeated the action three times. He drew with stiff lips and, satisfied, lit the tobacco with a match. He sucked on his pipe in silence and Mrs. Wilton also went quiet, perhaps reading some marital cue that he needed a moment of reflection.

Struthers sat there with them, ensconced in blue smoke and inherited wealth, and wondered how she would manage to root for these folks—so rich they had staff for their pets, so rich they'd lost count of their horses, so rich they wore moderately priced clothes from L.L.Bean and drove twenty-year-old cars, because they knew they were wealthy with such conviction they didn't have to perform it for anyone. How could she root for people who shielded themselves from every struggle the rest of mankind had to deal with?

From her sweater pocket Gail withdrew a translucent linen handkerchief and dabbed the tears from under her eyes. Struthers took note of the maternal unraveling. She had worked enough cases to have observed that intuition was rarely wrong. She glanced at several dozen framed photographs of Chet on the polished circular table. Politics aside, Struthers reminded herself that these people were looking for their son. At least she and the Wiltons had that in common. When her son turned eighteen, he moved out and cut her off completely, like he'd been planning it for years. The image of him dragging his overstuffed suitcase out the door and into a friend's pickup truck still felt like a blade right through her gut. She sent him money through his father, letters, books, anything she thought he would like. But everything came back unopened. Even the checks.

She removed her near-empty wallet from her back pocket and flipped it open. From one of the slots she withdrew a photo of Franky hanging upside down from a jungle gym.

"This is my guy," she said. "He's twenty-four. I don't know what I'd do if I lost him."

The Wiltons looked at each other briefly, as if jarred by the unsolicited visual of Struthers's personal life. Gail finally caught her drift. "You understand our urgency, then."

Struthers nodded. "I'll get right to it," she said.

THAT NIGHT STRUTHERS WENT HOME and called her son. Since leaving the Wilton manse she couldn't shake the sting of her imagined grief. What she wouldn't give to hear him talk, or sing, or even tell her off. What if the last time she spoke to him was the last time she'd *ever* speak to him? To the sound of the never-ending ringtone, she was visited by sweet, painful memories of holding him. How hard he'd try to climb up into her lap, and how rarely she would help him, insisting he figure it out on his own. It hadn't taken him long to learn how to scale her knees and slip quietly into her lap, so strong was his need to be held. She'd kiss him and let him stay while she worked. How still he would sit. Now she wished she hadn't made him work so hard for her love.

CHAPTER 25

For two days after the killing, Twyla threw herself into a frenzy of useful activity from the moment she woke until she hit the pillow at night, as if the memories alone would kill her. She raked leaves, poisoned anthills, changed the oil in Mimi's car, organized her receipts from the previous ten years, cleaned out her closets. For anytime she slowed down—to bathe, to eat, to tend to herself in any way—vivid scenes returned. The look on his face before he knew he'd been stabbed, the blood sliding down his neck. And with these scenes a sickening feeling without name, so abhorrent she hurled herself against it, pushing it under, so deeply that it dragged all other feelings down with it.

On the third morning Mimi sent her out to the market with a list and an envelope full of coupons. It would be the first time she left the house since that night.

"I'm short this week, but I'll get paid tomorrow," Mimi said. "Tell Mr. Kaiser to put it on credit. And if he gives you a hard time, you have him call me." Mimi affected a carefree tone, but her eyes were watchful.

"All right." Twyla tucked the list and coupons into her pocket, anxious to leave. Her voice still sounded froggy, and it hurt to speak.

"I gotta get on the horn with Dean," she grumbled. "I swear that man would sooner see me starve to death than give me one cent more than he owes me."

Mimi said something but Twyla was well on her way. She hadn't the strength to pretend.

Twyla drove on high alert. She halted completely at every stop sign, minded the right of way. She let her hair crowd her face, fearing being spotted—by whom? She couldn't think of one person who would be looking for her. But it was the unknown she feared. What had she overlooked?

Still, there was relief in having a mission to complete. She chose the most beautiful produce, inspected every item and made sure she was getting the best price per ounce. On checkout she caught the cashier double-scanning an item and made her correct the mistake. Although Mr. Kaiser did balk at adding to Mimi's growing debt, she persuaded him to spot her one last time.

As she wheeled the cart out of the double doors, she noticed a flyer in full color flapping in the rush of air from outside. She stopped astride the threshold and leaned over the handlebar to get a better look, though she knew from the jump in her gut exactly what it was. The word "MISSING" was printed above a picture of a man in a suit and tie, his hair clipped and combed, much as it was the last time she had seen him.

Shaking, she pulled the leaflet free of its tack, and studied the picture. The last time she'd seen him he'd had his hands around her neck, veins in the shape of a Y on his forehead; and later, in the water, the animal violence of panic, the swinging arm, the lack of recognition in his eyes. Here he looked composed, respectable, his blue-blood features heightened by the crisp white collar. There was a $50,000 reward for his safe return. Someone missed him. His parents, Gail and Chester—how had she remembered their names? They feared for him, were leveled to the same helplessness as anyone, rich, poor, or wealthy. And the worst of it—they didn't know he was dead.

But how could she alone carry the burden of such a gruesome crime? She did not believe herself that powerful. She groped for other sources to carry the weight with her. She blamed Lorelei for using him, his parents for raising him to be entitled, her mother for keeping her small, for teach-ing her to hate her body and fear sex, to suppress her appetite, for shaping her into the type of person a guy like him would take advantage of. She blamed Chet for making a fool of her, then worming his way back into her life. For daring to lay his hands on her, and for pushing her under-water after she had tried to save his life. She seethed, furious now for so many injuries. This rage burned her from the inside. She'd take it any day over guilt.

"Miss?" someone said behind her. "Miss!" She was blocking the doorway. She apologized and took the flyer with her into the parking lot, then, thinking better of it, threw it away.

CHAPTER 26

Something came unhinged after Twyla saw the missing persons flyer. Where Chet had pinched off her breath, her voice, there was now a rupture between her brain and body. Her stomach felt cool and dead. She ate but took no pleasure in it. The thrust of her initial mania petered out until she scarcely had energy to get out of bed. Thoughts turned to sludge. She struggled to express herself and often heard her own voice at a remove, like she was talking in another room. She was cut off at the neck, a floating head.

Mimi switched her days around so Ollie could spend Halloween with her. Twyla could hardly make eye contact with him. She turned on the television to keep him busy, but he then pressed her to help him make his pterodactyl costume. She went through the motions of cutting felt wings and stitching the pieces together, but her mind was a slab of stone.

Friday night Mimi returned from her job at the ad agency to find Ollie agog in front of the television and Twyla staring into the open microwave. She said nothing. Only flicked off the television, picked up her son, and carried him to the bathroom. After she'd bathed him and put him to bed, Mimi confronted Twyla.

She stood there, dead center of the kitchen doorway, like she was giving Twyla a chance to preempt the discussion. She seemed to want to be wrong about whatever was bothering her.

"Twyla, what is *up* your *ass* lately?"

"Sorry?"

"You should be sorry. Why did I come home to find Ollie watching the tube at seven o'clock at night? He should have been bathed and brushed and tucked in for storytime."

Twyla knew she should apologize. Instead she shrugged.

Mimi came into the kitchen, then raised her voice.

"Ollie tells me he watched television all day," she said. "I thought for sure he was exaggerating, but he said, 'No, Mama, I watched it for seven hours,' and then I asked him which shows. Wanna know what he said?" She paused for effect, then counted off on her fingers. "*Good Morning America, The Price is Right, The Young and the Restless, Guiding Light.* Dammit, Twyla, he gave me the entire *TV Guide* lineup, all the way to the evening news."

Twyla tried to contort her face into an understanding shape, one that might conceal how little she cared about this issue right now.

"Yes, ma'am, that's true." Her voice came out dry and cold. "Sometimes I get a bee in my bonnet and get to cleaning. I know he'll be safe while I'm busy if he's watching TV."

"You're his nanny, Twyla. Your job is to take care of him."

Well, that's actually your job, she thought but opted not to say. Mimi both narrowed and widened her eyes in some private realization, as if she could hear Twyla's thoughts, or perhaps was thinking the same thing herself.

"I'll cut down on the shows from now on, I promise."

Mimi looked frustrated, like she was looking for more resistance. She tightened the lock on her crossed arms.

"That's not the point, Twyla. What's even going on with you? Ever since the day you came back from Writer's Night you've been odder than a three-dollar bill. Dressing for winter when it's still warm out, wearing pancake makeup when you never used to wear any. And I'm not one to talk you out of cleaning up, but I can't put a glass down for a second before it's washed and put away. Makes me feel like I'm in a restaurant and not my own house. It's putting me on edge, Twyla. I won't have it."

Twyla nodded to show that she was listening but the sense she was making of it was spotty.

"Well? What *gives*?"

I killed my first love, then left his body to the fishes.

"I'm sorry," she said. "I'll do better." Twyla understood Mimi might not trust Ollie in her care anymore. She wasn't sure if she trusted herself.

"Honey, you're starting to worry me." Mimi approached her and lowered her voice. "You got a desperate look in your eye. I know that look, I've been there, do you get me? Right on the edge of . . . of checking out." She waited for some sign that Twyla was computing.

Twyla didn't reveal anything, but it was taking everything in her power not to do so.

"Right after I lost full custody. There was so much ugliness between me and Dean and I could see it wearing on Ollie. He got quiet and played alone. And that first night without him this house echoed like a goddamn tomb and I felt as good as dead. Like I'd be better off that way. Even convinced myself Ollie would be better off without me, too. I don't cry about that anymore. I put that behind me. I'm a bitter bitch, but I'm not hopeless anymore. Listen, if you're in trouble, you can tell me. I can't do much to help, but I can listen. Sometimes that's all it takes."

Something warm and painful bloomed in Twyla's throat. She wanted to cry. She had come to care deeply about Mimi and Ollie and now realized looking after them was keeping her afloat. If she was caring for someone, maybe she wasn't all bad.

MIMI SPENT THE WEEKEND TAKING Ollie to Halloween things, a pumpkin patch, a fall festival, and mostly steered clear of Twyla. By

Sunday she was missing them both. The ten o'clock news was a litany of updates on reports of crime on the rise and petitions for parents to keep their children indoors. The police chief making forceful statements, families clutched in solidarity. Mimi sat on the couch all wrapped up in a comforter Ollie had used to roof his fort. Twyla unloaded the dishwasher keeping one ear cocked for any news of Chet. She set each cup down gently so as not to draw attention to herself, though Mimi was well aware of her. Every so often she would glance in Twyla's direction and shake her head, bundle herself tighter in her cotton wrapping.

"More news tonight on the local musician and son of banking heavyweight Chester Wilton gone missing . . ." Mimi leaned toward the television. Twyla held her breath. Her guts churned. She couldn't be caught staring at Mimi, her mouth agape, surely looking as guilty as she was. But her feet were glued to the linoleum. Mimi blew out her lips and stood up, still in her bundle.

"I can't take all this maudlin news. I'm gonna go read something trashy and hit the sack."

Twyla closed the dishwasher door and nodded to Mimi in acknowledgment.

"Now where did I put that thing?" she said, searching for the remote control.

"I'll find it—you go on," Twyla said, hoping to catch the end of the segment. Mimi shrugged and went to bed.

Twyla kneeled a few inches from the television and turned the volume down so only she could hear.

". . . just off Clarksville Highway where a vehicle was found in a wooded area last Tuesday and towed by request of the land owner. Thanks to a tip from the impound employee, the vehicle, a 1976 dark green Ford Bronco, was identified as belonging to Chester Wilton. Anyone able to provide information . . ."

She slapped off the television. She had wiped her prints from his car, but what had she missed? Faith would be sucking her teeth and shaking her head right about now. *Serves you right, Twyla Jean. What else did you expect? Lusting and fornicating and carrying on like a homely Jezebel.* All at once Twyla felt the weight of her actions tumble over her like a truckload of dirt. They would find her soon, she could feel it. She couldn't imagine going to prison could be any worse than waiting to get caught. Her time was up.

CHAPTER 27

Twyla slipped out that night and took a taxi to the police station. As she stepped through the main entrance, her heart was leaden but calm.

A drunk doubled over on a bench drooled into the trash can between his legs. Two fratty-looking boys yelled at each other, both bleeding from the nose and eyes nearly bruised shut. A heavyset man in handcuffs was being shoved, stumbling through a turnstile that didn't quite accommodate his size. The young, hollow-cheeked man helming the front desk looked distraught, shouting commands upon deaf ears.

Afraid her nerve would soon expire, Twyla elbowed her way to the front of the line.

"Hey!" she shouted. She tried to get the young man's attention, calling out *sir*, tapping the service bell repeatedly, but all she got was a passing, exasperated glance. They were in triage, and she did not appear pressing enough to acknowledge. She searched for a friendly face, in the broad-chested guard manning the turnstile, or the small and trim officer exiting an administrative office, but everyone was absorbed in the wrangling of one or more people, or answering a phone, or bustling with purpose.

Finally, a man came up to her.

"Here to report a crime?"

Twyla startled. He had light brown skin, and army-short hair, and there was a badge clipped to his belt. Her throat closed up again, squashed, collapsed. Not a word or sound could escape. At her reaction, his expression turned kind.

"I'm Detective Cortez. You don't have to be scared. We can help you."

Still, nothing. Her arms locked at her sides. This was the moment. She could unburden herself of her secrets, her guilt, the horror of her actions, she could do right by Chet's family and start her long road to atonement. If only she could open her mouth, she might say it.

I did it.

The officer gave a sympathetic look. "Would you like to speak to a lady officer?"

She wanted to cry for his misspent kindness. *You've got me all wrong*, she wanted to say. The detective was youthful, handsome. A gold band on his finger. She imagined a home, a family, weekend sports, church on Sundays. The life she could have had if she had stayed put in Fort Worth. The life she thought she never wanted.

SHE LEFT THE STATION IN a hurry, chanting to herself *It's not my time, it's not my time. Please, God, forgive me, it's not my time.* A young man sheathed in a sleeping bag called out to her from a bus stop bench.

"Look out for yourself. There's bad intentions on the streets."

A chill. *Bad intentions.* He went on about a vortex and baby killers and a pox on the federal government and she kept walking past, unable to shake the truth of his reading. Had he sensed the darkness around her? The darkness gathered volume as she put distance between herself and her penance. How close she had been to turning herself in, only to flee. She was a coward. She had only the flimsy excuse of some cosmic wrongness. It was not her time. But when *was* her time? And what would she do with herself until then?

Some ill compulsion—to punish? To wallow?—led her to haunts she had visited with Chet. She peered in the window of Tubb's record store but the blinds were drawn; she stepped inside the phone booth in Printers

Alley and remembered his face, first devilish, then dreamy; she sat on the park bench at the end of Broad, taunted by the mellow rush of the Cumberland before its awful sound drove her away. It was difficult not to solve the equation her mother had laid out for her. Sex before marriage equals death and disgrace. How could she have proven her mother so right? Whether she turned herself in or carried on in a prison of her own guilt, she could not imagine feeling free or happy again.

Even if she had cab money to get back home, the thought of sleeping on the street was preferable to returning to Radnor Lake and bringing this darkness with her. She walked all night and dozed by the warmth of a bakery alley, drifting in and out of dreams, not violent, but disoriented, meaningless, fractured, awaking to the smell of yeast and flour, smells familiar and comforting, of church bake sales and Mother's store-bought frozen rolls brought miraculously to life in the oven. She could not trust the happiness of these memories.

The sun long risen, she finally slept enough to get up and look for something to drink. There was a pretty church with orange mums bursting from their flower boxes and music trailing out from the open door. A thin Black woman in a Sunday hat stood at a table on which sat a coffee urn with some cups and a stackful of programs. The woman smiled politely and filled a Styrofoam cup, then handed it to Twyla.

Twyla thanked her and asked to listen to the music issuing from the open doors.

"Go on in, if you like."

"I'll just stay here if that's okay." The woman nodded and turned her attention to the sidewalk, perhaps for faces she knew or another soul more open than Twyla.

There were nine women and two men in the choir and when they opened their mouths they unleashed a sound as exuberant as a big brass band. The old, sorrowful hymn had been arranged around a lively beat, an inevitable force, in relentless pursuit of joy. They sang in four-part harmonies, choir robes hanging over their plain clothes, swishing in relaxed unison. Love bounced off the vaulted ceiling and the walls and into Twyla's heart. It was impossible not to be affected by these voices, impossible to explain them as anything but divine. When the rehearsal ended the singers grabbed at platters of donuts, drank their bitter coffee, and clumped together to chat after shaking hands with the choirmaster. One ducked quietly into a pew, knelt down, and prayed.

That church music vibrated through her, like a pang, a spasm, all afternoon and into the evening. There was goodness in those voices, or goodness passed through them right into her heart. There was easy joy, but joy that sprang in equal measure from sorrow and from suffering. And she held on to that feeling greedily, playing the trumpeting voices in a loop, yearning for that burst of feeling from church. But each time she replayed it, the sounds in her head lost some of their vigor.

She returned to Mimi's, grasping for one handful of what flowed through that choir, and by the time she laid her head down that night, the feeling was gone. The emptiness she felt when she could no longer summon the charge of those perfect harmonies made her wish she had never heard them at all. She wept in self-pity, grinding her face into the pillow. And then, bitterly, she prayed. She begged God to protect her from harm, to let the laws of nature mete out Chet's justice; she prayed his body to the bottom of the river. She begged for asylum, that her victimhood would protect her from getting caught. That all the good she ever did would tip the scales of worldly justice in her favor. She prayed for her soul to be saved, that she be scrubbed clean of her wickedness. And when she was spent, utterly carved out and dry as a gourd, she rolled over and stared up at the ceiling through the slits of her swollen eyes, and she prayed for a song.

CHAPTER 28

Someone was listening.

Who, she couldn't say. Mother would suggest it was a guardian angel. She hoped it was Daddy. Like a wound debrided, only the raw, living part of her remained, and she felt warmed by the tender presence of another. And with that warming, the music flowed through her.

All her songs had felt holy, but usually they came in sparks, a melody here, a verse there, which she would shield and kindle and fan until they set alight and lived without her intervention. But tonight, the music and lyrics arrived hand in hand, fully formed. As they poured into her, her worries lifted, her mind sharpened. She remembered Mickey's words, that every song is a soul that wants to be born, and she leapt out of bed for a pencil and paper, singing all the while to keep this little soul from wandering off to someone else. She would give this song a home. And in return, the song would set her free.

She found a nub of pencil and went to the living room in search of paper. She fished through the trash can and pulled out a crumpled envelope. After she wrote down the lyrics, she took Pearl into her arms and played, resisting the urge to fiddle, for deep inside she knew this song, like a newborn, was perfect just the way it came.

It was like discovering some priceless antiquity. She wanted to tell someone, urgently, but it was risky. Some treasures were better left buried. When Mimi came home from work, Twyla knew she could not share it with her. It would invite too many questions. But she did wonder about singing it in a bar, some sleepy dive where no one knew her. To a room of strangers it would just be another country song.

Twyla greeted Mimi, then pulled a frozen potpie from the oven, now bubbling hot. She served Mimi a generous portion and took a small amount for herself.

"You precious angel," Mimi said and blew on a steaming forkful.

After she'd had a few bites, Twyla asked to borrow her car.

"I sure as hell don't need it," Mimi said. "I'm beat. But I gotta ask, what you need it for? You haven't stepped out in a while. Are you back on the prowl or something?"

"No," Twyla said, blushing hotly. "But I am feeling a little better. I wrote a song last night."

Mimi grinned. "So that's why you've got that just-got-laid glow."

"Yeah, it's been a while," Twyla said. "I'm thinking about maybe going up. I don't want to go to Irma's, though. Too crowded."

Mimi thought for a minute. "There's El Toro over on Edgehill. Used to be a rowdy honky-tonk, but they do a steak luncheon with a live band for the Music Row crowd, so most of their business happens during the daytime these days. Might be worth checking that out tonight."

Mimi tossed her the keys. Twyla slotted her plate in the dishwasher, grabbed her guitar, and left. She stood on the front step for a moment, briefly unsure of herself, then she heard the lock click behind her and began walking toward the car.

The drive to El Toro was quiet and the streets were mostly empty. Twyla sang, softly, in rehearsal. Then she noticed a pair of headlights in her rearview. There was nothing unusual about them except the vehicle seemed a little close to the Daytona's rear. A little knot formed in her chest. She squinted against the glare. She turned left and lost sight of the car behind her. The knot loosened. She exhaled and reassured herself that she was not being followed.

Then the bright headlights swung back into view.

She stepped on the accelerator, juicing the engine, and pulled far away from the trailing vehicle. The appearance of the car solidified her fears. She *was* being watched. Or investigated. She gripped the steering wheel, afraid to turn back, afraid to stick with the plan. How could she go out into the world, guilty as she was, and not give herself away? She should go back inside and draw all the curtains and forget about taking the stage. But as she gained speed and the headlights faded in the distance, she calmed a bit, enough to realize two cars going the same way did not mean she was being followed. She slowed down, put on her blinker, and took the exit for El Toro. The other car passed by.

She found the bar, pulled into the parking lot, and idled. Even if tonight was an overreaction, maybe it was wiser to wait a few months for the investigation to blow over. She had much to lose if she was discovered and nothing to lose if she waited.

Nothing to lose. She felt the rhythm of the Daytona's engine, looked over and saw it vibrate the strings of Mickey's guitar. Win or lose, she could not contain the music inside. All those songs. The ones she'd written and yet to write. And this one in particular, there was thrust behind this song. Now that she'd written it, it pressed at her. Pestered. Yearned to be sung. Threatened to harrow her if she did not let it out. The thought of *not* singing it, owning it, delivering it to even one other person caused her neck to feel like it was being cinched shut.

Twyla tucked her chin and flipped up the fleece collar of her borrowed jean jacket and approached El Toro. The parking lot was empty save a dually pickup and a late-model Pontiac sedan with a boot on one wheel. The bar was a stucco box dressed up with terra-cotta shingles, fake windows painted in trompe l'oeil and an arched, intricately carved door. Next to the door stood a felt marquee announcing an Orbison Tribute Medley.

A top-heavy man with a jet pompadour and dark glasses sat on a stool beside the door, whittling. She walked up to the entrance, expecting him to notice her, but he was absorbed in his task. As she got closer, she could see he was carving an anatomically precise statuette of a nude man. When she was two feet away, he gasped and dropped his knife and carving.

"¡Ay! Pinche diabla!"

She apologized, reflexively, in twangy Texas Spanish.

"My English is fine," he said with a sort of hurt pride for having been startled and left his stool to recover his things. "It's a dollar to get in."

"Oh," she said, caught off guard. She fished in her hobo purse and came up with a handful of change.

He looked at her through a suspicious squint.

"Are y'all letting anyone go up and play tonight?" She dropped the coins in his hand. The man was silent.

"No?" she said as he counted and pocketed the money.

Her courage began to wane. Perhaps it was a sign to stay home. The headlights, now this. There must be another way to get this song off her chest.

"Maybe another time," she said. She waited for him to return the coins but he went back to his statuette and began carving an ear with the tip of his knife. Now she would either have to ask for her money back, or leave it there, which she wasn't going to do. Then she looked at the felt marquee by the door, and the man's pompadour, and put two and two together.

"Really, I came to hear some Roy Orbison," she said. "I'd listen to his covers all night."

The hard line of his mouth relaxed.

"It's not *covers*," he corrected. "It's a tribute." He rubbed his sideburns, receiving her flattery. "But I was only planning on a short set," he said modestly. "I don't like to stress my voice. Maybe when I'm done I let you up for a song."

He opened the door for her.

"My name is Carlos, by the way," he said. "This is my place."

"Nice to meet you," she said and followed him inside. She did not offer her name in return.

Now, having gained entry, her anxieties refreshed. *If it doesn't feel right, just walk away.*

She ducked between heavy curtains into a near-empty room with a half-moon stage dead center and western-looking wooden tables and chairs. A long bar on the left with a margarita machine churning neon slush. A drunk snoozed on folded arms down the bar from which a reedy pair of men in Wranglers and cowboy hats shared a bucket of beers. On the right a modern jukebox played a familiar ranchera song. She loved the sincerity and passion of the vocals, the crisp trumpets and soaring violins above rapidly strumming guitars, and the complex old-world sound of the accordion. His anguish, and hers, swelled with the singer's voice.

Then she noticed two old cowboys at the bar sitting intimately close to each other, face-to-face, knees interlocked. The one with a mustache slid his hand along the bar and borrowed the other's drink, tasted it, and puckered his lips like it was too sour or too sweet. He said something and the other laughed, and the look on his face—chiding, knowing, alert to his lover's flawed perfection—bore the mark of a long-shared past. These cowboys were not only lovers, they were mates. Bound together just as her parents had once been, loyal, a bit tired, relaxed in the lack of mystery between them. She'd seen it on Mother's face when Daddy broke out his dusty fiddle and her mother's feet would start to jig without her permission, it seemed, and she'd cast him a look like *You bad thing,* and then throw up her hands, like *Oh, what's the harm in one little dance?* Twyla ached now for this closeness. She had felt it with her mother before she found the church, with Mickey before he left and died. She had dreamed of growing into it with Chet. Then she saw him, black-eyed and deadly. Three jabs and the mask of rage slipped and suddenly she was the monster.

She sat at a table near the stage and touched her throat, willing it to open. She couldn't leave now, in fact. The song and the moment had chosen her, and if she refused it, it would haunt her. *He* would haunt her.

Carlos punched a song in the jukebox and took his place in the spotlight. "You Got It" played over the speakers and he sang along. His voice held up in his vocal sweet spot, a very tight octave in the tenor range, but as soon as the song drove in the upper register he cracked, and instead of switching to falsetto, he just pushed through, straining and breaking until the end of the note. The cowboys left between his first and second numbers. Seeing him belt out these songs so crudely, so sincerely, she felt more forgiving about performing her own.

Halfway through his second song he got a tickle in his throat. His eyes watered and he hacked and waved her onstage to take over. She pointed to herself, stupidly, as if there were anyone else around he could be addressing. She scanned the room again. Still nearly empty. The bartender gone, on break? The drunk still unconscious on a pillow of his arms. She climbed up, took a seat, and adjusted the mic. She removed her guitar from the case and warmed up her strings with a few gentle strokes of her thumb. She was as ready as she'd ever be.

Just as she started the opening chords, the door swung open and a tall, slim figure came in, blurred by the glare of the can light. His footsteps struck loud against the old wood floor, shaking her concentration. When she opened her mouth to sing the opening verse, her throat closed up. She flushed, sweat forming at her hairline and under her arms. She swallowed hard and tried to start again, but the words vanished. She drew her guitar nearer and closed her eyes to block out the room. Then she remembered the lyrics written on the envelope in her pocket. With a long glance at what she'd written, the song returned. She set the envelope on the floor, ready now. She coughed, her voice cleared, and then she sang.

I grew up in the church, singing in the choir,
"Praise your Father's name, and blessings He will bring."
But Mama showed her love by telling me I'm nothin'.
"She may be ugly, but at least the girl can sing."

Then I met a man, thought he was an angel,
He told me I was pretty, so I gave him everything.
He must've told his girlfriend something even sweeter,
'Cause when I saw her kiss him on her finger was a ring.

I should have faced the music,
But I just ran and hid,
The devil made me do it,
The devil made me do it.

I never meant to hurt him, just to write a love song,
He reached around my neck before he fell into the sea,
Even if I'd saved him, what's the point pretending,
A guy like that could love an ugly girl like me.

I should have faced the music,
But I just ran and hid,
The devil made me do it,
The devil made me do it.

The body of her guitar resonated, trilled with the sound, transferring the vibrations to the spaces inside her, filling the emptiness at her center with its music. The song welled up between them, Twyla and her guitar, and then spilled out across the floor, flooding the room. She imagined being surrounded by people, a listening jury. She wanted someone to know what she had done, but also what had been done to her. She was guilty. She was innocent. She was contrite. She was impenitent. For this one moment, her song released, she was free.

She threw her whole heart, her whole body into the final verse. Though no one in this room could know what the song was about, or why she'd written it, the weight of her lyrics heightened every sound, every vibration in her strings.

As the water swallowed up the only one who'd loved me,
I fell upon my knees and prayed He'd understand.
And I opened up my mouth, and belted out that love song,
And then I wrote it down on the backside of my hand.

I should have faced the music,
But I just ran and hid,
The devil made me do it,
The devil made me do it.

When her wet eyes opened a full minute after she'd stopped singing, the bar was empty; even the slumbering cowboy was gone. There was no clapping or acknowledgment of what she'd released into the world—the only sounds were the grinding of the margarita machine. Then she heard muffled laughter from Carlos outside the front door. Her song had fallen on an empty room. There was relief, but also disappointment. She laid her guitar back in its case and secured the buckles, then stepped off the stage and headed for the door. The floor was tacky under her shoes and the grungy smell of beer and lime and smoke hung heavy in her nose.

She stepped into the fresh evening air.

"No encore?" Carlos said and winked to the short, younger man he was speaking to.

"Maybe another time," she said, heading to the car. She was not keen to sit and talk.

"¡Oye, gordita!" he shouted. She turned around. "Sounded pretty good from out here," he said. "You should come back and play again at lunch when there's a crowd. Maybe I throw in a steak dinner."

A complicated smile curled her lips. Someone *had* heard her.

CHAPTER 29

Whatever chance remained of Twyla singing again at El Toro vanished as she watched the grainy crime scene footage on the next evening's news. She had just loaded the electric popcorn maker and turned on the machine. Mimi, seated on the floor with Ollie between her legs, turned up the volume just as the kernels began to detonate.

"The body of a young man was retrieved from the shores of the Cumberland this afternoon. Thought to be the son of a Nashville banking heir, Chester Wilton was reported missing just five days ago." A stretcher on wheels, a human form barely suggested under its vinyl shroud. Men in blue milling about with walkie-talkies, clipboards, plastic baggies, and a long-haired man with a camera, squatting, framing his shot.

Twyla's breath locked into her chest. They'd found him.

The video cut back to a suntanned woman with frosted lips and a picture of short-haired Chet on the screen. *"Police on the scene are withholding comment until the body is formally identified and a preliminary autopsy report is complete."*

Twyla held on to the counter, scanning Mimi for signs of recognition. Had Mimi ever met Chet, caught a glimpse of him through the window? If so, could she identify him from this photo? Or the name? The newscaster called him Chester, a name she'd never used.

"That's a shame," Mimi said, twirling a lock of Ollie's hair around her finger. "What a looker he was."

Twyla exhaled when Mimi did not make the connection. The popcorn had filled the machine and was now tumbling out of the clear yellow chute and onto the counter. She shoved a wide salad bowl beneath it to catch the popcorn. Ollie had gotten up and was now stuffing the fallen pieces into his mouth.

"Needs butter," he said through his cud.

"Body turns up in the Cumberland," Mimi said, "usually it's a suicide."

Twyla couldn't find the words to respond. Tears pricked at her eyes. Another layer of reality was setting in. Now people were speculating about what killed him. Saying things about him. There would be theories. She felt an odd protectiveness over Chet. She couldn't imagine he'd kill himself, but then she didn't even know him well enough to be sure he wouldn't have tried.

"But a young man like that?" Mimi said after thinking for a bit. "Handsome, rich, what's he got to kill himself for?" The speed at which she came to this conclusion made Twyla realize, selfishly, that ruling his death a suicide would solve the problem of an investigation. She'd have to live with her guilt, sure, but on her own terms.

"His poor parents," Mimi said and stretched her legs. She got up and draped herself over the counter to reach the bowl. "All the money in the world don't mean boo if your baby is dead." Ollie looked up from his clawful of popcorn, chewing.

"Babies can't die," he said plainly. "They're too young."

Twyla couldn't think about Chet's parents right now. She couldn't think of him as someone's baby. He was a grown man, and he had tried to kill her first.

CHAPTER 30

Struthers wouldn't wish the loss of a child on anyone, not even the Wiltons. When she heard the news of Chet Wilton's death, delivered by way of the family accountant, she experienced a genuine pang of compassion followed by a sliver of satisfaction that even they could not escape the humiliation of suffering. It wasn't schadenfreude, it was more like kinship in the democracy of death. She stretched a brown turtleneck over her head, gargled with mouthwash, and made haste to Belle Meade. The Wiltons joined her in the living room and received her condolences with the well-trained expressions of the aggrieved and repressed. Gail's hand was as cold and inert as a long-dead corpse, and she appeared to have crumpled in on herself, her height seemingly inches shorter than when last they had met, just one week prior. Chester II was a straw man, held up by the stuffing of his pedigree.

"Well, good a time as any for a gimlet," said Mr. Wilton abruptly. He popped out of his club chair to pour a drink.

"Another?" Gail said, then swallowed her lips inward, as if the reproach had slipped, a habit of marriage she realized too late did not apply to a time like this. On his way across the campus of their living room, which had not one but five discrete conversation areas and two fireplaces, he tripped on a wrinkle in the runner and lurched forward, losing his grip on the tumbler in his hand and bracing himself on the

sofa in front of him. In the deliberate way he unfolded himself from
this position, she guessed he was drunk or humiliated, or both. Turning
away from the women, his back convulsed once, twice. He was sobbing.
Then he straightened and continued toward the bar to mix them all a
drink.

"Right," said Mr. Wilton, his long, thoroughbred face scrubbed of his
earlier emotion. "Down to business. We want to keep you on to supple-
ment the police investigation. They're underfunded and, pardon my saying so, but their chief is a hillbilly. You have our full support. Whatever
you need to find out what happened to our son."

Mrs. Wilton looked up bitterly at her husband.

"We know what happened to him," she said. "We need you to
prove it."

Struthers slipped her notepad out of her back pocket and felt for her
pen, but remembered seeing it on the floor of her car. Before she could ask
to borrow one, Mr. Wilton handed her a glossy, gold-trimmed black pen
that must have weighed a pound.

"The cap *twists* off," he said impatiently when Struthers was unable
to remove it.

She let out an "Ahh," unscrewed the cap, and poised the fountain pen
over the notepad.

"You were saying you think you have a suspect in mind?"

"We have a theory," Mr. Wilton said. His wife shot another searing
look at him and turned her attention back to Struthers.

"It's not a theory," she said. "We know who did it."

Struthers held her pose, pen aloft, expectant.

"It was that grifter, Lorelei Ray." Gail threw down her conclusion
like a gavel.

"His ex-girlfriend—*fiancée*, in fact," said Mr. Wilton distastefully.
Mrs. Wilton shook her head at the word.

"Why do you say 'grifter'?" asked Struthers.

"Because that's exactly what she was," said Mrs. Wilton. "From the very start she had Chet pegged for a fool. And she had this *striving* quality about her. Chet brought her to a party here one time and she spent the whole evening ignoring him and passing out her 'demo' record. I asked Chet to take her home, thinking she was intoxicated, but she wasn't. That was just her way. Driven, self-promoting. It was unsettling."

"So she was a musician, then?"

"If you can call it that; she didn't have much talent. It was obvious to me she was after his trust fund since the minute they met."

Struthers noted a possible motive here. "I see, and does he currently have access to his trust fund? Er, *did* he before his passing?"

"Well, he was supposed to when he turned twenty-five last year, but we had attached a condition to the release."

"And what was that?"

"That he be gainfully employed."

"And he was not?"

"Well, not until right before he disappeared. We offered support, of course, because he didn't make enough to live on. It was a lark. It was never going to last."

"You said not until right before his disappearance . . . What changed?"

"It was wonderful, really. He came to us and said he was ready to take a job at the bank, working for his father. It's what we'd raised him to do. We were so relieved, we didn't question it. He started right away and cleaned himself up, stopped with the late nights and the marijuana. It was"—she dabbed at the corner of her eye to absorb a leaking tear—"it was like he came back to us. Like he was one of us again."

"So you released the trust fund to him."

"Yes."

"How long before his death?"

"About two weeks, maybe less."

"And did he withdraw money from the trust?"

"Yes."

"How much did he take?"

Both the Wiltons looked at Struthers as if she'd asked them to pull down their pants.

Mr. Wilton cleared his throat. "If this is pertinent to the case, I will have my accountant share the numbers with you."

"It is very pertinent to the case," she said. They remained silent, apparently sticking to their guns about the accountant bit. "Well, then, can you just tell me if he had enough to inspire someone to kill him?"

"Not enough for someone from *our* world," he said. "But someone from hers?"

As Struthers looked around the room, which was twice the size of her bungalow, she concluded that her question had been stupid, and of course there was enough money to inspire treachery; even if it had been chump change to this family, it could have meant the world to someone like her. She thought of the growing stack of unpaid bills, the daily calls from her landlord, the power she could only keep on three weeks out of every month, the gas she had to squirt in her car a few bucks at a time until she was coasting on fumes.

"And do you know where she lives, this Lorelei Ray?"

"No," Mrs. Wilton said. "I hate to imagine it. Last I heard she was living on top of a porn shop. Or a pawn shop, one of the two."

"We'd give you the key to Chet's house, but the police department has it," added her husband. "I had hoped to have it back by now, Detective Struthers." His face burned red all of a sudden. "They brushed us aside," he said. "When we reported him missing. Gail knew something was terribly wrong."

Struthers took minor joy in the squad's shortcomings, but declined the opportunity to exploit the moment, much as she might have liked.

"They've got their hands full down in homicide, but I'm sure they're doing their best. I used to work there myself."

"Yes, that's why we called you."

"Good on you taking things into your own hands," Struthers said, clapping Mr. Wilton on the upper arm. Then she delivered the line people like this ate up with a silver spoon.

"The boys in blue work for the taxpayers," she said, "but I only work for you."

Struthers smiled at the thought of solving the case before the Metro police. That they might, as a result, hire her back was a fantasy she would not entertain. Not just yet.

CHAPTER 31

Struthers would have preferred not to start from scratch on the investigation. Had she any of the resources or access to the case files, she would have a couple of days' head start. But then again, with the Metro Police Department's C team at work, she probably couldn't trust much of what they'd gathered. Sloppy as a bunch of two-year-olds eating soup. In her time there she had witnessed investigators contaminating evidence in ways she couldn't have dreamed up. Taking coffee shits in the crime scene toilets, eating tuna salad on the crime scene counter. One fella had brought his date to the scene of a strangling, hoping to impress her. It had worked so well they had sex on the victim's goddamn bed, mixing their fluids with those of the killer.

Although no one would accuse Struthers of keeping a neat home, she had created for herself in the rented bungalow a haven from her fevered existence in the outside world. She had painted the walls by hand and bricked them over in books. Everything was old and steady and beautiful. She nuked a couple of wieners and poured herself a cup of jet fuel with sweetened condensed milk, then brought her provisions to the kitchen counter. She spread out the new map she had purchased for this case directly under the hanging sconce and sharpened her favorite pencil. First, she circled what landmarks she could glean from the television reportage including where the body had been found and the rough location of his vehicle, somewhere near the northern bend in the river. She'd tried to shake down the coroner for a TOD to no avail, but then received a call from the Wiltons. The coroner had informed them his time of death was sometime after the family dinner on the night of October 24 or early on the twenty-fifth. Roughly seven days after his death, the corpse was recovered washed up on the east bank, about three miles northwest of downtown and one mile from the wooded grove where his vehicle was found. According to his parents, he had no business far from town. He worked in the Financial District between Third and Fourth, which was a stone's throw from the river. Perhaps he had met a colleague after family dinner, had a few too many drinks, a fight had ensued, and he fell or was thrown in. Or killed nearby and dumped. He was a big man, too heavy for anyone but another large man or two to carry. If the crime had taken place on a bridge, he would have been easier to dispose of.

The location of the car was curious. From what she could see from the chopper news footage, it had been lodged in a wooded area well off the riverbank, and there were no nearby businesses within frame. Perhaps he'd had a shady meeting gone wrong. Killed near the car, dumped in the river. Or perhaps he was killed elsewhere and the culprit relocated the car and hid it from view. If this was the case, the crime scene could be anywhere but most likely near the water. She'd begin her search with the most likely locations downtown and would work her way outward.

She circled a few scattered businesses with access to the river where he might have been seen or recognized, then called to verify their opening hours on the night he disappeared. The bait-and-tackle shop, boat dealership, and pleasure boat rental did not bear fruit as they were all closed by six p.m. The ones that were open in the later hours after his family dinner were mainly bars and restaurants, plus one pharmacy and a movie theater. Half of working a case was a process of elimination, and she got a kick out of crossing names off a list. The jet fuel slipped into her bloodstream. This was the shit she lived for. Knocking on doors, conducting interviews, funneling and sifting the granules of information until all she had left were the facts that mattered.

SHE HIT THE PAVEMENT, INTERVIEWED friends, acquaintances, employers, anyone who might have had contact with him in his final days and hours. The first round of interviews, it seemed, yielded only eliminations. His immediate superior, a besuited, dry-mouthed man, indicated that Chet had fulfilled his duties as a new hire, which consisted mainly of shadowing, taking notes, and reading up on several semesters' worth of finance books that most of their hires had read in college. He did no more or less than what was required of him.

The Chet Wilton Band members had not seen him since he went square. She sensed neither animosity nor grief from the trio, more like a rattled sobriety, as if slapped by the knowledge that death could come for them, too. They were older than she had expected, the youngest in his forties. When she asked whether one of them might take over as lead singer, her jealousy theory took a nosedive. They had already started auditioning for other lead performers. They were career backups. Not a shred of ambition in the lot.

As a precaution, she showed Chet's picture from the missing person flyer to the business owners on her "probably not" list. Most had seen him on the news but never before that. The marina owner, a man of retirement age, barely glanced at the flyer. Around the time of the murder he was out of town, had closed up shop that morning and wouldn't have had any customers until he opened again the Thursday following Chet's death.

She stopped by one of Chet's bar hangouts and interviewed the owner, a grandmotherly type with dated cat-eye glasses and a strong set of shoulders. The old woman cleaned the bar litter from her wooden floor with more vigor and efficiency than a brand-new Hoover.

When she saw Struthers, she brushed a strand of hair from her face and leaned on her broom.

"We don't open for another hour, but you can have a seat if you like."

"T. Lynn Struthers," she said, "here to ask a few questions about a case I'm working."

"Irma," the woman said.

"Miss Irma, have you ever seen this man around here?" Struthers held out the flyer, which, she noticed too late, was already posted on the bulletin board.

"Oh, sure, Chet used to come by pretty regular. Not usually on Writer's Night, though." She grimaced in an attempt to adjust her top dentures.

"Oh, no? Why's that?"

"It's none of my business," she said and resumed sweeping.

Struthers could tell from her tone that this was only the beginning of her sentence, that a woman like this made everything her business.

"But," the owner continued, "he didn't write his own stuff, far as I know. Seemed to me he was in it for the girls and the glory. Those young songwriters, some of 'em have a long way to go, but ever' one of 'em is putting their heart out there. Takes a lot of nerve to get up in front of people and work out a song you wrote. Might make a guy like him a little green-eyed."

"A guy like him," Struthers said, pressing. "A guy like him didn't like to see others doing well?"

"Let's say he was used to things coming easy to 'eem." She got back to her sweeping, the strap of her apron slouching off her shoulder. Then she stopped and leaned on her broom again without facing Struthers.

"We were short-staffed that night with my waitress out with the flu. But come to think of it, there was a fella with a slick haircut that made me double take. I was taking orders faster'n I could fill 'em, so it was just a little thought. Didn't occur to me till now. But that fella looked a lot like Chet Wilton."

"What time was that?"

"Golly, I don't know . . . early, I think. A little after eight o'clock? Hard to say, like I toldja, I was busy."

"And was he with anyone?"

"Not that I saw, but—"

"Busy night," Struthers said.

Irma sighed and turned her back to signal she was done talking, and Struthers took the hint.

"Here's my number. Holler if you think of anything else."

Struthers stuck around, thinking maybe she could find someone to corroborate Irma's account. If he was really here, she might get more eye witnesses to his final hours. Find out about how he seemed that night, whether he was with anyone. A handsome guy like that, somebody might have remembered. But it was a slow night and though she found a couple of leads, one who had seen him in concert and another who remembered him from Tubb's, no one had seen him on the night of the murder. She got a list of everyone Irma remembered being there that night and left.

She ended the night combing the streets of downtown. She crossed over the Sparkman Street Bridge and peered into the green-black current below. Did it happen on a bridge? Would someone see it at that time of night? Did he jump? What would it take for a guy like that to snuff himself out? She thought of his parents, the suffocation, the expectations, the Samsonian gesture of cutting his hair, his potency for a payout. If only she could get a cause of death from the department.

The Cumberland whorled and coursed beneath her. After two solid days of legwork, she had found plenty of dead ends but not many leads. She was hungry for the vigor and friction of working with a team. Crooked and bungling as they were, she loved those guys. Worley and Mankin, Smith and Cortez. She even missed the razzing—about her size, her haircut, her two-dollar words. She lifted her glasses and cleared the tears from her cheeks. Was she crying now?

"Goddamn it, Struthers," she muttered, "get a grip on yourself." The hormones had her moodier than a teenager on the rag. She had been looking forward to the Pause. The freedom! Freedom from blood, freedom from beauty, from being of childbearing age, that dreary mantle she had carried so long. But so far this great transition had made her feel un-stable, muddy-minded, bloated, and ironically caused her to bleed more days than not. "I'll never wear Easter whites again," she'd lamented after a gusher had made a murder scene of her favorite ivory slacks.

Staring into the churning river, she had the irrational wish for Cortez to pick up the phone and apologize. They weren't only partners, after all. They were friends. They had bonded over their criticism of the department. Her own trajectory had been similarly uphill, more like the sheer face of a cliff, and she'd always been one mistake away from falling right back to where she started. Struthers began her career at the police force as a secretary, as any woman did. It was the best place to learn about the job she actually wanted. She started combing the case files after hours and casually working her theories into conversation with her boss, making subtle suggestions about leads he could follow up and why. Then she put herself through police academy courses on evenings and weekends, by which point she knew the trade better than any rookie. Still, it took her twice as long to get hired as any of her male peers. The cops treated her like set dressing, and they'd say the damnedest things in front of her, revealing how a police station actually ran. Mostly she'd learned what not to do, how the detectives she worked for would form a theory first and then let that shape how they pursued the case. It was like they couldn't hold all the moving parts in their heads at once. It was a common, unspoken practice to sacrifice the real culprit for the one they could convict. And it made her ill to think of the fools they'd put away who may have been guilty of something, but certainly not murder. Some might have been disillusioned, but for Struthers it was an awakening. Despite the power they wielded, most of these knuckleheads weren't all that smart. And all she had to be was smarter than them.

She picked up a stone the size of a potato and weighed it in her hand. Then she took a step away from the railing, wound up, and chucked it as far as she could. She watched it arc and fall and vanish in the river. It didn't even make a sound.

"I'll find you," she said. "Don't think I won't. This old bag ain't got shit else to do."

CHAPTER 32

For the first time since she got the boot Struthers cruised into the station like it was just another day on the job. Chip at security tipped his hat, Janine at the front desk lifted a sympathetic hand in greeting. Sergeant Morton, an old drinking buddy from the police academy, stepped into his office and closed the door.

When she reached her former office in homicide, she stood in front of the glass door that used to bear her name and now was painted with that of her replacement and former partner, Detective Paul Cortez. If his promotion hadn't been at her expense, she'd be proud of him. Despite his stellar marks at West Point and perfect service record, the good ole boys' brigade of the upper ranks had needed some arm-twisting to give a shot to their brown-skinned colleague. She'd gone to bat for him, helped him rise up the ranks. But as she predicted, he had proven himself within his first six months as her partner, and together they started slamming cases shut quicker than killers could deliver the bodies. With her grit and flair for creative thinking, and his practicality and procedural know-how, they were unstoppable.

She'd never taken him for a rat. With Struthers gone, Cortez had been promoted to lead detective. On the surface it sure looked like he had ousted her to advance his own position, but when she was honest with herself she believed he had been doing what he thought was right. She was the last to admit her private life was a wreck. She had blamed it on menopause, but even she knew the excuse was horseshit. The problem was the more she neglected her problems, the more she thrived at work. Weeks before she framed the wife beater, Cortez had referred her to HR, who'd referred her to a shrink. He knew the business with Franky was killing her from the inside. But she'd taken Cortez's concern with her emotional well-being as an affront. They didn't say such things about men. Men, she'd noticed, could self-destruct in peace.

Today, she crossed the hall to the lounge, which was merely a converted storage closet containing a microwave oven and a musty coffee-maker shoved on top of a mini fridge. She poured herself a scalding cup, into which she dumped milk powder and four sugars and stirred it with a pencil she found on the counter. When she turned around, her old partner was standing there.

Cortez eyed her up and down, giving her a visual inspection before greeting her. He was on the boyish side of thirty-five, with smart black eyes and a tidy mustache dressing his upper lip.

"Struthers," he said, guarded as a truck full of money. "You come here in peace or do I need to pat you down?"

Struthers made a V with two fingers to show she meant no harm.

"Nice to see you, Benedict Arnold." She gestured at the office behind him. "You gonna invite me in, give me a tour?"

Cortez shifted in front of the door, as if blocking it.

"Hallway chat. Got it. Listen, no hard feelings on my end," she said, not quite truthfully. Cortez bit his lip, holding back. She could see he wasn't ready to talk. "I saw the news about the Wilton kid. That your case?"

"You know it is," said Cortez. "What's it to you?"

"To me?" She considered her next play here. If he knew she was getting paid to work the case for the Wiltons, he'd make sure she was blocked out of the investigation. If she offered to help out, pro bono, he wouldn't buy that either. He knew her too well to believe she had a charitable heart. First, the bait.

"I thought you could use some help," she said, knowing the phrasing would trigger suspicion. "It's your first big case since I left and I don't think I could bear to see you blow it."

Cortez crossed his arms and puffed up his chest a little, hardened his mouth.

"Look, no offense, I'm sure you have it under control, but I know Captain Russo has your men spread thin." She paused to gauge his reaction. A flicker of the jaw muscle, a quickening pulse so visible on his athletic throat. "Don't tell me you couldn't use a pinch of the Struthers magic. Just a little dash?"

He didn't change position. But she could see in the slight movement of his eyes that he was thinking it over, perhaps imagining what motives she was concealing, and what he would have to lose—or gain—by getting mixed up with her. She let her outstretched arm fall slack against her thighs and exhaled.

"Listen," she said and looked around, lowered her voice. "Cortez. Amigo. Here's the deal. I'm struggling out there," she said.

Cortez loosened the weave of his arms and shifted his weight to one leg. He was listening.

"I miss homicide." She let the statement sit with him. As tough a front as he was putting on, she knew he felt guilty for taking her down. "I'm doing workman's comp P.I. work for two shits less than nothing, do you understand? I'm sober as a priest and I'm about to lose my mind on these stakeouts. I've never been so bored in my *god*damn life."

Cortez cracked a reluctant hint of a smile.

"C'mon, think about it, will ya?" she said. He forced the smile away.

"I'm not asking for pay—yet—I just want back in the game. It'll be off the books. Consider me an anonymous source. I'll do my thing, you feed me what you're turning up on your end, and I'll make you wish you had come to me sooner. If you say no to that, well . . ." She trailed off, not wanting to insult him before she'd closed the deal. He held his ground.

"*Workman's comp*, man!" she shouted. His poker face was as hard as ever, but he had a tell.

He was still here.

"Just think about it, okay? You know where to reach me." She downed her coffee in a long gulp and screwed up her face like she had swallowed whisky. She crushed the Styrofoam cup and tossed it behind her. The seed was planted, but whether it would take root was beyond her ken. Goddamn cipher, that one. It was just like Cortez to have a whole conversation with her without saying a word.

CHAPTER 33

Since seeing Chet's bagged body on the news, Twyla had done everything she could to avoid leaving the house, feigning fatigue, illness, and her old standby, cramps. When the pantry was properly barren she called the grocer and spent a chunk of her wages paying the bag boy to deliver.

She could picture him there on the slab, his expression flat, features melted, perhaps some bloat, a purple tint. A model in clay. What story would his body tell? He had drowned, she was sure of it. They would see that in the autopsy. They'd find the holes, too, though, from the jab of her pen. What would they make of these marks?

When Mimi finally said she couldn't pay her anymore unless she snapped out of her funk, Twyla rallied enough to complete the minimum of her responsibilities.

She went out to do an errand for Mimi and was stopped in traffic when she heard a familiar song from the car in the lane next to her. Despite the cutting chill outside, she rolled down the window.

I should have faced the music,
But I just ran and hid.

Her heart seemed to stop, her chest locked, every muscle tightened as she strained to hear the rest of the song. Then the chorus hit, right as the traffic picked up and the driver pulled ahead of her. *"The devil made me . . ."* There were a few differences in the melody, but she knew. The song was *hers.*

Her hands trembled as she twirled the radio dial, searching, searching for her song.

She found the right station just as the song faded out.

"—*do it, the devil made me do it . . .*"

"Who sang it? Who?" she shouted at the radio. The DJ had just started to answer when she turned up the volume dial and the signal went dead. She had mistakenly changed the station. By the time she found it again a new song was playing. She whacked the seat next to her in frustration.

Who had stolen her song? It didn't make sense. Could Carlos at El Toro have heard it and sold it to this woman? He hadn't seemed interested enough in her to take down the lyrics as she sang. And if he had, why invite her to come again? No, Carlos didn't make sense. When she had opened her eyes after the song, there was no one in the room. And the timing—how long had it been, two weeks? Not even that. How could someone steal her song, record it, and get it on the radio in so little time?

And yet. *The devil made me do it, the devil made me do it.* Those words she'd written, trailing out of the speaker like they belonged there. It was so bizarre she started to question whether the song was hers or if she had heard it on the radio first and in some crazed fugue state conjured a memory of having written it herself. Or had she heard it on the radio at all? Had that moment been a hallucination, a haunting?

LATER THAT WEEK MIMI FINALLY landed a job working on an album, not just a one-day gig spiffing up a single, but a solid twelve tracks from an artist Twyla hadn't heard of but was apparently known around town. Perhaps as an act of charity, Mimi took her to work as a gopher girl on the days Ollie was with Dean. Twyla knew this was a professional gift, and if she kept her head on straight she might learn something useful. The artist, Laurie Kane, was young, pretty in an angular way. She entered the room in corduroy overalls and a university sweatshirt, her face and hair untouched, yet lovely. She drew looks from the male producer and the session players but seemed oblivious or bored of their attention.

During a break, Mimi went out to stretch her legs and the producer turned on the radio, betting everyone in the room they wouldn't go three songs without playing one of Laurie's. Laurie stretched luxuriously on the tweed couch and smoked a cigarette, ashing into an empty peanut tin that rested on her abdomen, again indifferent to the fuss being made over her. Four songs went by as Twyla ate her cheese sandwich in the corner, and then the last strains of "Unchained Melody" morphed into the opening chords of "The Devil Made Me Do It." She looked around, as if for a witness that this moment was really happening.

Her song, sliding up against the same airwaves as the King.

The soft-spoken radio jockey chimed in to recap the lineup and introduce the debut single by singer-songwriter Lorelei Ray.

Twyla forced a sticky wad of sandwich down her throat.

Lorelei Ray. She knew that name. She'd heard it at Irma's, preceded by "the future *Mrs.* Chet Wilton"; then, weeks later, uttered by Chet moments before she stabbed him. She went suddenly cold.

Then Laurie sat up and waved at the producer. "Turn it up, Ron!"

"Have you heard this one?" Laurie said. She flopped back down and took another drag. "It gives me the chills."

Mimi came in then, cheeks pink and nipped by the wind.

"What are y'all talking about?" she said. Then, before anyone could answer, said, "Who is this again? I *love* this damn song."

Twyla listened to them rave about her song. They called it eerie, gritty, heartbreaking. Laurie talked about doing a cover. Mimi criticized the mix, of course.

"If I could just get my hands on that track. It's a mess. The vocals are tinny and the drums are muffled. But that song." She shook her head. "It's got me by the throat and won't let go."

Twyla shrank into the corner, overwhelmed by a feeling of illicitness, like she'd walked in on them admiring a nude photo they didn't know was hers. The first time she had heard her lyrics drifting out the window of a passing car, she'd only felt shock, her mind scrambling around trying to understand how her music was coming out of the radio. But to overhear a room full of people—people she admired—praise the words she wrote left her desperate for more.

Then a voice splashed ice water on her excitement. *Wicked girl. Sinner, you. Taking pride in your own evil.* This wasn't good fortune, it told her, this was punishment. How else could she explain the coincidence? Lorelei had heard the song and recorded it as her own, knowing Twyla could not claim it. *That's what you get, Twyla Jean.* She could see all the eyes of the congregation upon her, feel their scorn and judgment, and Pastor Horton, prowling across the dais, his own eyes filled with menace, looking like the devil himself.

CHAPTER 34

With little to show for her first round of interviews and crickets from Cortez, Struthers had entered a familiar phase of the investigation, what she liked to call fermentation. It felt like nothing was happening. The case seemed stalled. Rotten. But past experience told her magic was at work. She just had to keep feeding the starter. This trust in the process was difficult to communicate to the Wiltons, who had been calling daily for updates. Her optimism may have been slightly overblown, but people like that were so accustomed to paying for progress, she didn't want them to get too antsy and take their business elsewhere.

She forged ahead, gathering information on the victim. She looked into his records at Vanderbilt and discovered he was a popular, if academically disappointing, student and, apart from being the beneficiary of nepotism (a research library bearing the Wilton name broke ground the year before he matriculated), did not seem to be guilty of any behavior that would earn him a lethal enemy. The only problem with her findings was that there were no problems. Hunky athlete with a squeaky-clean record didn't sit right with her. There was too much caveman in his brow to believe he had coasted through life without putting someone in the hospital. There should be DUIs, drunk and disorderlies, suspensions—*something.*

She tracked down the man who served as ombudsman handling complaints at the university, but he revealed nothing she could use. His dean of students and academic advisor were similarly useless. Then she went down to the infirmary and found a nurse who remembered Chet. And the woman's look when she heard his name—like she'd just bitten a wad of gristle—suggested something darker lurked beneath. She slipped the woman her card with assurances of anonymity and a wink.

HER MIND, NOW CALMED BY peaceful surroundings, began to prickle with thoughts of the conflicted nurse. She brewed a fresh pot of Folgers and dumped a can of sweetened condensed milk into a lumpy glazed mug made by Franky in the fourth grade. Then she thinned it with coffee and took it to her reading chair.

There was something here, Struthers thought as she chuffed over her mug and took a sweet sip. Handsome son of a banking tycoon floats ashore a few miles downstream of the heart of Nashville seven days after his death. His car abandoned upriver from the location of his body. Cops won't disclose cause of death yet but she knows they're playing it safe till the autopsy comes in, and there's sure to be foul play. Parents suspect the fame-hungry fiancée. But she'd be after his money. Why not kill him *after* they tied the knot? The band members seemed a little checked out for having lost their lead singer, but the fact that they were merely guitars for hire, with no ambitions to take center stage, made them unlikely as suspects.

The phone rang. She stretched over the arm of her chair in hopes she could answer without leaving her seat, and just grasped it with the tips of her fingers.

"T. Lynn Struthers."

There was a pause as whoever had called was deciding whether or not to proceed.

"This is anonymous, right?" a woman said in a sweet, thick southern accent. It was the infirmary nurse.

"Yes, ma'am, completely."

"You promise this won't come back to me?"

"I can't make promises, and I can't protect you. You'll have to decide for yourself if what you have to say is worth the risk."

The nurse took a long, quiet breath.

"There was a young woman who come in, back when you were asking about, '71 or thereabouts, and she was *visibly* distressed. She wasn't crying or nothin'. She was real quiet. Closed-up like. I talked to her for a bit, and come to find out she was looking to terminate, you know, her pregnancy. Of course, we don't do that sort of thing, but I counseled her for a while like we're supposed to and then I get the feeling she wanted to keep the baby."

Struthers was not remotely surprised at the direction the story was taking.

"All right, so what does this have to do with Mr. Wilton?"

"That's what I was getting to. Chet comes in a few minutes later and thanks me, all genteel, and then he walks her out of there. And the next day I get this lawyer calling me up—"

Then a man's voice called out from the background, and the woman mumbled something and hung up.

"Damn!" Struthers called back but there was no answer. She leaned back in her chair and reviewed the conversation. So he knocked a girl up. Surely that wasn't all . . . Had he raped her? And what of the lawyer? She was scribbling down what the woman told her when the phone rang again.

She picked up to a different woman in midsentence. She could tell within seconds that the caller was Mrs. Wilton. She was huffing and sputtering, her words in the wrong order, like a mess of schoolchildren falling out of line. Finally, she pieced together something Struthers could understand.

"Turn on WSM!"

"What?"

"The radio—turn it to 650—now!" Struthers tripped on the phone cord on her way to the stereo.

"She's written a song about it!"

"Who?"

"That girl," Mrs. Wilton shrieked. "Lorelei *Ray*."

A song? She twisted the AM radio dial to 650. A high-pitched voice she didn't particularly like was singing, "—*should have faced the music . . .*"

"A song about *what*, Mrs. Wilton?"

"Chet, for goodness sakes, *Chet*! She's singing about killing my son!"

CHAPTER 35

Twyla was fixing her hair when Mimi burst into Twyla's room in a lizard sheath dress, rolling deodorant into her pits.

"What gives?" she said looking around the room. "People are gonna be here like now!"

She was throwing a cocktail party for the team behind Laurie's album and Twyla had promised to play bartender and keep the hors d'oeuvres coming. Twyla had lost track of time. In fact, she'd been in and out of a daze since overhearing everyone talking about her song.

Mimi aimed her finger down the hall at the kitchen, where Twyla had left grocery bags on the counter. Twyla stuffed a white shirt into black trousers as she headed down the hall. She mixed the onion dip, fired the oven for crab toasts, and set up the bar, then left a dozen martini glasses in the freezer.

Soon the doorbell gonged and guests in silks and cowboy hats began filling the living room. Twyla took their coats and furs and passed around crab toasts. Laurie arrived in a gold lamé dress with spaghetti straps and handed her overcoat to Twyla without recognizing her. Twyla took that as a good sign. It was unnerving to be among so many people, and she was more than happy to keep a servant's profile, barely noticed, a vehicle for food and drink. But as she studied the crowd of Nashville music makers—producers and publishers, sound technicians and managers—

she soured a bit thinking what could have been if she hadn't done what she'd done.

Mimi, on the other hand, came to life. She circulated, joining groups and firing up blasts of laughter with a purple joke. Twyla wondered if Mimi was putting on an act or if this vivacious, social being was actually her true self.

A healthy-looking seventy-year-old man who had power shooting off him like rays of light sidled up to the bar and ordered a martini. Mimi joined him.

"How you been, Lester?" She kissed him on both cheeks in greeting. "Still looking for your next act?" This was Lester Buck, Twyla realized. According to Mimi, a big-time manager.

"Always looking, Mimi," he said. "Speaking of looking, you're looking fine." He popped his bushy eyebrows at her. "Still divorced, I hope?"

"Still a dirty old man, I see," she said good-naturedly. She gave Twyla a look, like *Get cracking on that drink*. "What kind of act you looking for, then?"

"Mimi, maybe it's the age talking, but I'm sick of the same old horse-shit. I'm going rogue. I want someone surprising. Someone to put Nashville's panties in a tangle."

Mimi's gaze sharpened just slightly.

"Now, I don't like to meddle but Twyla here has some chops."

She now understood Mimi was setting her up. Something she swore she'd never do. All Twyla had to do was take the ball.

"That so," he said, a touch bored, and eyed the status of his cocktail.

"Just the other day I heard her working on something. She's got style, Lester. How would you describe your stuff, honey?" Mimi asked.

Take the ball, Twyla. Take it and run.

"Gosh, I don't know . . ." Twyla waffled. It was kind of Mimi to give her an opening, but she felt ambushed. She could take the leg up, and then what? How could she live in a spotlight knowing what she'd done, her deeds ever creeping behind her?

"Bobbie Gentry meets Bob Dylan," Mimi said as if she'd landed on the right way to sum up Twyla's music.

Lester took note, leaned in.

"You think you want a piece of Nashville, huh?" he said. Twyla smiled, noncommittal, fetched a martini glass from the freezer. Just like Mimi showed her, she mixed gin and ice and a dribble of vermouth, then shook it with a violent intensity and strained it into a frosted glass.

"Odd, idn't she?" he said and took his drink. "I don't mind odd."

Then the doorbell rang. It was a quarter to eleven.

"Who do you think has the nerve to show up this late?" Mimi said. Lester shrugged and bit into an olive.

Reluctant to leave Lester hanging, Twyla excused herself and opened the front door.

There stood a tall, slender woman, her face just hidden under the brim of her cowboy hat. She wore a sweeping coat of rabbit fur over a silk blouse and jeans. She lit her needle-thin cigarette, and exhaled into the doorway.

"Hello, Twyla."

She knew this woman, but her brain was so flooded with emotion—of fear and excitement, jealousy and intrigue—that it took a moment to link the woman's lovely proportions to the figure she'd seen kissing Chet, to link her clear, cutting voice to the one she had heard on the radio, wrapped around Twyla's lyrics.

Lorelei Ray projected confidence, as if she had every right to be standing there on Mimi's doorstep, another guest arriving late to the party. Twyla stepped outside and shut the door behind her.

"Do you know who I am?" Lorelei asked.

Her thoughts bashed around in her head. What was she doing here? How did she know where Twyla lived? How long before Mimi got curious and came to the door?

Twyla nodded.

"Come take a ride with me," Lorelei said.

Twyla shook her head. "I can't . . . There's— I'm working."

Lorelei tightened her gaze. Then she reached out and opened the front door.

"Or we could talk inside—"

"No!" Twyla blocked Lorelei from entering and pulled the door shut. She needed time to think. "I'll go make something up. Wait somewhere else. I'll come find you."

She slipped back inside and looked for her keys and purse in her room. A meeting with Chet's ex-fiancée so shortly after his death seemed unwise. If she ignored her, Lorelei might out her to Mimi, or worse. If she had proof that Twyla killed Chet, why hadn't she taken it to the police? She had tracked her down and of course she had the song. She was motivated.

Then she returned to the bar where Mimi and Lester were still chatting.

"Ah! There she is. We were just saying—Lester was just saying—we ought to set up a time to get together, maybe you can show Lester what you've been working on?"

Twyla hesitated.

"Oh," he said, leaning toward Mimi, "she's probably thinking, 'Who is this ole fart?'" Lester put on a show of good humor but she knew there was serious business at hand. Moments before, she had been dying to see where this conversation went. But any opportunity with Lester could be ruined if Lorelei walked through that door. As she considered what to say in response, an urge grew within her, one that defied her common sense, one she knew meant trouble. This woman was parading that ballad around as her own. Whatever Lorelei's agenda, Twyla had one, too. She needed to know what, if anything, Lorelei had on her. If she could do that, maybe she could figure out how to get her song back.

Twyla looked at Lester and got ready to shoot herself in the foot. After a quick glance at Mimi, her eyes saying sorry, she told Lester she had somewhere else to be, hoping to God that one day she'd get another chance like this.

She pulled Mimi aside and explained she had been invited to sing at a bar in town and, since guests were buzzed and blithe and serving themselves, Mimi, reluctantly, released her. She whipped up another bowl of onion dip and left a pitcher full of premixed martinis next to a tray of clean glasses. Then, with a curious look from Mimi, she slipped away.

CHAPTER 36

Lorelei led Twyla to a candy-coated tangerine Datsun Z parked askew and blocking the driveway completely. Twyla debated whether she should say anything at all. Although she was hungry for answers, she figured if Lorelei had something to say, she'd better let the woman offer it up on her own. Lorelei finished her cigarette and flicked it into the trees.

"All right, enough beatin' around the bush," Lorelei said. "I saw you that night."

Twyla closed her eyes, lost her breath. Lorelei knew. She *knew*. Still she wouldn't offer up anything. "Which night?"

"You know, *that* night, during his set at Irma's."

Twyla let out a little breath.

"The whole time he was playing I had my eye on you. You homely types think you're invisible but I saw you clear as day, staring at him all doe-eyed. You might be thinking a woman like me has nothing to worry about, but you'd be wrong. I'm always scanning for who's gonna try to take me down." She punched her finger toward Twyla without quite touching her. "And there's always somebody."

Twyla couldn't get a hold on what Lorelei was suggesting. She seemed to be implying that she knew Twyla had been running around with Chet, but hadn't revealed any knowledge of the murder. If Lorelei had been at El Toro that night, she must have known what Twyla had been singing about. She must have.

Twyla found her hands in fists and flexed them open. She had no leverage here. She should let Lorelei take the lead and see what she knew. But as she stood in front of this woman, who was drenched in God's blessings, who slipped through life like an eel through water, a feeling came over her. The feeling of other people's heels upon her back. Of words caught in her throat.

Twyla opened her mouth and blew her cover.

"You stole my song."

Lorelei's eyes widened just slightly, then relaxed, and she cocked her chin, into which had been pressed the most beautiful little dimple.

"Maybe," she said, eyes bright and fearless. Lorelei didn't have shit. "But it's my song now."

Lorelei looked down on Twyla, but Twyla didn't for that moment feel small. She had written a song that every radio station in the Nashville area was playing. It belonged to her. And it was time to claim it.

"I want it back," she said, emboldened by the sound of her own voice. Lorelei laughed.

"Get in," she said. Twyla didn't move. "Get in, or I'll come over there and shove you in myself."

"Why would I get in that car with you?" Twyla said, and as soon as she did she could see on Lorelei's face that there was something else.

"Because," Lorelei said, then let out a gusty sigh. "I know you killed Chet."

Twyla felt sick in the back of her throat. Her mouth filled with salt and her ears rang.

Lorelei, on the other hand, was casual, bored even. "Not only do I own your goddamn song," Lorelei said, "I own you."

Twyla wanted to flee but her feet were riveted to the ground.

"I don't know what you're talking about," Twyla managed, eyes wet, stomach turning flips.

"Just get in, woman, this drizzle is making my hair fall." Lorelei opened the passenger door and shoved Twyla inside. Then she took the wheel, started the engine, and peeled out.

"Where are we going?" Twyla asked. She'd straightened the wobble out of her voice.

"My place. I'm putting you to work," she said, and caught her own reflection in the rearview mirror and wiped a dab of something from the little dip under her nose. Noticing Twyla's confusion, she frowned. "Well, you didn't think I was gonna make it with just a single?"

Twyla closed her eyes. Lorelei wasn't making sense. Why weren't they talking about Chet? "You want me to what now?"

Lorelei blew straight out in frustration and gave Twyla a look like she was stepping on the train of her evening gown. "Good lord, Mama Cass. Keep up. I need a whole goddamn *album*."

Twyla shrugged off the comment on her weight. She was struggling to make the leap between being told Lorelei knew she'd killed Chet and this—proposition? Demand?—that Twyla help her write more songs. A soup of dread and fright sloshed around in her stomach. It seemed she had been found out, and the knowledge of this heightened her shame. And yet it wasn't going the way she expected. No threats to turn her in, no outpouring of grief or vengeance for killing Chet. Lorelei knew what Twyla had done, and was leveraging this knowledge against her, but there was no feeling behind it. If anything, she was smug. It all seemed so transactional. Lorelei sped north up Granny White Pike at what felt like g-force speed. On the radio, Diana Ross belted silky high notes over a dizzying disco track.

Twyla cranked down the window and caught a fresh breeze to ward off the sick.

"Stick your head way out of that window if you think you're gonna boot," Lorelei barked.

Twyla had admitted to nothing. And Lorelei had offered no proof. If she was only inferring from the lyrics, she'd be right, but her hunch wouldn't hold up in court. At least Twyla didn't see how it could. Without proof, Lorelei had nothing. Twyla rolled her head back inside the car and stole a glance at Lorelei, who was singing along in her thin falsetto, her sticky, cherry-pie lips lewd in the streetlight.

"We should talk about how this is gonna work," Lorelei said. "First, you're gonna have to ditch the chick you're living with and move in with me."

Twyla pinched the bridge of her nose, even more confused. "You've got the wrong idea—"

"My meeting with RCA is a month from now, which gives us three weeks to write and a week to record and mix the tracks. It's not enough time but it'll have to work." Lorelei sped up to a red light. A late-night trucker sailed across the intersection right in front of them.

Twyla threw her arms across her face, bracing for impact. Lorelei stomped on the brakes.

Twyla cried out. "You're out of your mind! You're—" She wrestled with the door handle. She'd had enough. She didn't want to hear any more of what Lorelei said. Or learn more about what she knew. Finally, she tugged the lock button up, opened the door and started to lurch out of the car.

"Get in here," Lorelei said and snatched her by the hair. Twyla reached back but the woman's hand was ensnared. She threw her weight forward, releasing Lorelei's grip along with a spray of her hair, and stumbled toward a twenty-four-hour diner. Lorelei idled there with the door open, breathless and frazzled. She seemed to be contemplating whether to give chase, then she laid on the gas so that the passenger door snapped shut, and in seconds she was gone.

CHAPTER 37

Twyla spent the following days agitated by Lorelei's words. She couldn't think of a way for Lorelei to connect her to Chet or prove she'd been the one to murder him. But she found no solace in the absence of proof, only a gnawing dread that the delicate film of safety was about to give way. By Tuesday she was anxious to see Ollie. She kept herself busy shuttling him to and from preschool, fixing his favorite meals, building forts, and even replacing the brittle rope on the tree swing.

On Thursday, Dean came by to pick up Ollie and strode through the front door, sifting through the mail like it was his own. He stood over a brass trash can into which he deposited a messy sheaf of junk mail and circulars, then stacked some bills on the narrow hall table. One letter he inspected more closely, then, sniffing, handed it to Twyla.

"It's for you, apparently."

She didn't recognize the handwriting. A little slash of nerves opened up in her chest. Dean was gathering Ollie's backpack and a tote full of his "always toys," the ones that stayed with him from house to house. She quieted the feeling and drew Ollie into her arms and hugged him.

After Dean had loaded Ollie in his car, he returned presumably for some final words with Mimi. Twyla sensed in his stern but avoidant expression that she was no longer needed and retreated to her room. She shut the door to muffle the sound. Mimi seemed to shut down, with Dean badgering her for an answer. It was a pattern she'd observed over these past few months. He'd notice something out of order, an offense to his worldview, and would then interrogate Mimi like a child. She would avoid his questions, and the less she gave the more he sought to take.

Twyla lay on her bed and felt for the envelope. On the front, someone had hastily, or angrily, written her name and spelled it wrong. *Twila.* No stamp, no address. Her stomach burned, her eyes watered. She knew it must be from Lorelei.

She set the letter aside, certain that in opening it she would release an even worse fate than the one she was already living.

TWYLA FOUND MIMI CURLED UP on the sofa staring at the stack of ash on the tip of her cigarette. Her face was plump from crying, and tears had carried mascara in charcoal tracks down her cheeks. Though it worried her to see Mimi so torn up, Twyla was glad for a moment to reach out of her private misery and sit with her friend.

"Why do you put up with it?" Twyla asked.

Mimi ashed her cigarette, took a drag, and blew a haze of smoke between them. She didn't seem to want to answer. Twyla waited it out. Mimi sent a tight little smoke donut hurtling upward and then erased it with a sigh.

"I guess the short answer is, I owe him," she said. "Big time."

"How's that?"

Mimi followed the thread of her cigarette up to the ceiling and rested her head against the back of the couch.

"I wasn't always the upstanding citizen you see here. When I met Dean, I was two weeks out of prison for possession and sale of narcotics—*cocaine*, if you must know. I was living in a halfway house bagging garbage for a cleanup crew at the Nashville Fairgrounds. When I tell you I was down and out, I was *all* the way down and *far* out. Probably sounds pretty grimy to a nice girl like you." Twyla's hands went cool. *If she only knew.*

"But I clean up good and I can charm the lies right off a car salesman when I want to. One night I was nursing a 7 Up wishing it was Everclear and he sits down next to me asking me if I ever dated yet-to-be success-ful record producers, and I said those were the only ones I knew, and he liked that. I liked the hair on his chest and the three little freckles below his right eye. And he liked my jailhouse humor and my watermelon butt, which, sadly, I lost in the divorce. We met in June and were married by the end of August. I came clean about my mishaps and thought he'd hightail it, but it was almost like he loved me more *because* of it. And that shocked the hell out of me. He gave me a job, he took care of me, taught me how to work. I was always looking for a shortcut, and he showed me how to push through and do it right. He's not *all* asshole. And I'm not all idiot for loving him."

Twyla offered a smile of encouragement to show she understood the love of a difficult man. For a moment she set her personal horrors aside and was able to enjoy being here, talking woman to woman about hard times and the mysteries of love.

"But he was controlling, too," Mimi said. Her tone sloped down-ward, signaling the turn in her story. "He didn't want people to think he was dating a junkie. So that's why he dressed me like Mary Tyler Moore. It's probably why he lets me stay in this house, because he wants to keep an eye on me. He wouldn't trust me to get my own place. I'm pretty sure he thinks left to my own devices I'd just end up where he found me. But the thing of it is, after all we've been through, his affair, the divorce, the custody dispute, I'm still grateful." She laughed darkly. "I'd take a bullet for that son of a bitch."

Twyla didn't like hearing about the power Dean had over Mimi but she understood. Mimi had been vulnerable, and Dean strong. He'd taken care of her. He'd made her feel worth the trouble.

"I did seventeen months in prison. I was totally unprepared. At the time, I was so hard up, the thought of regular meals, a chance to get clean, a guaranteed place to sleep every night sounded like a step up. It was ghastly, Twyla. I'd seen some rough women on the streets—hell, I was raised by one—but the mentality in there . . . Something happens when you lock people up. And the guards, most of them treat you like livestock. Worse than. It was awful. Every day was a year. Every month a decade. See this?" she said, stroking the silvers at her hairline. "Prison did that. I still don't sleep easy. You never know when someone's going to steal from you or prank you or punch you in the head for looking at their girl. One time I woke up scratching myself, and when I pulled back the sheet I was covered in ants. My bunkie had emptied a dozen sugar packets in my bed in the middle of the night. And she was hanging there from the top bunk, laughing her ass off upside down."

Twyla shook her head in disgust.

Now that Mimi was being so forthcoming, her secret pressed down on her even more. She imagined the way she might feel if she were able to tell Mimi the truth. Was it naive to hope she would understand? Mimi's confession about her past seemed like a sign that it was safe to open up. Perhaps it would be as if a cancer had been carved out of her throat. Raw, painful, but one step closer to healing.

TWYLA COULDN'T SLEEP THAT NIGHT. She twisted and shifted and rolled around the bed for hours, wired by currents of dread. She couldn't put the envelope, or Lorelei, out of her mind. Finally, she sat up and pulled the chain on the sconce next to her bed. The envelope lay face down on the bedside table. Only the tip had been licked and sealed. She slid her finger under the flap and pulled out what was inside. A square-shaped photo in black-and-white. A boat on a river in which two figures seemed to be fighting. The man, clothed but for the pants around his knees, hovered over the naked woman, whose right hand was clenched at his neck. The photo evoked in her a tense, but detached, state of vigilance. She stared at the image, as if further inspection would reveal in its details a sign of its fraudulence, or some other couple unknown to her, engaged in an act that hadn't ended in death.

A cursory knock as the door was pushed open and Mimi appeared, bedraggled and curious.

Twyla slapped the photo down on the bed. Mimi smiled, amused.

"Whatcha got there?" Mimi teased. "Twyla Higgins, you looking at a nudie pic?"

Twyla remained frozen, blood rushing to her head, heartbeat in her ears.

Mimi took a step toward her. "Oh, come on. Is it your boy? Lemme see."

"No!" Twyla said, and held the photo to her chest. Puzzled, Mimi stopped, waiting for further explanation. "It's private is all." Twyla stuffed the photo in the envelope and into the bedside drawer. "Sorry."

Mimi seemed alert to something beneath the surface of Twyla's reaction, but she did not comment.

"None of my business," she said. "Anyway, I couldn't sleep for shit. When I saw your light on I thought maybe you could use some company."

At this kindness, Twyla's eyes stung with tears, and she was filled with remorse. She stuck a sharp fingernail into her thigh to tame this emotion. For the moment it seemed she had eluded Mimi's suspicion, but in the long run she would not survive this acid guilt. How it ate away at her, dissolving her creativity, her peace of mind. She wanted too much—to evade punishment for what she did without suffering the weight of the secret. She ached to tell Mimi, even as she feared it. Perhaps Mimi would understand. She was no saint herself. And she loved Twyla, had even pledged her devotion after she had saved Ollie from drowning.

"I'm in trouble," Twyla said. Her voice was hard and small. Mimi straightened up. "I did something I can't take back."

Twyla could only think it would be better when she wasn't alone with it. Mimi searched her face. "All right, go ahead."

"That Writer's Night last month," she said, wondering if she should tell the whole story or get right to it. "I ran into my ex—you remember the boy . . ." Mimi nodded, her eyes brimming with worry. "We went on a boat ride and messed around and then . . . we had an argument. It got nasty and then he jumped on me. I fought back and I—" She looked around like there was something she could hold or touch that would make it easier to say. Finding nothing, she cradled her face in her hands.

"Twyla, *what*?" Mimi said. "You can't stop now, honey. Just tell me."

Twyla took a breath and saw herself saying the words, and the weight of a boulder began to roll off her. "I stabbed him."

Mimi drew slightly backward and her hand went to her stomach.

"And before I knew it, he was in the water. I tried to help him," she said, and both women thought of Ollie. "But he was heavy, and he was pushing me below the water, too. I thought I might die. And then he just . . . he went under." She was crying, furious at herself for the way it sounded. "There was no one around. I couldn't call for help, and by the time I got back here, I wasn't myself, I was out of my mind, all I could do was sleep. And then it just seemed like it was too late to go to the police—"

"Why are you telling me this?" Mimi said into her hands, which were clasped over her mouth.

"I don't know," Twyla said, panicked. Mimi wasn't sympathetic—she was horrified. "I thought maybe you could help. Maybe you know a lawyer or something. When you said you'd been to prison—"

Mimi put her hand up as if to stop Twyla from lumping their crimes together. "This is *way* out of my league."

"Mimi, you have to understand," she pleaded. "He had his hands around my throat. He was going to kill me. I had to."

Mimi looked conflicted. She buried her face in her folded arms and kept it there for a long time. Twyla was quiet, hoping the silence might give way to a change of heart. When Mimi looked up, the conflict was replaced by resolve.

"Look, I'm sure you did what you had to do . . . I don't guess I have reason to doubt what you're saying." She held out her open hands. "But I can't let you stay here anymore."

Twyla shook her head. "No, please, Mimi."

"It's not safe for Ollie, and frankly it's not safe for me. I can't be seen getting mixed up in something like this. Do you understand? I've worked hard to live straight. If Dean found out I was harboring a— He'd take Ollie without a second thought."

Twyla reached out for Mimi, as if she could transfer some kind of understanding, or urgency, through their skin.

"I'm sorry, Twyla," she said and withdrew her hand. "But you've got to go."

Her eyes pricked and she forced down the urge to cry. She needed Mimi and Ollie, more than she knew until this moment. She felt so helpless because Mimi was right; she should leave and keep the two of them out of it. But she had to try, and there was only one card to use.

"But you *said*—" Twyla pleaded. "You said you'd never forget what I did for Ollie, you said if I ever needed anything I should come to you."

Mimi looked slapped. "Well, *shit*, Twyla, I didn't mean murder!" She clawed back her hair in disbelief. "I mean, *how*?" she said, looking for signs of her character in the face she'd always thought to be innocent. The girl who saved her son. One life saved, another taken.

"Twyla, don't you dare make me feel bad about this. Think about Ollie. How could any mother leave her child with—"

"Please don't," said Twyla. She couldn't bear to hear the rest. She wished she could take it all back. She should have known better than to open her mouth. From now on she wasn't saying a word about it. But would Mimi? Twyla had to make sure. She held up her hands to show she was cooperating.

"I'm leaving, okay? But can you promise me something?" Mimi didn't answer. She was trembling, blinking back tears.

"Mimi, please, can you just pretend I never said anything? I'm sorry to bring you into this. I shouldn't have done that. Just please don't tell anyone. Can you promise me?"

Mimi blew out a breath and stalked over to the sliding doors, pressed her forehead to the glass. She shook her head *no*. When she spoke, her tone was yielding and weary.

"I won't say anything," she said. "Because of what you did for Ollie." Then she pointed toward the closet. "But you can't take anything of mine with you. Put your old clothes on and leave what you borrowed. I don't want any ties to you."

Twyla did as she was told. She packed her bag and left Mimi's clothes in a pile on the dresser. Twyla knew she hadn't any right to her boss's things, but putting on her old white blouse and clunky shoes was humiliating. Like she had been pretending to live a life that was never hers, and was now returning to the ugly truth of herself. Dressed and loaded up with the few belongings she had come with, Twyla lingered by the door, wishing she could hug Mimi before she left. Mimi was wooden.

"Good luck, Twyla."

Twyla nodded and tried not to cry.

"Can't I call you?" Twyla said. "When things settle down?" Mimi was her only friend here. And Ollie. She hadn't even gotten to say goodbye.

"No, Twyla," Mimi said, jutting her head back, incredulous Twyla would even ask. "We can't ever hear from you again."

CHAPTER 38

The devil made me do it. Struthers gazed deeply, blindly into her frothy orange drink as she worked the lyric over in her mind. The confession written into Lorelei Ray's song suggested a tortured mind, a woman possessed. A woman not ready to claim responsibility for her deeds. Lorelei *did* seem like the type to deflect guilt. But in every other way the lyric did not add up to a legitimate confession. First, according to the Wiltons, homicide had already cleared Ms. Ray as a suspect. It was possible she had Chet killed, but Struthers didn't have enough information to say whether it was a professional job. Second, if she was the culprit, why would she admit to killing him, even under the guise of a song, and risk drawing attention to herself? Was it hubris? Hiding in plain sight? It was too flamboyant to believe, even for Struthers. She left the Orange Julius shop and strolled the six blocks back to her bungalow, with Lorelei Ray heavy on her mind.

When she got home she checked her messages. One from Gail left at four that morning, urging her to triple-vet Lorelei's alibi. She suspected Ms. Ray might have someone covering for her. Struthers called the Elaine Powers Figure Salon franchise number twenty-nine. Lorelei's boss, Blair McClaine, a no-nonsense woman with finishing school elocution, said her employee had swapped shifts that day to be on a radio show.

"It appears," said Ms. McClaine, "that she may be advancing her position in the world."

"Does that surprise you?" Struthers asked.

"No, it does not. I happen to know that she is fastidious when it comes to her career and her physical appearance. Unless it pertains to a performance, as I understand, she avoids the nightlife and has boasted to the girls about how she gets twelve hours of sleep religiously."

"Oh, me too," Struthers joked. "Twelve hours, every week."

Ms. McClaine acknowledged neither the joke nor the garnish of Struthers's own laughter, but waited primly for the conversation to improve.

"Lorelei was always going to land somewhere impressive, whether by invitation," the woman declared, "or by force."

"Ma'am, can you confirm for me that Ms. Ray was teaching her classes on the night of Monday, October 24?"

"Yes, I can. She clocked in at 7:00 p.m. and clocked out at 10:15. Police have my only copies of the time stamps, but I did note the times in my ledger. After that, I haven't a clue."

"People come work out that late?"

"Our women come after work, after tucking their children into bed. For many, the Figure Salon is a sanctuary."

"Do you know which radio station she went to?"

She didn't. Struthers gave Blair McClaine her phone number with instructions to call if she had any more information, then she immediately turned on the radio and began scanning stations. The needle landed on a screaming ad for motor oil. She continued searching and then, finally, *bingo.*

"Thank you for being here, Miss Ray," the DJ said.

Struthers massaged the dial so that the sound came in nice and clear, then whipped around for a pen and notepad.

". . . all things considered. We certainly—"

"No, I wanted to be here," Lorelei interjected. *"I felt I owed it to Chet. He was so supportive of my career. I think he would have just killed me if I'd turned down a chance to play live on your show."* The DJ let out a nervous chuckle at the tactless use of the word "killed."

"Well, I surely appreciate that, Miss Ray. Would you like to tell our listeners a little about Chet? If you're up to it, that is."

"Yes, I'm okay." She took a deep, wobbly breath. Struthers took one, too.

"Chet was my fiancé. We were engaged just a few weeks when he went missing. We looked everywhere for him. It was torture, not knowing what happened. And then, when they found him, dead, and not on accident, I—well, I went a little crazy. You can understand that."

"I sure do," he said. *"Who wouldn't?"*

"Yes, and, well, I wrote a song. You may have heard it. It's called 'The Devil Made Me Do It.'" The title sent a chill through Struthers's scalp.

"Now some people might be thinking, 'Forget about the devil—did Lorelei Ray do it?'" the DJ asked. *"You have to admit, it's a little suspicious, you writing a song about your boyfriend's murder, telling everyone just how you did it. What do you have to say about that?"*

Struthers leaned in to make sure she heard this part. Why didn't she have her tape recorder handy?

"Well, I suppose I'd say, first of all, that the police have cleared my alibi." Her tone was falsely sweet now. *"But I would just like to explain a little more about my thinking. It's about what I imagined might have happened to him, what might have been going through the killer's brain. That probably sounds like I'm some kinda kook, but it's how I deal with things, you see. I put it all into my music. It's how I understand the world, really. Through my art."* The radio went silent. Struthers wiggled the dial to see if she'd lost the signal.

"It's okay, take your time, Miss Ray."

Lorelei sniffled. *"I'm sorry,"* she said with a hitch in her voice. *"I just wish Chet could see me now."*

Struthers mentally threw tomatoes at Lorelei. The Wiltons weren't wrong to suspect her. She was a ham, and she was exploiting a horrific situation like a seasoned opportunist.

"He'd be mighty proud, Miss Ray," said the DJ. *"I understand you've got a song prepared for us today?"*

"Yes, Carl, thank you." She took a deep, theatrical breath through her nose. *"This is 'The Devil Made Me Do It.'"*

The girl had the nerve to perform a cappella on what had been a heavily altered recording, and now that she was hearing the complete song, Struthers had a moment to assess it for both its forensic and artistic value. She sang sweetly, lilting and high. A blend of Joni Mitchell and Karen Carpenter, without their vulnerability or depth. A polished voice, maybe *too* polished, with the childish formality of a middle-school recital. But those lyrics, and that haunting melody, caused every hair on Struthers's body to stand on end. Struthers had to admit that Lorelei Ray could, in fact, write a hell of a song.

CHAPTER 39

The prime suspect in Struthers's murder case looked like Wonder Woman in plain clothes. She had legs to her chin and a gait like a Tennessee walker, pulling her knees up high and setting her feet down way in front of her. Her black hair had bounce straight out of a Prell commercial.

"Shit," Struthers mumbled. "All of us made of the same atoms. All of us made of star stuff. And yet some people's stuff came out looking like *that*." She shook her head at the injustice.

Struthers had waited outside Lorelei's apartment in the hopes of interviewing her. Her chances of getting anything she could use were admittedly slim. The woman had already spoken to the police and been cleared as a suspect, and she wasn't likely to spill her guts to Struthers. But she couldn't get that song out of her head. And the interview . . . Lorelei was hiding something. Struthers started walking toward her.

"Lorelei Ray?" she called out to her. Lorelei didn't break stride.

"I spoke to police already and I've got nothing more to offer."

"I'm not police." She was about to explain she'd been hired by the Wiltons to pin the murder on her, get her to speak in her own defense, when Lorelei offered a cover.

"Press, then?"

Struthers pivoted. "How'd you guess?" Lorelei stopped and swiveled her torso without moving the rest of her. She pointed to the spiral notepad that was peeking out of her shirt pocket. "Hah, dead giveaway."

Struthers caught up to her and whipped out her pad, reporter-like.

"Ms. Ray, I'm doing a cover story for, uh, *City Beat Magazine,* a profile on the woman behind the song."

Lorelei narrowed her eyes, lifted her chin, and gestured for Struthers to follow her. She strutted half a block to a seedy bar that was open, but empty. A cigarette machine stood just inside the door like a bouncer. "I'm out of smokes," she said without explaining what Struthers already knew, that she was to buy her a pack before Lorelei would open her mouth. Struthers fed her last single into the machine and Lorelei yanked the knob to release a packet of Virginia Slims.

Lorelei sat and waited for Struthers to buy her a drink.

"Club soda," Lorelei said.

"Double vodka. Water glass. Rocks. Shot glass of grenadine on the side." The bartender held Struthers's gaze for a long moment while he gathered up all the qualifiers she had just thrown his way. Then he pulled a club soda off for Lorelei and filled a pint glass with Coors and pushed it in front of Struthers.

"So what's your angle?" Lorelei said, presumably about Struthers's story.

"You tell me—what angle should I take?"

"You gonna make me out to be a black widow or something? Or some opportunist after her fifteen minutes of fame?"

"Not unless you give me reason to. I just want to get to know you first."

Struthers asked Lorelei about her ambitions, her music, what she was working on next. About her relationship with Chet and what she thought of his parents. Were they supportive of the engagement? Lorelei paused in front of an opportunity to be honest and risk revealing some unflattering bit of information about herself. Struthers already knew their relationship was adversarial.

"They were set against me from the start. It wasn't about me, though, you see, it was my background. I was trash to them. I'm sure they'd say as much after a few gimlets. They thought I was after his money."

"Weren't you, though? That's not so evil, everyone likes cash."

Lorelei shook her head. "Money is easy."

"Is it, now?" Struthers asked, intrigued. "So easy you're living over a pawn shop?"

Lorelei flicked away the insult like lint. "It's fame I want. All I ever wanted."

"Was Chet Wilton gonna give you that?"

"It wasn't his to give. But we were good together. He had the connections, I had the drive. We both had the looks. I had no reason to want him dead. His parents, on the other hand . . ."

Struthers laughed at the gall. This chick was kind of growing on her.

Maybe she was under the influence of Ms. Ray's charms, but she didn't like Lorelei for the killer. If she had done it, jabbed him and pushed him off a bridge when he wasn't looking, why would she put herself in the spotlight, and so soon after he was gone? She was an opportunist, all right, but all she could be guilty of was profiting off a dead man. Trashy, yes. Deplorable. But Lorelei wasn't her woman.

CHAPTER 40

Twyla filled a half-gallon milk jug with water before she left and, in a petty act of defiance, had snagged a thin pair of socks from Mimi, which protected her heels from the chafe of her loafers. By now she knew her way into downtown. She took it slow down the asphalt road, quiet now. It was too cold for the thin blouse and smock she'd worn that day in August when she'd taken a bus to Memphis, and she was sure to freeze if she didn't find shelter quickly. She'd lost weight the past couple weeks, and her old clothes hung on her like they belonged to someone else. Were her mother to see her now, she'd cluck approvingly and measure her waist with her hands and say something like "Now that's a whole lot better than potato chips, idn't it?"

Her own self-pity hung like a yoke around her neck, a physical weight, dragging behind it a burden of her sins. She didn't want to begrudge Mimi, but she was hurt, deeply so, that her friend would turn her out like this. It wasn't even that she had asked her to leave, it was the way she did it, like Twyla was something diseased she was snipping away so it didn't infect the rest of her life. Had she sent her off with a backpack filled with food and water, some money, a blanket, it might have taken away some of the sting. Her need sparked shame in Twyla. Mimi already had a child.

It surprised her how quickly her thoughts turned to survival. She shook from the cold and her stomach was empty. She hadn't enough money to last her the night. By the time she got to Irma's downtown, her feet felt like they'd doubled inside her loafers. It was only when she stood in front of the alley door and heard the drowsy chatter of the late crowd and smelled the good smells of beer and smoke and peanuts that she realized she couldn't be here at all. What if someone had seen her that night with Chet? They'd sat next to each other a minute, no more, before leaving one after the other. But there was a chance Irma, or someone from the house band, or any number of people who might have known Chet, had recognized them. She'd been onstage only moments before.

Another door closed.

She walked away from the warm bar in search of the boardinghouse Irma had mentioned on the first night she came to town. It didn't take her long to find the friendly-looking brick house in the Gulch with a porch full of hammocks. The woman who ran the place came down in her robe with an expression that suggested this sort of intrusion was not uncommon, but unfortunately for Twyla she had no room. "Try the Catholic Charity up on Jefferson Street." Noticing Twyla shivering in her cap sleeves, the woman disappeared into the hallway, then reappeared with a rumpled peacoat. "From the lost and found. Looks like you're gonna need it tonight." Twyla took it gratefully and followed the directions the woman gave her.

As she walked, she obsessed. She thought of Lorelei and for the first time really considered the proposition she had made in her car. It broke Twyla's heart to have her songs stolen by this woman, and she ached to perform them herself. She reasoned that maybe this was her penance. Or a way to get her music out into the world. Perhaps, if it meant her songs would actually have an audience, it was better to hear them performed by Lorelei than not at all. A few weeks ago she was picking tunes alone in her bedroom and now she had an original song on the radio. Plenty of artists had songwriters. There wasn't any shame in it at all.

So why did it hurt like she was giving away her child to be raised by someone else? It was unnatural. And Lorelei was doing it all wrong. She sang it like a folky love song, emphasizing the wrong words, changing key for dramatic effect when the real drama unfolded in the lyrics and in the steady, grinding delivery of the notes. The fact that the song was gaining traction on the radio was both flattering and insulting. Lorelei's version was popular, not hers.

If she agreed to work with Lorelei it would be as though she admitted to killing Chet. Though perhaps there was nothing more or less she could do to implicate herself than the proof revealed in that photo. She removed the photo from her back pocket and held it up to a streetlight. Seeing it again she couldn't imagine how Lorelei had managed the shot. It was dark, and they were drifting, the banks of the river thick with overgrowth. But the photo was conclusive. At the very least it put Twyla at the scene of the murder with the victim when she hadn't any other known connection to Chet. And though the image was grainy from the low light, their faces were recognizable, and the way her hand met his neck could only be interpreted as the moment of his death. She stared at the photo even as it made her ill to do so. She wanted to be rid of it.

Though surely Lorelei would have her own copy, Twyla couldn't bear to be in possession of this vile image, the worst moment of her life. She ripped it, and again, and tore the pieces into smaller bits until they looked like snowflakes in her hand. She dropped the bits in different places along her walk so they could never be pieced together. Her ruminations powered the last thirty minutes of her journey, and it wasn't until she heard the sounds of laughter and country music that she saw she had walked straight to Printers Alley. She would have passed by the small marquee easel outside the pub if the name of the third billing, scrawled in hot-pink chalk, hadn't jumped right out at her.

Lorelei Ray.

CHAPTER 41

The name appeared as if summoned by her thoughts. She stood rubbing the backs of her arms to strike up some heat, debating whether to go in. Hearing her song on the radio had been one kind of horror, but seeing Lorelei perform it live might just do her in. Yet, in a hateful way, she was curious. How badly would the woman butcher her song? Would she receive applause? Indifference? An angry shower of popcorn? Twyla stood there, frozen by indecision.

Thick odors of fried fish and hush puppies snaked up from the kitchen below and stoked a hunger she could no longer ignore. The possibility of food and shelter from the cold pushed her forward. She took the stairs to the underground club and found a seat toward the back, ordered a double margarita and a bowl of free peanuts. The bar, barely half full, did not appear to be the hottest joint on Printers Alley.

When her order came she ate savagely. She funneled the sweet-sour drink into her mouth until her head ached. Two women who looked like sisters shared a mic and sang an old folk song in piercing harmony. The taller one played guitar while the other lowered her fiddle to harmonize the chorus. For a moment Twyla was held by the song, suspended in the strains of someone else's heartache, which tonight felt very much like her own. She took refuge in their song, spun herself in its silver threads. When the music ended they left the stage, and she was redelivered to her grim reality.

A portly man in suspenders appeared and invited a round of applause for the Tarry Sisters.

"You may know our next act," he said, reading from a card. "From her first single, 'The Devil Made Me Do It.' Ladies and gents, put your hands together for Miss! Lorelei! Ray!"

Twyla gripped the edge of her seat. A couple people whistled from their seats, and someone in front elbowed her seatmate to pay attention. Did she have fans already? A sleepy-looking drummer and a teenage red-haired guitarist took the stage and warmed up briefly before Lorelei strode into the spotlight. She seemed even taller standing there in her fringed stiletto cowgirl boots, tight Lee jeans, and a red sequin bolero. She was playing a pub known for their fish and chips, but she was dressed for the Opry.

She held the mic in one hand and the cord, like a train, in the other.

"How's everyone doing tonight?" she said. Sultry she was, and poised. The sequins sprayed ruby light across her chest, up the clean lines of her neck and jawline, in the blue-black tresses of her hair. Twyla imagined she would open her mouth and bray, mule-like, and leave the stage in shame. She willed it to happen, she bargained, she prayed. She needed her to fail.

By the time she finished the first verse, it was clear Lorelei would not fail tonight. It wasn't that she was a great singer—her voice lacked character, her delivery was studied but basic—but what she lacked in soul, she recouped in a deft manipulation of the audience. By the time it ended it appeared she had won them over. A round of applause fired up, one Twyla would have been grateful for, but Lorelei, in a stroke of vanity or showmanship, went back to the mic.

"I can't hear you," she said. Her tone was stern. Admonishing. It worked. They yipped and whistled and cheered.

Lorelei bowed and reveled in the attention, then she stepped down and crossed the room, drawing stares and comments from onlookers as she passed, until she reached Twyla's table. She did not stop, but clipped Twyla's shoulder and kept walking.

Maybe it was the tequila, but Twyla was ready to make a move. She waited a moment for the next act to be announced, for fear she'd be noticed with Lorelei. After a minute or so she pushed away from the table and charged out the door. Being jostled by Lorelei tickled an animal urge in her, an urge to pounce. She scanned the alley and saw Lorelei turn the corner onto Church Street. She followed her, watching. Both women seemed to be aware of each other, yet not quite eager to meet. After a few blocks, Lorelei stopped in front of a short flight of stairs beside a pawn shop. Twyla approached and called out her name.

"I got your message," Twyla said, heart racing and breath coming quickly. Then Lorelei whipped her dark waves around and gave Twyla a cool, cutting look.

"What . . . in the *hell* are you wearing?"

Twyla resisted the impulse to look down at her plain frock, then gathered up her dignity. It was base of Lorelei to disparage her outfit. But she couldn't help taking Lorelei down a notch, too.

"You're ruining the song," she said. Twyla knew she would not be expecting criticism after that show.

Lorelei played nonchalant, but there was a spark of injury in her eyes.

"Well," she said, "every radio station in Nashville would beg to differ."

Twyla let the moment breathe. She didn't have to explain why. She could tell by the way Lorelei narrowed her eyes and sucked in her cheeks that she knew she was right.

Lorelei stamped her high-heeled boot. "Goddammit, that's why I wanted you to help me in the first place!" Lorelei whined. Twyla held her ground, enjoying the sight of this woman losing her cool. Then she seemed, in the span of a moment, to recover. "Honestly, Twyla, the way I see it is simple: either you agree to help me, or I drive down to the police station and tell them all about what you did."

The photo appeared in her mind. A keepsake of her savagery that she could hold in her hand. One single frame. Damning. Reproducible.

Twyla looked around. The street was not crowded but there were plenty of people around, drifting in and out of bars, smoking in circles. She had left the asylum of Mimi's and was now exposed. Anyone could hear them.

She sat down on the steps next to her bag and guitar, pondering through the slush the margarita had made of her brain. She had nowhere to go, no money, and was one false move away from arrest. Her options had narrowed down to two. Go write for Lorelei and turn over her music without credit, without pay. In exchange, she would have a place to stay and Lorelei would refrain from sharing the evidence that would surely convict Twyla for her crime. Or she could flee Nashville, somehow, and live in fear of the truth catching up to her.

Finally, she stood up and faced Lorelei.

"So," Twyla said, her voice low, a little rubbery from drink, "you want me to write the rest of your album. One you think is going to make you famous. And you think I ought to do it for free because of what you think you have on me?"

"I'd say I'm offering you freedom to do what you'd be doing anyway. Only difference is, I can actually make your songs famous."

"How do I know you're not just going to hold this over me for the rest of my life?"

"Soon as the album hits number one, I burn the photo and the negatives."

Twyla examined Lorelei for a sign she was telling the truth.

"So why cut me loose? They'll want more music after the first album. You can't write, you said so yourself."

"I can't write but I know the market. And I know talent. You're good, Twyla. And this song will take the album to the very top. And once it does? Honey, they'll hire me the best writers in town. Even better than you."

There was a dim and flickering light above the apartment door. Fat bugs circled and bashed it drunkenly. She was so full of hatred for this woman she didn't dare open her mouth for fear of what would come out.

But she was tired and cold and drunk and Lorelei was sounding more right by the minute. All she wanted now was a warm place to crash and something to eat.

Lorelei smiled, a penciled eyebrow arched in smug satisfaction, the look of a woman who knew she'd won.

"I knew you'd come around."

CHAPTER 42

Lorelei led her up the stairs to her third-floor walk-up, a scant studio with a hammered tin ceiling and a tall window that looked out onto the street below. She went to the window and jiggled it violently in a seesaw motion to coax it open. Fresh, cool evening air replaced the stuffy heat of day.

"I'm gonna do my toilette," she said. She shrugged off the sequin bolero and hung it neatly on a garment rack, then shut herself in the bathroom.

Twyla swayed on her feet and reached for the kitchen counter. A deep, unsettled feeling arose in her, and it wasn't just the alcohol. There was something about the intimacy of being here among Lorelei's things. She hadn't even known where Chet lived, and now she found herself in a place he had frequented. She looked for traces of him. A pair of shoes, a framed photo, a rumpled shirt heaped in a corner. There was a closet into which Lorelei had stuffed a thin twin mattress. The mattress, which was bare but for the tangle of a green blanket and a pillow, stuck out width-wise, with only a curtain on a dowel for privacy. Had Chet installed it? Had they slept there together, spooning to fit in the cramped space?

The kitchenette appeared unused but for three dark-pink cans of Tab and a cardboard box that doubled as a trash can. A TV on the floor, a beanbag chair, and a papasan arranged around two milk crates pushed together. All the color in the room came from the garment rack and four more milk crates beneath it overflowing with clothes. Dresses in satin, sequin, spandex, and pleather, trimmed in feather, fringe, and fur. Dozens of shoes—go-go boots, high-heeled cowgirl boots, strappy heels, glittery platforms, pumps, and wedge sandals stood mated and straight in their original boxes. The most elaborate furniture in the whole apartment was a simple rattan writing desk under the front window, which was flanked by two matching bookshelves.

The shelves on the left held a bold collection of motivational books with titles like *How to Get Ahead in a Man's World*, *Improving Voice and Articulation*, and *Seven Secrets to a Sleek Physique*. The other shelf held three rows of spiral notebooks and several shoeboxes filled and catalogued with cassettes and Betamax tapes.

The aspirational quality to these belongings surprised Twyla. In every other way, Lorelei had seemed indifferent to the opinions of others. But perhaps her persona was crafted and not innate. It occurred to Twyla, through the seasick feeling in her head, that another copy of the photo might be hidden among the pages of these books, or between their covers, or taped inside the dust jackets. She removed the books one by one and fanned through their pages, inspecting them inside and out.

A cool, uncomfortable sweat formed on the back of her neck.

"How stupid do you think I am?" Lorelei said.

Lorelei stood in front of the bathroom wearing nothing but a thick layer of cold cream on her face. Twyla was so startled by Lorelei's nakedness, that it took a moment to realize she had been caught. She noted the strange proportions of Lorelei's body, her long limbs, childlike in their thinness, her heavy breasts, and the hollow under her rib cage, as if she were sucking in. She looked to be descended from a different species.

"Go ahead and look if you want. You're not gonna find it here."

Twyla returned the book to its gap on the shelf and stood awkwardly in the center of the room while Lorelei dragged the papasan cushion onto the floor and laid a sheet folded in two over it. Then she squatted beside the mattress, adjusted her alarm, and turned out the light.

In the abrupt darkness the room tilted sideways and smeared itself

across Twyla's eyes. Double margarita, in reverse. Twyla lunged for the
bathroom and emptied her evening into the toilet.

WHEN SHE FINALLY BECAME AWARE of her surroundings again, her
head was in Lorelei's lap. She was stroking and shushing Twyla gently and
her face bore a concerned and uneasy expression. The room was lighter
than before, and she had been draped in Lorelei's green blanket. The green
funk of the river lingered on her tongue.

"Did I pass out or something?"

Lorelei seemed relieved, even moved, at this sign of improvement.
She continued stroking her hair, sending a flood of warm feelings through
Twyla. She had not imagined Lorelei could be kind.

Then, almost as if Twyla's pleasure triggered a shut-off switch, Lorelei stopped stroking Twyla's hair.

"Well, you beefed all over my bathroom, for one."

Twyla was ashamed and looked away. There was a cruel feline quality
to the way Lorelei lured her into a sense of safety, then struck. Lorelei
seemed aware she had spoken harshly and, again, revised her tone.

"Look, honey, let's clear the air. I need you, you need me. Why don't
you just tell me what happened with Chet, so we can move past it and
get to work?"

Twyla was in no condition to discuss the details of that night. She
was queasy and cotton-mouthed and as far as she was concerned, the
fewer details exchanged, the better. But the worst of it was already known
to Lorelei. And there was an appeal to giving her a fuller picture, in case
Lorelei thought she'd killed him in cold blood. She sat up and wrapped
her arms around her knees.

"He had his hands around my neck," she said. She recalled his features, dark and furious, hovering over her. "I—I couldn't breathe." Lorelei looked guarded. "You must have seen he was going to kill me—didn't
you?"

Lorelei chewed on the inside of her lip and stared at Twyla for a long time.

"I didn't know what I was seeing," Lorelei said. "Sometimes it's hard to know the difference between passion and violence."

Lorelei opened her mouth again and looked ready to elaborate, but then something stopped her. She stood and went to the kitchen, stared at the empty fridge, then cracked open a Tab and swallowed two diet pills. Twyla couldn't understand Lorelei's cool in all of this. She had witnessed the *murder of her fiancé.*

"Here's what I don't get," Twyla said. "You were *engaged* to him. I don't see how you could just move on. Didn't you love him?" Her old feelings for Chet bloomed now against her will. She had been so convinced that they, Chet and Twyla, were in love. How could those feelings have survived what she did? What he did? And yet here they were, warming her heart, making her want to stop time so the sweetness could linger.

"No," Lorelei said. She was calm, but her tone was heavyhearted. "I didn't love him."

"So why were you going to marry him?" There was an anxious, hurt feeling in her chest as she throttled back to the night she'd found out they were together. That Twyla was not his girlfriend, but a dirty secret.

"It was business," she said, relenting. "For both of us. I was the arm candy, and he had the connections. Honestly, don't be so naive. You're looking at me like I'm some kind of ghoul, but I didn't invent the marriage of convenience."

Twyla did feel slightly relieved to hear how little Lorelei cared for Chet, one life fewer ruined because of her. But her nonchalance was nonetheless unsettling. Was she really so coldhearted, or just a skillful actor? There was a long silence as the two women attempted to move past the discussion of Chet and orient themselves to the task before them.

"Let's get some sleep," Lorelei said. "Tomorrow, we work."

CHAPTER 43

Struthers stopped at home to check her messages. There was one from the Wiltons, inquiring (again) about her progress. She had been reluctant to share her findings for fear they would (accurately) conclude her investigation was stalling out. Another, from Cortez, asked for a meetup at 7:00 p.m.

It was already 7:30. She hung up and booked it to their usual spot at McFerrin Park. As she pushed her little Beetle to the limit, she wondered hungrily whether he had called to loop her in or reprimand her for stepping on his turf. Either way she hoped she could get something out of him that would nudge her own investigation along.

By the time she jogged up, Cortez was getting ready to leave. "I've been waiting for an hour, Struthers."

"I didn't get the damn message until just now," she said, panting. "Sorry, why so cryptic?"

"Look, I didn't want to get into it on the phone. I can't be caught consulting with you."

Struthers tried not to look too eager. "Consulting?"

He raised his palms out to her in surrender. "You gonna make me say it?" he said.

She smashed his cheeks between her palms and brought his face close to hers. "Ohh, I could kiss you on the lips for this." He pushed her off like a kid rejecting his mother. She laughed at him, their old cat-and-mouse dynamic a sweet comfort. "All right, I'm cool, I'm cool. Fill me in—what have you got so far?"

"We've got a homicide with no murder weapon, no viable suspects, no crime scene, and next to no resources. It's basically just me working the case and I can't do it alone." He shoved his hands deep in his pockets and looked around. This was really getting to him. "I don't want to be paranoid but I think they're setting me up to fail; the captain has been sticking his foot out every time I walk by, just waiting for me to fall on my face."

"Some things never change," she said with an edge, and wondered if he could see the irony of his confiding in her about his mistreatment when he had taken part in her own. But she couldn't rub his face in it now. He was making nice, and so would she. They needed each other.

"Autopsy report come in?"

"COD was drowning."

Struthers took this in. Not what she was expecting. "Drowning . . . but you're sure it's a homicide?"

"There was an injury that could have been fatal if he hadn't drowned first. Multiple stab wounds to the left side of his neck," he said, touching himself at the corresponding part of his throat. "The wounds were strange."

"How so?"

"Shallow, barely an inch deep. And irregular. Nothing like a blade. Maybe you can take a look." He reached inside the open car door window and pulled out a large brown accordion folder.

"Paul Cortez, did you smuggle the case files out for little old me?" she said, with a cheeky pull of her eyebrow. She could hardly wait to get her hands on the coroner's report. He held the file to his chest a moment as if reconsidering, then removed a manila folder that held a stack of color photos.

Struthers shone a penlight on the pictures, scouring them one by one. The matinee idol from the Missing posters lay before her in a flaking, swollen mass of tissue. Before consulting the coroner's notes, she took some time to form her own impressions. There were postmortem abrasions on the forehead and backs of the hands and tops of his feet from where the body had scraped the riverbed, and his eyes, nostrils, and lips had been nibbled on. Sloughing of the skin from water absorption could be seen on the palms and soles of the feet, typical in bodies recovered from the river. Then Cortez showed her the close-up photograph of his neck. The macerated skin looked mottled and bruised, and just where he had described, there were three pea-size puncture marks near the carotid artery.

"Any guesses on a weapon?"

"Tough to tell. The critters and things had gotten to the tissue, but they did pull a sample from the deeper-down layers."

"Well?"

"There was dark discoloration on some of the tissue inside the wound."

"Like gunpowder burn, or what?" she said, moving the information around in her mind. "Or something in the water, maybe?"

"Not sure," he said. "The examiner said it could be extra-fine silt, but he was surprised by how dark it was, and how deeply embedded it."

"Are they testing for composition?"

Cortez shook his head. "The lab is backed up till Christmas."

Struthers was practically running in place. "Give me a sample. I'll get it done independently. I'll take it to Memphis if I have to."

"No, that's the thing. I've reached out to every contact I have. The labs are completely slammed. We're up to our eyeballs in bodies and evidence."

There was a moment where they both paused. Struthers knew at least part of the reason they were in the red was because they had fired their best detective.

"Look, I've got money," she said and rubbed her fingers together. "I can make things happen." He raised an eyebrow, prompting her for more. She realized she may have revealed too much. She was never flush and he knew that. She'd have to stage a distraction and circle back to the sample when she could think of a better setup.

She shuffled through the photos and returned to the first, the full body, for another look. His pants were gathered at his knees. No underwear.

"What do you make of that?" she said, pointing the penlight at his groin.

"Let's keep this one above the belt, Struthers," he said.

"No, you cretin, why are his pants down?"

"Could be the current dragged them down. If they were loose fitting."

"Hmm."

"Why?" he said, intrigued. "What are you thinking?" She savored the feeling of a hunch not yet shared. His anticipation to get into her head. It was the thrill of having a partner that she had been missing since going solo. Not just the hunch, but working a case together. Feeding off each other's curiosity and inching closer to an answer together.

"I don't know. It's odd. The button and fly are undone *and the underwear* are down. The current didn't do that."

Cortez took her observation in without adding to it. He could be coy sometimes. She didn't belabor the point, not yet, but carried on with her analysis.

"He was a big hunk of meat, that one. Burly."

"Look, I know it's been a long time since you had a date, Struthers," he said.

"No, I mean they must have caught him off guard, right? A husky guy like this would have held his own in a struggle. But look"—she held up the close-ups of his hands—"no defensive wounds."

"You're right—none were found by the coroner either." Cortez thought for a minute. "So, what, you think someone jabbed him in the neck while he was taking a piss and dumped him in the river?"

"Does that sound like a tight theory to you?"

Cortez kept his mouth shut. She hadn't meant to snap but her gratitude at being shown the files had suddenly worn off and she was now stressed at how much time had been lost.

"I'm saying I don't know, but his size and bare genitalia give me pause."

"Jesus, Struthers, 'bare genitalia'?"

"I think they are relevant. And I need more time with the files."

"That might be a problem."

"I'm taking these home with me," she said, holding them to her chest. "You'll have them back tomorrow."

"Absolutely not."

"I need more time." She was not above begging.

He looked her over and then glanced at his watch. "You've got two hours."

CHAPTER 44

Twyla woke up scattered across a bare floor. Unfiltered light drove through her eyelids, and her pasty mouth had nearly glued itself shut. It felt like someone was swinging a hatchet to her head. Lorelei emerged from her den, the green blanket draped over one shoulder like a Roman senator, and dropped two aspirin in Twyla's hand.

"Well, shall we get started?" Without makeup, the length of her nose and the angles of her face gave her a masculine bearing. This and the look that seemed always on her face, as if she would trample any one of God's creatures to give herself a boost, triggered in Twyla both fear and admiration. She tossed the aspirin into her mouth and forced them down.

"I have one question," Twyla said, taking a chance. "How did you get my song? How did you even know I was going to sing, or who I was—or any of it? And how in the world did you get that picture?"

Lorelei smiled like she'd been waiting to be asked.

"That's more than one question," she said. "If I tell you, that's it. Then we work."

Twyla nodded, bracing herself for whatever she was about to hear.

"That night at Irma's, when I caught you looking at Chet in that special way, like you knew exactly what you were missing, I confronted him. I can always tell when he's messing around, sure as shit wasn't the first time. But when I saw *you*, well, it didn't make sense. He's never been with someone so ordinary before. Like attracts like, you know? And so I thought, well, there must be something more to it. So I got him a little drunk, and then I pressed and pressed him, I threatened him a dozen different ways, and finally he gave in and told me about you. Sweet little Twyla Higgins, Texas bred and bound for fame. He kept saying you were *different*. That you *had* something, not like all the desperate wannabes Nashville eats up every damn day, but something—God, what did he say? Something precious. Or timeless. I could gag just thinking about it. And his face lit up, like he'd found a lump of gold."

Twyla felt hot and flushed in her face and her hands went cold. She had so wanted to believe Chet cared for her.

"And so of course the woman in me was jealous as hell and you being homely just made it worse, like you were so great it didn't matter how you looked. I couldn't get it out of my head. I guess I was a little fixated on you. I had to know what was so goddamn special."

Twyla remembered then what Chet had said about Lorelei. "She is one crazy bitch. . . . She'll fuckin' track you like an animal."

"I tried to put it out of my mind, but after we broke up I started tailing him here and there. Not every day, mind you, just, you know, casually. At first it looked like he'd cut things off with you, too. But then—bam—I see you with him and I don't know what came over me but"—she paused here, assessing Twyla—"I needed proof. So I followed him to the river, and I had my camera in my car, a good one. I used to bang a photographer in my modeling days."

Twyla shook her head. "But we were in the middle of the river. How did you get the photo of us?"

"It wasn't easy, I'll tell you that. Scraped myself trying to keep up on the riverbank."

Twyla let the image of Lorelei stalking them downriver sink in.

"Okay," she said, piecing things together. "You had the photo, and there was no song at that point. So, why didn't you turn me in?"

Lorelei looked thrown off. She squinted like she was trying to find her way back.

"To be honest, I don't know. I was in shock. I've been around the block but I'd never seen anyone get killed."

This made sense to Twyla. Shock.

"And how did you steal my song? Do you travel with a tape recorder, too? Were you just waiting for me to sing something good enough to steal?"

"That's not a bad idea, actually," Lorelei said, thoughtfully. "After you killed Chet, I guess I was just looking for answers."

"What kind of answers?"

Lorelei paused and looked upward, searching for the right words. "I couldn't get it out of my head. What in the world did he see in you? What did you have that I didn't? I guess a part of me was thinking, 'What in the hell will she do next?' I didn't know you would be singing that night. I was just spying on you."

Twyla took in Lorelei's analysis, how bizarre she thought it that a woman as beautiful as Lorelei could be upstaged by the likes of Twyla. And how Twyla had felt similarly, that Chet had chosen Lorelei's looks over Twyla's more modest assets. But then, he hadn't really chosen one over the other. He had singled out the qualities he wanted in each woman and tried to keep them both. Perhaps that was his mistake, failing to see these two women as they were.

"But boy," Lorelei went on, "when I heard you—and that song—it just about knocked me to the ground. I tried to write it down but it went so fast, and it was all I could do just to hold on to the melody. I wasn't even thinking about stealing the song at that point—I just wanted to remember it. God, it was beautiful."

"So how did you? Reproduce it, I mean?"

Lorelei smiled again, wickedly at first, then with pity.

"Oh, darling," she said. "You made it easy."

Twyla dug her nails into her palms.

"Your lyrics—they were right there, on the stage, like you'd left them for me."

CHAPTER 45

She could get lost in the grim luck of it all, this revelation that she had—in her haste to leave the bar—gifted the lyrics to Lorelei, who had then had used the money Chet gave her to record "Devil." That Lorelei had marched her shitty recording up to every DJ in town and, with her pageant smile and a coy mention of her connection to the missing man, had landed a spot on the radio lineups. And now she had less than three weeks to deliver the remaining nine tracks to RCA. Somehow, Twyla had to be able to put it all behind her. In this moment, she clung to the work ahead of her, grateful to have something to focus on other than her own crushing stupidity.

Lorelei had prepared a fussy-looking graph with song titles in one column, mood words in the second, and lyric ideas in the third. For each she went through and sang a melody for Twyla. Twyla let her run through the entire presentation. She would have stopped her sooner, but she had to figure out a tactful way to tell her they couldn't use any of it. They were all, every last one of her ideas, garbage. Tuneless, vapid, clichéd. Devoid of imagination, passion, curiosity, insight into the human condition. Boring. She clamped her teeth down on the side of her cheek to keep all of these comments from spilling out. Fortunately, Twyla's mother had trained her well. Faith could be thick-skinned at times, open and cooperative at others, then, out of nowhere, easily bruised. Reading the moment correctly would be the challenge.

"Well, what do you think?" Lorelei asked. Her expression betrayed a knowing—a rare humility for this otherwise intimidating woman. Something about her revealing this weakness leveled things between the women. Twyla could see Lorelei truly needed her. It felt less like coercion and more like a plea for help.

"How about this," she began. "Would it be all right if I asked you a few questions about yourself?"

Lorelei straightened her spine a couple inches and left her arms crossed. She raised an eyebrow to suggest the smallest unit of cooperation.

"If I'm going to write for you, I need to know what makes you tick. What do you want? Who are you writing for? Who broke your heart? Where'd you grow up? Were you good in school? All that stuff."

As she considered the string of questions, Lorelei sucked in the flesh of her cheeks, setting her cheekbones in lovely relief. Jealousy aside, Twyla could appreciate Lorelei's beauty as a gift.

"Well, we weren't the trashiest family in Louisville, but we weren't Kentucky's finest either. My mother did my schooling, Daddy worked for the railroad as a welder. Wasn't home much. Had a mess of older brothers but they were all pretty big by the time I came along. Mama always wanted a girl, so she made the others wear last year's shirts so she could keep me in new dresses. Put me in a beautiful baby contest when I was six months old and I won first place. Pretty soon she was hooked. The prize money was good, and my daddy wasn't home enough to notice what she was up to." Her speaking voice was a studied mix of Scarlett O'Hara's flouncy, antebellum lilt and Faye Dunaway's icy gravitas, though never both at the same time. She'd careen from one to the other in the same sentence. One moment she was hyper-articulated, the next her blue-collar roots would emerge.

"What about you? Did you like it?"

"Pageants? I didn't like standing still with a stretched-out smile on my face. But I did like winning. Look at this," she said, and pulled a large

wardrobe box out from behind the garment racks. In it she had piled
dozens of tiaras, crowns, and trophies. "Last title I got was in 1973 when
I was twenty-two. Miss Kentucky."

She rummaged around in the box and pulled out a photo. A girl of
four or five in full makeup, wearing a petticoat poodle skirt and gleaming
tap shoes. Her mouth more grimace than smile. Twyla wanted to feel
sorry for her but she envied her power; even then she looked like she
owned the world and everyone in it.

Twyla took the graph, balled it up, and dropped it in the trash.

"Hey, I worked hard on that!" Lorelei looked hurt but perhaps not
surprised.

Twyla ignored her, picked up her guitar, and started playing around
with melodies.

"Let's make something fresh, okay? Together. It'll be better than trying to force old ideas."

Lorelei did not argue, though she still seemed to be struggling with
the loss of her work.

Twyla pushed ahead, assuming a borrowed confidence. She recalled
things she'd heard Ron, the music producer, say to Laurie Kane.

"Let's start with our first track. What mood do you want to set? How
do you want the listener to feel?"

"I want that first song to make a splash," she said. "I need a radio
darling with a sharp hook and a chorus everybody's gonna remember."

Sharp hook and memorable chorus felt like pressure to Twyla. She
never started with a formula. She always let the mood or the idea drive
the song.

"Pop country isn't my strong suit," she said, trying to temper Lorelei's
expectations. "But let me play around with some licks." She strummed
out something bluesy, just to warm up the strings.

Lorelei listened for a while, skeptical, then shook her head. "No way,
you're putting me to sleep. Cut the rhythm in half." She pounded on the
table with an open hand. "One, two, three, four—like that."

Twyla pressed her teeth together. "I'm just warming up, Lorelei, you gotta let me breathe or this isn't going to work. It might take me a minute, but we'll get there."

She freestyled a bit, feeling out the rhythm, getting the lay of her guitar, until she landed on something simple, playful, a pretty loping intro. Her daddy's picking style seemed to work perfectly for this one.

"That one ain't half bad," Lorelei said. "Do we need to write it down or something?"

"Don't worry, I won't forget."

Lorelei listened for a while as Twyla nailed down the lick and felt her way into some progressions. She seemed impatient. "Well, should I write some lyrics, then? How's all this work?"

"If you like," Twyla said, distracted. She now wanted to be alone with the music.

"Can't we use some lyrics you already wrote?"

Twyla put down her guitar. "Lorelei, you can't play the songs I wrote for me. It won't be believable. You're take-charge, you know? Confident."

"I'm not some *libber*," she said like it was a dirty word.

"I didn't say that. It's not about politics. It's about voice. Tone . . ." She got an idea. "Let's try something . . ." She jotted down a few phrases that captured the feeling of a woman who has had enough. "Okay, you're a housewife—"

"I would *never*—"

"It's okay, *you're* not the housewife, you're singing from her *perspective*. Let's try and get into this woman's head. She's fed up, all right, and she's telling her husband to scram."

Lorelei eyed her. "I'm listening."

She played a few bars of the first verse, thinking up lyrics as she went. "How about this . . .

"*I fry your eggs up crispy, serve your coffee piping hot.*

"*Bring your paper to you promptly . . . at . . . seven on the dot.*"

She put her guitar down and scribbled down some lines, scratching out and rewording, until she had a couple verses, then she set them to the music she'd started with.

Lorelei did not meddle. She seemed to respect that something was underway.

Twyla was immersed in the process, but she was vaguely aware of being observed. When she finished, she turned the lyrics so Lorelei could see. The whole thing took her ten minutes.

"This one's called 'Kiss My Ass Good Mornin'," Twyla said and began to play.

> *I fry your eggs up crispy, serve your coffee piping hot,*
> *Bring the paper to you promptly at seven on the dot.*
> *You got everything you wanted, so what you complaining for?*
> *You can kiss my ass good mornin', on your way out the door.*
>
> *Kiss it hard and kiss it wet, then pack up all your stuff,*
> *Kiss my ass goodbye, son, I've finally had enough.*

Lorelei hooted and slapped her hands together. "Shit, sister!" Her eyes twinkled with possibility. "You put that together just now?"

"I guess I did," Twyla said. She hadn't expected such enthusiasm for a first attempt.

"Well?" Lorelei said, impatient. "Go on, sing me the rest of it!"

> *You were bein' friendly, you didn't mean no harm,*
> *When you stayed out at her house till seven in the morn.*
> *I know I'm not your keeper, but I'm settling the score,*
> *So kiss my ass good morning, son, and please don't slam that door.*
>
> *Kiss hard and kiss it wet, then pack up all your stuff,*
> *Kiss my ass goodbye, son, I've finally had enough.*

Twyla flipped the page for the last verse. Lorelei was keeping time on her thigh.

My mother told me, "Sweetie, a man is wont to roam,"
You just look the other way, and make sure he comes back home.
But life is short, and I got more important things to do,
Than sitting 'round and wasting all my precious time on you.

Lorelei let out a rodeo yell and stomped her foot. "Git it, now!" And Twyla barreled into the chorus.

Lick your lips and pucker up, I don't need you no more.
Hell, my ass is tired of being kissed, so git your ass out that door!

Lorelei kissed her on the cheek and shook her by the shoulders.

"God*damn*, woman!" Lorelei's Kentucky accent had burst wide open. "You just wrote a goddamn hit in less time than I need to take a shit!" Twyla laughed at herself, at the ludicrousness of the situation, but the song, and the way Lorelei seemed lit from within, faded everything else away.

"Oh, honey," Lorelei said, playfully, though it sent a ripple of nerves through Twyla. "I'm never letting you go."

Lorelei went to the fridge and produced an open bottle of champagne. She poured the half-fizzy drink into a couple of jelly jars and brought one to Twyla. "I don't know what kind of black magic you're practicing, but—" She stopped talking, seemingly at a loss for words, and took a long sip. "How the *shit* did you do that?"

Twyla couldn't help being pleased. Lorelei's reaction reminded her of the part of songwriting she had been missing. Sharing it with an audience. It also gave her hope that she might be able to work with this gorgeous tyrant.

"I can't explain it," Twyla said, proud. "I just do." It was coming back to her, as natural as opening up a door and letting the breeze roll through.

Why she'd found her knack again, after these weeks of stagnation, she wasn't sure, but she wondered if it might be on account of writing for someone else. Her inner life had gotten so jagged and unkind, she'd exceeded her abilities to render it beautiful. There was no bright side to this guilt, to the memories of what she'd done. All she could do to keep herself afloat was to live in the day she was in and leave those feelings behind. Writing for someone else was like leaving herself altogether, like putting on a disguise. She could get used to wearing someone else's skin.

CHAPTER 46

It had been over a month since Chet's body was recovered and two weeks since Struthers reviewed the files. Cortez was apparently still bogged down in interviews, paperwork, and all the red tape Russo could throw at him; meanwhile, the case was getting as cold as the weather outside. She'd left him a message, a dishonest one, saying she might have a break in the investigation. She had to be sure he'd call her back.

While she waited for his call at home, she tried to revisit the Wilton case as if she'd never seen it before. She transferred her jumble of notes to index cards. The ritual of recording her data points this way, then tacking them to her trusty six-by-eight bulletin board, one she had made herself out of massive sheets of cork and wood trim and mounted on her dining room wall, had the effect of calibrating her thinking, calming her nerves, clearing the debris of irrelevant facts.

In reviewing the photos of Chet obtained from his parents, she'd observed that he wore his pants fashionably tight around the thighs and hips, which had led her to conclude that his jeans did not get dragged down postmortem. They were down when he was killed. Now she opined that unless he had the extreme misfortune of getting whacked while taking a dump by the river, he was likely stabbed peri-coitus. Either by his lover or by someone who caught him in the act. It stunk of a love triangle. The strange location of the Bronco could point to this theory—maybe they'd parked somewhere private for some late-night necking. This brought her back around to Lorelei. Though her timetable didn't allow for it, perhaps she had hired a hack for the job. One of her Kentucky cousins or a suitor trying to gain favor. Someone who simply didn't know what they were doing.

So, she mused, lovers sneak away to make love on the banks of the old Cumberland. Bubba follows them on Lorelei's orders, shanks him while his attention is elsewhere, pushes him into the water. Explains how a big guy like that didn't defend himself. Maybe the guy drives the car deeper into the trees to hide it from view. So where is the girl? She would be a witness. Why would she keep quiet? Maybe Lorelei and her cousin scared her into silence. Or maybe they got rid of her, too.

The trouble with this theory was the stab marks on his neck. Nothing like a knife wound. And the strange black stains deep in the tissues. The puncture marks just didn't line up with a hit, no matter how bumbling. The guy would have brought a knife, gun, garrote, something lethal. Wilton's wounds almost seemed accidentally deadly.

Struthers rubbed her eyes. The note cards were beginning to bleed together. She brewed a stout pot of inspiration and called Cortez again. It was four p.m. He could be anywhere, knocking on doors, following up leads, but on the second ring the operator patched her through and her old partner picked up.

"Jesus, didn't you get my message? Never mind—just stop what you're doing and spitball this case with me. I'm getting lightbulbs."

The sound of papers shuffling. "What do you got?" He was playing it cool, but she heard a quiver of curiosity.

She explained the country-cousin love-triangle-hit theory, then the funky wound confusion.

"Well, maybe *lightbulbs* is too strong," she said. "One minute I think it's a bungled hit, then next it's spur of the moment."

"Spur of the moment . . . What's your thinking there?"

"Improvised weapon, for one. No gun, no knife, not even a proper bludgeoning. The body wasn't weighted, and they threw him in before he was even dead. How did they know he wouldn't swim to safety? If they really wanted him dead, they would have finished the job."

"Maybe someone was coming, scared the killer off."

"Way off there in the woods? At that hour?"

Struthers had a theory forming but she wasn't sure how it would land with Cortez.

"What?" he asked, sensing something in her pause.

"It's not fair, I shouldn't say it."

"What is it?"

"You got a photo of Chet Wilton handy?" She waited for him to rummage through his files and find one. He came back and described one of him in his college football team portrait, another from a publicity photo for his band.

"He just doesn't look like a victim to me," she said.

Cortez groaned. "Aw, come off your soapbox, Struthers. This is a murder. He is the *victim* as evidenced by the fact that he is *dead* by someone else's hand. That is our baseline. We do not deviate from that assumption. It is a fact."

"Don't get your feathers ruffled, chicken, I'm just calling it like I see it. He's a big hombre. And I have a witness who may or may not testify to some ungentlemanly behavior. I'm starting to think self-defense."

Cortez took this in for a moment.

Struthers kept going, pieces coming together as she spoke.

"Big, good-looking guy like this, found dead with his pants down, with no defensive wounds. Either it was a surprise attack from behind, or it was someone he knew. Trusted, even. And he just didn't see it coming."

If Cortez had anything to counter this line of reasoning, he kept it to himself.

"Talk to me about the victim's car. Can you tell if it was left there by Wilton or moved by someone else?"

"Oh, definitely moved there," Cortez said. "We dusted every inch, inside and out, but it was wiped down. Squeaky clean."

Struthers took this in. "And you canvassed the area around the car? Were there marks showing where it came from?"

"It was all high grass. By the time we got there it looked like the car had been dropped right in the middle of the thicket."

"And the driver's seat?"

"It was set pretty far back. The vic was tall. Whoever drove it was either his size or left it where it was." Struthers nodded, chewing on the information. Pieces shuffling and reshuffling in her mind, forming nothing but a vague impression, a feeling.

"What do you make of the drowning?" he asked.

"Well," Struthers said, "he was stabbed near the water, that much is sure. Stab-stab, splash, is how I see it. They wouldn't have dragged him from the scene of the crime—how much does he weigh?"

"Two forty-five at his last doctor's visit."

"Shit, no. He fell. Or was pushed from behind. From a bridge, from shore, from a boat. I'm not sure which. Coulda been fishing, I suppose, though he isn't dressed for it. Nice blue Oxford shirt. Any boats recovered that I don't know about?"

"Nope, nothing."

"Cortez, go to the close-up of his neck. Were the puncture wounds on the right side or the left?"

"On the victim's left, with a slightly upward angle. Meaning the killer struck from below."

She slapped her thigh. "That's what I thought. Unless the killer was left-handed, which we shouldn't rule out, I'm thinking the person stabbed him head-on. They were facing each other. Either they were dancing, fighting, or—"

"Not bad, Struthers," Cortez said, understating the joy she could tell he was feeling at this new direction.

"My money's on a woman or a very small man," she said, and, remembering her coffee, went to the kitchen. "The jabs were not exactly death blows. I mean, they would have killed him, but not because of how deep they were—because of where they landed. Smack in the jugular."

She stopped short of the coffeemaker. "Cortez, any mention from your interviews of him seeing someone on the side? Groupie, ex-girlfriend?"

"No, although the bandmates did mention him skipping out on rehearsal a few times. And that he'd had them lie to Lorelei when she had called asking where he was."

"I like this love triangle," Struthers said. "A motive for Lorelei is obvious, but the window is tight. Too tight. What about the mistress? Tired of being kept on the side? Jealous of the beauty queen? You pulled phone records on everyone, right?"

"Yeah, I got 'em for Wilton, Ray, the bandmates, his parents, everyone," he said, then made a stalling sound in his throat. "I just haven't had time to deal with them yet."

"You're shitting me!"

"I don't have the manpower!"

"What kind of— Never mind, I'm coming over there. We'll go over them together."

"No, no—you can't come around here. *I'll* drop them off."

Struthers greeted Cortez with a mug of coffee and a stupid smile. She couldn't hide how glad she was to be working together again. They split the list and made good time digesting strings of numbers. Within the first hour, Struthers had a hit. Twenty-seven outgoing calls to the same number between August 24 and September 23, the last call being placed a month before the murder. Cortez called South Central Bell and used his rank to find the name, Mimi Dewitt, and an address that corresponded to the phone number.

Cortez declined an invitation to join her—it was risky to come to her house in the first place, and Belén was cooking. By dinnertime Struthers was on her way to a tony, but secluded, neighborhood near Radnor Lake.

CHAPTER 47

Struthers pulled up to the modern home under a canopy of thinning trees, wondering if the killer was behind those walls. As she stood at the front door, tucking in her shirt, she realized her pistol was at home. She noted a weapon within arm's reach—a garden spade planted in a bed of ferns—and knocked.

A woman, looking wrung out and wrinkled, opened the door. Not what she was expecting. Did Chester the Third have mommy issues? Or was there someone else living here, someone not listed? A woman this age could have an eligible daughter. She had to be open to both possibilities, but this chick with her European pits and beef jerky complexion didn't seem like Chet's type.

"Who are you?" the woman said, and when Struthers failed to answer she started to close the door. Struthers panicked. She smiled, too cheerfully.

"Hello!" she said. She spun, trying to think of a cover story. How did she not come prepared? A flailing attempt shot out of her mouth. "Sorry to trouble you, ma'am, I work for the National Census. We're doing a preliminary head count in preparation for the 1980 report."

The woman kept her heavily lined eyes pinned on Struthers. She wasn't buying it. Shit.

"Ma'am, is it just you living in the household, or are there . . . others?"

The woman shifted her weight and leaned into the doorframe.

"A teenage daughter, perhaps?"

Mimi Dewitt flung her a look that in the animal kingdom would involve teeth and a low growl.

"Or son! We're tallying the age and sex of each household member is why I ask."

The woman seemed to be calculating the risk of sharing her household information when a little boy crawled to the doorway on his hands and knees and barked like a guard dog.

"Whoa, there! Hello. You didn't mention having any pets." She pulled out her notepad. "One dog," she said and winked at the boy. She recalculated. Young son. A happy accident?

The women sized each other up and there was a shared sense that they were well-matched in the event of a physical fight. Struthers had the height and weight advantage, but Mimi wielded a mongoose-like fight-to-the-death quality.

"Just me and the boy," she said evenly. So there wasn't a daughter, or at least not one she'd admit to. Niece? What was the relationship here?

Struthers wanted to ask about Chet, show the photo and read the look on this woman's face. But she'd blown it with the cover story. Better take the info to Cortez and let him interview her.

Struthers walked back toward her Beetle but paused when she heard a strangled noise. She followed the sound to a cracked bathroom window and saw Mimi Dewitt hyperventilating into a hand towel.

With a juicy intuition she wondered how this woman had gotten so unnerved and what exactly she had to hide.

CHAPTER 48

Twyla wrote in pressured spurts in the nest of Lorelei's papasan, napping to recover and awakening with a lap full of scratch paper and Pearl at her feet. She subsisted on Tab and canned peaches and cottage cheese until Lorelei would bring leftovers from her mysterious dinner plans. Lorelei did not explain her whereabouts to Twyla, but she suspected her outings were related to the growing success of "Devil."

Even from her confinement, its success was undeniable. The song drifted in from passing cars, open shop doors, even from within the neighboring apartments. DJs indulged callers, one request after another. She had even seen, from her lonely perch, a timid fan approach Lorelei on the street, hold out a pen and paper, and ask for Lorelei's autograph. Lorelei had robbed her of any pride she might take from the song's popularity. The bitterness brought on by this loss made it painful to hear.

Twyla could tolerate jealousy, however, and for this reason chose to dwell on the ways she had been wronged, swindled of her creative currency. Guilt and shame and horror at her own actions were not compatible with survival. She could not afford to indulge her conscience, not now. Now her survival depended on the one thing she could do, and do better than most. And despite her captivity, writing songs was saving her life. She even started writing her own, building on the small collection she had developed after Chet left her, that beautiful period when she was coming back to herself. These were a far cry from the popular music she had written for Lorelei, with none of the thrust, swagger, or musical complexity. They were humble songs. Structurally simple, unadorned. She ached to develop them, to share them with an audience, to feel her music land in their hearts.

Lorelei slinked in late one afternoon having been gone all day. She looked more secretary than singer in the cream blouse knotted at the throat and pencil skirt, her licorice hair twisted low and tight in a bun. Twyla deduced she had met with someone from the label and sensed their lives would be very different soon. In what ways, she did not know.

Lorelei reached back and pulled off one navy pump, then the other, and set them down in their box under the garment rack, then she slumped down on the beanbag next to Twyla in her papasan.

"How's tricks, Mama Cass?"

Despite her reluctant fondness for Lorelei, Twyla found these transitions after her roommate returned tedious. Lorelei, on the other hand, was upbeat and even deferential, as if trying to uphold Twyla's opinion of her.

"I got news," Lorelei said. She was nibbling the corner of her nail.

Twyla sighed, heaving her attention from her work to Lorelei's prideful face.

"I just had a meeting with my manager . . ."

Lorelei extended her long leg and nudged Twyla with her foot. Twyla pushed it away.

"Okay, look—you don't have to be happy for me, but you should give yourself some credit."

"Oh, yeah? Credit for what?"

Lorelei sat forward and took her by the wrist. "They asked me. To play. The *Midnite Jamboree* at *Tubb's*." Lorelei's mouth hung open, face frozen in its enthusiasm to stake down her point. This was big news.

"That's something," she said, not able to land on a single feeling. Jealousy, mostly. But a shy ambition was there, too. She imagined herself on the little stage, warming up the crowd, teasing with a long intro, drawing them closer with the first verse, and then delivering a wallop with the chorus. But she would never get a chance to play "Devil" the way she wanted to. She shifted away from Lorelei, leaving her toes in the cold.

"So how are you gonna play it?"

"I'll play it like I *been* playing it. I'll give them exactly what they've been lovin'."

Twyla didn't know what she wanted out of this arrangement, or what she could even expect to have. If she could improve Lorelei's performance, it might give her an illusion of control. And to her credit, Lorelei was honest enough with herself that she knew her limits. They did need each other.

As for the fate of the album, she wished for its failure as much as its success. It pained her to see how proud and entitled Lorelei was of a song she only made worse by singing it, and it would be gratifying, if self-defeating, to see the woman's career vanish as quickly as it had appeared. But if all went well, as Lorelei had said, she'd have her pick of Nashville's finest, rendering Twyla useless, and, she hoped, free. She might be allowed to seek out a normal pace of living, somewhere far from Nashville. She could see herself playing local gigs in a mountain town out west, maybe teaching guitar to little kids.

"Listen, I have some thoughts on 'Devil' . . ." Twyla began.

Lorelei made a sound to show she had heard Twyla but wasn't interested.

"You need to work on your delivery," Twyla said.

Lorelei's arctic-blue eyes flapped open and she swiveled her head around to take whatever Twyla had to say head-on.

"What's wrong with my delivery?"

"I think we can make it better. Do you know where your diaphragm is?"

Lorelei sat with her mouth half open, head cocked at a perplexed angle. "Why would you ask something like that? Are you trying to get in my head?"

Twyla pointed at the top of Lorelei's head. "You're singing from here. It's high, it's thin. There's no foundation. You have to pull up from *here*," she said and jabbed Lorelei under the rib cage. Lorelei grunted, looking first shocked, then hurt, then furious.

"Sing out now," Twyla said, tapping her own center, "from right there. Like someone just punched you in the gut, and there's no fight left in you. It should sound like you're digging your own grave."

Lorelei sang out, her voice low and soaked in hurt. She sang like she didn't care if anyone heard. She sang like she had no other choice. When the song was over, Lorelei wiped her eyes and went to the kitchenette, then took a diet pill and drank from the sink. She turned around to face Twyla.

"Well," Lorelei said nippily, "how the fuck was that?"

Twyla considered the benefits of honesty here. Lorelei was not fragile, but she had opened herself up. She searched for a tactful evaluation. Her vocal cords were weak, her instincts were all wrong. She'd never be a great singer. But she *had* made Twyla feel something just now.

"Let me ask you this," Twyla said. "Did you feel different singing it that time?"

Lorelei nodded. Her eyes were pinned to her feet.

"And did you feel me feeling the song?"

Lorelei's lips pressed together, her eyes wet. "I wouldn't have put it so stupidly, but yes, I did."

"Then you did good. Even if you're off-key or you drop your line. Bring the hurt with you onstage, hold it close, sing from the very bottom of it. You can do that? You'll win them over." Twyla, too, was tearing up. Despite herself, she felt for Lorelei. A woman she'd feared and envied, now as gentle and afraid as a lost child. She marveled then at the strangeness of compassion, that feeling of kinship that wraps itself around people, no matter what they've done.

Lorelei seemed to hit her emotional limit and wheeled around to begin the hours-long process of making herself up. Twyla sat back down on the mattress and noodled with a new song over the sounds of the shower, then hair dryer, then products clicking together in Lorelei's makeup bag. She wove these into a sonic fabric and wrapped them around her song. The scents of burning hair and aerosol filled the room and made her think of Mother's elaborate rituals, the Velcro rollers and hairpins, the spritzing and setting, the rosewater she splashed on her neck and wrists and décolletage, the girdle she'd struggle into, followed by a lace-trimmed slip, and finally, the garment, pressed and tidy. A final kiss of lipstick sealed the look. Like a circus, she would erect herself each morning and dismantle at night, only to do it all over again the next day. It was the one part of Faith's old self she brought with her to the church. And in that sense her rituals soothed Twyla as much as they seemed to do so for her mother.

She wondered, then, what her sudden departure had done to her mother. Had she kept her room the same? Did she miss their moments together? Or had she carried on, refused to mention her daughter's name, as if she'd never known her at all? At this, she felt the truth punch her in the ribs.

And a sweet sorrow of loss and tenderness awoke in her breast, a humble feeling, a knowing that she wanted more than anything to just be special to someone. With this feeling, she took up her guitar and wrote slowly, giving the verses and their melodies time to emerge.

"Would You Still Love Me?"

You can fit your hands around my waist,
My blue eyes set your beating heart aflame.
When we make love you lose yourself in every part of me.
But if I weren't pretty, would you feel the same?

Would you still love me?

Once she had the main idea and a melody she liked, the following verses came easily.

When Lorelei emerged, beautified, Twyla played it for her. Lorelei stretched out on her side and watched and listened, a thumbnail between her teeth. When the song was over, they lingered in the silence. After a few moments Lorelei caught Twyla's gaze and nodded. They had their last song.

CHAPTER 49

There was nothing to gain in going to Lorelei's show at Tubb's and quite a lot to lose, but Twyla's curiosity got the best of her. She touched up her cheeks and lips with Lorelei's rouge and lipstick and rubbed some blue shadow over her lids. She found a suede poncho that covered her and kept her warm. Under that she wore her old pedal pushers and a borrowed pair of black cowboy boots that just fit with a clump of tissue in the toes. Just before leaving she added a black cowboy hat.

At a quarter to midnight the record shop was packed. She muscled through the crowd, glancing over at the counter where Chet had first offered her a warm beer and a chat when she'd needed it. Strangely the memory was still fond, unmarred by all that followed. She wondered how her life would be different if she had arrived a few minutes later to find Tubb's closed that first day in Nashville. Or if the rockabillies hadn't booked a gig in Atlanta and left her behind. Maybe she would be back in her childhood bed, or on a mission to El Salvador, or somewhere else entirely. She shuddered. Soon she was jostled deeper into the crowd toward the booming speakers.

Lorelei took the stage in a yellow jumpsuit with a V so deep you could see where her breasts rested on her ribs. Every man close enough to see her was looking like he wanted to slurp her through a straw, and the women were looking mad at their men. The emcee announced her. The house band started up, a little pluckily, for Twyla's taste. Then Lorelei turned back and whispered something to them. They started over from the top, this time with more sobriety. *Good instinct*, Twyla thought.

Then Lorelei moved toward the mic. Twyla felt nervous for her. As she sang the opening verse, the chatter did not die down. *Too high*, she thought. *You're singing too high.* Lorelei did not seem to notice, but still the audience carried on. When she finally sang the chorus, people started to pay attention. The man who had brought her onstage put down his drink and waved off the man he was talking to so he could listen. A young woman in front started to sing along and a few others joined her. The crowd tightened around Lorelei. As she pulled from the energy of the audience, her voice naturally sank into her body. Twyla watched as she dug down into her pain and pulled it out by the root.

The audience was in love.

The sight of all these bodies, these hearts, yearning toward music *she* had created was a thrill that verged on terror. And Twyla, who had clung to her talent in the face of Lorelei's blinding everything, watched helplessly as her one advantage slipped away.

Twyla ducked out the door into the cold, vibrating. She regretted helping Lorelei. At the time it had felt like a matter of pride. She could not stand to hear "Devil" butchered. Now it felt like she'd signed over the last of her powers to Lorelei. She was about to cross Broad and head back to the apartment to wallow when someone snagged her by the wrist.

"You're just like a little kid, you know that? Hiding behind a pole, thinking nobody can see you." Lorelei smiled. "I can see you, Twyla. Don't think I can't."

She had a proud, playful air. Twyla knew that feeling. She'd had it exactly once, onstage at Irma's, barely an hour before climbing into a boat with Chet.

"You really shouldn't have come," Lorelei said, a bit breathlessly. Then a giving smile brightened her face. "So why am I so glad you did?"

This unexpected praise brought some color to Twyla's cheeks.

Lorelei tipped her chin toward the stars, extending her long, beautiful neck. "Well? You haven't told me what you thought yet," she said. "How did I do?"

There was a part of her that wanted to take her entire performance apart. Lorelei had just stolen her dream and lived it, owned it, better than Twyla. But Twyla could not lie and, against all logic, had come to care for Lorelei too much to tear her down.

"You nailed it."

Lorelei looked over Twyla's head, and her eyes brimmed. And then she leaned down and hugged her. Twyla was so caught off guard she became emotional at being touched, at the smells and textures of another. She was taken in, held, wanted. The feeling existed out of place and time, beyond the circumstances that had brought them together—that however awful Lorelei had been, however twisted the arrangement, however gruesome the secret between them, that kindness could still exist here.

Lorelei pushed away and held Twyla at arm's length. "I wish you could sing it with me," she said.

Twyla was certain she was joking, but then, as if taken by the surprise of her own idea, Lorelei clapped her hands together.

"Cass . . . do you think it would work? What if I brought you in for a private session?"

"That's— No, it's playing with fire." Of course she would give anything to be in that room, to be part of this record, but it was cruel of Lorelei to give her hope.

"You won't have to say a word. Just sing. It just might work. The label—they're crazy about the other songs."

"You played the other songs for them?"

"Honey, I *recorded* them. Every one but this. Did you think I was just waiting around?"

Twyla was hurt and angry. Each word, each note had come from her. To have no control, no say in how these songs were realized, was a physical pain that started at her core and radiated outward, that mangled her voice. Even if it had to be, it wasn't right.

"You should have told me," Twyla said, her cheeks hot. "Why didn't we rehearse before you went in? I could have helped you. Now I have no idea what you did in there. For all I know you ruined them." As soon as she said this aloud, she considered the possibility that the label, for all their optimism so far, might not sign Lorelei.

Lorelei looked hurt now.

"I didn't screw it up. I just told you, they're crazy about it. I didn't want to say until I was sure," Lorelei said, now looking humbled, or regretful. "They're announcing the deal on Monday."

Twyla felt suddenly overwhelmed. Elvis Presley's label was signing Lorelei for an album Twyla had written. She would be a Nashville songwriter. That deal was hers to be proud of, but the night felt suddenly cold, and she was seized with a desire to be unconscious. There were no words left, no feelings, nothing to be done but go home, slide under a blanket, and fall asleep.

CHAPTER 50

Struthers stopped by the payphone to check in with her answering service. She'd been mulling over the encounter with that rode-hard woman from Radnor Lake, Mimi Dewitt. Twenty-seven calls to that number, yet there was no known connection to the victim. And the woman's re-action, the *panic*. She'd asked Cortez to run her through the system and learned she had a rap sheet but nothing alarming. She'd done some time for drugs, so maybe she was Chet's dealer? Even then, the intervals didn't check out. Nightly calls for several weeks, then nothing for a month lead-ing up to the murder. He'd have to have been using pretty heavily. And the only substance the autopsy found in his system was alcohol.

The phone booth smelled of piss. Ellen greeted her, not with the usual professional pleasantries, but by asking her if she was sitting down.

"I'm in a phone booth, Ellen. I can't sit—"

"Detective." She said it as if she could hardly believe herself the words she was about to say. "He finally called."

Struthers wedged herself in the corner of the booth for stability. *Franky.* She pressed the receiver hard up against her ear.

"He just left a number," Ellen said. "Are you ready for it?"

She patted her thighs for the pad and pen she always kept next to her wallet, but they weren't there. Her rear pockets were empty, too. Could she have left them at home? She told Ellen to hang tight and skipped over to her car where she was certain she had just seen a pen sticking out from under the curling floor mat. She retrieved the ballpoint immediately, its plastic crushed and shattered, and dumped her sack lunch onto the seat. Then she brought the paper bag and frayed pen to the phone booth and asked Ellen for the blessed number.

But the pen wouldn't write. She shook it, violently, to get the ink flowing. She scribbled and scored the paper, licked the point, warmed the inkwell between her hands. It wouldn't budge. She ran back to her car, searched all over, tearing it apart for a goddamn pen, going mad with it. She ran back to the phone where Ellen waited patiently, if incredulously.

"I'm sorry," she said, short of breath. "I don't have anything to write with."

"Detective Struthers, why don't you just call me back when you find something. The number isn't going anywhere."

"I need it *now*, though, don't you see? He wants to speak to me now. What if he changes his mind? What if I miss my chance?"

"If I read it out to you a couple times," she said gently, "perhaps you could memorize it?"

She did as Ellen suggested, repeating the number several times aloud, but the digits kept getting jumbled in her head, and her airway started closing up. She was hot to the touch and dripping sweat and couldn't breathe.

Cortez would have a goddamn pen. A whole army of matching, reliable pens lined up in his pocket. Where was he when she needed him? Then she felt with fresh remorse the weight of her actions toward him. She was wrong to put him in a position where he had to choose between her and the truth. To hold him responsible for her termination was a greater shame than the thing she'd done to get fired in the first place.

Admitting this to herself brought her a momentary peace. She breathed a little deeper and closed her eyes. When she opened them, she saw the filth on the phone booth window and had, in a stroke of simple genius, an idea.

"Ellen, are you still there?"

"I didn't want to hang up until I knew you were all right, ma'am."

"God bless you. Ellen, read me the number again. It's okay, I'll get it this time. Just go ahead."

Ellen said it slowly, and Struthers repeated it aloud, then went outside the phone booth and with one finger traced the number into the grime on its window. Then she read it, proudly, back to Ellen.

In the mirth that followed her mastery of that one, small task, Struthers had another revelation, one that compelled her to postpone, just momentarily, a phone call to her son. She remembered in a flood of sense memory the Montblanc, the beautiful, silken flow of the pen Mr. Wilton had lent her. How it relaxed in her hand and slipped across the textured, thick paper. It was weighty. Sharp enough, she thought, to pierce skin in just the shape of those odd puncture wounds. And its ink was dark and staining. Could it be? Even in the privacy of her own mind it was a bizarre proposition. Then why did it cause her hairs to bristle?

If a fountain pen were the murder weapon, whose was it? Chet's used against him? Or some other, unrelated person who happened to carry this antiquated, somewhat twee, device. An affectation, really. Could it, she thought with a start, be the *father* who killed Chet? But what would be the motive? Rage? Father-son fishing trip gone wrong? No. He wasn't the type to get his hands dirty. And why would he hire a brilliant (if disgraced) detective instead of letting the Metro police fumble the investigation? He had hired her *in spite of* her sour reputation. He had hired her because she was good, because he wanted to find out what happened to his son.

No, the father was out.

But the pen. The pen was a lead so ripe she could smell it.

CHAPTER 51

Struthers found in the yellow pages the name of the only pen broker in town and arrived at the store as soon as it opened. Samuel Taylor, proprietor of Old World Stationer, gave Struthers a long and serious appraisal upon receiving her at his door, no doubt clocking her day-old sweats and eau de desperation. But she lifted her chin. She had spent enough time mired in the snobbery of her parents' money-poor, education-rich social circles to speak in a language he could understand.

"Mr. Taylor," she said, "I am investigating a crime and am wondering if you can educate me on the finer points of your merchandise." Mr. Taylor's reactions were closely strung—first bemusement, then nervous laughter, then guardedness.

"What sort of crime, if I may ask?"

Struthers approached the glass display between them. She was distracted by an array of pens, gilded, etched, glossy black, and solid gold. The choice of presidents.

She returned her attention to Mr. Taylor. "An unpleasant one, I'm afraid. I'd like to know a few things about your fountain pens, in particular. Are they very sturdy?"

"Yes, of course. They're built for a lifetime."

"And the ink—is it staining?"

"We have dozens of inks with various characteristics, but most prefer this saturated, archival, fade-resistant ink that stands up to water."

He held up a squat little vial. In her mind, Struthers saw three shallow wounds tinged with black.

"This one here." She pointed to the writing end of a silver pen in the case. "May I test it?"

"Certainly." He ceremoniously unlocked the case and set the pen on a blue velvet pad next to a stack of heavy doodling paper. She uncapped it and pressed a finger to the nib. It was much sturdier than it appeared, and she wondered what damage it could do. To know for sure, she'd have to jab one of these into a raw chicken, see what kinds of marks it made. She held it to the flesh beneath her jaw and felt its sharp, thin teeth.

Mr. Taylor's intrigue deepened at the morbid gesture.

"May I ask," he ventured. "Would this have anything to do with the Wilton boy?"

Struthers snapped out of her reverie. "Why do you ask?"

"I've been following the case. And it's just . . . rumors swirl, and . . . well, I hear he was *stabbed*. When I saw you . . . with the pen there, I only wondered . . ."

This man knew something, coming up with that name out of thin air. She raced to assemble the pieces. These pens were for the rich—she had ruled out Mr. Wilton as a suspect, but perhaps he had gifted one of these pens to his son. Or perhaps Chester the Younger was a customer?

"Tell me, have you done business with the late Mr. Wilton?"

He cleared his throat and smoothed his hands down the front of his waistcoat, giving it a quick jerk at the end. "I may have."

Bingo.

"I'd like to see a list of Chet Wilton's purchases. And his father's, while you're at it."

"I'm afraid I can't disclose—"

"You can't *disclose*? Is there some kind of privileged relationship between a man and his pen dealer?"

"No," he said slowly. "It's simply how I do business." Struthers was about to bluff that she would seek a search warrant, when she noticed the slightest shift in the man's gaze, a fidget in his hands that revealed some conflict in the man's loyalties. She closed the distance between them. She could smell the splash of basil and mandarin aftershave common among men like him, men who wore garters and braces, who might not have claim to large sums of money but sure behaved like they did. Men accustomed, but not immune, to mistreatment by the very wealthy.

She moved a little closer. "And how would you describe the victim, Mr. Taylor? Affable? Polite? Timid?"

"He was none of those, I'd say. A touch . . ." He seemed to be at a loss for an apt descriptor. "He was not so much governed by his principles as his father."

She squinted. "Was he unkind to you? Push you around a bit?"

He paused, gauging perhaps the intent behind the question.

"No, no, nothing like that," he said. *Well, come on out and say it, you cocktease.*

Taylor cleared his throat. "He had not, upon his death, settled his debts, I'm afraid."

"Aha," she said, returning the lob. "Mr. Taylor, *perchance* . . . might there be an exception to your privacy policy for customers whose balances were unpaid?"

He met her gaze.

"Perchance," he said with a hint of conspiracy in the arch of his brow. Then he excused himself behind a low curtained doorway and emerged a minute later with a file folder.

"This," he said, "was the work order for Mr. Wilton."

You fusty old dotard, you. Struthers held the slip of paper toward the light. "Two hundred dollars," she said. "For Christ—"

Mr. Taylor intercepted whatever gauche ejaculate was about to emerge from her mouth and pointed at a sentence in the notes section of the invoice. "I think you may find this of interest."

Etched in elegant cursive, an inscription.

For Twyla.

CHAPTER 52

Struthers purchased a vial of ink and the type of nib sold with Chet's pen for testing and left the shop thrilled with the magnitude of this break. Twyla. *Twyla?* How many Twylas could there possibly be in the Nashville area? It was beefy, as solid as it got. A second woman, with a memorable name, inscribed on a mysterious pen that could very well be the murder weapon. This Twyla was a witness perhaps, at the very least, but maybe— just maybe—the hand that wielded the lethal, tiny spear. A pen! A little phallus. Perhaps, she thought cruelly, a poetic end for a man with a questionable history with college girls? An inferiority complex? Struthers was itching to call the Wiltons with this new lead, but their son's funeral was today. A big to-do at Mount Olivet Cemetery.

She hated to think what evidence had been overlooked before the remains were released to his family. Back in her day she had always taken her own set of photographs, separate from those of the coroners. And more often than not she had caught some subtle detail overlooked in their examination. But she had potentially solid evidence on her hands. All she needed was to find the pen and the woman. For that, she'd need cash in hand. But she couldn't approach the Wiltons at the funeral. It would be graceless. Obscene. Even for her.

She considered putting out an ad in the paper offering a reward for anyone able to lead them to a woman by that name. But such a specific, public appeal risked spooking the suspect. She'd need to be stealthy, but subtle. Then she remembered the abused-looking phonebook tucked into a shelf in the booth. *No*, she thought. *If I had a last name, it would be a cinch.* It would take days to look through all the first names in Nashville.

Unless she had help.

If the Wiltons signed off on another disbursement, she could call a temp agency and hire a couple detail-minded gals to work their way through the phonebook. If she could get enough eyes on it, she'd have a name and address by tomorrow morning. But she was clean out of money . . . unless she crashed that funeral. The Wiltons would forgive her for intruding if it meant advancing the case. She was sure of it. This was what she told herself all the way to Mount Olivet Cemetery right up until she heard the howl of a mother burying her son.

Struthers had never been a crier, not until menopause took its torch to all her inner structures and burned them to the ground. Still, the bouts of tears usually came for baffling reasons: during sappy coffee commercials, when a young person held the door open for her, an old man struggling with a button. Today, sitting in the cemetery parking lot in the familiar embrace of the Beetle, with the Wilton boy's funeral as her trigger, she cried for the right reasons. For the loss of her partner, Cortez, for deceiving him once again to serve her own ends. For the career she had sacrificed everything for, and for being a shitty mom. She allowed herself these tears, long and messy, growls of injustice, fists hurled at the upholstery, sending up billowing clouds of dust.

When her jagged breaths had smoothed, and self-pity exorcised, she looked in the mirror and admired the post-cry swelling in her face, how it smoothed the wrinkles around her eyes and contoured her cheekbones, amused that her minor breakdown had left her looking less haggish.

Then, on the subject of hags, she thought of Mimi Dewitt. Maybe she hadn't been spooked because of her past—maybe she knew just who Struthers was and why she was there. She wondered how she would react to the name *Twyla*. Was she protecting the girl? Hiding her, even? She had to go back to find out.

She consulted the phonebook she kept in her car for Twyla Dewitt but found none. Maybe the girl was a niece or a cousin or simply wasn't listed. She'd have to figure out another way to get the woman to talk. Or open the door, even. Certain she couldn't use the census trick again, she dug her old Police Academy badge out of the glove box and tucked it into her pocket. The department had stripped her of her real badge but hadn't asked for the one issued by the academy. Apart from the words TRAINING ACADEMY in all caps, it looked very much like the real one. At a glance, in the second and a half most officers spend flashing their shield, you couldn't tell the difference.

She left the cemetery and drove to the modern house in the woods again. A Mercedes was just starting to leave the property and tooted his horn as she drove up. She parked and approached, keeping a safe distance, and flashed her badge. The man was decent looking but had a weaselly bearing. He said he owned the place but didn't live there anymore, and his ex-wife wasn't home. That he knew a Twyla Higgins, she'd lived there from mid-August to mid-November, that she had helped out with Ollie.

Struthers did a little jump on the inside at this confirmation. She noted the last name, Higgins. "How old was she?"

"Early twenties, probably. Moody disposition but she was good to Ollie, and he loved her to pieces. Strong swimmer, too. Saved his life one time. Is she okay?"

"She's fine. I think she might be able to help me with a case I'm working."

This seemed to ease the man slightly. Casually, he asked if Mimi was in trouble.

No, she wasn't, not unless she was harboring a criminal. But she didn't say the last part.

"Do you happen to know where Twyla was on the evening of October twenty-fourth?"

Dean thought for a moment. "No, no, I wouldn't know that. What day of the week was it?"

"Monday."

"Sorry. All I can say is Ollie is with me Monday nights. So she wouldn't have been watching him."

"And what did she look like?"

"Huh. Now that you ask me, I'm having a hard time bringing her to mind. Unremarkable, I guess. Plain. Long hair, curly. A little plump for my taste."

Struthers bit back a retort about his choice of the word "taste."

"And do you know why she stopped working for your ex-wife?"

He paused, tipped his head to the side in thought. "It's funny, I usually keep track of these things, but I can't say that I do."

"Falling out with her boss, perhaps?"

"I'm sorry, I just don't know." He fidgeted with his house keys. "Listen, I just came to pick up my mail. Gotta go. Will that be all, miss?"

Miss. She cleared her throat. "Detective."

Without acknowledging the correction, he dipped into his car and raised a palm to the window. Not a likable man, but a helpful one. He had given her a last name, confirmation that Twyla lived in the home, that she was a little younger than Chet and could reasonably be the one receiving those twenty-seven calls from him in the evening hours. He had given her a rough description of the suspect, and one detail she hadn't asked for—one that on its own was useless, but taken with the whole of the case just might be useful. She was a strong swimmer.

CHAPTER 53

Struthers was hot, and she was getting closer by the minute, but she needed to massage these new bits of data. She decided to try a trick she sometimes used when she got stuck on a case, something she had learned from a much younger lover. Meditation. When she got home from Mimi Dewitt's house, she kicked off her Top-Siders and got down on the floor, crossing her legs. Then she closed her eyes and hummed to clear the air. At first, the stillness led to confusion. All the complications of the case frothed up and spilled over, a chaos of images, dates, names, relationships. The victim's naked pelvis, engorged and eaten by river life; the Montblanc, its surprising weight; Lorelei Ray on the radio, the song— the song! Why couldn't it be Lorelei? So tidy. So obvious. *For Twyla,* Twyla, that name, like an Appalachian river creature preying on naughty boys by the water's edge. The water, the river. The Cumberland River. Strong swimmer. Strong enough to drown a beast like Chet? Plain Twyla with handsome Chet. Motive, motive. What's the damn motive? It was in there somewhere. Plain girl, hiding in plain sight. A face no one would suspect. A face no one could love?

Again, her brain felt crowded. She hummed. Suspect: Twyla. Weapon: pen. Place: the river. *What is this, Tricia Lynn, goddamn Clue?* The pen that nicked his jugular was one half of the murder weapon. But the cause of death was drowning. The river was the other half. And she had to figure out where to place him. She could revisit the private boat

owners along the river. She could recanvass the businesses with a picture of Chet, though by now everyone had seen him on the news, so any
memory of him that night could be manufactured, an accidental mental
implant. On the night of the murder the marina had been closed and the
owner gone, so police hadn't done much more than gathered a statement
from the owner and canvassed the building and its property. But the
marina had access to the river and was close to where the Bronco was
found. A buoying energy lifted her upright. Her thoughts grew clearer.
Her mission more succinct.

Link him to the marina.

THE NEXT MORNING SHE RETURNED to the marina. There were a few
empty slips and the rest were filled with candy-colored rowboats, a few
with outboard motors, and two with fringed canopies. The smell of
bug spray and river muck was heavy despite the cooler weather. Amid
the intermittent calls of loons and the drone of traffic beyond the trees
she could hear the *tack tack tack* and grind of an electronic calculator.
She found the owner, a man older than she, wedged in his galley office
behind a screen door.

"You looking to rent a boat?"

"I'm not here to rent, but we spoke a few weeks back."

"P.I.," the man said and popped out of his chair, releasing a metal
screech from the chair against concrete. "Sure, I remember. How can
I help?" he said. He took his hat from a hook and stepped out to join
Struthers.

"I understand you weren't here the night of the murder," she said.
He nodded. "And that the marina was closed for business, is that right?"

"That's right."

"I'm coming back to you, sir, because of this location. Do people rent
out your slips, by any chance?"

"No, ma'am, all the boats here belong to me. I never liked the idea of
people coming and going while I wasn't here."

"I see," she said, mentally crossing that possibility off the list. "Hmm." The man seemed to want to help her out. She could see him thinking, scraping his memory for something.

"Is it possible," she asked, "that someone took a boat while you weren't there?"

"No, ma'am, all the boats were there, right where they should be, when I came back."

"But what if they put the boat back?"

"Come again?"

"Do you remember anything out of the ordinary when you came back that day—when was it?"

"October . . ."

"Twenty-seventh. Yes, try to remember that day. Were there any objects left behind, anything missing or anything at all that caught your attention?"

He stood there with a blank look, hands clasped behind his back. "No, I don't think so . . ." He said it very slowly as if he wasn't quite done thinking. She gave him time. It was important to give a subject room to breathe.

"Come to think of it . . ."

"Yes?"

"The knot was kinda funny," he said. "We always tie up the boats when the customers dock. Like this." He led her a few yards away to the dock, squatted beside a cleat, untied the rope and illustrated how to snake the line in a figure eight and secure it with a final loop over the top. "But when I got back, the *Li'l Banana* was tied up around the post. We never tie up to the post unless we're off-site and there's no cleat. So I just figured it was somebody coming in while I was in the office and I missed it. But it was odd. Not like me to overlook something like that."

"Can I see the boat?" she asked.

"It's just over here." He led her to a yellow rowboat on the far end of the marina. On its side in bouncy italics was *Li'l Banana*.

"There's one more thing," he said. "I don't know if it helps, but when

I got back from my trip, I had to hose off all the other boats. Dust, leaves, bug droppings. I'm saving up to build a boathouse, but for now I spend half my time cleaning these suckers out. But this'n here," he said, pointing toward the gleaming yellow boat, "she was clean as a whistle."

Struthers felt that spike of urgency she used to get when Franky was little and a glass shattered on the floor, and she wanted to stop time, freeze everyone in their place, and go over everything with a microscope.

"Sir," she said, as calmly and as gravely as she could without alarming him. "I'm gonna need to take a statement from you. But first I need some time with this boat." She looked at the sky. Charcoal clouds and a damp wind. "Is there any way we can get this thing under cover?"

She ran to her car and got the fishing tackle box that was her data collection kit. She brought out a wad of rubber gloves and struggled into them, then handed a spare set to the marina owner. Together they dragged the boat to the slipway and carried it to a covered area outside the office. Struthers shone her penlight from the nose to the rudder, inside and out, under the seat, in every crevice. She dusted for prints, took photos, scraped gunk out of cracks and bagged it. She documented every step and logged it in a notebook with date and times, in case the evidence was disputed. But there was nothing, on the surface, that she could use.

If the murder, or disposal of the body, did take place in the boat, the fact that the boat was cleaned so meticulously somewhat muddied her theory that the crime was impulsive. But the cleanup did deepen culpability. If it was an accident, let's say, why not call for help? Her guess was, however the murder happened, on some level the killer wanted him dead.

As an afterthought, she removed and bagged the rope. Perhaps, she thought, there was an outside chance of fiber or skin cells where the killer had docked it. As she coiled up the length of rope and slid it gingerly into an evidence bag, she noticed some discoloration. The blackish shadow soaked into the grain of the rope could have been anything at first glance. Mud, guano, tree sap, motor oil. Under the beam of her penlight the splotch took on greater significance. It was, to her eye, some kind of ink.

Her heart pounded as she fed the rope into the bag to preserve any mi-
croscopic evidence and sealed it with a sticker. Then she scoured it front
and back with her penlight and found several more flecks resembling the
first but lighter in color, closer to sepia, and finally, a chain of ruddy spots
that were darkest in the creases of jute and could only, in her opinion, be
blood.

CHAPTER 54

Struthers found Cortez raking leaves on his front lawn like the good Boy Scout he was. He was on a two-day suspension for sharing police business with her—an untimely slap on the wrist that was meant to send a message, as much to Struthers as to Cortez. She could see from across the street it was eating at him. She could take her evidence—the marina owner's affidavit, the rope with the blood and ink stains, the fountain pen invoice and inscription, the phone records and Dean Dewitt's testimony about Twyla—bring it all to the station and take full credit, but she didn't want to leave Cortez behind. He was in trouble because of her.

"Hate me, but hear me out," she called out to him. He stopped raking and straightened up. "I think I cracked the case."

Cortez looked weary and disappointed.

"*If* what you're saying is true," he said, "am I supposed to congratulate you for winning a game you're not even supposed to be playing?"

Struthers took the response as a favorable sign and lugged her shopping bag full of evidence to his front door and waited for him to let her in.

As tight as she and Cortez had gotten during their time as partners, Struthers had never been inside his house, despite numerous invitations from Belén. Here at their Amish dining set, she wondered if she hadn't wanted to see him as a husband or a father. If taking him out every day, putting him—and herself—in danger, required her to see him as independent of hearts that could break if something happened to him.

Or, she thought, with a pang of truthfulness, she wanted to see him as a stud. If she thought of the stack of diapers under his nightstand or the Betty Boop toothbrush on his bathroom sink, she might lose her favorite fantasy.

She spread out the evidence on his dining room table and walked him through every detail. He listened, nodding, eyes steely at first, then reluctant, then curious.

"There's even crowbar marks on the gate," Struthers finished with a flourish. "Owner didn't notice till later because the lock was intact."

Cortez looked at her with reluctant approval. "I'm not gonna stand here and say this isn't good stuff," he said.

"This chick, Twyla, she seems like a rube. Toddled into town, from Texas, for Chrissakes, stars in her eyes. She probably thought she struck gold with Chet Wilton, in more ways than one. I'm thinking she found out he had a girlfriend and whacked him with the first thing she could find. Or maybe he was getting frisky with her out there. In which case she might claim self-defense. But his parents are gonna make sure they throw the book at her."

"Why bring this to me, Struthers? I'm off the case, suspended—my hands are tied."

"Once you show them actual evidence, they'll let you pick it up for sure." She waved him off like he was wasting time even for broaching the topic. "When you're back, I need you to test this rope for the molecular composition of these spots. The black here, which I think is ink from the murder weapon, and the blood, which will match Chet Wilton's blood type."

"And why again?"

"It's all down to the rope. One: the marina owner noticed it was tied up kind of funny, not like they're supposed to be. Two: it has evidence of injury—the blood droplets—and the murder weapon, which I will argue was a two-hundred-dollar fountain pen given by Chet to his naughty lover, Twyla Higgins."

He laid a hand on her shoulder. "Struthers, you did good." *Patroniz-*

ing, she thought. Or apologetic. She rolled out a kink in her neck, already reading bad news on his face.

"Oh, hell. I can just tell you're gonna dump cold water on me and I'm telling you now it's not going to work. This is an airtight, gold nugget of a case."

"Don't get me wrong," he said, "I think they have a shot at convicting with all this. And I thank you for bringing it to me first."

"Oh, for Pete's—" She couldn't believe it. She stood up and started collecting her case files, shaking her head *no, no, no.*

"And when I bring it to the captain, I'll feel out the situation, see if it makes sense to tell them where it came from."

"Where it came from—? He'll know who it came from, he already knows we worked the case together. Can't you see? I want back in. This is my ticket. Please don't mess this up for me." She was begging. It disgusted her how wrong she had read her partner. The suspension really must have done him in.

Cortez took two steps back, putting distance between him and Struthers, and crossed his arms. When he spoke, his voice was mental-ward calm.

"Who knows, maybe we catch him on a good day and he brings you back. But if you want a shot at that, we can't give you credit publicly. We do this behind the scenes. You make NPD look good, you earn points with the captain and we look into expunging your record with HR. But I'm telling you now it's a tough sell. You have to let me handle this. Don't go talking to the press, don't try to do things your way, Struthers. Don't."

"Well, are you gonna make an arrest?"

"Yes, soon as I get all my ducks in a row. I have to log all the evidence, verify your sources, obtain my own witness statements. We have to do this right, or it's garbage."

"What the shit, Cortez—"

"I don't want to make an arrest and then have to cut her loose. Look, you just dumped this on me. I gotta sort through it and see what holds up and what doesn't."

"Christ Almighty, I just dropped a Triple Crown thoroughbred of a gift horse on your doorstep and you're trying to check its teeth?"

Cortez pinned his hand on the pile of evidence. "Leave it, Struthers. Let me handle it. I'll do what I can to take care of you."

Struthers gnashed her arguments between her molars. Short of a confession from Twyla, she had everything they needed and still he couldn't give her credit. Cortez following procedure would be a mistake. She could feel it like a rash. He was gonna blow it. She shoved his hand aside, gathered up her evidence, and dumped it in the grocery bag.

"Struthers, don't do this. I'll have to call you in for interfering with an investigation."

"Call it in, then," she said. Cortez moved for the door and blocked her exit.

"Hopefully I finish solving your case before they bring me in, you backstabbing *pendujo*," she said.

Cortez shook his head and took hold of the bag. "It's *pendejo*, stupid."

They wrestled with the bag. She threw her height into him but he held fast. Low-center-of-gravity son of a bitch. She let go and shoved him aside.

"Take it, then. And don't look so smug. I just don't want you to do something I'll never forgive you for."

Cortez straightened himself out.

"You're doing the right thing," he said, patting the bag of evidence. "Don't worry, okay?"

"Yeah, I'll try not to worry while you go over my work with your fine-tooth comb and run out the damn clock."

She left his house in a huff and locked herself in her car.

"I'm not done yet," she said to herself. They had her evidence, but they didn't have Twyla.

Struthers jammed on the ignition. She trundled aimlessly along the gridded streets of Cortez's neighborhood, hating their seasonal plantings and hand-lettered mailboxes. She rounded the cul-de-sac and rolled down the window. The wind lashed and chapped her face and drowned out the music. She found she could not leave. She was stuck gunning her engine, burning fuel she couldn't afford, nowhere to go but mad.

In obsessive loops, she detailed her grievances. She was on thin ice with the Wiltons, Metro had cut off her only source from within the department, and now Cortez had in his possession the whole goddamn case tied up with a bow, and she had nothing, *nothing*, to show for her efforts. Her whole life felt like a broken bowl, fractured and held together by wet glue.

She slammed on the brakes. The Beetle skidded forward to the smell of burning rubber.

She'd never called Franky back.

"Fool!" she cried. Derelict! He would never forgive her. Never.

Quivering, frigid to the core, she rolled up the window. She cried. She wallowed in regret. She was sorry.

"One thing," she whispered. "Can just one thing work out?"

Then, on the radio:

"*—everybody, you asked for it. Once again, for the nine thousandth time today—*"

Her ears perked in anticipation.

"*I give you 'The Devil Made Me Do It' by Lorelei Ray.*"

The song.

She turned the volume all the way up.

Of course. How could she have missed it? She had been carried away by the trail of evidence. She had followed it—shocking—like a hound tracking a single-scented path. But the song had been right there, the soundtrack to her investigation.

As the opening lines rang out in the cold little car, Struthers felt certain the answer was here in this song. For once her pen and pad were where they were supposed to be, and she scribbled down the lyrics as she heard them. When it was over she adjusted her seat back as far down as it would go. *The devil made me do it.* An imagined confession, a fantasy of what happened to her boyfriend. The fact that Lorelei wrote this song in the first place never sat well with Struthers. It was so maudlin. And to cash in on her boyfriend's death, to put it out into the world before the investigation was complete. Tacky at best. Something didn't fit.

An ugly girl like me. An ugly girl like me.

Most people would assume the kind of person who could take down Chet Wilton would be a man, and a big one. Why had Lorelei Ray imagined the killer was a woman? And why, specifically, a homely woman with low self-esteem? Struthers slapped her horn and scared a passing cat straight up in the air.

It was so obvious she could scream.

Lorelei knew Twyla was the killer when she wrote that song.

CHAPTER 55

RCA made a big to-do about Lorelei's record deal. They sent a car and alerted the press. As Twyla watched her ride away in Hank Williams's red Cadillac Eldorado she couldn't help but imagine herself in the back seat. The reluctant appreciation she had felt toward the album had gone rancid with news of Lorelei's recording contract, and all she could feel now was bitterness. Perhaps it was watching Lorelei spend three hours bathing, painting her face, rolling her hair into bouncy waves, and squeezing herself into a violet leather pantsuit so tight it looked like she'd been dipped in ink. Or hearing her, as she underwent this transformation, sing Twyla's songs in that treacly voice, or how she referred to *Devil* as "my album." Each song was a child she had nurtured and loved, and Lorelei was marching them out in front of the world, claiming them as her own. She had surrendered them out of necessity, but they were no less a part of her than her own flesh and blood. She understood, of course, the deal she had made. The songs were the price for asylum. In Lorelei's eyes, they were never Twyla's to begin with.

Which made Lorelei's kindness to Twyla all the more confusing. Ever since the embrace outside Tubb's, Lorelei spoke more openly, handled Twyla with tenderness. She even made references to their future together. It was almost as if she wanted to be friends.

When the signing was featured on the local news that evening, Twyla couldn't help but watch.

"RCA has a new act, the up-and-coming singer-songwriter Lorelei Ray. Ms. Ray signed her contract to much fanfare at RCA offices this afternoon . . ." Twyla suffered through descriptions of Lorelei's outfit, her former life as a beauty queen, and a brief interview in which she dedicated the album to her late fiancé, Chet Wilton. She was about to charge at the television and rip its cord out of the wall, when the anchor announced the next segment.

"In a related story, the investigation into Chet Wilton's murder has turned up a new lead. Investigators are refraining from comment but a source has told us the victim's blood was found on a boat at a local marina. Any tips or useful information can be delivered to the hotline number below."

Twyla's heartbeat tripled.

"Blood!" she shouted at the television. "What blood?!" Then her whole body locked up, and her mind began to whir through her memories of that night. How could they have found his blood?

Though her struggle with Chet was a frightful smear of images and sensations, she had a precise recollection of the aftermath. She had scrubbed and rinsed every surface, every crack, even the paddles. She'd retrieved the pen and returned the boat exactly where they had taken it from, had laid the paddles in a crisscross to match the others. A quick glance at her guitar and the silver wink inside its hole reassured her. But the fact remained that they had found his blood on the boat. And if his blood was there, some damning trace of her could be, too.

The key jingled in the lock and Lorelei pushed through the door looking dazed and champagne drunk.

"Look," she said, and let a long slip of paper flutter to Twyla's lap. "Thirty thousand, baby. More on the way."

Twyla was still reeling. She couldn't handle whatever game Lorelei was playing.

"You can buy a lot of hairspray with that," Twyla said.

"You ought to be nicer to me. I was thinking you could help me figure out how to spend it."

Twyla drew back. What did Lorelei think was happening here? "That's your name on the check. Winner takes all."

Lorelei rolled her head back like Twyla was harping on a technicality.

"Let's say I'm feeling generous. *Come on*, don't deny it. We're a corvette together, Cass. I'm the sleek body, you're the engine. Can't have one without the other."

Twyla was confused. "You said I was done after one album."

Lorelei's face, her whole spirit, fell. "You want to go, then?"

"That's the plan, isn't it?" She couldn't believe it but it seemed like Lorelei was serious about bringing Twyla up with her. For a moment she let herself wonder about the possibilities. If Lorelei really meant to make her a partner, pay her, there was a chance Twyla could see her dream right up close. She could go everywhere, meet everyone. If they played it right, she might even take the stage one day.

Then she remembered the bloody rope.

"I think they have something on me," Twyla said, her eyes full. Saying it aloud to Lorelei made it difficult to hold back her tears. "I saw it on the news, they found his blood. I think it's just a matter of time before I open the door to a badge and a pair of handcuffs."

Lorelei dismissed it. "I have the only proof and I wouldn't use it against you. Not now."

"But why are you so sure of that?"

"If they had anything real, they'd be here by now. The police know where to find me—they've probably been staking me out this whole time."

Twyla was crying now, getting frantic. "But you still have proof. If you don't need me anymore, what's to stop you from turning me in, or letting them find me?"

Lorelei's eyes watered, too, and she reached out for Twyla's hand.

"What do you want me to do, Twyla? Just say it."

Twyla thought now of Lorelei's promise. That as soon as her album hit number one, she would take the photo and negatives and set them on fire. It was earlier than they'd agreed, but if the cops had something on her she couldn't wait. Lorelei's response would tell her exactly how afraid she ought to be.

"You could destroy the photo. Right now. Light it up and be done with it. If you're right and you have the only link between me and Chet, then you have to set me free." She considered her words before sharing them. She wasn't sure if she could hold to them but they might be worth the risk. "I can't trust you as long as that photo exists. If you burn it, maybe we have a chance."

Lorelei looked surprised, then vulnerable. She seemed to know what was being asked of her was fair, but it meant a voluntary loss of power.

She went to the closet where she slept and pulled the photo out of a little slit in the mattress. Then she brought out an envelope and showed Twyla the negatives inside.

"Here," she said. "You do it." Then she lit up a cigarette and handed the lighter to Twyla.

Twyla went to the mattress and slipped her hand into the opening and felt around for duplicates of the damning image, but there was nothing. She turned the mattress over and inspected all the seams, just in case.

Lorelei set the negatives and the photo in the sink. Twyla forced herself to look, to make sure it was indeed the right image. She held the negatives to the light. Pictures of Lorelei posing in her living room, amateur headshots. A shot of Lorelei onstage. Chet was not pictured in any of the photos. There at the end, the final image followed by a chain of blanks, was Chet, hovering over Twyla, their reversed faces the color of black pearl against the white water. Just as she remembered, Twyla's fist was planted against his neck. She felt weak, her knees liquid. She propped herself up on the counter. That Lorelei had agreed to let her destroy it signaled to her the depth of her caring. Whether Twyla could match her feelings, she wasn't sure. The corner of the photo caught fire and curled; its surface bubbled and peeled, then levitated, before falling, collapsing into ash.

"You know what I see when I look at that picture?" Lorelei said.

She ran her fingers through Twyla's hair, stroking, parsing, fingering the knots. "I see you fighting for your life."

TWYLA COULD BARELY SLEEP THAT night. Even with the photo gone, Twyla couldn't imagine living freely. Lorelei's fantasy of the dynamic duo, so tempting when she had presented it, now struck Twyla as ludicrous. Shameful, even. And it called to mind the curse of her own fantasy making. She wondered how much of what she had felt for Chet was real, or if it was fueled by her determination to believe what she wanted to believe, that someone like that could open up his heart to her. And here Lorelei was, deciding against evidence to the contrary, that the woman who murdered her ex, who she had coerced to write songs to further her own career, could be her friend.

Twyla had nowhere to go, but she couldn't stay here. She could stay at the Catholic Charity or hop on a bus. It was strange to think it didn't matter where she went, only that it had to be far from this apartment. She checked the clock—nearly seven a.m.—and got herself dressed. She laid her old paisley duffel on the papasan and stuffed the rest of her plain, ugly clothes inside.

Lorelei stirred, then pushed herself up in bed. She seemed to take in the duffel, Twyla on her feet.

"Where are you going?" She asked it with a fullness that suggested she already knew, and dreaded, the answer.

"I'm just going out for a bit."

"With all your things?"

Twyla didn't answer.

"Cass, wait," Lorelei said, holding out a beckoning hand. "I'll give you credit. We can change your name, put it on the record. You can sing your songs with me. Please. Please stay. We can make it work. We'll do it together." There was sorrow in her voice, but she was too proud to cry.

Twyla took in her words, and though she didn't believe them, she

CAROLINE FROST

warmed a little at the fantasy. She kept walking toward the door, not answering, not turning.

"I get it," Lorelei said, biting her tears away. "I'll always be the one who stole your song."

Twyla was glad to hear she understood this. Lorelei got up, rummaged in her purse, and crushed into Twyla's hand two twenty-dollar bills. "For a bus or whatever. I'm guessing you're not gonna hang around Nashville."

Of her own free will, Twyla stepped out of her cage and hugged her captor goodbye.

CHAPTER 56

Struthers sprinted down the block to the pawn shop above which Lorelei Ray lived. She jammed the buzzer once, twice, and after an excruciating minute a third time. But there was no answer. The implications of her discovery—that Lorelei had *known* Twyla, even written her story into her song—were dizzying. Had they planned it together? Had Lorelei sent Twyla to do her dirty work? But why? Who were they to each other—friends? Sisters? Lovers? And to sing about the crime, well, it was utterly *wanton*. The motive was still out of reach. There was certainly enough to detain Lorelei long enough to get Twyla's coordinates. Hell, Twyla could be in there right now for all she knew. Standing here in the biting cold, she wished she could call Cortez so she could make a proper arrest, but if she did, the case would be, once again, out of her hands.

She had been waiting an hour when Lorelei slumped up to the door, sucking on a champagne bottle. Eight fifteen a.m. Was she drunk from last night or had she just gotten an early start?

Lorelei yanked on the handle.

"You might need your key for that."

Lorelei flashed an acid smile. She wasn't wasted yet, but looked pretty well on her way. She found her key and stabbed at the lock a couple of times, missing her mark.

"Why do you keep showing up, *sir*?"

Struthers was filled with a kind of hungry joy and a watchfulness, like she'd just hooked a fish that might at any moment thrash itself right off her line.

"Ms. Ray, I'm not a journalist. I'm a private investigator hired by the Wiltons to find their son's killer. They are convinced you did it. I disagree."

Lorelei turned to her, and here Struthers could see her eyes and nose were swollen from crying.

Lorelei seemed to lose strength at that moment and lowered herself to the step.

Call it prejudice, but she hadn't thought Lorelei capable of the complexity of emotion she now witnessed in her features. Outrage, heartbreak, and the beginnings of resignation. She removed a spangled, disco-type handbag from her shoulder and considered it deeply.

Struthers sat down next to the woman, not too close.

She could press her, question her. She could threaten arrest. That she must have known about Chet's murder when she'd written the song. But something told her to wait.

Finally, Lorelei pried open her purse and pulled out an envelope. Struthers waited. The trust was tenuous. There was something important inside. She considered how to act if Lorelei changed her mind—whether to wrest it from her hands and run back to her car. But Lorelei passed it to her. Her downturned lips, the tears in her eyes, the tug on the envelope as Struthers removed it from her hand, all reeked of regret. Self-hatred, even. She was betraying someone she loved.

"Her name is Twyla Higgins," Lorelei said, wiping her arm across her eyes, "and she'll be leaving town soon. I'd check the bus station."

Struthers opened her mouth to offer the girl platitudes like *It's a proud day for justice* or *You've done the right thing*, but Lorelei had already unfolded herself and staggered away.

CHAPTER 57

Struthers sailed over to the police department bearing the beautiful, irrefutable evidence that would reverse the fetid tide of her misfortune, breezing past security, skipping down the hall past scowling familiar faces, and into Captain Russo's office where he was just arriving for the day. She slapped the photo down on his desk.

"No time to explain, but I just solved your goddamn case."

Russo stood to his full, midsize height, tucked in the tail of his shirt, and leveled his dark eyes at the intruder.

"Struthers, what the hell are you talking about?" He was flustered at her sudden appearance, but in the curl at the edges of his mouth she could tell he was glad to see her.

"I've been working the Wilton murder, as I'm sure you know, and I just got a big break. It's going to make you look like hot shit, Russo. All I need is one thing."

The captain made himself busy scraping a streak of Wite-Out off his desk blotter. But she could see his hairy little ears perk up. He was tuned in.

"Oh, yeah? What's that, Struthers?"

"You know what I need."

Russo sighed and swept away the scrapings.

"I can't give you your job back. You went behind my back and teamed up with Cortez just to make yourself look good. I could lock you up for interfering—"

"Interfering! I was helping."

"If I needed your help I would have asked for it."

"Bull honkey. You assigned the case to Cortez with next to nothing, just waiting for an excuse to cut him loose."

"I assigned him to that case because I knew he could get the job done."

"He's good but we're better together. You know that. And you'll keep that in mind when I show you what I have on the Wilton murder."

"We're doing just fine without you, Struthers. Cortez brought us some solid evidence. Just came back from the lab. We think we have a murder weapon identified and we're closing in on the perp."

He was bluffing. She could smell it like the splash of Aqua Velva coming off his five o'clock shadow.

"The labs are backed up, Russo. You're not hearing back from them for weeks. And we *both* know where Cortez came up with the goods."

"Fact remains, whatever you think you're doing for this department, you being involved will put a stink on it." He stole a glance at the photo, paused as he inspected it. Once he had identified the general category, he turned friendlier.

"Look," he said. He eyed her again and weighed his words. "Depending on what you got here—*if* it's as useful as you say—maybe I can send you side work when we're short-staffed. We hire out sometimes. Money's decent, no commitment. Think it over."

"I solved the case without you, I'm not handing it over for you to take credit. Give me the job back. It'll make us all look good. Otherwise I'm taking it to the press."

"I don't get it, Struthers. Why even bring it to me? You could make a hell of a lot more money in the private sector."

"Honestly, Russo?" Her voice caught up on itself. Damn, damn hormones. "I *miss* you sons of bitches."

He exhaled and massaged his mustache.

"Give it to me or go to the press, just don't slow this thing down.

You think you've got the guy? Hand him over so his family can get some peace."

She gave the table a loud rap with her knuckles. "You shouldn't have fired me. You know it. Your boys fuck up all the time and you cover for them. And that guy was a criminal through and through. If that was your daughter he was smacking around—"

"You're out of line."

Struthers held up the envelope. "I'm calling WNGE in an hour. I'm gonna tell 'em how I came to you with irrefutable evidence and you turned me down because of an old beef. How's that for interfering with an investigation?"

"I'll say you were a failed cop and you tampered with evidence to serve your own selfish agenda."

Struthers brushed it off. She had him right where she wanted him.

"All right, Cap'n, you do that. But how's that gonna look when it's *me* hauling the perp to the station?"

CHAPTER 58

Twyla traveled on foot to the bus depot, crying, headfirst into the driving sleet, with only grief to keep her warm. This penetrating, layered, permanent loss. Of her parents, of Mimi and Ollie and now Lorelei. Even Chet. The loss of her dreams and all the songs she had loved. The loss of her self. She sobbed as if her pain could be shaken, heaved out of her. By the time she arrived and asked the teller for a ticket, she was soaked through and spent.

"Where to?" asked the ticket agent.

She hadn't decided where she would go, and the answer she gave surprised her.

"I'm going home."

The teller straightened her glasses. "That's nice, sweetheart, but where's home?"

She was saddened to realize she did not know. Home to Mother and Lloyd? Even when she lived there, she hadn't fit in. And as battered as she felt right now, at least she could put a few chords together, open her mouth and sing.

"What's the next bus out of here?"

The woman checked her schedule and turned it around so Twyla could see.

"There's a nine a.m. bus going direct to Bowling Green, leaves in, oh, forty minutes."

She sold Twyla the ticket and told her where to wait. After using the restroom, Twyla sat on a bench until the bus pulled in, its tires squealing as it came to a stop. She climbed the steps and showed her ticket to the driver, advancing to an open spot in the very front.

The driver closed the door and called out their next stop. As she raised her guitar strap over her head to load it in the overhead compartment, she saw, with a clap of horror, that it had been her duffel, and not Pearl, hanging across her back. She spun around and scanned the aisles and seats, but there was nothing. Then she realized her mistake.

In her rush to leave Lorelei's, the weight on her back and the thick strap against her collarbone had felt like her guitar. An efficiency of the mind. A mistake unforgivable. The bus was moving. There was no turning back, not now. Safety lay ahead. A second chance. She had paid her dues with Lorelei, she had bartered for her own escape. But then—without thinking, she shouted for the driver to stop, to let her out at once. She abandoned her bag, which was filled with things she had never wanted in the first place, and ran from the bus and out into the cold. She dashed across traffic and pounded up the hill, her feet numb and bashing against the toes of her clunky, homely shoes. But she didn't feel the pain or the cold. She only saw Pearl where she'd left her, standing in the corner by the window, waiting. She felt she was flying, legs strong, lungs brimming. She moved so fast she thought Mickey might be pushing her along, so fast she was certain she could make it, could feel the shape of his guitar in her arms.

CHAPTER 59

Twyla had run a half mile from the station when she heard someone call her name.

Her lungs burned and her ribs seemed ready to crack. She slowed down, then stopped, doubled over to catch her breath. A tall woman swaggered toward her, an ID thrust out in front.

"I'm Private Investigator T. Lynn Struthers. Are you Twyla Higgins?"

Twyla found herself nodding.

"Is this you?" The woman reached into her pocket and withdrew a photograph, then showed it to Twyla.

Twyla raised a hand to her cheek. She had seen that photo burn. Every trace of it, negatives and all, turned to ash in Lorelei's kitchen sink. But Lorelei had looked out for herself, just as Twyla had done in leaving. Whatever she did with her face must have confirmed the investigator's question.

"I am making a citizen's arrest on suspicion of the murder of Chester Wilton."

For a moment, Twyla considered running. The woman was not police. Maybe there was a way.

But when the investigator took her firmly by the wrists and cuffed them together behind her back, Twyla found she did not want to run. Struthers turned her around and looked into her eyes. Her expression was not unkind.

"I'm not police, sister, but I used to be. You're about to be in big trouble, so listen carefully. You have the right to remain silent . . ." Twyla nodded, suddenly overwhelmed, and collapsed into Struthers's arms. How easy it was to submit to being taken away. Relief. A breath.

She didn't have to hide anymore.

CHAPTER 60

Twyla kept quiet and tried not to think about what lay ahead. After Struthers turned her in at the station and she had been fingerprinted, stripped, sprayed, and numbered, Twyla got in line and placed a call, not to her mother, but to Mimi.

"Goddammit, Twyla, I've got nothing to say to you. I'm hanging up."

"Mimi, wait!"

Silence, but to Twyla's relief, the call did not end. She could hear cartoons on in the background and imagined a cross-legged Ollie too close to the screen, his stuffed elephant in his lap.

"I'm in jail," she said. She was ashamed to hear it said aloud, but she hoped Mimi would understand.

"I know where you are," Mimi muttered. "They told me before they connected your call. I'm lucky Dean didn't—"

"Look, I need help. I don't know what to do." She could hear her old boss thinking, fighting with Twyla in her head. "Mimi, I'm scared."

"Shut up. Okay? Just don't say another word. I mean it. Not to me, not to the guards, not to your bunkies. Just keep your head way the hell down." The cartoon sounds faded. She was walking the telephone into another room. The door closed. "Here's what's going to happen. They're gonna assign you an attorney. You can't afford a good one, but I'll see if the guy who represented me can request you. He's competent and he'll

give you a fair shake—that's all I can say for him, but it's better than rolling the dice with the court-appointed pool."

"Thank you."

"Listen here, Twyla. That's the last word you're gonna say. Don't even
say hello. Just keep your mouth sealed shut until you talk to your lawyer.
Talk to him and only him. There's snitches in prison, there's people who
want to see you go down. You're a mute, okay? A mute."

Twyla nodded her head. She was scared of this place, and the sound
of Mimi's voice, however gruff, only made her want to run to her. She
thought then of her mother, those long minutes each night and morning
when she would run the brush through her hair, moments she had always thought of as comforting. But it struck her now they were marked
only by the hope of connection. Each time her mother took up that
brush Twyla thought today might be the day things turned around between them.

As she hung the receiver in its cradle her face filled with heat and
her eyes watered. She missed her mother. She missed Daddy. She missed
being someone's child. She blinked back her tears and there was a hard-
ening at her throat. Cold, deep, clenching. Like the way it felt between
Chet's hands, but worse, somehow, with its cause unseen. She could not
swallow it down, nor could she release it. She couldn't speak now even if
she wanted to.

CHAPTER 61

As Mimi had instructed, Twyla kept to herself and didn't say a word to anyone but her lawyer. Brett Copeland was friendly enough and did her the favor of not asking if she was guilty. Some people pushed Twyla around, provoked her, called her stupid, slow, deaf, and dumb. Others were friendly, asked her questions about her life, offered to help her out. They were the hardest to ignore. Her relief at being caught was short-lived. Every night was haunting, an obsession over how she ended up here in a human cage, friendless, in trouble with the law, without even Pearl to keep her company. Did it all boil down to that moment, a flick of the wrist? Or had her trouble started the second she decided to think for herself?

She had only been in custody five days when she received an un-expected visit. As she entered the visitation room, she saw her mother perched on a nailed-down chair, done up like always, a touch thinner, eyes brimming, arms outstretched, and she was seized by an urge to run to her. Her never-good-enough mother was suddenly the best she could hope for. Lloyd stood behind her, hands on her shoulders. The guard made a sound between his teeth that was meant to warn her against physical contact. In a show of obedience, Mother dropped her hands and clasped them in front of her.

Twyla swallowed the lump in her throat, but it stayed put.

"Baby, what in God's name?" Mother said. She looked from the guard to her daughter, to Lloyd, and back to Twyla. "Well, it isn't true, is it?"

Remembering Mimi's advice, she kept quiet. Anything she said could be used against her.

"My God, Lloyd, she's worse than I thought." She looked lost for a moment, then resolved. "Twyla, we're here to help." Twyla teared up at those words.

Mother smoothed her hands across the table. Her cuticles gnawed to tatters. "Here's the deal," she said. "First Tab pooled up some money to retain an attorney. A reputable one, darling. Not this public servant you have. He thinks we have a good case."

Twyla wasn't sure what kind of a case this attorney thought they had when she hadn't even spoken to them yet. Still it was nice to hear. She smiled a little in thanks.

"It's all lined up. He can see you as soon as tomorrow. All we ask," her mother said, tilting her head just so, her eyes pinched in an entreating way, "all we ask is that you allow yourself to be saved."

Twyla sat back against her chair. There was a catch. She should have expected it. Then she furrowed her brows at her mother. *What do you mean "saved"?* she wanted to ask. She had already been baptized.

"I don't know what you've done. I'm not asking. Lord knows I've imagined every scenario. But, Twyla, the Lord forgives all who accept Jesus Christ. You get yourself baptized, *for real* this time. And then you'll get out—the lawyer was quite confident—and come home to us." She looked up at Lloyd for confirmation, then back at Twyla.

Twyla held her mother's gaze, waiting for the rest of the offer. What would happen if she didn't comply?

Lloyd squeezed his wife's shoulders, fortifying her. At his touch, her mother's mouth pursed.

"If after all of this, you still cannot see this as the miracle it is— people digging into their pockets, going without just to help you—if that does not make you want to turn to God, well . . ."

Twyla eyed her defiantly, daring her to draw a line.

"If you won't be saved, then you're on your own."

Twyla slammed down her fist. *But I'm your daughter*, she thought. It was childish, but Twyla hadn't considered that her mother was capable of shutting her out completely just as she had Mickey. She could run away, but her mother was supposed to be there for her, always.

Mother hardened her eyes.

"You don't have one word to say to your mother? After all you've done? Not one apology, 'Sorry for worrying you,' nothing?" Twyla looked down. Her mother manipulating again. Trying to be the center of all suffering.

"I never could talk to you anyhow," her mother said.

Lloyd finally butted in. "Faith, baby, go easy on her."

Twyla pinched up her face, confused. There was a time when they talked, before her father died. Didn't that count?

"I've got some things to tell you," Faith said. "Things I've been meaning to say for a long time. So I wrote them up in a letter." She handed Twyla an envelope, which had been torn open by security and the letter stuffed in askew. Twyla pulled the paper out.

"For heaven's sakes, not now, Twyla." She took Twyla's hand in hers. It was soft, recently moisturized.

"I'm sorry you won't let us help you, baby." She squeezed her daughter's hand as if for the last time. "But won't you let God?"

CHAPTER 62

As soon as Twyla was back in her cell, she ripped the letter out of its already-opened envelope. The first two pages were written on her mother's best watermarked stationery, and the following eight pages were on frayed spiral paper, yanked out in haste, as if she had realized midway how long it would be and economized. Twyla pressed out the folds on her thigh and began reading.

Dearest Twyla Jean,

I tried to do good, always. I tried to show you a righteous way of living. But I haven't been honest about your father. In light of what's become of you, the path you've taken, I think you ought to know. You can be like him, like you always wanted; or you can choose better.

What you need to know is this:

Mickey was a good man until he started drinking. He was always a night owl on account of being a musician. Work kept him out late and road life is tough, I knew all that when I married him. Goodness, my father was a proud alcoholic, so it wasn't like I didn't know how to live with one. Who knows, maybe that's why I picked him. He was the life of the party and everyone loved him, most of all me, but as long as he was drinking, which was most always, he was lazy, forgetful, unreliable. If you found yourself needing him for something serious, well, you could almost guarantee he would not be there. His life was music. It was the only thing that made him push through a hangover and face another day. He stayed out late and left all the running of the house to me, and I didn't mind because that was my kingdom. I couldn't keep him home, but I could manage my homestead. Seems silly seeing it written down.

I wanted an education so badly, but before I knew it, I got pregnant and then you came and all my life just . . . well, it's not your fault, but I gave it to you. I know my story's not special, and it's the way of women to put themselves last, but I guess I hated everyone for it. Myself included for letting it happen. His drinking began to wear on us when you were about four and that's when I made up my mind to get my teaching degree. I took some community college courses, made straight As and got into Texas Woman's University. But the week before I was set to start classes your daddy got arrested in a brawl. Had to pay his fines and come to find out we were three months behind on the mortgage too. He'd been pouring his paychecks right down his throat. He'd been selling things, including his wedding ring, to keep the lights on. I was so mad I kicked him out. He was living in your uncle's garage for the better part of a couple years, I bet you didn't know that.

And maybe it was the grief or maybe because of you, but Mickey straightened up some after that. He spent less time on the road and he fussed over you and bought you things and took you everywhere with him. You missed a lot of school in those days because I didn't have the heart to tell him he couldn't see you. Those are probably the times you remember, seeing as how you love him so much. It got to where I felt all right asking him to live with us again. He could help me watch you while I did a thing or two for me. Your grandaddy found him a job at the packing plant and he was on the straight and narrow. I never told you this but I was taking an accounting class at the community college at night during that time. I don't know why I kept it a secret. Could be I was afraid of what everyone would think if I didn't follow through.

But you remember the day he hurt his hand? He was breaking down a side of beef with a cleaver the size of a windowpane and he hacked his left hand right across the back. He sliced through all the tendons and bones except for his thumb. They wrapped it up quick and got him to the hospital in time to sew it up, but that cleaver was covered with beef blood and a week or two later gangrene set in and they had to remove it from the wrist. You can imagine what it did to him, losing his hand. When he tried to switch and play the other way around, he'd get so frustrated he couldn't stand it for more than a few minutes. I think it broke his heart losing that hand, because with it he lost the only thing he had ever been able to give to the world.

They put him on morphine in the hospital, but I don't know where he got the heroin. His boys wouldn't have done it, they kept their noses pretty clean as far as I know. But he was in more pain from the injury than a fifth of bourbon could ever cure. Anyhow, the reason I kicked him out . . . I'm not sure if you're gonna hate me for telling you or hate me for not telling you sooner. I've been holding this back from you, Twyla, because you loved him so. And it's a cruel thing to rob someone of their hero. But you're grown now, and you can see things in gray.

One day, I had to run some errands in Dallas, and when I came home you were cross-legged on the floor, about six inches from the television screen. I called out for him but there was no answer. Then I checked all the rooms and found him curled over in the bathtub with a needle hanging from his toes. I could scarcely feel a pulse.

I turned the shower on him, ice cold then scalding hot, until he woke up sputtering and cursing like a demon. Made a few phone calls until I could get his fiddler, Bert, to come pick him up and as he was leaving I told him as long as he was using he better find somewhere else to live. Right then I'll say it, I never wanted to see him again. To betray me like that, when I trusted him to keep you safe. It was unforgivable.

What I'm trying to say, why I'm writing you now, is to help

you understand why I couldn't bear to have Daddy or anything that reminded me of him in the house. It made me sick, just sick to my stomach, to think of what he could have been. He wasn't some deadbeat. He was a wonderful man, a loving father, a brilliant musician, who could have given us the world, but instead he gave himself to the drug.

Twyla, I've been praying every waking moment, begging God to help me understand how you could get into trouble like this. I know you could never do such a thing, I have to believe you didn't . . . or if you did, it's not in your nature but some fluke. But it does feel like a cloud of darkness hangs over this family. We've been on this path, and I've been wrestling to steer us in another direction and I'm exhausted. I can't do it anymore. That's why I won't fight for you, baby, if you won't choose a life in Christ. Mickey didn't accept the Lord. He just wouldn't. His God was music, then booze, then the stuff that killed him. After he died, God was the only one who wouldn't let me down.

I know it's not fashionable to be churchy, and I know you probably think I changed when I joined First Tabernacle. But I didn't change. I became more myself, more joyous, more free than I ever was when Mickey was my god.

I pray you'll take this letter to heart. And I can't begin to know God's will, but I will leave you with this, my precious daughter. If you do not accept my offer, I cannot be in your life. I'll be praying for you, loving you from afar, just as I have done all this time.

In the love of Christ,

Mother

CHAPTER 63

Twyla strangled the letter and dropped the pages to the floor. There was just enough kindness in her mother's words to open her heart right before she stabbed it. It was just like Mother to twist the situation to suit her. Make herself out to be some kind of saint, when for all she knew her mother had driven her father to drugs. Why did Faith think this would be helpful, to see her daddy as a strung-out, negligent dad? Mother never saw her part in things. And to coerce her into being saved when she was facing murder charges? How dare that woman demand something so personal, Twyla's surrender, in exchange for support that could set her free? What was Christian about that? What about giving without expecting anything in return?

Now she thought of Daddy and a chest of memories cracked open, from after the accident and the loss of his hand. The grim set of his jaw, eyes glazed, the raw knob he kept stuffed in his pocket. "Tired eyes," she'd call them, not knowing, of course, the real cause. His long trips to the bathroom; the bruising; the sickly, chemical smell. A glut of memories, colored now by what her mother wrote in that letter. She thought of all the times Faith made her feel wicked, bad, perverted. Now reading the letter Twyla thought all the damnation brought down on her was meant for her father, that Mother had chosen not to grieve but to scour him from her heart. The shame, that buckshot to the gut. She had felt its leaden sting every time she stepped outside the lines, asked a question she shouldn't, every time she yearned for touch, for someone to look at her like she was cherished and desired. That old familiar feeling turned over and seemed to push up into her chest, into the muscles of her arms and legs, not hard but molten. Could it be that all this time the feeling she confused with shame, or guilt, was only hot, righteous anger with no place to go? Fury turned inward, hardened to a solid state? Only the act of making music created the friction needed to set it free.

She pictured the moment that night in the boat, then her thoughts returned to her mother, so easy to hate now. To hold responsible.

How am I different?

Like Faith, she turned away from painful feelings, ran from trouble, silenced herself to keep from saying the wrong thing. She'd turned her life over to a man, forgotten herself, traded her talents for love.

How am I different?

I am worse.

Now she thought of that night on the river and held herself to its flame.

A strong moon. An oar to the gut. The boat tipping. Hands around her throat, spit on her face. A small, hard weapon. Fighting back. Thank God she had fought back. She only did what she had to survive. More than once that night he had tried to snuff her out. Lorelei had seen it, too. *You were fighting for your life.*

That was the story she told herself. The one she *had* to tell.

Another story emerged now, as she unearthed her anger. Old hurts, reanimated, clawed and clambered to the surface. The feeling at her throat, the strangling, was not only the pressure of his hands but a lifetime of protests withheld, of opinions swallowed, a whole book of music unsung.

CHAPTER 64

It was just after Christmas, and Twyla's attorney appeared before the glass window, looking hale and happy, and spoke into the phone.

"I have some news that I think you'll be pretty pleased to hear," Copeland said. His bow tie was slightly crooked, and the lump of his belly strained his shirt buttons.

"I have something to tell you, too." The feeling in her throat was gone. She felt serene. She had even begun to imagine making a life here in prison, the books she would read, the songs she would write.

"You're going to want me to go first," he said, his eyes wide like he couldn't believe what he was about to say.

"The DA is dropping the charges."

Twyla went very still. She asked him to repeat what he'd said. He said it again.

"They have exculpatory evidence," he said. "There's no case."

He looked giddy. She couldn't put his face and the words he was saying in meaningful order.

"How can that be?" Copeland seemed irritated at her lack of reaction. He repeated himself.

"Twyla," he said, softly now. "You're going home."

Home. The word landed strangely in her ear. Had she heard him correctly? The visitation area was unusually loud. An inmate was yelling at her husband, and an infant cried so pitifully from her stroller Twyla could hear it through her attorney's receiver.

"Going home? But how?" she asked. He'd already told her the prosecution's case was said to be strong. The marina owner's testimony. The photo. The bloody, inky rope. She couldn't imagine a way out.

He slid two pictures in front of her. One was the blackmail photo. Chet hovering over her, her murderous hand upon his neck. She turned away. Knowing Lorelei had turned her in was painful enough, but seeing the shameful image in the hands of her lawyer felt like a new violation. The other photo was from the crime scene. She willed herself to look, though her insides bucked and twisted. Chet laid out on a tarp, waterlogged, his whole body a bruise, skin shedding from muscle. His pants around his knees, filled with twigs and river muck. There was a slip of paper taped to the photo over Chet's face.

"Why would you show me this?" Her throat went dry, her stomach unwell. "Just tell me what the hell is going on."

The attorney raised his eyebrows and smiled slightly, like the best was yet to come. "Look at his hair." Then he sat back and waited for lightbulbs.

She leaned over the two images. In the autopsy photo, his hair was closely cropped, trimmed with tiny snips around the ears. He'd had it slicked back that night. In Lorelei's photo, taken what looked to be twenty feet away, his hair looked the same, though the image was grainy and in the light of the flash, which made his face recognizable, his near-black hair blended into the darkness.

Then she saw it.

A long, wavy strand cutting his cheek in two. Now she looked more closely, held the image to the light. It was faint, but she could see now his hair was not short but long and gathered up in a rubber band.

The blackmail photo wasn't taken on the night she killed Chet.

The realizations staggered in, one after another. The night they first made love, their first time in the little yellow boat. How his hair kept drifting into her kisses and she'd given him her elastic, a ratty, stretched-out pink one she wore around her wrist. One her mother had tied into her hair the night she left for Memphis. And then, the flash. A pop of light she could not place. At the time she had thought it was a sudden flooding of her senses, pleasure made visible, a celestial wink. A chill skittered up her spine and across the tops of her arms as she transposed onto that memory the image of Lorelei, clandestine, watching, pouncing with a pulse of her finger. Then she recalled how, earlier in the evening, Chet had seemed shaken, had confessed to having had a fight with his bandmate. Now Twyla understood. While Twyla was planning on giving herself over to him, Chet had fought with Lorelei, stormed off, and met with Twyla, allowing her to think she was the only one. Furious, Lorelei must have followed him to Mimi's, then the marina, and all the way downriver. One part of her story had been true. She had brought her camera to catch him in the act.

Then another sudden drop in her stomach, as she realized that Lorelei never had anything over her. Had she taken more time with the photo, Twyla would have noticed the wisp of hair. She would have told Lorelei to get lost and made her way out of town, returning home or starting over with her guitar and the gift of a second chance.

"Their case is weak, Twyla. They've got nothing."

"Nothing?"

"Not enough to convict. As soon as the photo is authenticated, they will undoubtedly drop the charges."

"What about the stains on the rope?"

"It's still circumstantial. O-positive blood type. It matched the victim but one in three people are O positive. Could be anyone's, a nosebleed. The photo ties you and Chet to the boat, but not to the boat on the night of the murder. Sixteen people had rented the yellow boat in the month leading up to the murder. Any one of them could have nicked a finger and bled onto the rope. The marina owner was gone the night Chet died, and he wasn't able to say when the crowbar marks happened to his gate. The DA won't try it. There's no witness, no murder weapon, nothing to locate him or you when he died."

He waited for her to join him in celebrating this unfathomable turn of events, but she couldn't switch gears so easily. Moments before she had been ready to accept her life behind bars.

"There's more," he said, with a kind of prurient relish. "Turns out there are now allegations from a Vanderbilt grad who accepted hush money from the Wiltons to terminate her pregnancy."

Twyla felt sad but not surprised.

"It's materially irrelevant to the case, but it does shift the public opinion."

"Public opinion?"

He flopped a copy of *The Tennessean* in front of her. "THE DEVIL MADE HER DO IT: KILLER PICS SHOW WILTON MURDER" above the blackmail photo and a leaked mug shot of Twyla, eyes puffy, hair spun wild around her shattered face. Twyla scanned, picking up bits of information.

Below the fold there was a smaller article on Lorelei, how she rose to fame on a song that accurately imagined her fiancé's killer. A quote from Lorelei: "I suspected he'd had someone on the side, but my song was just a fantasy. I had no idea I was so right. I wish I weren't."

"Sorry to have to show you those, but I thought you should know. But don't worry. Once you're cleared they'll be singing a different tune, so to speak." He pushed up his glasses and snickered at the turn of phrase. "The investigator who arrested you—you remember—she's protecting her source, so we don't know who took the photo. I expect they'll keep looking into Ms. Ray. It's just too uncanny she wrote a song about his murder before anyone knew he was dead." He shivered. "Eerie. But you gotta admit," he said as he packed up his things, "it's one helluva song."

CHAPTER 65

Twyla burned up in her bed that night. Though her bunkmate had rolled herself into the covers to keep warm, to Twyla the cell was a kiln. She kicked off her sheet and then removed her pants and top and wadded them under her bunk. Even naked, she sweated into her mattress. Her insides felt like a churning, overheated engine. Metal grinding metal, sparks and hot grease. No part of her could rest. Her fingers tapped an anxious rhythm, her heels scuffed shallow trenches into the bed, her mind whirled and snapped from topic to topic. The news that she would be set free had had the strange effect of dashing her hope into pieces.

How could she just carry on living with the knowledge of that night, the sounds and sensations ricocheting through her body? The light suck on the pen as she pulled it out of his neck and sank it once more into muscle. Another sound now, one she only just remembered. Something he'd said when the first blow landed. He'd looked at her, not frightened, but confused. "What?" he'd asked her, as if she had mumbled and he hadn't understood. Had he meant *Come again? One more time?* No, it was more like *How can this be?* His sense of what was possible now expanding to include sweet, passive Twyla jamming a sharp object in his neck.

Until this moment she had clung to his aggression, framing the stabbing as self-defense, but there was more, she could feel the details she had avoided, could sense herself now yielding to their truth. His grip relenting, shifting to her shoulders. Words of concern. He had checked on her, snapped out of his trance and seen the fear in her eyes *before* she brought up her hand. She had struck just after the moment he realized he was hurting her. While his hands were around her neck she was a victim, but as soon as his rage withdrew hers flooded in its place. He was the target of her outrage, a vital fury that she had framed as self-preservation. He had misled her, lied to her, squandered her heart. He'd taken her out alone, undressed her, insulted her, then when she dared speak up he had walloped her with the oar and wrung her neck. He'd left bruises to prove it. Should she have tried harder to save him? No. She had every right to save herself, even if he showed remorse. What was she supposed to do? Simply lie there and be grateful for his change of heart? Scurry away to safety? No, as soon as she was able, she drew up her fury, sharpened it to a fine point and drove it into his throat.

She obsessed over the new insight, her rage, landing always on righteousness. She was right to protect herself, she was right to use force. He deserved to die. But each time she considered her imminent release, she returned to the most pressing question.

Did she have the right to be free?

In singing "Devil" at El Toro she had sunk back into herself, finished what she started when she left for Memphis. She was compelled to take back her ballad, because it was the only way to restore order. She had killed a man and tried to get away with it. The story, and the blame, belonged to her.

The song had been stuck in her throat since the night she vowed not to sing it again, instead being forced to listen to its false cousin, from radios and windows, a perversion of her words, toothless in another woman's mouth.

Now she struck up a beat on the tops of her thighs and hummed the opening hook.

Then, she sang.

She sang out what she had done, a tale so much a part of her it was etched in bone. She sang the opening verses and could smell the old car-

pet and warm armpits of First Tabernacle, could feel the risers bending
beneath her feet:

> *I grew up in the church, singing in the choir,*
> *"Praise your Father's name, and blessings He will bring."*
> *But Mama showed her love by telling me I'm nothin'.*
> *"She may be ugly, but at least the girl can sing."*

Then she was falling in love with Chet, the epiphany of sexual desire
matched and returned, the shamelessness of being with him anytime,
anywhere. She felt even now the hunger alive and rasping for him, or
someone. The jolt of seeing him onstage with Lorelei, her impossible
beauty, the cold realization that she could never be enough.

> *Then I met a man, thought he was an angel,*
> *He told me I was pretty, so I gave him everything.*
> *He must've told his girlfriend something even sweeter,*
> *'Cause when I saw her kiss him on her finger was a ring.*

> *I should have faced the music,*
> *But I just ran and hid,*
> *The devil made me do it,*
> *The devil made me do it.*

> *I never meant to hurt him, just to write a love song,*
> *He reached around my neck before he fell into the sea,*
> *Even if I'd saved him, what's the point pretending,*
> *A guy like that could love an ugly girl like me.*

> *I should have faced the music,*
> *But I just ran and hid,*
> *The devil made me do it,*
> *The devil made me do it.*

The next verse struck her like a burst of cold wind, chilling under the skin. The callousness of her taking this crime and making it into art. And a knowing that this one act might be part of her nature. It was brutal, but true.

> As the water swallowed up the only one who'd loved me,
> I fell upon my knees and prayed He'd understand.
> And I opened up my mouth, and belted out that love song,
> And then I wrote it down on the backside of my hand.

And as the chorus "the devil made me do it" passed across her lips, it changed, righted itself, shifting the blame where it belonged.

> I should have faced the music,
> But I just ran and hid,
> The devil didn't do it . . .
> I did.

She went on, buoyed—liberated—by the truth.

> Most days I am sorry,
> and sometimes I just ain't,
> But one thing is for certain,
> I'm nobody's saint.

> All the prayers I've spoken,
> All the hymns I sang,
> Won't amount to nothin'
> The day they watch me hang.

> The lawyer says I'm innocent,
> Just a helpless kid,

The devil wasn't there
When I did what I did.

I should have faced the music,
But I just ran and hid,
The devil didn't do it . . .
I did.

CHAPTER 66

Up until the moment Gail Wilton descended her imposing front steps toward Struthers with murder in her eyes, the investigator had slept easy, had practically waltzed through her days knowing she had put a killer behind bars. The fact that Chet had deserved his fate, that maybe his parents did, too, considering the way they'd gagged that poor college girl, could no longer be part of her calculation. Their punishment had been served, and so, too, must Higgins's. The Wiltons had been thrilled at her achievement, had even toasted her at their annual Christmas party, a dull but costly affair with all the caviar Struthers could snort.

The weeks following the Higgins arrest had brought a swell of interest in Struthers's skill set and, to her personal delight, in her story. The aging, intrepid, she-cop-turned-private-dick-bringing-down-a-killer story proved tasty fodder for local news outlets. "Ousted Cop Solves MNPD's Murder Case," read one headline. Another, her favorite: "Lady P.I. Beats Boys at Own Game." The $50K payout from the Wiltons, which would arrive soon, according to their accountant, would be the seed money for her new investigative services, and would allow her to take clients on a sliding scale, help out the everyman. She had even secured, as her office manager, dear Ellen, who was more than ready to drop her night shifts at the answering service.

Now, at her professional zenith, it seemed she was about to hit the deepest bottom of a year filled with bottoms. To hear the vile slurry of epithets coming from Mrs. Wilton's mouth, Struthers might have placed her in a nuthouse or prison brawl, not, as she was today, in a tailored pantsuit, jabbing a freshly glazed nail right where she might point a gun, if she'd had one: squarely over the detective's heart. The truth was, in that moment, Struthers felt similarly enraged to hear the news that the photo, that cherry piece of evidence, the lynchpin of her case, was a fake.

Mr. Wilton laid a hand on his wife's shoulder, subduing her. She wiped the spittle from her mouth, smoothed the front of her outfit, and followed her husband inside.

Struthers came home from the startling exchange to discover a crank call from one of the boys at Metro and a message from the accountant that the massive, life-changing check had been revoked. She closed her eyes, exhaled deeply, then picked up the phone and called Cortez.

A long silence. "You didn't vet the photo?" he finally said. "Just handed it over?"

Struthers opened her mouth, then shut it. No excuses this time. She knew she'd blown it.

"Look, we're going to try to keep it out of the papers," he said. "Metro isn't thrilled about this either."

Struthers knew better than to trust the underpaid officers to keep this under wraps. "That's a nice thought, but this story is too big to hold. We've got hours, not days."

Cortez agreed.

"Just don't let her go, not yet. I need more time—I know it's her. It has to be."

"Struthers?" Cortez went serious.

She bristled at his change of tone. He was going to rub it in.

"Man, the last thing I need is a lecture on procedure, okay? I know you would have vetted—"

"*Shut up*, will you? I'm trying to say I'm sorry, okay?"

Struthers sat back in her chair. Where was this coming from?

"Are you yanking me around?"

"No, listen," he said. "I saw her."

"What do you mean you *saw* her? Higgins? In lockup?"

"Struthers, listen to me. She came to the station. Weeks ago. I never would have clocked her, but she looked, I don't know, messed up. I thought maybe it was a domestic situation. I tried to get her to report but she wouldn't say anything, then she turned around and left."

"You had her in hand?" She jammed her thumbs into her temples. This was big.

"I know . . . *Pendujo*, right?"

She rolled her eyes. "No—don't you see? She came to you, she looked guilty. Cortez—she was turning herself in! You were right there. This is just what we need to hold her. I swear to God if you can get me in a room with her, I'll make her confess."

CHAPTER 67

Twyla's lawyer came back for another meeting the following day. Copeland breezed into the room without greeting her and began talking.

"I know you're anxious to get out but we're almost there. We had one little holdup—doesn't even matter. They'll keep you another forty-eight but they've got *nothing*. I'd be shocked if they release you any later than Monday. I have something in here for you to sign if I can just find it . . ." He opened his briefcase and fingered through a stack of documents in lively distraction. "You are one lucky gal."

"Wait," she said. "I'm not leaving."

He stopped and cocked his head, puppylike, batting his eyes as he tried to make sense of her.

She braced herself. If she kept her mouth shut, she could leave this place and start over, wiser for her mistakes, loaded with purpose. She could love again, have children. Change her name and sing again. She could be anyone she wanted. If she kept her mouth shut. As she considered this life one last time, she had the sensation of hands around her neck, pinching off her oxygen, trapping her voice, only this time they were not Chet's hands but her own.

If she could not sing the truth, she could not sing at all.

"I want you to tell the police I have something they've been looking for."

"Twyla," he said, his merry mood now sobered as he turned his attention to the document in her hand. "What . . . is this?"

"Just read it."

She slid the paper toward him. He held it out and read what she had written. And as she tracked the subtle cascading emotions on his face, her lungs cracked open, her throat unclenched, and she breathed.

CHAPTER 68

Cortez, the prince, stuck his neck out for Struthers and it worked. His account of Twyla's visit to the station provided grounds to hold Twyla Higgins. In exchange for his statement, Struthers agreed to butt out—for the time being. But they just had word from Higgins's attorney that she wanted to speak to investigators, that she'd prepared a statement, which gave Struthers the delicious feeling of a coming break.

Now—*of course* now—she longed for her son. She had treated him like an impediment when she was working, always trying to skirt away from him, unload him on sitters and family so she could do what she really wanted. She had taken his love for granted. Three weeks passed before she finally got back to him. How the case had eclipsed him so instantly, so completely, was a mystery that kept repeating itself. She managed to swallow her guilt and call him back, daily, for a week, until he finally answered. Oh, the teeth she pulled to get him to say hello. So stubborn, so punishing, but she had resolved to be bigger, and kinder, to shove the olive branch down his throat between his teeth if he wouldn't take it on his own. He finally agreed to meet her for coffee.

She arrived ten minutes late, flung the door open, and then stopped, arrested by the sight of her baby beneath the window. Broad-shouldered, like her, complexion Irish white like his father, the mess of his dark hair and the elven point to his ears signs that he was still the boy she

remembered. He was eighteen the last time she saw him. He looked
up. A brightness in his recognition, a loving he couldn't hide. Then he
tightened up and she sat down in front of him. After an agony of small
talk, she finally spoke straight.

"Listen, I'm here with a target on my ass," she said. "Pull back your
bow and let the arrows fly."

Franky stared into the blob of cream in his coffee. "I don't feel the
need to enumerate your failings, Mother."

She smiled in silent amusement, and pride, at the little nerd she had
raised.

"I can take it, bubs. I know you've got a thousand things to say to me.
I'm not here to fight. I came to hear you out."

He gnawed the inside of his cheek, hinting at anger unspoken. Let
him stew. She'd broken a hundred witnesses. Sometimes it took hours.

"Maybe we need an icebreaker, huh? Where you living these days?"

"I'm living with my girlfriend, Liz."

"Girlfriend?" Her eyes pricked to hear he was with someone.

"Yeah, she's a social worker for the county."

"No shit . . . I bet she's seen some things."

"Yeah." He was quiet again and she let him be. He went on. "She's
been helping me understand some things. About how I grew up."

Struthers tensed. This woman was filling out a report on her parent-
ing? From her son, she'd be happy to hear what she'd done wrong. But
from the shrink he was boning? Shit no.

"Okay, give it to me. What, in *her* opinion, was wrong with how you
grew up?"

Franky looked up, maybe surprised she didn't know, or that she'd
stuck around to hear it. He took a deep breath and let it out.

"Murder scene photos at the dinner table."

Struthers laughed. "You loved those!"

"In *kindergarten*? They gave me nightmares. I wet the bed till I was
ten."

Struthers shook it off. She had broken him but now she wanted to put him back together.

"Rolling up to school with your siren and lights flashing just so kids would notice you. You never cared how stupid that made me feel. It was all about you."

Struthers crossed her arms and looked away.

"You asked for this," he said. "Waiting around the station with drunks and criminals in handcuffs. I didn't want to say it then but I was really freaked out. And you left me alone."

"Oh, come on, I—"

"No, see? This is what I mean. You only care about what *you* think is important, and you would glaze over whenever I asked you to do anything outside your idea of fun. Especially when you were working a case, I just felt like I wouldn't exist until it was solved. And then there was always another case right behind the first."

She protested, she tried to talk him out of his position, even as his words pierced her with their truth. Even as she knew how right he was, she couldn't bring herself to tell him so, because it would mean the wobbly scaffolding beneath her would finally list and come crashing down. If she hadn't been right to follow her ambition, to claw her way over the backs of lesser men, to fight for her good name, if all of this had meant nothing because she hadn't been the mother he wanted, then it called every choice into question.

"I'm sorry for trying to be something," she said, stupidly, her sentiment stinking dead on arrival.

Only Franky's eyelids moved as they closed, briefly, wearily, to shut out the lameness of her retort.

"Mom, did you ever think it was possible to do both?"

It wasn't. It couldn't have been possible, or she would have done it.

"I didn't need more time, even," he said. "I wasn't asking for much. It's just when I had you it never felt like you were really there."

They sat there in silence, Struthers doing target practice at the platitudes that came to mind: *I'll do better from now on.* BANG. *Turning over a new leaf.* BANG. *If I could do it all over again, I'd choose you.* BANG-BANG. And Franky simply sat, waiting for her to make it right, sullen, but unsurprised when she didn't.

She would never forgive herself for admitting defeat so quickly but nevertheless set her bag by the door and went to Franky to say goodbye. It was time to go. Some things couldn't be undone. She had been ready to trash it all, the job, the heat, the spotlight, for one more chance to win back his favor, but maybe this wasn't what he was asking for in the first place.

Maybe it was better to return to her life and do what she knew. Leave now and spare them both a messy goodbye. But something drew her to where he sat brooding. She leaned over, hesitated, hoping he would signal whether he wanted her or not. Then she remembered who she was to him. And as she took him in her arms, her whole body lit up with the memory of that movement, the gathering up of his limbs and scattered feelings, the initial stiffening, leaning away, then melting. She felt her size over his, his tenderness, her strength, his need to be taken up by her and held. Or was it now her own need that she felt so keenly, his having expired long ago, after he found a new person to tend to him? She smelled his day-old hair under her cheek, felt the straps of muscle along his back and shoulders, lax at first, then when she did not release her grip, he reached up a hand and lay it on her back. New hope caught fire and guttered in her breast. Her failure was not complete.

THAT EVENING THE CAPTAIN HIMSELF called to tell her she had been right. The Higgins girl had confessed and even told them where to find the murder weapon.

"They found the pen."

"It *was* a pen! I knew it. Where the heck was it?"

"Taped to the inside of her guitar."

"Sneaky devil . . . Was there blood? Tissue?"

"Tissue lodged in the nib, matched the vic."

"And the inscription?" She closed her eyes in wait of those two, sweet words.

"*For Twyla.*"

Struthers pumped her fists like Rocky Balboa.

"I wanna hear you say it, Russo. Starts with a *You* and ends with a *Right.*"

Russo stalled. "How about you come back and work for us again. On a *trial* basis."

She put the phone down and looked up at the ceiling to catch the tears. Here it was. The chance to work with those crooked bastards, to be back in the mix. She could dance. She could kiss him right on his lips. But she thought of Franky and hesitated. Getting back to the department, now that it was being offered to her, wasn't everything.

Winning was sweet, but she wasn't sure now if she wanted to keep the prize.

CHAPTER 69

Nineteen seventy-seven rolled into 1978 and Twyla spent the dawn of a new year in deep reflection. Prone on her bunk, she rubbed a knotted muscle in her neck, one that grew angrier and more punishing as she took stock of what lay ahead and what she'd left behind. How long would she be here? How would it change her to wake up every day to concrete and iron, to sad smells and angry looks, to meals better suited to hogs? She thought of the small taste of performing her songs, the guts it took to walk on stage, the hush as she went to the mic. She recalled the precise moment when the audience went from casual interest to rapt attention. Or when she stopped worrying about her appearance or the lyrics and the music swept her away. That feeling, when time stopped and the song took over, if she could have *that*, she could survive.

But she was here, behind gates and checkpoints and barbed wire. How could she share what was in her heart with the world outside? Then she thought about "Devil," her longing, the torture of hearing another woman sing Twyla's words as her own. And how singing the truth had stitched her back together. Her powers were few, but one thing was certain. "Devil" belonged to her.

When she reached out to Mimi asking for a visit, she figured her friend would continue to ignore her and rue the day she let Twyla into her home. But darned if Mimi didn't come. She entered the room like an angry cat. Guarded and edgy, her eyeliner thick and smudged like a battle mask. She sat down across from Twyla and took up the receiver.

"I told myself I was never coming back to this shithole," Mimi said.

Twyla smiled bleakly.

Mimi's expression moved from defiance to fear to an angry sort of pity.

"Dammit, Twyla, I had all sorts of things I wanted to say to you."

"Go ahead and say them," Twyla said.

"How am I supposed to kick you when you're already as far down as you can get?"

"That's the thing, Mimi, I can't fall any farther than all the way down. Go ahead, I deserve it."

Mimi reached for a cigarette and remembered they had been confiscated.

"Double damn." She scratched at a peeling shard of laminate on the table, gathering her thoughts. "Well, now you went and took all the fun out of it. Goddamn ruined my life and now I can't even chew you out. Dean only allows supervised visits now, you know. Of course he brought the near-drowning and the murderer thing back on me. I didn't fight it, didn't want to put Ollie through the heartache. So now he lets me visit every other day for two hours while what's-her-tits looks on, watching where I put my feet, as if I would dirty or break anything I touched."

"Oh, Mimi . . ." She suddenly felt so ill-prepared. She had nothing to give, no way to comfort her friend. "I don't think I've felt worse about what I did until this moment."

The women sat there together in silence. There was much to discuss but not enough time.

"Listen," Twyla said. "I need you to record a song for me."

Mimi looked up from her pile of laminate, slow and awestruck, as if Elvis himself had just risen from the dead. Then she scrunched up her face with all the questions that statement provoked.

"How—? With what equip—? Why me, I only mix—" But Twyla could see the intrigue flickering in Mimi's eyes.

"'The Devil Made Me Do It' is mine. I wrote that song."

Mimi slumped back in her chair, a sort of amused wonder on her face. "You wrote—" Her head tipped back as she let the realization settle in. "The murder ballad about Chet Wilton. God, of course! Twyla, that song is *hot shit*. How—?"

"Lorelei Ray took it from me, and sang it as her own. Now I want it back." She filled Mimi in, about the song, the empty room at El Toro, the weeks living at Lorelei's writing an album she'd never be allowed to sing. Mimi started to hush her up, worried someone would hear, but she went on. She didn't want to be quiet anymore.

"I'm fessing up now. My lawyer's trying to get the rights back and it's looking good."

Mimi put a hand to her lips and shook her head slightly. "You're confessing to killing that boy," she said. "You don't have to do that."

"It's already done."

"Oh, honey."

Twyla drew close to the glass. "Mimi, I can't survive in here with nothing to show for myself. I want to record the song, and I want you to do it."

Mimi looked stunned.

"My lawyer cut a deal with the warden to let you bring in equipment. You'll have a guard on you at all times. I'll be on the other side of this glass."

Mimi held up the receiver. "You want me to record an album on *this*?" She laughed darkly. "What do we get, forty minutes at a time? It'll never work."

Twyla started to lose heart. Mimi might be right, maybe it was technically impossible. "I just want to get it out, Mimi. I'm not trying to win a Grammy."

Mimi shot her a conspiring look.

"Well, maybe *I am*."

CHAPTER 70

After the Higgins confession, the phone at Struthers's P.I. firm started ringing again. Business grew slowly but steadily, and she even teamed up with Cortez consulting on a new case, a poisoning in the Gulch, this time with Russo's blessing. It was good to be in the fold without all the oversight and paperwork of being an MNPD detective.

In late January, she received a call about a lead in a cold case. A landscaper had dug up a crushed pair of glasses resembling the ones the victim had worn, and she had to get out there before they contaminated the evidence more than they already had. Glancing at the clock, she realized she would be fighting the morning rush hour. Still pumping a toothbrush over her teeth, she called back the number the man had left and yelled at him not to touch a thing and walked him through securing the perimeter in layman's terms. She wiped the foam off her mouth with the back of her hand and hung up. The phone rang again.

"Look, I'm a half hour away at least, just do what I said and don't—"

"Mom?"

Her mind was already whirring, ten steps ahead of where she was right now, working with the PD to unearth the body she was certain lay under the broken spectacles. A smudge of dark clouds on the horizon looked to be racing east and could, in the time it took her to inch through traffic, be dumping rain all over her crime scene. It took several seconds for the sound of Franky's voice to cut through the noise and find her. It was as if she had already dived off a cliff, headed inevitably toward an ocean, and was now tasked with diverting herself backward, defying the laws of gravity and momentum, and meeting him back on land.

"Hi—hey there," she said, stalling. *The evidence would not wait.*

"You busy?" he asked.

She would reason herself out of staying to talk to him. He was an adult, he could handle it, she could schedule a time instead of being caught off guard like this. It was frantic, this need to attend to her work. And only now did it occur to her she might not be running toward her work, but away from Franky. Something slugged her in the gut. She sat down. She pinched at her eyes, now damp with tears. She gulped down her shame and cleared her throat.

"Me? Busy?" she said and in the archness of her tone tried to communicate that she knew why he had to ask, she got why this was wrong, and she knew she must do better. But of course, she didn't know how to say these things, much as she wanted to.

"Franky. I was just sitting here thinking about giving you a call. How you been?"

CHAPTER 71

No one expected forty years. Against her attorney's orders, she had admitted in her confession to stabbing him *after* he stopped strangling her, that she had, for a moment, wanted him to die. The charge was downgraded from Murder One to Murder Two, defined as a knowing killing without premeditation. Still, the prosecutor took her to trial. Twyla's cooperation and clean record, combined with the size of the victim, and the lack of planning evidenced by the impromptu weapon, all but ensured the judge would give her the minimum—fifteen years—or close to it. Her story, her song, had won over the public, and the press. If they loved Lorelei's "Devil," they were rabid for Twyla's. The grit, the simmering rage, and her otherworldly vocals touched women all over the country. That her song had been stolen and used to blackmail her only added to its mystique.

But the judge, rumored to have been cozy with the Wiltons, wielded Twyla's own blade, her song, against her. Whether or not her crime was an act of self-defense, the judge reasoned that she had turned murderer when she failed to report the death and instead wrote a "craven tribute" to her crimes. The judge accused her of exploiting the boy's murder by cashing in on the popularity of the song established by Lorelei Ray. She could have just confessed, he'd said. She didn't have to sing about it.

In exchange for her freedom, Twyla won back her song. She filed a separate suit against Lorelei Ray for the rights to "Devil." She did not ask for money, just the song. Lorelei settled immediately but asked to keep

the other tracks from her debut album and Twyla, in a fit of sentimen-
tality, allowed it. They were written for Lorelei, after all. A few months
after the settlement, RCA released a new version and "Twyla Higgins"
was credited as songwriter on every track.

Mimi came two weeks in a row to record Twyla's first single, now
titled "The Devil Didn't Do It." Lester Buck was in on it, too, and made
sure she got the right equipment. He quietly signed her as his client, then
tipped off a reporter at *The Tennessean* about their plan and pitched it as
a redemption story. The story went national. The headline read: "Killer
Reclaims Stolen Murder Ballad, Admits Guilt, Tops Charts."

The story drummed up a storm of interest, and Lester eventually
brokered a two-album deal with EMI Records. It was so much more
than she could have asked for. The attention won her some enemies in
prison but even more friends, and as long as she sang to the inmates every
Sunday, she was untouchable.

Mimi came to visit every month, even as she grew old and ill. She
recorded and mixed each of Twyla's fifteen albums, the last one wrapping
just two months before the lung cancer she'd been treating finally took her.

Twyla had tried to give it all away, the "Devil" money, every year
divesting to causes supporting the arts, programs that purchased instruments and lessons for children, even bought a bus to take kids in need to
their music lessons. There was so much money she had reached a limit to
finding places to put it, and so for the last decade had let the mountain
grow. Merely thinking of the burden of figuring out what to do with it
tightened her chest. She often wondered if it was guilt, not goodness, that
made her give it all away.

Eventually, Twyla found contentment behind bars. In a way, she had
been in prison all her life. She'd served time in a prison of religion without grace; a prison of shame, of insecurities; a prison of secrets and of
silence. Here at the penitentiary she did not fashion her outsides to be
seen, but rather lived fully in her body, in its rare pleasures, in its hungers,
in its ever-changing contours, and even in its waning abilities. Here she
made music and so was free.

IV

CHAPTER 72

Twyla steps outside prison and feels as though the eyes of the world are upon her. The way she felt on her first day of middle school, the burn on her cheeks, the sweat under her shirt, the conviction that life would not carry on as normal after this great, humiliating, thrilling moment. And yet, there were few goodbyes as she left her cell. The yard is empty, the guards ignore her, even Roland, whom she has known for nearly twenty years, only nods and returns his neutral gaze to the barbed-wire fence.

Advancing toward the town car, her manager, Sherry, takes her arm.

"They're *waiting*," Sherry says, forgetting to welcome Twyla to her new life beyond the prison gates. Sherry is all business. She informs Twyla the press are staked out at another entrance, that they'll be here any moment.

Twyla catches the driver staring as he holds open the door.

"Congratulations, Ms. Higgins," he says. Sherry looks up from her phone.

"Oh, yes, big day, Twyla! Isn't it fab? Hurry, hurry, though!"

Her attorneys insisted she hire Sherry to manage the transition from prison to public life. She will be a buffer, a facilitator, a filter. She has arranged for housing, credit cards, phone service, cable TV, utilities, a car, even driving lessons. Twyla welcomed these dependencies, reasoning that it allowed her to give all of herself to the music, but here in the light of day, with her whole future mapped out by people she paid to make problems go away, she feels more like a child than when she left Fort Worth.

Indeed, she has gone from being her parents' charge to Mimi's, to the prison's, and now to her keepers'.

They arrive two hours early, plenty of time as far as Twyla can see, but based on the blue veins snaking across Sherry's temples and the tone she uses on the phone, they are late. A woman in cargo pants and a headset meets them at a back entrance and leads them through a series of turns to the well-lit dressing room. A comfy chair, a squashed love seat, a dressing table, a cheese tray, and an icy bucket of champagne. Sherry pours two glasses to the brim and hands one to Twyla, toasting somewhat awkwardly to freedom.

There is a knock at the door, and a brassy redhead pokes her face in the crack. "Hair and makeup?"

Over the next hour several people dance around Twyla, fussing, snipping, smearing, to wipe away prison and make her sparkle. When the makeover is complete, she looks in the mirror and barely recognizes this elder pixie.

A sharp bob grazes her earlobes, a cat's-eye flick lengthens her round gray eyes, rendering them mysterious and coy. The meticulous tailoring on her suit is obvious even to her, despite having worn government-issued, one-size-fits-all for the last four decades. But she does not know how to be this phoenix she sees in the mirror. With a comfortable sadness she acknowledges to herself that all that is left of her is the music. This isn't a comeback. It is a homecoming.

Then another someone knocks, and when the door is opened a courier holds out a big garment box tied up in crinoline ribbon. The harried stagehand leans it up against the wall and passes her the tag.

It reads: *Did you miss her? xo L.*

She tugs at the ribbon and lets it fall away, pulls open the brown paper box, and draws aside sheets of tissue paper. Waves of heartache and gratitude crash over her.

Pearl.

Twyla opens the case and holds her daddy's guitar close, smells the old wood and strums its tuneless strings. How like Lorelei to extend a gesture both flamboyant and kind. She wonders what her instrument has been up to all this time. Has it remained in Lorelei's care, stowed in her case until now? Or has it been in some evidence locker, retrieved from a careless clerk? Wherever it's been, unlike Twyla, Pearl hasn't changed. She takes up the old guitar, heavier in her weakened arms. Her fingers, knobbed and curled palmward, lack the calluses she played so hard in her youth to build, but she can really feel the strings and frets now as her hands skate up and down its neck.

"Can you find me fresh strings?" Twyla says to the woman in cargo pants. The woman gives her a quick nod and speaks into her headset.

She knows Lorelei sold her story for six figures and published a celebrity tell-all, *My Story* by Lorelei Ray. They had tried to call it *The Devil Made Me Do It*, but Twyla's lawyers had threatened to sue faster than the ink on the press release could dry. Then, one November in the early nineties, Lorelei appeared in the visiting room like a grand dame of Broadway at curtain call. She stood there in a dramatic winter coat, shiny black hair stacked on her head, lips bloodred. She hadn't come to apologize or even rehash old wounds. She had brought Twyla her cassette tape. With childlike pride, Lorelei explained it had taken her over a decade to write the eight original songs on it. She had even learned intermediate guitar, enough to accompany her own vocals, and recorded her songs in her apartment bathroom. Twyla was amused, but also touched, that after so long Lorelei only wanted her approval. The music itself, which she was allowed to play on the library tape deck, was not terrible. Earnest, literal, thematically a bit scattered. But the melodies were true and Lorelei's voice had acquired a certain luster in her maturity.

Questions remain, of course, and Twyla could spend hours combing over the particulars of their strange union, the meaning of this gift. But today the details don't matter.

As TWYLA WAITS FOR HER call backstage, she struggles to absorb the fullness of the moment. She notices grit and dust underfoot, smells of paint, grease, and electrical parts. The hollowed-out sound of the announcer onstage and Sherry, whispering into her cell phone while simultaneously typing something on it. The milky cone of the spotlight and the bright circle where it hits the floor, waiting for her.

Then she hears her name, just the first, clear as light. Followed by cheers. Her knees lock up. Her voice goes cold. She isn't ready. She gazes, trembling, at the long walk to the stool that waits in the spotlight. Fearing the band she's never played with, the sound check she missed, the new strings that need stretching, the pain and stiffness in her strumming arm. She has been making music for decades, but she hasn't performed, not like this. How long has she dreamt of this moment, this very theater? The Opry. How many heroes have crossed the floor to center stage and sung their songs right into her kitchen radio? Why does she think she can do this? Then, what makes her think she can't?

The producer leans in and says, "Take your time. They'll wait all night for you."

With Pearl in hand she carries all the nerves and fear and upset over to the stool at center stage and sits down. The room gapes open like something into which she could fall and disappear. She adjusts the mic, clears her throat.

"Old guitar," she says. "New strings. Mind if I break them in while we talk?" She begins to stretch and tune, stretch and tune. "I never thought I'd get to sit where you're sitting," she says. "Let alone all the way up here." Silence. Her heart speeds up. "To tell you the truth, I'm scared half to death."

Less than silence. A vacuum.

She props one foot on a dowel of wood between the stool's legs, giving support to her guitar, then looks outward. The audience is wrapped around her, their faces blurred, but she can feel them as if they are inches away. They are scared, too. What will this haggard old woman do? Can she still sing? She doesn't want to let them down. There is a brimming.

Cheers erupt, then quieten. A yip here, a whistle there. Faces waiting. Maybe they aren't scared; maybe they are giving her time.

They hold up their phones. She pats them down with her hand.

"Put those away now," she says. How her voice travels. Lit screens begin to wink and disappear. "Makes it hard to see your faces." The holdouts remain, resolute. No use trying to stop them. She sees a girl in front, tears pouring down her face. Her black hair is ironed straight and she's covered in makeup, though she can't be more than eleven. Twyla wishes she could kneel down to her but her knees are useless. Instead she stretches out her hand.

"Why are you crying, honey?" she says. The girl is too overcome to say anything. Her mother strokes her back. The girl lifts up on her toes and sniffles and says something Twyla can't understand. Her mother helps, "She says she just loves you so much, Miss Twyla." Now Twyla wants to cry, though she won't, not yet. Not before she's even had a chance to begin.

TWYLA PLAYS THE OPRY LIKE it's her first, her last, her everything. She plays the three sets she's agreed to, then, when the audience nearly riots for an encore, she comes back for another two hours. In fact, she only stops when the announcer appears onstage and holds up Twyla's hand like she's won a boxing match, shouting to the crowd, "I don't know about you but I've been waiting for that for forty years!" At the roar that follows she imagines a wild sea bashing a cliff. Then the audience begins to chant. *De-vil, de-vil.* She has not yet played her most famous song.

The announcer turns to her, awaits her response. How strange. She didn't mean to leave it out. Perhaps she hoped to exist, this first day of freedom, outside of her crime. She limps to the edge of the stage to thank them, and when she lifts her hands they are sticky and rusty with blood. The pads of her fingers have split and soaked the bare patches of wood on her guitar and coated her strings. In the trance of her performance, she did not notice the injury. Here, palms out for all to see, she knows her hands will never rinse free of his blood. She lowers her arms in shame. They are all thinking it—how can they ignore what these hands have done?

Her crime is the reason they know her name.

CHAPTER 73

Twyla has never been on a plane, and she isn't about to start. Against Sherry's orders, she boards a Greyhound with a backpack loaded with snacks, clean underwear, a steel bottle that makes her water taste of pocket change, and on her back, Pearl. Sherry thinks she'll be mobbed and tries to send a bodyguard along with her, but Twyla is confident no one will notice an old woman traveling alone. She will take the bus home, just as she left.

She finds a seat at the back and arranges her things. She enjoys the rhythm of the road, the cool air pushing up from the vent on the window, the blur of green foliage ribboning past her. Today she hopes for a song. Fragments of lyrics, and half-formed melodies flirt with her, appearing here, tickling there. Then, just when she has a little something in hand, the lyric or the melody vanishes, leaving only a spritz of their essence behind. A sense of beauty but nothing she can hold.

She is anxious to write another album, her first outside prison. In fact, she can't remember a time when she wanted to make something so badly. Inside, with her sentence yawning in front of her, she was patient. Some albums arrived so fully formed she could write the songs in one weekend and lay down tracks the next; others gestated for months before she found their truest expression.

But with the meat of her years now gone, and the clear line of her release demarcating her body of work, she fears she is at last out of material.

Like the thinning of her hair and the loss of cushion between her bones, she worries her creative flow is waning, a signal of the great, inevitable End. Save "Devil," her entire catalogue consists of the prison songs. And now everything that follows, if anything follows at all, will be the songs she writes as a free woman. She worries her containment, her boredom, gave her the freedom to create. Out here, there are so many distractions. How can she block them out long enough to make her music? And does she want to? How little time remains, she cannot say. A part of her wants to recreate her confinement. Hole up and write until she has something worth recording. Another wishes to sink her hands into the soil, chew on grass, taste fountain water, try acid, find a mate. Now, she realizes with grim irony, anything can be had except the one thing she truly desires.

When she arrives in Fort Worth eleven hours later, Twyla hires a taxi to drive her around. She wonders, as she rolls down the window, how a city can smell the same after forty years. Of dust and grass clippings, grill smoke and gasoline, and when the wind blows just right, as it does now, the slightest whiff of animal rot. She asks the driver to take a detour past her old haunts: the high school, same as ever; First Tabernacle, shuttered and condemned, its congregation now swallowed, according to the driver, by a nearby megachurch; and finally, New Groove. She has kept in touch with Eli, who she calls every year for updates on the details of his life, from grandchildren, to sales, to the fluctuations of his rheumatoid arthritis. He franchised New Groove in the nineties but kept the original shop. Now they sell vintage vinyl, cassettes, and CDs to young people with a sense of irony and codgers who never upgraded their sound. Eli's daughter and her husband bought the appliance store next door and built it out into four state-of-the-art recording studios, which are frequented by local artists. She will go to Eli's soon, but she has someone she needs to see first.

She finds the door to her childhood home unlocked and lets herself in. Despite its age, it has an air of impermanence, of shoddy craftsmanship, of thin surfaces seldom cleaned. Wallpaper veiled in a resin of grease, the carpet grayed and natty and footworn.

Lloyd is long gone. He died of a heart attack ten years before, and Faith shared the news by sending Twyla his obituary. No phone call, no note. Now Faith has a roommate, Frederica, who intercepts Twyla and briefs her on her mother's condition following the stroke. That she is able to communicate by pointing and sometimes writing, but often the words are incorrect. As Twyla makes her way to her mother, Frederica hangs in the doorway casting suspicious glances and territorial vibes.

Twyla follows the hall past the living room and around to the kitchen, at the center of which sits a woman Twyla scarcely recognizes. She sits erect in her chair, one hand in her lap, and spoons Malt-O-Meal from her bowl, giving no indication she knows her daughter has arrived. She is clearly stricken—one side of her face chews, the other rests—but there are marks of her vanity, too. Lacquered red nails, vulgar against her brittle skin. A freshly laundered nightgown, both prudish in its cut, and suggestive in its transparency. *That's Mother.*

Twyla approaches the table and Faith turns stiffly toward her, her eyes lit up with interest. She reaches her good hand out to Twyla's waist, cinching it, raises her eyebrows approvingly at her weight loss. No hug for her long-lost daughter, no tears. Then she motions for Twyla to come closer. She rubs Twyla's coarse gray hair between her fingers as if assessing the quality of a length of cloth.

"Yes, Mother, I'm old."

Faith frowns and sighs like nothing can be done and flits her hands to shoo Twyla away. Then she stabs a finger in the direction of her makeup bag on the counter. Twyla brings the embroidered pouch and unzips it for her. Faith fishes out a compact, flicks it open, and dabs some powder with the pancake-shaped puff and dusts her nose, forehead, and chin.

The back of Faith's hair has matted together in a loose patty. Twyla finds a brush among her things and coaxes out the rats. Her mother grunts complaints but does not stop her. In prison, girls put margarine on their hair to moisturize and make it shine. She finds some canola oil and rubs her finger around the lip, then warms the oil in her palms and runs it through her mother's hair, which fans out in a wavy, unruly mane.

"All these years, Mother . . . I never knew we had the same hair."

Her mother tuts and shakes her head slightly.

"I thought you *hated* my hair, the way you'd yank it and braid it tight to keep it down. Why did you do that?" Twyla asks, knowing she will not receive an answer. "There was nothing wrong with the way it was." Why Twyla chooses to focus on this grievance, and not the way Faith had abandoned her when she needed her most, is a mystery. Perhaps it is all the same. She rejected her hair, she rejected Twyla.

Her mother lashes out with a look that surprises Twyla. Hard eyes that say *Don't test me.* Twyla wishes she could talk so they could have it out. Her mother cries out and crumples her face like she is chewing. She wants to say something but can't seem to get it out. Mother slaps her own cheek in frustration.

"Sorry," Twyla says, not sure what she is apologizing for and then realizes it is for her own benefit, an old trick to prevent one of Mother's tantrums. Her mother shakes her head *No.* Does she mean *No, don't be sorry*? Or *No, I didn't hate your hair* . . . She waits for Faith's meaning to become clear.

She points at the counter by the phone. Next to the scratch paper and a cluttered mug of pens is a framed picture of Twyla when she was little, seven or eight, dancing with her mother at a wedding.

She picks it up and turns to her mother. "Where did this come from?"

Faith stares back intently.

She looks at the picture more closely now, and the feeling of that day returns. Her itchy, sagging stockings and the coconut cake. The jazz band in white tuxedos playing like it was the end of the world.

"I remember that wedding. Daddy was away in San Antonio so you took me as your date."

Her mother closes her eyes, a little smile on her lips. She seems to be swaying.

"We danced to every song, even the slow ones," says Twyla. Eyes still closed, her mother nods. Tears in the outer corners of her eyes catch the overhead light.

Frederica enters the room noiselessly, clears the bowl, then washes and puts it away.

Twyla finds herself hoping for a sign that her mother is proud of her. She crosses over to the living room. There are only Christian albums by the turntable, CDs by the stereo, Twyla's music conspicuously missing.

"Didn't you listen to my records?" She asked the label to send early copies to her mother every time they released a new one. "Where are they, even? Didn't you want to hear what I've been up to?"

Mother purses her lips. She seems resentful that Twyla has called attention to this. She impales her heart with an invisible dagger.

Twyla pinches her eyebrows. Wasn't it just like her mother to feel victimized by a gift.

Her mother stabs herself again. Twyla winces at the gesture. But her mother is old and ill, and after forty years, this may be the last time she sees her. She offers her mother some grace.

"Too painful?" she says.

Her mother looks away and nods very slightly. At this, Twyla's face reddens and tears come to her eyes. She recalls now her mother's letter. Many years passed before Twyla could read it again, and when she did she found buried in its pages a woman who was begging her daughter to come closer.

"I was mad about Daddy for a long time," Twyla says. Her mother nods. "You made him disappear. Didn't you see you were erasing a part of me, too?"

Another look from Mother, eyes wet and sharp. Is she hurt or ashamed? Twyla wonders: If her mother could speak again, what would she want to hear? That she is sorry? What can be said to make things right? And who here needs to change, her mother, or Twyla?

Faith tugs at her shirttail. Then she points to a yellowed filing box with a bent lid.

Twyla rises and looks inside. There are pictures—of Mickey and Faith when they first met, hiking in Big Bend for the honeymoon, then Daddy holding a newborn Twyla tight against his chest. Him singing loud, hat askew, at a crowded bar. There is a trophy from a music festival, a child's fiddle, its strings brittle and slack. And a ream of yellowed papers rolled and tied with a frayed department-store ribbon.

Written across the scroll in her daddy's hand are the words:

"Songs for My Daughter."

They are dated just weeks before they got the news her father had died.

Frederica somehow knows to usher her mother to bed. Twyla hugs her, promises to stay a few days, and says goodbye. Then she picks up her guitar, once his, carries the songs down the hall to her room, and spreads them out on the bed. The music is scored in a rushed, unsteady hand, but she knows her daddy's marks and can decipher its rhythms, the length of each note. She takes Pearl in her arms and feels, with fresh intimacy, Mickey's presence beside her as she plays. His voice in her head, his cantering rhythm on the strings, the stutter in his picking that seems at first like a mistake but as the song goes along creates a moment of reflection.

She is grateful just to glimpse into her father's heart, but these songs—they are the best he ever wrote. The bitterness of "Remember the Bad Times," a song he clearly wrote after Mother kicked him out; the hangdog hurt of "I'll Say I Love You by Saying Goodbye." There was "This Is When You Love Me Most (When You Don't Know I'm Here)," a crushing lullaby he wrote about holding Twyla while she slept. The crisis of faith in "Lord, Are You with Me?" and the panic of growing old in "Hurry, Mercy (There's Not Much Time for Me)."

His lyrics, like a prophecy discovered too late, express feelings she has tried to write ten different ways but always felt out of reach. The simplicity, the broken, humbled honesty. She thinks about what her father said about songs floating along, looking for a home. There is a shattered feeling when she realizes he had this music in him and never got to share it, that he died buried under his regrets.

After Daddy died, she never saw his body. And lacking proof, there was always a slim little drawer in which she stored her hopes that maybe he had only stepped away. Maybe this tour was a terribly long one, to which he kept adding dates, and that someday the tour would end and he would pull up to the driveway, pockets full of souvenirs, and bursting with stories to tell from the road. She would wrap herself around his reedy frame and beg him to teach her a new song.

She is determined now to bear them forth. These songs, and the album she will make of them, will be her proof, not that he died, but that he lived. That she lived. She will ferry these souls across the chasm to the other side. Then she pushes herself up and begins to play his last, an unfinished song:

"The Cut That Will Not Mend"

Twyla, you forgave me
Soon as I had sinned,
But I'm the only one,
I can't seem to forgive.

The only one alive it seems
Who'll hold me to my sins,
My own damnation against myself,
That's the cut that will not mend.

I thank you for your grace
But now this song must end
And today I'm making sure
I never sin again.

Twyla sobs over Pearl as she absorbs the lyrics, words of a man whose pain had overtaken him. Who knew he would soon be dead. *Every song is a soul that wants to be born*, he'd told her. Daddy managed to write them down, but there had been no one around to hear them—no one to hear *him*. She leans into her hands and weeps for her father, for his weakness, for the pain so great it made even his blessings unbearable. She weeps, too, for the beauty of his songs, that even in his anguish he put pen to paper and offered up all he had to give. And for her mother, who could not speak, but who finally gave her what she needed. Something to make meaning of the greatest loss of her life.

It occurs to her then that she has been on a treadmill of musical penance, never stopping, writing to save her soul. She hasn't slept a single night from start to finish for all the songs that rouse her, and with each record she hopes that this one will bring her salvation.

And then a title for their album arrives. She scratches over "Songs for My Daughter" and writes her own, "Songs for the Unforgiven," and then she writes a verse that comes to her, imperfect and shining, as if whispered in her ear.

Some cuts never mend,
And I've done my share of cutting.
Maybe I won't know how to forgive,
But all that's left to do
before my dying breath,
Is believing I had every right to live.

When she finishes singing she is electrified. Compelled by that familiar urgency to make music, to share it, to capture the souls before they pass her by, but this time she knows she is trying to beat the passage of time, the coming of the end. Now she will call up her friend Eli and record her daddy's songs, etch them in wax before they spirit away. She will do this for him, for Mother, for her own damned soul, for fear today or tomorrow, or someday soon, she will, without knowing, sing for the very last time. She wonders where her songs will go when she's dead, if they will find someone else to bear them forth, or if they were never hers to begin with and all she has done is gather the souls and play them back to God.

ACKNOWLEDGMENTS

Thanks to my editor, Liz Stein, who pushed me to write something daring, then held my hand as I made my way. To my agent, Liz Winick Rubinstein, for her fierce support and savvy. To my whole team at William Morrow for trusting me with another book. For your keen eyes, Linda Sawicki, Christine Vahaly, and Rachel Weinick. To Ariana Sinclair, for all your support. Thanks, Michele Cameron, for the interior design, and Yeon Kim, thank you for another beautiful cover, the face of all my hard work.

I'm so grateful to my people in Nashville for rolling out the red carpet—Jim Thomas for shuttling me around town, bringing me to The Bluebird, and introducing me to his very fancy friends; Karen and David Conrad for welcoming me to their home and telling me the most wonderful stories (I'll never forget that photo of Johnny just days before he died); Michael McCall for the tour of the Country Music Hall of Fame and for letting me dig in the archives; Brownlee Ferguson for his many gracious invitations, connections, and offers to help; and my mother, Lucy, for sharing her friends—and love of music—with me.

To Mary Gauthier for her lovely and sincere memoir, *Saved by a Song*, which made me cry all the way home from Nashville. Everyone, read this book.

To my rocker brother, Will, for his guitar.

To Hunter Perrin and Paul Beebe for being my on-call music experts.

To the good literary citizens who took time to read my book and share their impressions: Amy Meyerson, Eli Cranor, James Wade, Katie

Gutierrez, Laura Warrell, Jami Attenberg, Emma Brodie, Katy Hays. Please join me in thanking these authors by reading their beautiful books.

Thanks to my country music heroes (an incomplete list): Loretta Lynn, Dolly Parton, John Prine, Johnny Cash, Kris Kristofferson, Maybelle Carter, Marijohn Wilkin, Thom Schuyler, Brandi Carlile, Brittney Spencer, Alison Krauss, Emmylou Harris, Lucinda Williams, Mickey Guyton, Tanya Tucker, The Chicks, Miranda Lambert, Robert Earl Keen, Bonnie Raitt, Charley Pride, Don Schlitz, Marshall Chapman, and Willie Nelson.

To Paty, again, for your grace and kindness—we are lucky to have you in our lives. To Jakey, for lifetime bear hugs, walks around the yard, and laughs that hurt. Sometimes I think I dreamed you up. And kids, guess what? I'll be thanking you for the rest of my life—for sharing your joy, for testing my character, for growing my heart.

ABOUT THE AUTHOR

Caroline Frost is the author of *Shadows of Pecan Hollow*, which won the Crook's Corner Book Prize, was a finalist for the Golden Poppy Award, and was longlisted for the Center for Fiction's First Novel Prize. She has a Master of Professional Writing degree from the University of Southern California and lives in the Los Angeles area with her husband and three children.